An East End Girl

Maggie FORD

3 5 7 9 10 8 6 4 2

Ebury Press, an imprint of Ebury Publishing
20 Vauxhall Bridge Road,
London SW1V 2SA

Ebury Press is part of the Penguin Random House group of companies whose addresses can be found at global.penguinrandomhouse.com

First published in 1996 as *A Better Life* by Judy Piatkus (Publishers) Ltd
This edition published in 2017 by Ebury Press

www.penguin.co.uk

A CIP catalogue record for this book is available from the British Library

ISBN 9780091956271

Typeset in India by Thomson Digital Pvt Ltd, Noida, Delhi

Printed and bound in Great Britain by Clays Ltd, St Ives PLC

Penguin Random House is committed to a sustainable future for our business, our readers and our planet. This book is made from Forest Stewardship Council® certified paper.

For my brother Harry Lord and his wife Christine

An East End Girl

Chapter One

The Thames sweeping round the Isle of Dogs flowed smoothly. Deceptively smoothly. Tidal, the cold North Sea ebbing and flowing twice daily past Southend on the east Essex coast and Sheerness on the Kent side, the movement was noticeable right up to Teddington Lock seventy miles up.

At low ebb, with tide-left mud and water-worn posts exposed, the river could have a drab look; it looked almost too inadequate to carry all the world's trade up to the Pool of London – the hinged road of Tower Bridge opening up like a great steel and concrete butterfly flexing its wings to allow tall-funnelled freighters through.

It was very different at flood tide; the sense of space and freedom took away a man's breath, made him want to gulp in huge lungfuls of its fresh feel, made him proud to be part of it, proud to be a Londoner.

Charlie Farmer stood gazing at it, enjoying the sight on this fine August evening. From his vantage point where Westferry Road became Manchester Road, Greenwich foot tunnel under the Thames not a mile away, from which he and Doris had emerged a little over half an hour ago, he could see clearly across to Greenwich Observatory where they'd spent the afternoon. Between him and Greenwich, the wide expanse of water, flowing smooth on the ebb, glowed translucent bronze in the liquid evening light. There were greater rivers in the world with mouths so wide that their banks were totally lost to sight. But this was his river. London's artery. It was in his blood, flowed as his blood flowed – reliable, steady, tranquil.

A smile wrinkled his broad, weathered face at the word tranquil. On the surface perhaps. To the eyes of a landsman perhaps. He knew from experience that beneath its sleek surface lurked undercurrents waiting to sweep away anyone silly enough to try swimming from one bank to the other – young men, full of drink, doing a dare, the white corpse popping up days later on the outside of a bend circling among the old rope and driftwood after the Thames had done playing with it. Only when you took a craft upstream against a falling tide did you appreciate its pull, traffic passing fast the other way; only when you squeezed between the abutments of arches of its many bridges, the current swirling in treacherous rips, could you truly know the brute strength of this old river.

Charlie Farmer's grin broadened. Like life in a way, hiding from eyes the turmoil that surged beneath a placid surface.

Not that much surged beneath the surface of his life. He was proud of his family, his wife, Doris and their children: Cissy aged twenty, Robert, eighteen, May just fourteen, left school last month; then Sidney, ten, and Harry, eight. No more children now – he and Doris were past all that, hopefully.

They'd never truly known poverty. Struggled a bit at times, but never starved. He'd always been able to provide. A Thames waterman and lighterman, a Freeman, balding a bit now, but strong as ever, he loved his life, loved his work – something few men could boast.

'Ain't no better life,' he murmured, his gaze sweeping the wide expanse of water flowing smooth as silk.

Doris, her waist thickened by childbearing, her fair hair going gently grey and her open features placid, tightened her hold on her shopping bag with its empty Thermos flask and sandwich wrappings.

'Maybe not, but I've got supper to get when we get 'ome. And it's turning chilly. It'll take us an hour getting back, and I've got no big coat. Come on, Charlie, before we freeze to death.'

It was an exaggeration. It had been a lovely sultry hot August Bank Holiday Monday, but a breeze had sprung up with the sun's going, not cold, but compared to the earlier heat felt cooler than it was, and Doris's fleshy bare arms had begun to show goose pimples.

Charlie put an affectionate arm about her shoulders.

'Right, ole gel, time to go 'ome. Me ole tum's beginning to rumble a bit, I must admit. It's been a lovely afternoon, without the kids.'

It had been lovely. Away from the family for once, Cissy giving eye to the children, although not too happy about it. Arm in arm like a couple of youngsters, they'd made their way through the foot tunnel under the Thames, sat in Greenwich Park with other Bank Holiday families, the stewed tea from a Thermos flask tasting wonderful after plodding uphill, Doris puffing behind all the way, to where the shiny-domed Observatory stood. Once up there they had sat with their tea and sandwiches, enjoying the views of London basking in heat haze on the far side of the sleepy Thames.

Trains bound for Southend and Margate for the day would have been standing only; Hyde Park, like all London parks on bank holiday, would have been crowded with hardly a pin being put between each group; the Serpentine a seething mass of bathers. But in Greenwich Park all had been peaceful, a breath of countryside.

It was getting late. Tomorrow he'd be back on the river. Robert, too – in the boy's case, taking orders, still learning the skill, next year to apply hopefully to be a Freeman of the Company of Watermen and Lightermen of the River Thames.

Bobby, as Charlie called him, had been apprenticed for nearly four years, bound to him as he himself had been to his father some twenty-odd years ago around the turn of the century. Life was tougher then, Bobby didn't know the half of it. Six years since the war had ended, dumb barges more often towed by tug now, in double lines of three, saving lightermen that hard row against the current.

But he was a good lad, was Bobby. Quick to learn, willing, doing well. One for the girls, of course, with his looks – but a good lad.

'Coming then?' Doris's voice betrayed faint impatience. Charlie gave her a grin, nodded, and followed her away from the river wall.

'I just 'ope Cissy ain't 'ad much trouble from them kids of ours,' she said as they made their way along Eastferry Road. 'We've left it a bit later than we intended, starting back.'

Charlie grinned down at her lesser height. A bit of a worrier was Doris. 'Won't take us long. Put our best foot forward, eh?'

It was a longish walk back to Poplar. They started off at a brisk pace, her arm through his, she in her best blue crepe and her straw cloche hat with the cherries, he in his good suit and Sunday bowler. By East India Dock Road, their steps had slowed. A No. 67 tram took them the couple of stops to Canning Town and saved their feet, but it was still a plod the rest of the way to Fords Road and home, Doris sighing at her aching feet, Charlie moderating his pace to match her flagging one, lifting the arm she held to help take up her weight.

'Soon be 'ome, old gel,' he encouraged. 'Not far now.'

To which she sighed, 'I can't wait to put me feet up.'

Compared to the bank holiday quiet of the river, the back-streets of Canning Town rang to the cries and laughter of children with minds on that last game before being called in for supper and bed.

Charlie thought of the supper awaiting him. Boiled bacon and pease pudding – not butcher's pease pudding but lovingly cooked by Doris herself. She'd left the small half hock to simmer in the same water as the potatoes she'd parboiled for yesterday's Sunday dinner before going off to Greenwich, leaving Cissy to turn it off when done.

They'd had a bit of lamb yesterday, enough left for cold tomorrow with bubble and squeak – leftover potatoes and cabbage mashed and fried together. Doris said the bacon and potato water would make a nice broth for another time. She was a thrifty woman and a dab hand at making the pennies stretch. All thanks to her they ate better than many of them around here. He often felt a little guilty for not praising her more.

'We're lucky you an' me.' He followed his train of thought. 'Me comin' through the war. Not like some – thousands 'n' thousands – all gorn. Us gettin' through that 'flu epidemic like we did. Remember that? Five, six years ago? Did away with 'ole families, that did. I reckon it's your feeding keeps us so well, old gel.'

Doris gave a whimsical smile as if to say, 'Whatever brought that on?' But she only said, 'I just thank the good Lord for it.'

He gave a deep rumbling laugh, 'No, it's thanks ter you, old gel. Supper for most of them kids'll probably be bread and drip.'

Perhaps with a bit of meat jelly in it which, as the week wore on, would degenerate to plain dripping. Few were able to afford meat enough for it, so dripping came mostly from the pork butchers: 'ap'orth without (jelly) or, if you were well off that week, a penn'orth with. Bring your own basin, large enough to last until next pay day, if your man was in work that was. Even if not, it was cheap on bread and filled hungry bellies.

The man of the house might do better. As a special person, there was poached haddock for him bought, more often than not, by popping the family china into Uncles and making do with tin cups until it was redeemed. Bread dipped in the salty yellow liquid made a meal, the kids waiting for the earholes, the stringy flesh around the gills, to suck as a treat.

'Bobby and Cissy working brings in a bit on top of me own wages,' Charlie continued, still feeling for the less fortunate. 'We'd be in queer streets without them, way costs've gone up since the war.'

No one could call a lighterman's job exactly steady. There were days when waiting around for something would bring bouts of concern, and other days when it all came in a rush, keeping a man so busy he wouldn't see home for several days, loading, driving a craft (as barges were known), unloading, always the tide dictating the hours.

Much of the time these days he was on tugs. A four-man crew, skipper, mate, engineer, fireman and a boy to look after them, doing all the deck work – the coiling and handing up of tow ropes, pulling down of the funnel to pass under the bridges, scrubbing out cabins, making everlasting cups of tea.

They were long hours, he was up at four-thirty and seldom home before seven. Sometimes there were twenty-four-hour shifts on the more powerful tugs and the much larger craft they towed, covering greater distances, working the bridges up to Hammersmith and downriver to Canvey Island, even as far as the River Medway, to the Isle of Grain. But the lads, like the rest of them, whether on tug or craft, developed a love of the river, a feel for their work that few on shore had. Breathing in the clean morning air while others had to rely on the streets for air before dragging themselves off to offices, shops, factories, there was something that made a man feel of importance when working up or down along the river.

There was compensation for those long shifts, a bit on the side to barter for baccy at Free Trade Wharf, the odd something rolling into a corner – perks of the job, mopping up the unclaimed – to exchange for a bit of something else. Kept life ticking over sweet, though it was a foolish man who let himself be carried away by greed.

Discovery meant dismissal, your licence taken away; it meant becoming unemployable. Wasn't worth it, and it wasn't honesty that kept him from over-pilfering, as much as the risk of being caught. And then there was Doris, wont to get herself in a flap about things coming into the house that weren't come by honestly.

She had let go his arm to fish for the key in her purse among the empty sandwich wrappings in her shopping bag, but his own key was at the ready as they reached their door, one of a row of identical doors.

'Got mine,' he rumbled, inserting it into the keyhole.

'Bin out fer the afternoon, Mrs Farmer?' a voice crackled.

Old Mrs Turpin, a few doors along, stood gripping a tatty coconut-fibre doormat.

'Thought we'd take advantage of the weather,' Doris obliged.

'Anywhere nice?'

'Greenwich Park.'

'Wish my old man'd take me out. All 'e ever does is snore 'is 'ead off.' She began pounding the mat against the wall, raising puffs of dust with each collision. 'Be nice ter go out now'n again.'

With an offered nod of agreement, they stepped inside and closed the door on the lovely evening. It had grown dark enough to light the gas in the kitchen. Removing the single round glass bowl, Charlie carefully turned the key until the gas began to hiss. The mantle plopped as he applied a match. Its delicate chalky mesh gave forth a sickly hue but grew steadily incandescent with the glass shade replaced.

Sinking down on one of the four kitchen chairs, Doris emitted a huge sigh. 'My feet are killing me.'

Charlie smiled, dropping the matchbox on the table and going to hang his coat on one of the cluttered hooks in the passage. 'Don't wonder at it. Bin on 'em all day,' he called.

'Just need to take the weight off me legs for a bit,' she agreed, but as he returned, she was already up, going for the kettle to take it to the sink. Filling it noisily and transferring it to the stove, the gas lit with his box of matches, she announced: 'A nice cup of tea,' as if such activity could mean anything but that.

Cissy had come from the front room. Her clear grey-blue eyes and pretty features bore a somewhat peeved look.

'You're home, then?'

Compared to her parents' flat Cockney vowels, hers were rounded, obviously and painfully studied. Cissy took elocution and deportment lessons from a one-time opera singer who boasted of having gone much further in her vocation than her pupils actually believed she had. Madam Noreah Addiscombe, who wore black velvet always – a dusty black victim-of-age velvet – beneath which her bosom bulged mightily from her past operatic exertions and looked like a pregnancy in the wrong place, taught singing too, at sixpence an hour. Cissy couldn't afford to sing as well, so only took the elocution and deportment.

'Fat lot of good that'll do you, working round 'ere,' Charlie had said when he heard. But there wasn't much he could do about it being as she paid for her lessons out of her own wages.

Cissy was a machinist at Cohens just off Burdett Road. Piecework on dresses and skirts brought in good money if you were quick at it. And Cissy was quick at it. After giving Mum her keep, the rest was hers, and Dad's views were – to coin one of Madam Noreah's beautiful phrases – mere chaff blowing on the wind.

What Cissy wanted most in this world was to escape, to flee this poverty-striken East End for ever. She dreamed of it constantly. But it was only a dream. Girls like her, for all the elocution lessons at a tanner a time, did not get to flee to any better life.

Slim and upright, she stood in the doorway of the kitchen. For all Dad's efforts at decorating it with layer upon layer of wallpaper to hide the outline of bare brick-work, the paper soon became stained from cooking, necessitating another layer. But even that did not stop the summer invasion of bugs from not too clean homes on either side, the bane of Mum's life. Beyond, was the outside toilet and washhouse, the brickwork there well in evidence through the whitewash. How she loathed its miserable, mean look.

'Did you have an enjoyable afternoon?' she asked wearily.

Dad was looking at her in the manner of one taking the rise. But it was done with humour, loving her dearly for all her foolish ideas.

'Yes, we h-ad a very enjoyable h-afternoon,' he mimicked.

'Thanks for looking after the kids, luv,' Mum said, gently guilty. 'We wouldn't've had time to go nowhere if you 'adn't. Didn't give you much trouble, did they?' she added hopefully.

Cissy gave a non-committal shrug. 'Out playing most of the time. But had Daisy Evans called I'd have been unable to go out with her.'

Her mother looked crestfallen. 'You didn't say you 'ad anything perticler to do today.'

'I might have had. If she had come to ask me to go out with her.'

'Did she come?' Charlie asked, lighting his pipe.

'No.'

'Then it don't matter, do it? You 'ad nothing perticler to do.'

'Have the kids had their supper?' Doris asked with a quick glance at her husband. 'Where are they now?'

'Upstairs, gone to bed.' No sound came from upstairs. She crossed her fingers that Mum would not go up just yet to see them. If she did she'd find her youngest boy's eyes probably still red. Cissy trusted Sidney to heed her warning that if he told on her, she would get him next time, well and truly.

May had been good enough, playing hopscotch on the corner with girls her age, had come in willingly when called. But the boys. . . . The pair of them had played up something horrid, scowling and rude to her when she'd called them in, rebellious at having to scrub the black off their fingers where they'd been popping tar bubbles in the kerb caused by the heat of enclosed streets under a mid-August sun.

By five o'clock she'd had enough and belted into both of them. They'd scurried upstairs, Sidney calling her names from the safety of the closed bedroom door, neither daring to come down lest she belted them again. Mum wouldn't be happy if she knew, but one can stand only so much when it's not really one's role to play nursemaid.

At twenty, all she wanted in life was to be like those privileged little flappers who frequented the West End. She and Daisy Evans often went up West. Daisy too went to Madam Noreah, for singing, but not every week, as she wasn't so dedicated as Cissy.

Both at the same firm, most of their wages were spent up West each Saturday, dancing until the last bus forced them to leave those rich bright young things to dance the rest of the night away. The next six days would be spent eking out what was left, but it was worth it, pretending to be one of those to whom money was no object. Hair shingled on the cheap, spit-curled over the cheeks, fake jewellery matching the real thing, dresses homemade – worth it all.

Come what may, putting by for her elocution lessons was a must, even if it meant walking to work to avoid paying fares. One day, Cissy thought, one day I shall be part of those bright young people, if it kills me.

Another shilling or so went religiously into her Post Office Book. Saving since starting work six years ago, it held nearly fifty pounds.

Making her own dresses on Mum's old sewing machine helped. Luckily 1924 had brought a fashion for the simple straight chemise. A couple of yards folded end to end, neck and armholes cut out, shoulders and sides stitched, satin band around the hips – nothing could be simpler. With dangly earrings and two strings of fake pearls, it was easy to look a million dollars on a few pence. Although, the pale beige rayon stockings had to be bought, of course. And shoes – never the best on her money. Only looked so, leaving her coming home half-crippled by their ill-fitting pointed toes, narrow-waisted heels and unforgiving bar straps. But it was all worth it. She looked as good as any of them. And one day . . .

Chapter Two

Madam Noreah held the one-eyed ginger tomcat close to her unevenly bulging bosom as she stared through the window of her room on the ground floor of one of those somewhat neglected Victorian houses just off the Mile End Road. Once home to middle-class families of business men and a handful of domestic staff, now most of the long terraced rows of houses each accommodated several tenants.

Since the Great War, the moderately wealthy had moved out to urban perimeters to enjoy modern detached homes surrounded by those leafy walks and long gardens pictured on the hoardings and brochures of estate agents. Living the healthy life away from the smoke and dirt of the City, they commuted to it by sooty train instead.

The forsaken mansions had been taken over by all sorts and all professions, of which Madam Noreah, who gave singing, elocution and deportment lessons at sixpence an hour, was one.

She shifted her gaze from the dusty street beyond the grimy window to the ancient ormolu clock – a present from an admirer more years ago than she cared to recall – squatting in pride of place on the mantelshelf over a fireplace of once shining marble now more a shade of dirty grey.

Five to eleven. Miss Farmer would be on the dot as always. Madam Noreah bent her large face to look down at the subdued head of the one-eyed cat she called Nelson, for want of anything better.

'Miss Farmer is never late, you know,' she told the animal who purred its response in a welter of wet snuffling. 'I wish she could be, just for once. We must hurry and feed every one of you in the five minutes we have to ourselves, or you'll all be around her feet the whole lesson, purring at me for attention. Ah well . . . Come along, my little ones. Let us see what we can find to give you.'

Putting the cat down beside two others, a black and white and a ragged tortoiseshell, both of whom had been rubbing against the long skirt of her black, seen-better-days velvet, she moved off to the kitchen to distribute a series of saucers upon the grubby brown and white tiled floor; half a dozen to be filled with milk, the other half with bits of yesterday's fish, precooked offal obtained from the cats-meat man every Monday and now going a little bit off, and whatever other bits and pieces she had left from her own meals.

There was hardly any need to give her usual twittery call: 'Here-come-come-come-come!' as the sound of fork scraping against china had already summoned some dozen or so feline bodies of all sizes and in varying conditions of health, arrowing in through the open back door and from the parlour where some had been curled up on the sagging armchair, the sofa, the scratched sideboard and dining table whose polish had long since disappeared.

She watched them as they fed, the hungrier, fitter ones snatching up chunks larger than they should, while the less fit sniffed the fare and turned away, skinny but off their food.

Madam Noreah sighed and felt the tears prick her eyes for these poorly ones. She tried to tend them, but she knew little about cats beyond feeding them and giving them shelter; the poor strays who bred incessantly, the poor thrown-out kittens fending for themselves, the too-young mothers slowly starving as milk was drained from their thin teats, the one-eyed, one-eared denizens of rooftile and backyard.

'Eat as well as you can, my little ones,' she told the twelve, or was it fourteen? She never counted the same number twice. They came and went as they pleased.

A hollow pound on the front door told her it was exactly eleven and Miss Farmer was here for her elocution lesson. Leaving the cats to themselves, Madam Noreah went to answer it.

Cissy's nose twitched at the offensive odour of cat urine that met her as the door opened. She hated this place. But where else could one be taught to speak nicely at sixpence an hour?

Madam Noreah had once tried persuading her into taking up singing. 'You say you have no voice, Miss Farmer, but I believe you have, and I could develop it for you.' But Cissy knew it was the extra sixpence she was after, and anyway, the mere thought of taking in deep breaths of urine-tainted air to reach that high 'C' was a great deterrent to singing lessons.

'I just want to speak nicely,' she said. 'I can't afford both.'

That was enough to dissuade Madam Noreah from pursuing the question again, thank God.

Madam Noreah, seeing Miss Daisy Evans had arrived too, gave her singing pupil, quite her most favourite singing pupil, a toothy grin.

'Ah, you have come this week, dear. So nice. *Entré*, my dears.'

She opened the door wide for the inseparables, that was when Miss Evans deigned to come which wasn't as regularly as she'd have wished, but when she did come it was always with Miss Farmer even though she must sit and wait for an hour until her own lesson.

Cissy in her turn would sit and wait while Daisy went up and down scales and arpeggios and on to one of the easier arias Madam Noreah had set for her, accompanied on the piano by Madam Noreah who also gave piano lessons, before the two girls finally left together.

With the outside air coming in and diluting the cat smell a little, they made their way down the dim passage to the back parlour, now empty of cats still feeding in the kitchen. Cissy was grateful for that.

Cissy was first, taking reluctant deep breaths through her nose and, as her lesson progressed, growing slowly inured to the cat odour, taking her cue from Madam Noreah's powerfully resonant vowels.

'Oww . . . oww . . . Howw – noww – browwn – coww. Whom – loom – bloom. Repeat after me, "Ai have every hope of having a happy afternoo-oon."'

By the end of her hour Cissy's lips ached, but Madam Noreah was well satisfied.

'Very good. Excellent. *Parfait*, my dear, *parfait*.'

But what good did it do? Who . . . no, on whom was she to practise her excellent vowels? On Eddie? He'd only look stunned, as always. Edward Bennett lived a few streets from her. Shy, but down-to-earth, he saw himself as her boyfriend, and often took her to the pictures where he would hold her hand as they watched the flickering silent screen, forgetting to laugh at Charlie Chaplin or Fatty Arbuckle for gazing at her the whole time. She'd feel his eyes on her all the while she was laughing, almost spoiling her enjoyment of the slapstick.

Not that she didn't like Eddie. Just twenty-one, he was quite tall when he didn't stoop, good-looking, though he would more likely think he was being mocked should anyone say so. Cissy had to admit he had a natural grace and could have had all the girls flocking around him. But he was so sure he was the ugliest man alive. He'd told Cissy as much, confiding in her as one he could trust.

'No one's interested in a chap what's got mousy 'air all over the place,' he said once. In truth the colour was more gold than mousy, but he couldn't see it, nor that it waved gently. 'And piggy eyes,' he'd said on another occasion, totally unaware that those soft-brown orbs of his were his very asset. If only he'd acknowledge himself as halfway good-looking, Cissy thought, as she followed Madam Noreah's aitches, he would be a wow with girls instead of backing away from the first hint of admiration, shy to a point of idiocy.

He was different with her, at ease with himself. They had grown up together, played in the street and gone to the same school, and somehow she had allowed it to go on until, too late, it was becoming accepted by everyone that they would team up together as the saying went, even though she now cherished her dream of one day escaping all this.

He'd call round, welcomed in by Mum, who made him at home in the certainty that one day he'd marry her daughter. Dad approved of him – a lighterman like himself, made a Freeman two months back.

'Nice ter know you'll wed to one of us,' he had said, proud Cissy was continuing the family tradition. He too assumed that they would finally pair up.

Cissy thought otherwise, though she kept that to herself. She liked Eddie well enough, in a way she loved him. There was no doubt that he was in love with her. But she could not let herself love him back in the right way, because that way her dream would go pop, be lost for ever. She would be turned into a housewife, a drudge, a mother, all her ambitions would go out of the window.

'One last time,' Madam Noreah was saying. 'Repeat after me . . .'

The lesson coming to an end, Cissy went to perch on the edge of a bucket-seated velveteen armchair, aware of the stain in the centre – a faint ring of something nasty, probably an ancient accident by some cat or other – to wait for Daisy to go through her paces.

At the piano Madam Noreah said, 'I think in this instance we shall begin in the key of A, Miss Evans,' and as Daisy took a stance, the appropriate chord chimed out from the ringing piano.

Daisy filled her lungs, unmoved by the smell of cats – she was accustomed to smells, her house always smelled of cabbage water – and emitted the purest opening, 'oo, oh, aw, ah, ay, ee,', filling the shabby room with magic. Cissy felt a shiver of envy thrill through her as she sat listening to the clear crystal notes overcoming the dubious tone of the piano. Proceeding from the key of A to the key of B and thence to top C, Daisy could make the very air sing. It was an hour of rapture, finalised by the sweetest rendering of 'Kiss Me Again' from the operetta *Mlle Modiste.*

'Another Saturday morning lesson over,' said Daisy. The summer was now long past and Cissy took great gulps of smoke-laden London fog, even that was fresher than the odour of cats. 'Another sixpence down the drain.'

'Surely you think it worth it?' Cissy said, the diction she'd been working on so hard, lingering. A few hours with her family would of course, blunt it, though she'd be annoyed with herself hearing it happen; but it was embarrassing to sustain when friends and family, whose speech never rose above the gutter, were forever having a dig at her. Easier to forgo all she had learned for the while. She could always put the polish back on when the need arose – which was usually up West.

'I'm thinking of giving up singing lessons,' Daisy announced out of the blue, as they boarded the tram home.

Forgetting to hand her fare to the ticket conductor, leaving him hovering impatiently, Cissy stared amazed at her.

'You can't! You have such a beautiful voice. Whatever put an idea into your head of giving it up?'

Beside her, the ticket conductor coughed. Cissy came to herself. 'Oh, sorry, two threepennies please.'

The tickets in hand, Daisy giving up her threepence, Cissy turned back to her. 'You can't mean it. Why?'

'All that practice,' Daisy explained, gazing out of the window onto the Commercial Road where they had got on. 'It's not doing my figure any good. All that deep breathing. I'm developing a chest and I can't let that happen.'

Cissy knew what she meant as Daisy glanced down at her bosom still flat beneath the loose V-necked georgette jumper bought second-hand down Petticoat Lane. The fashion these last few years dictated that the perfect figure was the perfectly straight figure, the tiniest of curves in those vital statistics of 30-30-30 considered fat. And now even Cissy thought she could see a bulge on that stick-thin shape despite the flattening brassiere. But to give up with such a lovely voice – to sacrifice it to fashion.

'You don't really mean it, do you?'

Daisy shrugged and looked back out of the window of the noisy, juddering tram. 'I could carry on, I suppose, but I shall be careful doing the exercises she sets me. Fancy ending up like her!'

'That won't happen,' Cissy said, horrified by the mere thought of it. 'Not with all the dancing when we go up West.'

Tonight, though, they wouldn't be going up West. Daisy's parents had relations coming and Daisy was expected to stay at home and be sociable. Not brave enough to venture alone into the West End, Cissy too would stay in, content herself doing a bit more to the jumper she was trying to knit and hope Eddie might call, offering to take her to the pictures. Better than nothing.

As if by some sixth sense that was exactly what he did. Soon after tea, came a rap on the doorknocker. Mum went to answer it, the next thing was Eddie's tall stooping figure at the front room door where the family had settled for the evening to listen to Dad's gramophone records. The grin on Eddie's narrow handsome face was full of hope.

'Thought you might like to go to the flicks, Cissy,' he ventured.

'Sit down, Eddie, dear,' invited Mrs Farmer. 'Fancy a cuppa tea, luv? The pot's still 'ot. We've only just this minute 'ad ours.'

'Very nice of you, Mrs Farmer,' said Eddie, and sat up to receive his cup, then turned back to Cissy. 'Fancy goin' then?'

The way he spoke made her cringe. It was a problem she faced when with him – whether to keep up her cultured speech or moderate it so as not to sound out of place or show him up. It was a dilemma that followed her now whatever she did around here.

She teetered on the point of refusing his offer, but anything was better than sitting at home, Dad putting on one gramophone record after another, most of them comedy ones which got everyone giggling; Mum and Dad taking up the armchairs, May and Sidney sprawling across the settee – Harry gone to bed at his age – leaving her hardly any room to sit at ease. Cissy made a quick decision.

'What film had you in mind?'

He grimaced into his cup, his next words an obvious almost painful effort to improve himself, which showed he could when he wanted to.

'Whatever you fancy.'

There was not much she fancied this Saturday. There was a Buster Keaton film on at the local. She certainly needed a bit of a laugh to offset the disappointment of not going up West.

Eddie nodded readily. The Keaton film, *Our Hospitality,* wouldn't have been his first choice, she knew that, but so eager was he to take her out that he'd have suffered four hours of opera for it. And anyway, the big picture *The Covered Wagon*, was one he had said he'd missed last year in the West End. Now showing locally, this was his chance to see it and he was all for that, she could see by the way he leapt up, handing his empty cup back to her mother.

He stood waiting while she went to put on a dab of face powder and apply a coat of deep pink lipstick before coming back into the room, coat and handbag at the ready, her stiff brown cloche hat hiding shingled fair hair and eyebrows plucked to a thin pencil line. Her mother eyed her with some disapproval as well as anxiety.

'You shouldn't pluck them eyebrows of yours like that. It ain't nat'ral. Could 'arm your eyesight, tearing 'airs out like that. Then you go an' paint it all in again, and then 'ide 'em. It's daft.'

'You can take some of that lipstick off too,' Dad put in his two-pen'orth at the vividly coloured bow lips. 'In my time, young . . .'

But Cissy chose to ignore it as she swept out of the house with Eddie. If Dad knew she used deep red up West, wiping it off before reaching home, he'd have a fit.

*

Going to the pictures with Eddie was always a mixture of enjoyment and irritation. Relaxed with her, he was lively and could even be witty sometimes, but it was his moments of earnestness that spoiled it all.

The programme was a popular one. They joined the queue outside and, armed with a bag of still warm fresh-roasted peanuts to while away the waiting, moved up in twos and threes, thankful the evening was dry for November. Finally entering the vast darkened cinema a few minutes into the continuous programme, they felt their way to their seats, near the back. 'Don't want ter muck up yer eyes,' said Eddie, of the small square screen. 'Can be 'armful sittin' too close.'

More likely so he could be cosy with her nearer the back, but she submitted to that, because it was true what he said: the flickering, stark black and white screen was hard on the eyes close to. It could give you such a headache. For another threepence they'd have gone upstairs in the circle seats, but Eddie was saving, so he'd said on more than one occasion – rather too pointedly for Cissy's peace of mind – for the day when he'd have to provide for a wife. 'It's a big responsibility when you have to take care of a family, which I hope to one day, Cissy.' A statement she chose to ignore.

The full house was already rocking with mirth at Keaton, the air thick with cigarette smoke and it reeked of packed bodies and the perfume of disinfectant the usherettes had sprayed along the aisle. Cissy soon forgot Eddie's apology and its connotation for not going in the circle seats, as hardly had she sat down than she too had joined in with the laughter.

From beginning to end, Keaton's deadpan approach to every form of adversity kept her in stitches, especially in the steam-engine scene. Yet all the time she laughed, Eddie's gaze was riveted on her in obvious pleasure at her laughter as if he and not Keaton were responsible for her enjoyment, which had the effect of dashing her laughter.

'Stop staring at me!' she hissed angrily and went immediately back to doubling up at Keaton in a top hat footing along on a wooden bicycle without pedals, stopping at a crossroads in an embryo 1830s New York to let a cart go by. But she was still aware of Eddie's brown-eyed gaze watching her every outburst of laughter.

'Will you stop it! Watch the film, Eddie, for goodness sake!'

She was glad when the interval brought on an entertainer doing a turn with jokes and a song or two.

The Covered Wagon finally came on, interpreted by some dramatic piano playing, along with protests of 'Siddown' from an enthralled audience, to anyone daring now to fumble their way along a darkened row to go to the Ladies or Gents. Eddie's attention was at last distracted. Except that in the love scene, his arm stole around her shoulders, drawing her to him and making them ache through having to sit awkwardly. She resisted the temptation to ask him to take his arm away. It would have hurt his feelings. Instead she tried wriggling into a more comfortable position, hoping he'd take the hint, which of course he didn't, and gritted her teeth until it was time to leave.

'I'm sorry if I upset you in there, Cissy,' he said, as they joined the tram queue for home.

She remembered her sharp words. 'You didn't upset me.'

'It's just that I love watching you.'

'Don't be soppy, Eddie.'

Their tram drew up with a diminishing whine and a low moan. The queue moved forward, taking them with it. Eddie helped her on.

'I'm not being soppy.' He turned avidly to her after he had paid their fares. 'Cissy, I'm in love with you.'

She smothered a laugh. In fact she realised suddenly that she didn't want to laugh at all. A sidelong glance at him made her heart bounce for an instant. The sight of the lean face beneath the trilby hat threatened to steal that heart away; the strong hard muscles she imagined beneath the formal buttoned jacket made her shiver and there was a tightness deep in her chest. She looked quickly away, blessing the protection of the cloche hat that hid her eyes.

'Not here, Eddie. You can't say things like that here in a public place.'

For a moment he was silent, chewing over the remark. Then he said slowly, quietly, 'You're right, I shouldn't. Things like that should be kept private.' But it spoiled any further conversation.

They sat side by side, swaying to the jerky progress of the tram, its rattling, moaning din preventing any chance of talking, passengers having to shout over the top of it. She, with her mind going round and round, unable to cope with this new situation, and he – the good Lord alone knew what he was thinking, she contemplated dismally.

Walking home through the quiet streets, Cissy's thoughts were still in a whirl and she put her arm through his in an attempt to make him feel better. Each time he attempted to broach the subject again she managed somehow to parry it with some comment about the film they'd just seen.

Reaching her doorstep, she leapt in with a quick goodnight and, before he had a chance to declare his ardour afresh, had her key ready, turning it in the lock and pushing open the door.

'I've had a lovely evening,' she said, from the safety of the two steps up from the street. 'Thanks for taking me to the pictures. It was nice. See you tomorrow, perhaps.'

'Cissy.' He looked at her and in the reflection of the street lamp two doors down, she saw pleading in his eyes. Even with her being two steps above the pavement, her lesser height only brought her eyes on a level with his. 'Cissy, what I said earlier . . .'

'Mum and Dad are waiting up,' she interrupted brightly, looking away. Parents, decent-living parents that was, always waited up for their unmarried daughters, unlike their sons. Woe betide the girl who didn't come home on time. But a son out late was a man about town, given licence. Not that she didn't respect the strict regime Dad set for her – home by eleven, not a minute later, unless given leave by special arrangement – but why should Bobby have rope and not her?

'They're probably waiting to go to bed,' she said firmly. 'I'll have to go in now.'

Eddie capitulated, shoulders sagging. 'S'pose so. See you tomorrer, then? If it's nice, we could go down to the river for the afternoon?'

'Yes, that would be nice.'

Quickly, she moved back as he looked hopeful, half closing the door against the suggestion of his leaning forward to snatch a kiss. She had let him kiss her before on a couple of occasions, but very briefly, more to be sociable than anything, all the time hinting at the fact that she still only considered him a friend.

Friend or not, on each occasion she had felt herself melt, and it had alarmed her. There was danger in melting. It led to other things, and that led to commitment, and marriage, and getting stuck in a rut, never to get anywhere beyond summer trips to Margate for a week's holiday, in time with two or three kids in tail. That wasn't for her. Feel something for Eddie though she might, it wasn't for her.

'Goodnight, Eddie.'

She shut the door forcefully and went to announce herself to Mum and Dad. Bobby, of course, wasn't yet home, but they would go to bed now she was in, leaving him to wander home in his own time.

Bobby boasted a string of girlfriends, with his looks he could take his pick. Not for him the nagging to settle down. When he finally married, he would still be allowed to follow his own path to success, his wife, whoever she would be, encouraging him and bathing in the life he cut out for her.

Not so her. She would be required to follow in the shadow of her husband's success; whatever ambitions she'd had before marriage would be sacrificed to his. It wasn't fair. She wanted her own life, her own success. And no man was going to come between her and that – at least not for a long time.

Chapter Three

On this clear November evening, surprisingly clear after the fog that had lingered for two days, Bobby sat on a bench in Tower Gardens with Ethel Cottle, watching the reflection of street and house lights from the other side shimmering in the night-black water. Romantic . . . it deserved beautiful phrases – the sort of things Cissy said. He murmured into Ethel Cottle's pretty ear and was rewarded by a wistful sigh.

'Oh, Bobby, you talk so nice, you really do. I wish I could talk like that, all romantic like.'

'You do, Ethel. You do.'

The closeness of her, the feel of her, her gentle voice, that elusive perfume she wore – Devon Violets, she'd told him when he had asked – swept away thoughts of all other girls. In his time he'd taken out quite a few pretty girls, but Ethel topped them all. If he played his cards right, he would soon be courting her properly.

He leaned his head against hers as they sat with the Tower looming like a dark mountain behind them. With just a flickering street lamp several yards away, he couldn't see her very well, but the three times he had taken her out, a record for him with any girl, he could recall in every detail how she looked. Not tall, but willowy, her face a delicate oval shape, her narrow nose up-tilted, her rouged lips soft and sweet, her eyes the bluest of cornflowers and her hair the colour of burnished gold that glinted in the sunlight. Her laugh was tinkling and she laughed often at what he said. A girl of eighteen with a tender, loving nature, she was filled with the sweetness and love of life.

His thoughts on her waxing strong, later on, when he became more confident of himself with her, he'd tell her all these things. Until then, he would keep them wrapped up safely in a velvet and golden box in his mind. But he was prompted now to divulge just a little of what he felt. Not too much in case he frightened her off.

'You're the loveliest gel I've ever known, Ethel.' Ethel. What a wonderful name that was.

Her head moved away from his sharply and turned to regard him, the cornflower-blue eyes startled, accusing, taking him off guard.

'What d'you mean, Bobby Farmer – the loveliest girl you've ever known? I s'pose you've known lots, then? I s'pose I'm just one of your long string? And there's me thinking I was special to yer.'

'I didn't mean that at all, Ethel,' he burst in, horrified. 'You see the most beautiful girls passing by in London, but you top 'em all – straight you do.' He made his voice soften. 'And to think you've condescended to let me take you out . . .' He got the long words from Cissy, the way she used them, so sophisticated, they were worth saving up for use.

Ethel melted, giggled, then shivered as she let her head fall back against his.

'I think you're the nicest boy I've ever known, Bobby. . .'

It was his turn to draw his head away. 'What d'yer mean, Ethel Cottle – the nicest boy you've ever known? I s'pose you've known lots, then? And there's me thinkin' I was something special to yer.' But his lips had begun to curve upwards. She saw it and realising that he was joking, mimicking her, she burst out with one of her tinkling giggles and gave him a small shove.

'Oh, Bobby, you're a caution, you really are.'

'Come here,' he murmured forcefully, his voice soft, his purpose now full of confidence.

She did as she was told, her face turned towards his, and in the darkness the kiss was long and ardent, and the lights twinkling across the quiet dark Thames went unnoticed by the budding lovers.

'Why do *I* have to be in by eleven, when you can come home any old time you please?' Cissy burst out at breakfast on the Monday morning. 'My alarm clock showed twelve-thirty when I heard you come in on Saturday night – Sunday morning to be more precise.'

'Exactly twelve-thirty?' Bobby grinned over his cornflakes.

'Does it matter how exact? As a matter of fact it was nearer twenty-five to one. It's unfair. Just because you are a boy and . . .'

'That's enough, you two,' Mum said sharply. In a couple of hours she'd be calling May and the boys to come down for breakfast, the boys ready for school and May for work. She felt harassed and tired, always having to be up so early to see her menfolk off. With Cissy going on at Bobby all through Sunday and again this morning, it was too much.

For much of Sunday dinnertime Charlie had been down the pub with his waterman chums, something to do with union matters. He'd come home to snooze all afternoon leaving her to cope with Cissy nagging on and on at Bobby, throwing herself around the house, pouting, and refusing to let the matter drop. Bobby took it in good part, but Cissy . . . she could be a real madam when she wanted to.

'Do a bit more eating and a bit less nagging,' she told her now, 'or you'll end up late fer work.'

In reality it'd be two hours before she'd be late for work. There had been no need for her to get up as early as this. Only Bobby and his dad needed to rise at five o'clock. Still dark outside but they'd be on the river by the time dawn came up. Dad was out the back now, emptying himself before leaving. Bobby, having finished his cornflakes, was waiting for his turn for the lavatory. Their lunch boxes, with good thick doorsteps of cheese and pickle sandwiches and their flasks of tea, stood waiting on the dresser, while their haversacks were at the door to be picked up on their way out.

Cissy didn't need to be in work until eight; she could have had another couple of hours in bed. But, oh no, she just had to get up to continue nagging at Bobby, hoping to get her own way.

Charlie came back into the kitchen, his coat, cap and choker dotted by the first drops of rain that Doris reckoned would become a downpour. No shelter for a lighterman at the oars; rain, snow, fog, wind, they withstood it all while office and factory workers complained to high heaven whenever the weather was the slightest bit inclement, and even dockers and the like skulked under sheds out of the worst of it. But Charlie never complained. He'd come home after a wet day out on the river, shaking his cap and spraying everyone in reach, the grin on his ruddy face as broad as ever. This morning, however, he wasn't grinning.

He glared down at Cissy, toying with her bread and marmalade like a duchess, her lips a pout as Bobby made his way out to the lav.

'You'd do better, young lady, goin' back ter bed and gettin' out of it again the right side, instead of annoying yer muvver. It ain't got nothing ter do with you, what Bobby do and don't do. I don't blame 'im fer wanting ter be wiv 'is fiancée as many hours as 'e can.'

'Fiancée!' Cissy scoffed. 'He's taken her out twice as I know of.'

'More'n that. Nor do it take long ter know when you've got 'old of the right gel. A lighterman's gel, Milly Lee, and I approve of that.'

Cissy stared up at him. 'Milly Lee? He's not going with Milly Lee. He gave her up ages ago. She told me when I met her last week. And she wasn't too happy about it either. Bobby's been going out with someone called Ethel. Ethel . . .' she thought for a moment. 'Cottle, I think Milly said the name was.'

Dad was frowning at her. Mum stood looking bewildered.

'He never told us nothing about an Ethel Cottle,' she said quietly. 'Who is she?'

'I don't know. Milly said she lives in Jude Street.'

'I don't know no Cottles in Jude Street,' Doris said, a person who knew everyone for streets around, as did most women, in receipt of all the gossip circulating in the local greengrocer's. Jude Street was only a few streets away, the name began to ring bells at last.

'Yes, I do know! They moved in last year. I think someone told me they was evicted from their last place. They said he'd not been too well. 'Adn't had no work at the docks 'cause of it. That's the trouble – they lay 'em off for the least thing and then they leave 'em hanging around them gates until work comes in. Poor devils.'

'You mean she's a docker's gel, this Ethel whatever 'er name is?' Charlie's face was full of horror. 'Our Bobby ain't found hisself a docker's gel?'

He turned abruptly as his son came back into the room, checking his fly buttons with one hand, dragging his choker on and trying to knot it with the other.

'What the hell did you stop seein' Milly Lee for?'

For a moment, Bobby stared enquiringly, then his broad and solid features tightened. 'I don't 'ave ter account to you, Dad, for every gel I take up with.'

'You'll account ter me if you take up wiv one what's got a docker fer a father. Never got money, them. Standin' around waitin' fer piecework like andouts to a tramp. And then workin' like bloody navvies. And spendin' what they do get like water.'

'What d'you know about it?' Bobby's blue eyes blazed. 'Her dad works 'ard, she told me. All right, bin a bit poorly lately, but when he's well, 'e works as 'ard as we do. Harder.'

'Will you both get off to work?' Doris put her spoke in, seeing matters between father and son getting out of hand. They so seldom had arguments, at least nothing more serious than football, Charlie's team being Millwall and Bobby's East Ham which his father thought pathetic, that she glared at them both in alarm.

'Sort it all out when you get 'ome. 'Urry on now, both of you. It's starting to come down cats an' dogs.'

The rain could be heard rattling against the tiny square window of the washhouse. Difference of opinion cut short, Bobby snatched up his cap from the back of the chair and crammed it on his head with both hands, settling it well down, picked up his lunch box and trudged out through the front door with his haversack in the wake of his father.

Doris closed the door after them with a sigh, coming back to her daughter. 'Now p'raps, madam, you can get out of me way an' go up an' tidy yer room till it's time fer work.'

Shrugging, but still petulant over Bobby's licence, Cissy went.

Charlie Farmer sat on the edge of the narrow bench in the open aft cabin out of the rain and unstoppered his vacuum flask. Doris had made the tea good and hot, as always.

Slowly, savouring the brew's bitter aroma, he poured it into the Bakelite cup and stirred in a spoonful of condensed milk from the tin on the cabin shelf. The top of the thick syrupy stuff, left open in its tin by the craft's previous occupier, had developed a crusty sugary skin, adhering to the spoon which he gave a lick before taking a gulp of the boiling whitened tea.

He sighed with satisfaction. Doris maintained he had an asbestos stomach. She took everything lukewarm; working around the house, always feeding others before she fed herself, she ended up with her own meals near cold. But she was used to it and preferred it that way, eating quickly so she could get back to ironing, mending, washing or whatever.

Leaning forward on the bench, Charlie looked up at the sky beginning to pale to a flat watery grey. Rain before seven, clear before eleven. But in November English weather lore seldom held any sway – a few slits of washed-out blue to give a false sense of hope, then down the clouds would come again to drop yet more rain on London. Horizon and sky all awash with weather. Dramatic around the mudflats and creeks of Canvey Island or Erith Marshes maybe, but here at Beckton with the gasworks and the cranes and gantries, wharves and warehouses around the Royal Albert and King George V Docks, just plain dismal.

The tea finished, he went up on deck to wait for young Willy Barnes to show up. The rain had settled into a steady downpour, bringing up the clean smell of the river as well as the pungent tang of the gasworks. On nearby craft, others were busy coiling ropes, drinking their own morning cuppa; one or two hailing him, remarking on the weather. As yet, no sign of Willy who should have been here by now.

Orders from the foreman Sooty Wilson – so named due to a fall of soot over his face from the stove smokestack of his tug a few years back while in the act of dismantling it to see what had blocked it – were to take on sugar from the *Jonathan Lang* moored at the Charlton Bouys for the Tate and Lyle sugar factory.

Charlie grimaced. Rotten stuff, sugar, when it rained. You finished feeling proper stuck-up – not the snotty kind like Cissy with her posh talk and her fancy manners – but the uncomfortable kind.

That was in winter. In summer, September, Charlie recalled, it was wasps. Vacating every bakery in London, they came to swarm all over the craft, covered it, ropes, everything, until they were crunched underfoot. They were always too drunk with sugar to sting. But it was never a pleasant experience.

Sugar had its benefits – spillage, a couple of pounds wrapped up in newspaper for Doris's larder. Not that coal didn't have its own good side, a decent lump for the grate at home. Not much could be done with grain unless you kept chickens in the back yard. One good thing, today's load wouldn't leave a massive cleaning-out job afterwards like coal or cement, something Willy out in the rain would be glad of this morning. And there was Willy at last.

Clambering aboard, the sixteen-year-old had his jacket collar turned up around his large ears, his far-too-big cap dripping water. Willy had just obtained his Watermen and Lightermen licence. Allowed to work in the tideway now, today he'd be kept busy hauling tarps over the cargo to avoid weather spoil, working to get the barge away quick to make room for another. But for the moment, Charlie took pity on the lad looking like a half-drowned wolfhound.

'Cuppa?' he offered. Willy nodded gratefully, glad to go down out of the weather for a few moments until they poked off. A gangly youth, he stood lighting a ragged hand-made smoke with one hand, with the other stirring in his condensed milk. He too had a cast-iron stomach, taking it scalding, had to when there was work to be done. Charlie made sure of that.

Up on deck, Willy unmoored, letting go stern rope then headfast, and poking off from the wharf with a twenty-nine-foot oar. Very soon the craft was pushing out quietly in the rain to work its way up river on the flood tide, Charlie aft steering with one oar, Willy walking for'ard with the other, along the narrow gunwale, the craft manoeuvred between others of all types and sizes lying at rest. Then, with both oars getting into the rhythm, they swung out and pulled steady.

It was peaceful now, the banks gliding by, but an hour from now would see every wharf a chaos of lighters, tugs towing barges, craft pushing off from ships' sides; cranes swinging, dockers and stevedores yelling, nets being swung over, crates humped about, gangplanks bouncing to the tread of porters. For the time being, it was good to savour the tranquillity of this young day, rain or no rain.

A busy day had left it too late to get away on the ebb tide with yet another order for Barking Creek loading timber. It meant waiting for high water and Charlie saw no point going home just to come back. He went ashore for a cuppa at the local coffee shop, then over to the *Roadsman* where there was a good cabin built on that permanently moored barge with somewhere to sleep and a good cooking stove with an oven – home from home. Doris was used to him being away twenty-four hours on the trot. Bringing in overtime, she never complained.

Very early the following morning, the rest of the world hardly astir, he was picked up by a tug with several other barges, then it was down to Barking Creek taking on timber.

It was there he saw Bobby with another apprentice. Bobby didn't look too happy in an old, beaten-up, flaking barge with splintered bow-boards, dents and a few caved plates, good enough for dock and canal work, but obviously not to Bobby's taste. Bobby saw him too, there was no doubt of that, but as Charlie threw him a wave, he turned away.

Charlie's ready grin straightened. The lad was clearly still full of sulks about his opinion of the tuppenny-ha'penny daughter of some flopped-out docker. He'd put paid to that quick as kiss your hand when they got home this evening. He wasn't having it and that was final.

He turned on Willy, who was absorbed rolling himself another gasper instead of looking out.

'Watch that bank, you bloody fool!' he roared, quite unnecessarily, he realised, the moment he had. Yet couldn't help himself.

'Poke off, you daft sod!' To which Willy, seeing the bank not that dangerously near, nevertheless jumped to attention, his look one of amazement at the sudden change in this normally mild-mannered man.

Nine o'clock. Dad still wasn't home.

'I 'ate these long hours your dad does,' Mum said, eyeing the clock on the kitchen mantelpiece, she and the rest of the family having had their own meal around five. Afterwards Cissy had gone out for an hour, round to Daisy's to trim her hair. They had giggled and chatted in Daisy's bedroom, talking of Saturday and what dance-hall they should choose to go to, reading magazines together until Daisy's younger sister, having to come up to bed, made them vacate the room.

Back home now with not much else to do on a damp November evening, Cissy got on with a bit more of the jumper she was knitting herself, Dad's dinner was still gently steaming under a plate, but no sign of him.

'Be like soggy sawdust by the time he do get in,' Mum said, as Bobby came in to inform her that he'd seen his father at Barking Creek, as he sat down to his share of the shepherd's pie she put before him.

'Well, let's 'ope he won't be long,' she said mildly.

Grabbing a knife and fork, Bobby chose not to reply to that. 'Looks good, Mum.'

'Was good, you mean,' she put in. 'Time you two ever get at it. Shame, seeing good food go ter waste,' she remarked, as she bent to wriggle the poker among the coals behind the grating of the kitchen range, making the coals glow brighter and emit more heat, enough to make Cissy push her chair further away from it.

'I don't know me rear end from me elbow, never knowing when you two are doin' overtime,' Mum went on, though her tone wasn't peevish. Overtime money was always welcome. 'Did 'e say 'ow late he'd be, when you saw 'im?'

'Just waved.' Bobby pushed his empty plate back with a satisfied sigh; well built, in a few ticks he could put away a meal that took hours to cook. 'What's fer afters?'

'Tinned pineapple an' custard.' She drew the jug of custard, now with a thick skin on top where it had been keeping warm on a trivet away from the direct heat of the hob.

'He didn't say anythink to you?'

'Too far away.'

'He could've done a bit of tick-tacking like you lot do when you're too far for someone to 'ear you. Didn't 'e signal he'd be 'ome late?'

'No, he didn't!' Bobby said sharply, leaning forward to gobble up the sweet she'd put before him; the tinned pines were free, brought home by Charlie last week, something got for the trade of something else as usual.

The plateful disappearing in five great spoonfuls, Bobby was up from the table before she could probe any further, a naturally slow-thinking woman, she was prone to taking her time whenever asking a question.

'Going upstairs to charge,' he announced, his chair scraping back over the kitchen lino.

'You goin' out then?'

'What if I am?'

Doris frowned at the unusually disagreeable tone. 'There's no need to talk to me like that, Bobby.'

He moderated his tone immediately, his broad, good-looking face penitent. 'Sorry, Mum. I'm just in a bit of a hurry.'

'That's all right,' she conceded gently, loving him in her heart, calling after him as he made it down the passage and halfway up the stairs, 'Who yer seein'?'

His deep voice floated back. 'No one perticler.'

'Not that Ethel Cottle?'

'It depends.'

'Better not let yer Dad know, that's all.'

There was no reply. The door to the bedroom he shared with his younger brothers closing with more force than was needed.

''Ope 'e don't wake them boys up,' she murmured to Cissy.

Within ten minutes Bobby was down again, in good suit, collar, tie and trilby. 'Cheerio!' came his call. 'Might be a bit late.'

'Remember you've got ter be up early for work in the morning,' Doris called, her warning cut short by the slam of the front door.

'You and Dad give him much too much rope,' Cissy put in her spoke, staring hard at her knitting, but her mother only smiled.

'He's young yet. He'll settle down with the right gel in time.'

And I'm young too, thought Cissy, her needles clicking furiously for the life she yearned.

She was in bed well before Dad got home. Mum, as always, stayed up for him, warming up his dinner yet again. Cissy, half waking from sleep, heard their voices coming from the kitchen below, muffled and indistinct.

At one point, Dad raised his, a storm threatening to blow up out of it, but almost immediately his tone returned to conversational level with nothing to spark it off. Mum never retaliated enough for any argument to mature, and though a storm might certainly be brewing up over Bobby, Cissy had never truly known serious or prolonged rows in this house, though she guessed he was the cause of Dad's raised voice on this occasion.

Later she heard the stairs creaking as they came up to bed, their door next to hers closing quietly. For a while their voices droned on, muffled, slow, then finally silence, Dad beginning to snore gently.

What time Bobby came home Cissy didn't know, she was already asleep.

Chapter Four

The storm broke the following evening. Dad could never abide anyone sulking, his policy was always have out with it then done with it, despite Mum's natural inclination to pour oil.

Cissy arrived home from work to a quiet enough household. Mum was getting supper, Sidney and Harry long since come home from school. May as always was giving her tongue an airing on some lengthy saga about one of the women at the cardboard box factory where she'd worked since leaving school in the summer, Mum was not really listening.

The boys had taken themselves off into the back room next to the kitchen to read their comics. No sound from them, *The Magnet* and *Gem* were avidly scanned from cover to colourful cover, the pair of them lying stomach down on the rag rug in front of an as yet dull fire banked up to burn through by the time the rest of the family migrated there for the evening.

Coat and hat off, apron on, Cissy, with a still chattering May to help her, set about laying the kitchen table. Its plain deal surface perpetually hidden by green patterned oil cloth fastened under the edges with drawing pins, she flapped the everyday beigeplaid tablecloth on top, set out cruet and cutlery for the seven people soon to be squashed shoulder to shoulder around its narrow rectangle. Mum would sit at one end, more for easier manoeuvring than a place of honour. The other end was flush against the wall for want of room. Dad, Bobby and Sidney always sat in a row on the open side, Cissy, May and Harry had to squeeze between the table and the back wall, above them the shelf where pots and pans stood upside down to stop cooking grease getting into them.

Cissy felt the tension come in with her father, who was home at a normal hour with no overtime. There'd been steady rain all day, but she was certain it wasn't that which gave his usually benign features such a tight look. He didn't even mention the weather or light-heartedly shake his cap about as he usually did. She was sure it had to do with Bobby, bad feeling lingering from yesterday. Mum too noticed it as he bent to peck her offered cheek. Her voice was touched by concern.

'Everything all right, luv?'

'We'll see,' was all he said, as he sat down in her chair out of her way, opening his evening paper to read until she had dished up.

Cissy went on helping, washing up the cooking utensils to save Mum the job, May still prattling on about her workmates, doing little.

Bobby, coming in a few moments later, dropped a kiss on Mum's cheek with an 'All right, Mum?' but said nothing to his father as he went out and straight upstairs to the room he shared with his brothers.

As Cissy got the plates down from the cupboard for Mum to ladle on steaming helpings of meat pudding, carrots and potatoes, she watched her father's face grow even tighter. She felt guilty that in a way it was she who'd started it in the first place by mentioning the Cottle girl. It hadn't been vindictive. She'd been taken by surprise that her parents hadn't known. Yet she felt partly responsible.

Dad looked up from his paper as Mum called the boys to come to the table, at the same time calling Bobby to come down.

'What's 'e doing upstairs?'

'I don't know,' Mum said mildly.

Cissy took her place at the table beside May. Her father folded his paper, got up from Mum's chair to take his own seat while the two boys did their usual scramble to get to the table before the other, their chatter interspersed by May still on about the women she worked with.

'They don't 'alf 'ave a life, some of 'em,' she gabbled.

'Half, have,' Cissy corrected, but a look from her father cut short any further correction.

'I don't know what's goin' on,' he announced to the thin air. 'Being snubbed by me own son a second day running and ignored by 'im at Barking yesterday. I know 'e bloody ignored me. It was plain as the nose on yer face. I 'ad his silence ter put up with at breakfast this morning, but goin' off ter work on 'is own, not waiting for me – if that ain't a snub, then I don't know what the 'ell you'd call it.'

He went silent as Bobby appeared. Where they'd have automatically sat next to each other swapping accounts of their day, talking shop, Bobby did a bit of signalling to a surprised Sidney to move up to let him sit at the end. Charlie gave a grunt, aware of the significance of the move, gazing as though mesmerised at the meat pudding Mum put before him, knife and fork idle in hand.

'What's special about upstairs, then?'

'Nothing.'

Charlie glared up at him. 'Don't come the old acid with me, son. Yer've bin sulkin' fer two days now. Nothing riles me worse than sulkin'. Specially from a boy what thinks he's a man. You was out with that docker's brat last night, weren't yer?'

'It's got nothink to do with you.'

His father thumped his knife and fork down on the table. 'Nothink ter do with me? It's got everythink ter do with me, lad. Cissy told us about you and 'er, and . . .'

'Cissy's got no right.' Bobby turned an accusing stare on her. 'It ain't none of your damned business, Cis, what I do.'

'Bobby!' Mum looked annoyed. 'I won't have strong language in this house – not from a boy your age.'

'I'm not having her mixing it fer me. She's got Eddie Bennett. All right for them ter go walking out together . . .'

'We are not *walking out* together.'

'I thought you were, dear.'

'Well, I'm not.'

'What's this got ter do with 'im and that docker's gel?' Charlie thundered.

'Just a minute, dear.' Doris gave him a mild look then turned back to her daughter, her faded brown eyes full of concern. 'I thought you two were going steady.'

'Mum, we're not. At least . . .' Bobby forgotten for the moment, Cissy fought to defend her motives '. . . I'm not. I don't feel I'm ready to start going steady with anyone.'

'Of course you are, dear. In a few months time you'll be twenty-one – old enough for any gel to start thinking of settling down.'

'I don't want to settle down.' Her voice was a wail. 'Not yet.'

'Well, I think it's about time you started thinking about it.'

'Mum, it's my life, not yours.' For a moment Cissy forgot to whom she was talking. 'What about what I think? It's my . . .'

The rest was cut short by a roar from her father. He who so seldom raised his voice that the sound startled her into silence.

'You mind what yer say to yer mother, my gel. While you're under our roof, you 'ave some respect, or get out and find yer own place.'

'Charlie!' Doris's voice was shocked. 'Don't say them sort of things, luv. She didn't mean it.'

'I'm still not 'aving that kind of talk in my 'ouse. And, as fer you, miss . . .' He turned on Cissy. 'What's wrong with Eddie Bennett? 'E's the nicest bloke anyone could wish ter meet, and 'e's a lighterman. A good respectable trade many'd envy. You could do worse than 'im, my gel. You think about that one. I'm not 'aving a daughter of mine turn 'er nose up at a decent-livin' bloke as if 'e was dirt under 'er feet. Too much of this ellycution stuff, that's what it is. It's doin' yer no good. My advice ter you is pack that lark in and get yer feet back on the ground if you don't want ter end up an old maid. Eddie Bennett won't always be there waitin' fer yer.'

Out of breath by unaccustomed and excited speech, he sat glaring at her, awaiting her reply.

But it was Mum who spoke first. 'You must admit, Cissy, you are being unfair to Eddie, dangling him on a bit of string. And he's such a nice boy. He works hard. He could give you a really good home. You could both be so happy.'

Cissy gazed from one to the other, tears in her eyes, wondering how this argument had transferred from Bobby to herself. Bewilderment made her tone harsher perhaps than it should have been.

'Can't you both understand? I want some life before I settle down. I want to see things, meet people, nice people. No one seems to want to understand. I don't want to be like you, Mum – nothing more than a housewife, a family of kids around my feet. I want to see a bit of life first.'

'Then yer'd best leave and find yer *bit of life*!' her father burst out, rising out of his chair, his hands on the table supporting his weight. 'Obviously yer can't find it 'ere. And if yer can't find it 'ere, yer'd better go elsewhere to find it.'

Cissy too had sprung up. 'All right – I will!'

'Cissy, Dad!' Her mother had her hands out, appealing to the pair. 'Don't be silly the both of you. Sit down and finish eating.'

'I don't want to eat!' Cissy shouted. 'If he wants me to leave, then I shall leave.'

With that she pushed past May to get out, almost knocking her onto the floor. In the passage, her heart beating sickeningly, she grabbed her hat, coat and an umbrella, swept up her handbag from the front room sofa where she had left it on coming in, and, ignoring Mum's worried calls, ran out into the rain shutting the street door behind her with a colossal crash.

She hadn't meant it to happen like this. Having taken herself off she had no idea where she might go on a wet Tuesday night. But there could be no question of going back indoors to make herself look a fool. The only solution that came to mind was to see Daisy and unload herself onto her, hoping she might be a sympathetic listener.

'I've had the most terrible row at home,' she said as Daisy took her into the front room by permission of her parents who usually kept this best room for guests and Sunday afternoons.

Daisy's house just the other side of Barking Road was a different shape to her own with a large kitchen where the family could live as well as eat, the front room used only for high days and holidays, and it had three bedrooms, the third box-like where her brother slept.

The rain and Cissy's frame of mind had made the walk seem longer than it was, threading her way through the dark deserted streets on a Tuesday night when sane folk found it better to stay indoors, but now she was glad she had come, Daisy was all sympathy as she'd hoped.

'Dad's thrown me out,' Cissy continued as they sat down together on the sofa. Daisy stared at her in horror.

'Thrown you out? Why? What have you done?'

'Nothing actually. Well, not actually *thrown* me out. I walked out, I suppose. It was a row with Dad. He told me to go if I wasn't satisfied with the life I had. Can you imagine, satisfied with *that*? So I just walked out.'

'What are you going to do?'

For a moment, Cissy gave herself up to silent debate. Just what *did* she think she was going to do? Her shoulders sagged in defeat. 'Go home again, I suppose.'

'Well, that's a relief.'

'Not just yet, though. Is it all right if I stay for an hour or two, then go home? Everything might have calmed down by then.'

Daisy was all for that. Soon they were wrapped up talking about dresses, latest fashions, make-up, thumbing through Daisy's mass of magazines and squeaking longingly over clothes they would like to be seen in but couldn't afford, planning where they'd go next Saturday.

'I've bought some absolutely divine fringe,' Daisy told her, already aping West End idiom. 'I'm putting it on that yellow dress. You know, the one I bought down Petticoat Lane a few weeks ago. It's gold, the fringe. Matches the yellow a treat. I'm going to put three rows round the bottom, and if there's enough I shall put a piece across the bust. You just watch it shake about when I'm doing the shimmy. What do you plan to wear? Hope we get lots of partners on Saturday.'

Heads together, short hairstyles identical, Daisy's dark, Cissy's fair, Daisy brown-eyed, Cissy's blue-grey, they studied the garment, visualising how it would look. Around eight-thirty, feeling a lot better, Cissy made her way homeward, letting herself in. She had her own key, not waiting for her twenty-first; trusted by Mum if not Dad, Mum's quiet will dominating his as it did in most things.

'Should have her own,' she said firmly. 'She always comes 'ome at reasonable times and I don't want to keep getting up out of me chair to let 'er in.' Meaning that he, working hard all day for his family, wasn't expected to get up out of his to answer a knock at the door.

Dad wasn't speaking to Cissy. Neither was Bobby, and the atmosphere was tense throughout the rest of the week. She was glad for Saturday and her brief escape to the environment she was sure was made for her.

No one could feel more a part of it than she did, surrounded by the glitter and the glamour. She and Daisy would perch on spindly-legged, gilt-painted wicker chairs near to the huge shiny grand piano where they might be more easily seen, the slim, flashing fingers of the pianist tinkled out dance music, backed by a trumpet and saxophone, while the drummer beat a rhythm to set the feet tapping, the heart racing.

Lips bright red, cigarettes fitted into slim bone holders – Dad ought to know – allowing the smoke to wreathe elegantly. Both of them pretty, vivacious, putting on the accent, exhilarated by their once a week jaunt where others more used to West End life looked perhaps a fraction bored with it all, she and Daisy never lacked for partners.

'What a devastatingly lively gel you are.' This from a long streak of Knightsbridge elegance who pronounced 'gel' quite differently to the way her father did with him leaving the 'l' out altogether.

Cissy allowed her eyelids to flutter as she wallowed in her current partner's attention.

'I'm never anything else.'

'How smashing. I say, do you think we can . . .'

The remainder of his question was interrupted by a firm tap on his shoulder. Startled, he looked round at the culprit, a little affronted.

'I say, old man . . .'

'This is an excuse-me, isn't it, old chap?'

The voice was light but commanding, and faintly derisive.

'Er . . . I suppose it is. Oh, blast!'

Thanked, he walked stiffly away, leaving Cissy to be passed on as slavishly as the slave bangle on her upper arm signified. But she went willingly, this new partner far more acceptable than the one wandering off already looking for someone else to excuse.

'May I ask your name?' The bluntness of it took her breath away.

'Cissy Farmer.'

It sounded smart on her lips, stylish, and she was gratified to have her partner confirm that point with a small appreciative nod.

'Delighted to know you, Miss Farmer. Langley Makepeace.'

'How do you do?' she said, hoping she didn't sound too formal for the situation.

Madam Noreah had taught her introductions. And she practised it to the full on the social world into which she occasionally stole, but never with so handsome a man as this. Dancing close to him, she noted he had grey eyes, unusual with such dark well-groomed hair, shiny with expensive brilliantine, but it was his smooth, regular features, certainly making him out to be younger than his mature demeanour and full voice would have him seem, that made her ecstatic young heart do a little flip. Surely not much older than she, but so very certain of himself that she wondered if he might not be of some titled family.

He was a lovely dancer too. Her heart flipped again, and she dared to hope, as he guided her expertly through the fast foxtrot without her faltering once, that he might ask her for another dance. Maybe even to have her as his partner the whole evening. If he did, she could ask him more about himself.

The foxtrot coming to an end with a crash of cymbals, he escorted her back to her seat, her arm on his. He would ask for the next dance, surely. But it wasn't to be.

With a polite bow, a small appreciative smile and a deep-voiced thank you, he moved away. Not a word about the next dance or any other.

'Who's he?' Daisy was all goggle-eyed as she joined her.

'He excused me.'

'He didn't! My God, he looks like he owns Buckingham Palace.'

Cissy shrugged. If he owned half that, to have been excused by him was marvellous in itself. Her hopes grew greedy, but while others came to invite her to dance, Langley Makepeace was seen only from afar, partnering with girls whose shingles and curls were expensively styled, whose dresses came from Chanel not Commercial Road, whose shoes hailed from Paris rather than Frieda's Footwear, Whitechapel.

Suddenly it was not fun any more, dancing with this one and that. Perched on the grand piano with Daisy nursing an abused foot, their previous seats taken by others, their light weight going unchallenged by the pianist who had music on his mind, Cissy cast a glance at the large gilt clock above the entrance door. Ten past ten.

At twenty-five past they would have to leave this glittering place and make their way back home by tube to the dingy districts of Canning Town and Plaistow.

Daisy was still nursing her foot, the short skirt of her dress with its new addition of gold fringe almost up around her hips, her face, with its diamanté circlet gracing her forehead, pouting as she bent over to ease off the shoe. She didn't see the handsome young man approach them as the musicians struck up a ragtime with renewed gusto. But Cissy did.

Her heart gave a leap of dismay. For most of those here, the night was still young. But for her, there were only fifteen minutes left – like Cinderella she must leave the ball, only Cinderella would have had another hour and a half to go before she cast her glass slipper on the marble steps of the prince's palace. This particular prince coming ever nearer was doomed to even earlier disappointment.

Cissy forced herself to brighten and smiled. Langley Makepeace bowed.

'Shall we?'

Despite her own aching feet, Cissy slipped easily and lightly off the piano, her lithe slimness apparent beneath the pale blue georgette dress with its diamanté dress-clips and the swinging row of artificial pearls. Her dangling pearl earrings joggled brightly and she prayed he wouldn't notice the fake from the real thing.

'I'd love to,' she gushed, to be whisked away in his arms.

Would she hear midnight strike? Would she run from those strong arms into the night, her splendid dress replaced by rags? Would she see the golden coach shrink to a mousetrap, one glass slipper left on the marble steps of this palace to be picked up by this prince to go searching through the poor districts of London for the one whom the slipper would fit, to be whisked off to rule beside him as his bride?

But all that happened, as the minute hand of the gilt clock moved on towards the fateful ten-thirty above the crowded dance floor full of noisy young things jerkily gyrating to ragtime, was that as the band ceased its crazy staccato rag, she thanked Langley Makepeace with what little breath she had, and went and grabbed Daisy. The two of them ran to the tiny cloakroom for their hats and coats, changing into their street shoes in a flurry of haste, thrusting their dance shoes into cotton drawstring shoebags and hurrying off into the damp November night to the tube station, coats clutched around them with one hand, fishing in their handbags for the ticket money with the other.

No prince. Cissy's shoes were firmly on her feet. Already he would have forgotten her. But oh, what a wonderful prince he had been. She would dream of him in her sleep tonight. They'd be lovely, romantic dreams, she knew.

Bobby too had lovely, romantic dreams that night. But his were based on reality.

For quite a while now, he and Ethel had been growing fonder, their kisses becoming more ardent, but hitherto she had always backed away should his embrace become too urgent.

Then this evening he had taken her to a party. One of his mates, Frank Bottomly, previously an apprentice like himself, had received his Freeman's papers, necessitating a family celebration. Frank had invited him, along with his girl.

With plenty of drink flowing, Ethel, whose family had nothing like enough cash to spend on wines and spirits, did a grand job on every glass she was offered, to the extent that later she didn't care what Bobby asked of her. Besides that, she was in love with him, as he was with her.

At the start it had only been a bit of breast-fondling, pausing near the quiet recreation ground on their way back to her home. But as he began to get up steam, so did she. Before they realised it, caution had been thrown to the wind.

Hidden from the street lamp by the shadow of a privet hedge and with no one around, he pressed her hard against the recreation ground railings and they came together awkwardly, Ethel sighing, he puffing, the pair of them fit for nothing afterwards but to walk home slowly, saying little, each wrapped in their own private thoughts.

He did love her and wanted so much to marry her, but he couldn't yet afford to, not on an apprentice's pay. Not even on a three-yearman's pay. Not for another two years at least. He'd told her this, and she had understood; was willing to wait. After Christmas, perhaps, if he went careful with his money, he'd buy her a ring. But first he must convince Dad that nothing was going to tear him and Ethel apart. They were made for each other.

None of this worried him. For love conquered all, and they would emerge victorious. And so Bobby's dreams were sweet and romantic.

Chapter Five

'Do you know what I'd really like to do?' Daisy asked, after going on about how sick and tired she was of running up seams for Cohens Garments, day in, day out. 'I'd like to go on the stage, that's what I'd like. I've got a good enough voice.'

'I know that,' answered Cissy, as they stood in the short queue for clocking on, but Daisy was already chattering on.

'It's such a waste, all that hard-earned money going on lessons – nothing being done about it. I want to sing properly.'

The clocking-on machine pinged the time against Cissy's card. She paused to stare at Daisy.

'Opera, you mean?' She put her card back in its slot. 'That will take you years yet.'

'Not opera. I mean proper singing. You remember that singer at the pictures last week? If I could be like her.'

Cissy remembered. Between parts one and two of the main film, the projectionist had got the reel upside down, tried to correct it amid cat calls and whistles and had mixed up the reels. It had taken some several minutes to sort it out, peanuts and orange peel being tossed around as a diversion. The singer booked for the interval had gone on to keep the audience quiet and she soon had everyone singing along with her, the film forgotten until it came on again.

'I'd love to be able to do that,' Daisy went on. 'I really could, you know. I wouldn't feel a bit nervous, because I know I could do it. That's what I'd really like to do.'

There was no chance to say more. Eight o'clock and time to start, the two of them parted company, each going to sit at her respective machine. All conversation ceased as the power wound up. The burr and buzz of fifteen sewing machines on piecework would drown all but the loudest shriek anyway. Such a cry came around eleven o'clock, bringing Miss Jakes, their beak-nosed forelady, hurrying over with an irritable and imperious frown to see what the matter was.

Rosy Goodman's thumbnail had caught under the power-driven needle and automatically stopped her machine, which of course held up production and Miss Jakes wasn't at all pleased by that.

With Rosy yelling and sobbing, the whole floor came to gaze in horror at the slow dark blood oozing all over one of Cohens pale garments – pale as the victim's face – while Miss Jakes lifted the foot with unusual gentleness to ease the needle up.

Sometimes the needle would break, leaving part still in the nail. Then it was a job for pincers and the sal volatile. Fortunately for Rosy, it came out smoothly, leaving the pierced and aching nail to be bound up with a bandage from the grubby first-aid box and Rosy to be comforted in the tiny closet they called the rest room.

It was said in the trade that you weren't a machinist until you'd had your nail under the foot. It had happened once to Daisy, but not yet to Cissy and she lived in terror of her finger being caught, even though she was one of the fastest workers there. Her eyes would ache at the end of the day from training them on each short or long burst of that sharp, furiously piercing machine needle.

'You're not the only one wishing you could get out of this trade,' she said to Daisy, taking up their earlier conversation at lunch time. 'Just think, never having to come back here. At least you could make a living on the stage. What could I do just learning to speak nicely? I should have taken Madam Noreah's advice to take up singing as well.'

She toyed miserably with her cheese and pickle sandwich.

'It's all a waste of time. I can't keep it up here. The women all think I'm stuck up whenever I try. Eddie goes self-conscious on me, trying to improve the way *he* speaks and making a mess of it. Then I get embarrassed for him. And Mum and Dad never stop telling me that I'm wasting good money.'

Daisy nodded understandingly, her family too queried the money she spent on singing lessons. As for wanting to put her talent to use, when she'd mentioned her wish to go into the theatre, they'd been horrified. Only loose women went on the stage.

'You'd think I was telling them I wanted to be a street walker,' she said, glumly stirring her tea. 'It would serve all of them right if we left home to seek our own fortunes.'

She stopped stirring to look up, eyes shining. 'We could, you know. I'll be twenty-one after Christmas. I could do what I like then.' But Cissy wasn't so happy.

'I'm not twenty-one until March. I can do nothing until then.'

Daisy frowned. 'Why not? You're the one always going on about making your own way in the world, not wanting to settle down. But the moment I suggest it, you back out. All that talk. I don't think you'll ever leave home. You haven't got the nerve. Talk about empty drums.'

Cissy took a great bite of her sandwich. 'That's not fair!'

'I'd be game if you were.'

Cissy chewed slowly. 'Wait until after Christmas. Then we'll see.'

Since her two dances with Langley Makepeace five Saturdays ago, she had hoped the experience might have been repeated. She daydreamed of being swept off her feet and in quiet moments made up little scenes of him proposing to her, declaring his undying love – she the cool femme fatale, one hand nonchalantly extended to push him aside, her painted eyes averted like the heroines on the silver screen, Gloria Swanson, Theda Bara, Pola Negri. He would beg her favour. Finally she would give in and on his arm be conducted to the best seats of theatres, the best tables in plush, chandelier-lit restaurants; all eyes would watch her lithe figure as Langley Makepeace held her close at tea dances. She would be the belle of the ball and at his grand family home his father would announce their engagement. Lavish wedding plans would be made, and she, a humble girl from the East End, would keep her secret safe.

But the smart little dance floor in Kensington with its mirrored wall to make it look larger, where she had met him, had not produced him again. She had persuaded Daisy to go there with her on three other occasions, daring Daisy's raised eyebrows, but Langley Makepeace had vanished completely.

'We'll see after Christmas,' she said despondently and Daisy gave a disparaging snort.

It seemed there was nothing he could do right this evening for Ethel. Bobby knew what it was. She in one of her moods, saying that he didn't care for her any more, that all he wanted was her body and now he had it he didn't care how she felt, that she'd cheapened herself.

'You ain't cheapened yerself,' he coaxed as they walked through the cold December evening, she huddled in her slightly threadbare winter coat with its motheaten rabbit-fur collar yet refusing to cuddle close to him for warmth. 'I love you, Ethel.'

'No you don't. You got what you wanted. Three times now. And now you're only saying that.'

'I'm not *only saying that*!' he retorted impatiently. 'I wouldn't say it if I didn't mean it.'

But the truth was, he *was* only saying that. Lately he was beginning to feel a bit tired of her constant worrying.

After that first time going together, he'd had a job to persuade her that everything was all right, that he loved her dearly. And he had at the time. The second time they'd gone together, this time in the recreation field, it was colder and more uncomfortable as the November fog came down. The ground felt clammy and his overcoat, on which they'd both lain, was muddy in places so that he'd had to wash it quickly in the sink before going to bed – that second time he had still been in love with her. This third time, he wasn't so sure.

Now it was Christmas, a thin skim of snow lay on the ground. If only they could find somewhere warmer. Pressing her against the recreation ground railings, with Ethel complaining they were cold and hard on her back, her skirt pulled up and her knickers down, somehow the romance had gone out of it. Not that he didn't love her so that it burst out of him as the moment of his climax came, but as it went so did the overwhelming throb of love.

They walked home in the cold. She was still shivering after baring her flesh to the elements as well as him, yet refusing to let him put his arm around her to keep her warm, he began to feel not love but irritation. A man could stand only so much nagging and moaning.

'What the hell's the matter with you?' he burst out at last.

She sniffled in misery, clutching her coat closer to her. 'I don't think you love me at all, Bobby Farmer.'

At that point all patience fled. 'All right! If you want me to say it. I don't. I just wanted your body. Does that satisfy you?'

The answer was a thin wail. 'I . . . knew . . . it.'

Before he could stop her, she was off, running like the wind. He started to follow, but something made him stop. All that whining on the way back from the recreation ground. She was cold. *He* was cold. She obviously felt disillusioned. He felt disillusioned too. Where had the romance gone?

He stood still, gazing at where the darkness had swallowed up her small figure. She was only a street away from home. He wouldn't catch her now. Disconsolately he turned and wandered away in the direction of his own house. He didn't think he would be seeing her any more.

Christmas in the Farmer household was like a gathering of the clans. Each family had its own Christmas dinner. That done, they put on their glad rags, locked the door of their own homes behind them, and made a beeline for Charlie's, this year being his turn to have everyone. By six o'clock, the tiny tenement in Fords Road was trying to accommodate not only his brother Robert's family and those of his sisters Amy and Lottie, but Doris's side too – her sister, two brothers and each of their families. If the walls could have bulged they would have been given a hefty push.

Except one armchair for Doris's old mother of eighty-two, out went the three-piece suite into the garden to be covered by a tarpaulin. In came orange boxes with planks to lay across them to be placed around the walls of the front and back rooms, supplementing the six kitchen and four elderly dining chairs.

With the old piano going, a couple of dozen crates of beer got from a general whip-round by the men, a few bottles of whisky, maybe one of rum and another of brandy if Charlie had been lucky with lightering and a couple of bottles of port or sherry for the women, who could ask for more of a Christmas party?

The women turned their hands to sandwich making; ham, tongue and tinned salmon, going down well with pickled onions and gherkins. Then there were mince pies and sausage rolls, a large basin of shrimps, another of winkles and enough pins to go round, with Doris's Christmas cake as the *pièce de résistance*, taking pride of place at the centre of it all.

Upstairs, the kids pinched the dregs of beer glasses and littered the beds with cake crumbs, rolled all over the coats strewn across the main bed, dressed themselves up in their parents' hats, and helped break each other's Christmas toys. The noise they generated went unheard for the shrieks and guffaws of laughter downstairs and the singing as the piano was wreaked havoc upon by heavy-handed, untutored fingers.

No neighbour came to complain of the noise of singing and dancing. If the neighbours weren't having similar parties, they were at someone else's house sharing theirs.

Boxing Day was a much quieter affair with the need to get over the previous day. Doris, still hoping Cissy and Eddie would eventually get closer together, invited him to share the Boxing Day meal of cold, left-over chicken, mashed potatoes, pickles, and the remains of Christmas pudding warmed up with hot custard.

Cissy wasn't most pleased. 'He might have had better things to do on Boxing Day,' she hissed to her mother as she helped wash up.

She received a querying stare. 'What better to do than to see you, luv? He jumped at the chance when I suggested it to 'is mum. It seems a shame, you not being able to see 'im, being with 'is own people all over Christmas. I thought it would be nice.'

'What if I didn't want him to come?'

'Oh, you silly! Of course you wanted 'im to come. I could see it in your face all yesterday. And besides, you two 'ave been goin' out regular once a week fer ages, when 'e takes you to the pictures.'

'That's all we ever do,' Cissy said bitterly, squeaking her wiping-up cloth around a wet beer glass, 'go to the pictures.'

'That's because he's saving, dear.'

'Saving?' Oh, no, not saving again, went the thought.

'Fer when you two get married. I know 'e wants ter marry you, but don't say I said so when 'e does get around to popping the question. His mum said ter me that this time next year he'll 'ave enough ter put down on a little rented 'ouse for you two and you could get married.'

'Nice if I was asked first.'

Her mother looked at her with surprise. 'Hasn't 'e asked yet?'

'He makes noises. I think that's what he's trying to ask.'

'He's a shy boy, luv. Ain't that easy for a young man to propose. It takes a lot of courage. It's up ter you, Cissy, to 'elp a bit. You 'ave ter give 'em a bit of encouragement. I did with yer dad.'

'I don't think I'd want to go that far.'

'Now what d'yer mean by that – you don't want to go that far?'

'If he hasn't the courage, then he's not the man for me.'

Her mother gave a small indulgent laugh. 'That's silly talk, Cissy! He's in love with yer. It's just shyness – that's all.'

'I want someone who's sure of himself, Mum.'

'Eddie's sure of 'imself, just shy about asking you to be 'is wife. It's understandable.'

'Well, I don't want to understand. And until he does propose, I'm not ready to push him in that direction.'

Her mother stopped washing up, stood with her hands in suds, gazing at her. 'You're a funny girl sometimes, Cissy. If you ain't careful, your Eddie'll get tired of you. You'll end up too late to marry. You don't want to end up an old maid, do yer?'

But Cissy only shrugged and went on wiping up, wondering how soon she could get rid of Eddie for the night so she could go on with her daydreams.

Eddie had sat talking to Dad most of the evening when he wasn't sitting next to her on the sofa, which had been brought back indoors with the rest of the furniture, the crates and planks taking their place in the back yard until Dad could get them back to Briggs & Co.

Eddie had tried to hold her hand, but she had extracted it gently from his grasp. His touch made her tingle, but if only he had taken her hand and pulled her forcefully from the room despite her parents' horrified stare. If he had taken her to some quiet corner of the house and there had kissed her with passion, bending her over backwards like Valentino or Navarro did with their women on the screen.

But he'd just sat, allowing her to withdraw her hand, his only reaction to look a trifle sad and disappointed, as he carried on talking shop to Dad, discussing tonnages and cargoes and timber going by the standard rather than the tonnage, the pair of them swapping tales. Eddie related a rather nasty collision that happened last week, a sidewinder from a towed barge coming downriver from under London Bridge and the consequent argument with the driver of the tug responsible. Cissy sighed. Surely there had to be something better in life than this?

'I tell you what,' Daisy said, as they made their way to work one Friday. It was early February, cold but dry and sunny. Spring was in the air and Cissy's hopes were up.

'I tell you what,' Daisy repeated, 'let's not go to Madam Noreah's tomorrow. Let's go up West for the afternoon. Take our dance shoes and our dresses. Have a real day up there. Have lunch and a tea. And then we can go on to Kensington, to that dance place you liked so much before Christmas. We haven't been there for ages.'

'I haven't got enough money for all that,' Cissy said, prematurely counting her pay packet due this evening.

'I have.' Cissy looked at her in amazement. 'My dad won on the dogs yesterday. A real good win. He came home drunk as a lord last night and – you know what he's like. He was so soppy as usual. He gave Mum a quid for herself and one each for me and Sam, but there were two pound notes stuck together and he didn't notice when he gave me mine. I said nothing. So we've got two quid to spend as well as our wages. What do you think of that?'

Cissy thought; felt excitement building up inside her.

'I think it's absolutely marvellous!' Her arm through Daisy's she gripped it tight. 'Let's do it.'

'Let's,' Daisy echoed, giggling as they turned into East India Dock Road for their tram stop, neatly sidestepping the gypsy who scuttled towards them from the doorway of the Red Lion like some skinny black spider.

'Tell yer fortune, young ladies? Buy a bit o' lace ter bring yer luck, dears?'

Slender Cuban heels clicking fast, they tripped hurriedly past, chins down into their turned-up rabbit fur collars and eyes thankfully hidden by deep-crowned cloche hats, pretending they hadn't noticed her.

'They give me the creeps,' Daisy said as they escaped, the black eyes gazing in their wake.

Cissy could feel them boring into her back even as she put distance between herself and the woman. It was imagination, of course. What would the woman have told her had she paused? She might have discovered if she were destined to meet that Langley Makepeace again. There was half an urge to turn back, as if she were being drawn. She could still do so. They were only fifty feet further along the road. She still could. Yet something inside said she would hear tidings rather not known. Why she felt that, she wasn't sure.

Risking a glance over her shoulder as they joined the queue at the tram stop, she saw the dark eyes still gazing after her where normally the woman would have shrugged and gone on to plague some other passer-by.

The tram was coming. Quickly they boarded it. Even as she settled in her seat, the tram whining off, a glance revealed the swarthy face still turned in her direction, as though the woman knew exactly where Cissy had sat. A shiver went through Cissy's body.

Daisy was chattering away, unconcerned, the gypsy long since swept from her mind. But Cissy, just enough aware of Daisy's chattering to nod in the right places, was thinking of Langley Makepeace.

She should have gone back to that gypsy woman; she might have learned something of her future, yet she had been afraid. Perhaps of the woman herself, accosting her with her lace and promises?

There was no shortage of beggars in London. Kerbs still harboured the unfortunate flotsam from the Great War – even after six years – pathetic victims heaving along on crutches, sometimes with half a leg, sometimes a whole leg missing. Just a sleeve pinned to the breast was reason enough for the card slung about the neck on string proclaiming 'Ex Soldger with Wife and 6 Children to Surport'.

She couldn't help thinking sometimes, uncharitably, even as she was compelled by pity to drop a penny into a tin, that the crippled war veteran was more capable of producing children than pennies.

Some were more talented than others, the ones with all their limbs but no job moved along the gutter in threes and fours, making music with cornet and sax and clarinet. Some sold matches, some shoelaces. They far outnumbered the professionals; the one-man band, the spoon player, the barrel organ with his dressed-up little monkey and hordes of children gathering around to dance to his tunes. But none of them worried her as much as the predatory woman outside the Red Lion this morning. Yet still she felt drawn to encountering her again. What had life in store for her? Washing clothes and raising children with Eddie Bennett or living the life of luxury with Langley Makepeace?

Somehow she felt she should know already, without consulting any gypsy. Resolutely, she turned her attention back to a still chattering Daisy.

*

Sidney had toothache. It was a back tooth and kept Doris on her toes most of the night. This wasn't the first time Sidney's back tooth had played him up.

'You'll have to go to the dentist in the morning,' she told him, which produced a drawn-out wail and an assertion that the pain had abated considerably. But it didn't last long and she enforced her vow as she made up a hot salt-bag to press against the offending molar.

'It's no good goin' on like this, luv. It'll 'ave to come out. I'll take you off to the dentist first thing in the morning. See what 'e thinks.'

Sidney, reduced to a cold sweat, knew only too well from previous experience that unless you had the money for gas, a child's tooth was considered a small thing, yanked out in a tick without it. If it needed only a bit of drilling, that too was considered too easy a job on young teeth to warrant a jab of cocaine or a sniff of gas – unless your family was rich enough to pay, and Mum, as loving as she was, thought the same way as the dentist. No point throwing money around when it wasn't all that easy to come by. It would be over in a jiff. To Sidney it would be an eternity.

Despite all his efforts to bite his lip, his moans grew louder until all, except Dad, who, after asking what was going on had turned over and left Mum to deal with it, were woken.

Harry, angry at being woken up, had hit his brother with a pillow, making his cries even worse. May, who shared Cissy's bedroom, began tossing and turning, complaining enough to disturb Cissy. But Cissy was already having a disturbed night, dreaming of gypsies.

Bobby's night wasn't so pleasant either. For him there could be no sleep after what Ethel Cottle had told him.

He had gone out with her a few times since Christmas, unable to bring himself to tell her that he wanted to break with her. She was hanging on to him so, he hadn't the heart. But he had steered clear of the recreation ground in preparation for telling her.

Then this evening, she had dropped her bombshell. 'Bobby, you've got to help me. I didn't see my . . . you know what . . . last month, and now I've missed again. Bobby, I think I'm pregnant!'

The last had been a wail, as great as Sidney's in the bed next to his. 'What am I going to do? My dad'll kill me. Bobby, we've got to get married!'

He lay in bed assailed by the dilemma. He supposed he did still love Ethel when it came down to it. She was exciting, so long as she didn't start moaning about little inconsequential things. She had a lovely figure and a beautiful elfin-shaped face and deep blue eyes a man could drown himself in. There wasn't a girl around here to match her, except perhaps for Cissy, but Cissy was only his sister and she didn't count.

He couldn't even pretend that, if she was pregnant, it was someone else's. Say what you like, Ethel was a loyal girl and hadn't looked at another chap since she and he had been going out together. It might have been better if she had, then he might have felt a little easier. As it was, it looked as though wedding bells would be chiming within the next couple of months to keep things looking right. He had just begun to reconcile himself to the idea not being such a bad thing, drifting off, when Sidney's crying woke him up to start the whole round off again – damn Sidney.

Chapter Six

In the eyes of both families, Eddie was assumed to be Cissy's young man. Any attempt to deny it was treated as a young girl's natural coyness. The slightest rebuff on her part had Mum and Dad making a thing out of it until, for a quiet life, it was easier to bite her tongue, even though she still managed to wriggle out of talk of engagement rings.

Weekends were becoming his by right and those lovely West End Saturday evenings out with Daisy earlier in the year were history. As for her Prince Charming, he too was fading into history. She had never seen him again, he was more likely haunting private parties in Belgravia or languishing in the south of France, his appearance in Kensington just one of those slumming expeditions bright young people of means were known to enjoy from time to time. Pity. She'd had such dreams.

On this lovely March Sunday afternoon Eddie was rowing her on the Serpentine, never happier than when he was on the water showing his prowess with an oar.

He rested on the oars now, his lean handsome face grinning across at her.

'Happy?'

She trailed a hand in the water. 'Hmm.'

The response was non-committal but he didn't seem to notice. His hazel eyes grew serious as he regarded her.

'I'm glad. Cissy. . . .' He faltered then went on purposefully, 'We've bin going steady together for a while now and . . . well, I wondered if it wasn't time we began thinking a bit more about our future together. And well, now . . .'

He took his gaze away from her to let it sweep across the peaceful scene, the sun warm on the Serpentine, rowing boats gliding lazily by. Not a breeze ruffled the water or stirred even the top leaves of the trees. On the banks, families sat with picnics spread or threw bread to the ducks and swans gathering in greedy masses, racing for the best and largest morsels to swash in the water before devouring.

Eddie turned his gaze back to her as though the scene had brought him the resolve to continue.

'And now seems the right time to say it. Cissy, I want you to be my wife. . . . Don't say no,' he hurried on, as she drew in a deep breath, half shaking her head. Quickly shipping the oars, he slid himself across to her seat to clasp her hand in his.

'Don't say no, Cissy. I know it's a big step fer a girl. It's a big step fer me too. But I love you. I've got enough money . . . well, it ain't a lot, but if I go careful we can rent a nice little 'ouse, 'ave a nice little 'ome – the two of us. I'd look after yer and see you 'ave anything my money can buy. You could give up work and all. Wouldn't yer like that? Please say you'll marry me, Cissy.'

She could not meet his gaze. 'Eddie, I – I like you tremendously. I think you'd make a wonderful husband . . .'

'So you will? You will marry me?'

'I never . . .'

'Oh, Cissy!' His arm was around her shoulders, the boat rocking. She managed to turn her head away as his lips sought hers, but he was too over the moon to realise and laid his face close to hers. 'You've made me so proud. So happy.'

'Eddie, listen . . .'

'Let's get 'ome and tell yer mum and dad. They won't 'ardly believe it when we tell 'em. I can't 'ardly believe it.'

He was back in his seat, a skilled waterman moving surefooted in the precariously rocking rowing boat. Taking up the oars, he bent his back to it, shooting the craft through the water, and a thought, totally unrelated to Cissy's confusion of his proposal, came to her. Talk about Oxford and Cambridge Boat Race held last Saturday, the dark blues sinking at Hammersmith Bridge to the rare delight of spectators with light blue rosettes.

Eddie was in training for the Doggett's Coat and Badge – four and a half miles rowing from London Bridge to Chelsea. He was hopeful of achieving his coat and badge and Cissy felt a surge of pride seeing the muscles ripple below his short-sleeved shirt with every pull on the oars. Then she thought of the days that would follow on after the wedding excitement had dissipated – she just another housewife, just another mother eventually. Eddie coming home each day to the meal she would prepare, she washing his clothes and tidying the house. She and

Eddie growing older together with no more to say to each other, all new ideas exhausted, even the sharing of bed no more than a habit. She almost shuddered. Where was the dream? Oh God, where was the dream?

Both their families were overjoyed. Cissy suffered being kissed and embraced by both sets and Eddie came round every evening after work to sit with her family, or to take her to his. Plans were made around her ears: 'Don't want a too long engagement, luv. A year maybe – to save up. A spring wedding. Next March would be nice. Give us all time to save up. Ain't it exciting? What'll you wear? Short dresses are all in this year. And a luvly veil over one of them lace caps brides are wearing. You'll look just lovely, Eddie'll be proud of yer.'

'I'll do the flowers, dear,' this from Eddie's aunt.

'We can do a lovely spread between us,' this from both mothers eager to show their cooking skills.

Everyone was riding on the crest of a wave and workmates were congratulating her after Daisy, in whom she had confided, had told them the news.

'I need to get out,' she pleaded to Daisy that following Saturday. For once, neither of them had gone to their Saturday lessons, they were too taken up by the impending engagement.

Daisy's mother was out shopping and her father was at work, Cissy sat in her friend's kitchen, gazing out of the window at the rain falling on the tiny patch of grass they called a back garden.

'I feel stifled by all this.'

'Isn't Eddie coming round tonight?' Daisy asked, but Cissy was desperate.

'Let him. He'll find me not in. I'm still entitled to a bit of freedom, surely.'

'What did you have in mind?'

'Let's go dancing. Perhaps we could go to that one in Kensington.'

'Not *that* one again. I don't know what you see in *that* one.'

'I like it. It's small and cosy.'

'Hmm!' snorted Daisy, sipping the sherbert drink her mother made. 'There's dozens of other places we could go. Let's just go up West – take our dance shoes – see how we feel when we get there.'

Insistence would make it look glaringly obvious that something in Kensington other than just a ballroom was drawing her. She shrugged, putting Langley what's-his-name to one side. After four months even the name was fading.

'All right,' she conceded. After all, what she really needed was to get away from the constant Eddie for a while, to savour one last evening of freedom.

Ethel's eyes were full of tears. 'We've got to do *something*, Bobby. I've missed my next you-know-what as well. I'm definitely pregnant. I just know I am.'

'How can you tell? Apart from your whatsits?' he asked morosely.

A feeling of being trapped was beginning to weigh on him. He was unsure if he'd ever really loved Ethel, except for what she'd stirred in him. Then again, perhaps he did love her in a way. But marriage was a big step; asked a lot of someone who wasn't sure. And yet they had to do something, and quick – if she was right – before she began showing.

It was a strange situation. He felt at once sick yet gripped by the realisation that he might be a father. And yet, the baby Ethel was carrying, if she was carrying, was his. A piece of himself. For a moment a tremendous surge of pride assailed him. If it was a boy, he could teach him to box and play football. When he grew up he'd be a lighterman, carrying on the river tradition of the family to the fourth generation. If it was a girl, he could protect her against all adversity. She'd be beautiful, that was for sure, like Ethel. His heart began to swell with thoughts of boys setting their caps at her, flocking around her. For that alone it was worth getting married.

'I *can* tell,' Ethel was saying waspishly, her tone fearful as if worried he was trying to wriggle out of it. 'Women know these things. But we've got to make it soon before people begin suspecting.'

'They'll suspect as soon as we name a quick day,' he hedged.

'They can suspect all they want then – long as we're married.'

That was true.

Bobby had the sensation of being swept along before a huge dark wave, threatened to be engulfed by it as Ethel began making her plans. Now assured of his support, she steeled herself to tell her parents.

'I'll face them on me own,' she said bravely, when he offered to go with her. He looked at her with new admiration – the most courageous girl he had ever known. And face them she did. Quite successfully.

Apparently relieved to have her off their hands, especially, he found out later, as her older sister by three years had been compelled into marriage in the same way two years previously. Family tradition with their daughters it seemed, he thought sceptically, his admiration of Ethel's courage dimming after having trembled on her behalf for nothing.

It was now his turn to face his parents, he had a premonition that it was not going to be as much a piece of cake as with Ethel's family. He was right. Dad's views on the matter were far from congenial. He rose from the breakfast table with a roar, startling the life out of the others around the table.

'You bloody what?'

'Me and Ethel plan to get married.'

'That docker's daughter? I ain't 'aving you wed no docker's daughter. That's flat. You can think again about that!'

Bobby gritted his teeth. 'We've got to, Dad.'

'There's no got to about it.'

'She's pregnant. I'm going to have to do the right thing by her.'

A moment of silence followed, his father's face growing ruddier by the second. As he took a deep breath, Bobby knew he was for it.

'You – bloody fool! If you 'ad ter get a bit of fluff into trouble, you could've looked about for better than that. I know 'er sort. Get 'erself up the spout and she gets 'erself someone with a good steady job and she don't 'ave ter work no more. And you . . . You silly arse. Fell for it, didn't yer? Didn't yer?'

'It's not like that, Dad.'

His mother was pleading for calm. 'Please . . . Let's talk about this properly.' But his father wasn't listening.

'Don't tell me. I didn't come down with yesterday's rain. You not 'ardly out of 'aving your bum wiped by yer mum, and there's you making a father of yerself. Really made a rod for your own back, ain't yer? You silly, soppy, ravin' bloody lunatic.'

Bobby sat very still, his gaze riveted on his plate. What could he say? Yet what could he do? Everyone would know he was the father.

His father was pacing the kitchen while the others sat very still, not eating. 'You ain't marrying 'er, yer know. Over my dead body.'

Mum got up and began clearing away half-finished plates in a spate of nervous energy, bringing a cry of protest from Harry that he still had some more to eat, but a look from her silenced him.

'He's got to marry her,' she said simply. 'I wouldn't be able to hold me head up among me neighbours if he didn't, them knowing.'

'That all that's worrying you?' Charlie turned on her.

'Everyone knows they've been goin' out together, even if you don't, Charlie. She don't go out with no one else. And I've got to face me neighbours. You're at work every day. I 'ave to live 'ere.'

Resolutely she scraped the enforced leftovers into a wire tray. The dishes clashed as she piled them into the sink.

'What's done's done. Bobby'll 'ave to make the best of a bad job.'

Her husband was defeated by her will, though he blustered on.

'Then all I say is – 'e'd better not ever come moanin' back 'ere about wishin' he'd never done it. I wash me 'ands of the 'ole thing. As far as I'm concerned 'e's made 'is bed, so let 'im lie on it. The silly idiot!'

That morning he and Bobby made their way to work, separately.

Cissy's wedding arrangements were forgotten in the flurry to get Bobby and Ethel wed. Ethel's mum insisted on a white wedding despite the girl's condition, the dress made purposely loose.

'Lucky for her,' Cissy said of Ethel, 'with a slim figure like that she won't show too much of a bulge.'

'She's only three months gone,' Mrs Cottle smirked. 'They can count on their 'ands as much as they like later. Once the kid's a year old, gossip'll die down. By then there might even be another on the way. Most people have short memories.'

Even so, the wedding was a quiet affair, celebrations half-hearted. The family, already wise to the unprecedented haste, attended briefly to hand the couple a gift and their good wishes, eat a sandwich, a bit of the hurriedly made cake and drink their health before leaving early.

There was no honeymoon. Money was needed for down payment on a rented flat so they at least had a roof over their heads. Cissy went with Ethel to inspect it just before the wedding. It was small and smelled faintly of damp, but Ethel insisted they would make it cosy.

'I'd die if that happened to me,' Cissy said to Daisy on their way to work on the Monday after the wedding. 'I don't let Eddie anywhere near me, in case it did.'

'Don't you ever feel you want him to?' Daisy asked, mystified. 'Not even when you know you mustn't?'

Cissy gave a wistful sigh. 'Sometimes . . .'

She let her voice die away, knowing it wasn't for Eddie's touch that she sighed, but someone far more romantic, with far more to offer in life; someone who would set her blood on fire with delight and send her senses reeling. Eddie was able to do that, but Eddie was Eddie, solid and dependable. A man a girl could rely on, his two feet planted firmly on the ground, his heart never given to seeking adventure or taking a risk; as a husband he would always be loyal for the very reason that he did not seek risks. But oh, how she yearned for romance, for a little bit of adventure, for the blood to be set alight.

The dance floor was filled with couples indulging in the one-step. The high ceiling echoed back the strident efforts of a small dance band to be heard. From the chairs set in rows three deep along the walls where girls not dancing sat in hopeful groups, giggles emanated, girlish eyes wistfully prowling the room. While from the crowd at the refreshment bar, masculine laughter rose in intermittent waves amid the buzz of voices as the boys measured up likely partners for an evening.

This was Hammersmith, large, impersonal, accommodating several hundred pleasure seekers. Not Cissy's idea of cosiness, but Eddie liked it here. They had danced every dance together, except for the excuse-mes, which they sat out.

She watched a knot of people come surging in, about a dozen well-dressed young things, their shrill, cultured voices reaching her even as they entered. Belgravia slumming it. A giggle. Throwing their expensive, high-spirited weight around, being gorgeously silly in their joy of life, they were never blamed by the management of any establishment for what disruption they might cause for the reason that they always threw lots of good money around as well as weight.

Eddie had gone to get her a lemonade, the bar was crowded now with the excuse-me coming to an end and everyone needing a short breather.

Cissy watched the bright young people move on into the hall. Envy consumed her. Oh, to be one of them. Never having to work. Having the freedom to enjoy every pleasure life had to offer.

She studied them, the girls were in dresses far too expensive for this place. They had it all; real pearls, real gold, dangly real diamond earrings, ostrich feather fans, Paris shoes. The men had proper evening wear; double-breasted waistcoats, bow ties, tails. They were elegant, debonair and oozing wealth, each seemed to stand above the herd even though several were not excessively tall – two of them quite puny.

Cissy's scrutiny halted at one young man. He was dark-haired and much taller than the others. Her heart gave a leap so that it was suddenly hard to breathe. Kensington. The man who'd asked her for a dance – Langley whatisname, Makepeace. It was, surely it was.

Hardly aware of what she was doing, moving purely on an impulse, she was on her feet, making towards the group. Only as she reached it, did she realise the foolishness of her quest. What on earth did she think she was doing? What on earth did she imagine she was going to say?

Coming to a halt before them, gaping like an idiot and having lost sight of her original goal, she found her entire length being surveyed by one haughty young thing wafting expensive perfume, whose wide blue eyes edged with kohl had widened even more in silent enquiry.

Cissy wilted, began backing away, to be stopped by someone behind her.

'Whoops!' the man's voice was light and faintly mocking as hands fell upon each of her shoulders. Turning to stare up into the eyes of Langley Makepeace, her reaction was as instant as it was ridiculous.

'Oh . . . fancy meeting you!'

He looked blankly at her. 'Do we know each other?'

'Er . . .' Oh, God, this was awful. She stood staring dumbly at him.

But in the grey eyes, stunning grey eyes ringed by a darker grey, recognition stirred. 'By golly, yes. Didn't I dance with you . . . now where was that?'

'Kensington,' she burst out, encouraged yet still stunned.

'Kensington.'

'South Kensington really.' Thank God for elocution lessons. She was as good as any of these rich little flappers. 'It was a smallish ballroom, just off Brompton Road. Last November.'

He smiled down at her. 'Yes, I recall now. I've a memory for faces. Not names. Faces. I couldn't forget your face. I remember thinking at the time – she's a peach. And then you disappeared.'

'Like Cinderella.' Silly thing to say. Why had she said it?

He laughed. 'My very words! Though I didn't find a glass slipper. Perhaps you will leave it behind tonight.'

'Perhaps.' She made a small effort to release herself from the grip still on her shoulders, but he held her. Behind her came a burst of giggles. They were laughing at her. He was laughing at her. Oh, God, she was making such a fool of herself. All she wanted to do now was to escape and huddle quietly on her own into her embarrassment.

The band struck up with a smooth foxtrot – 'Oh, sweet and lovely, lady be good . . .'

She could see Eddie coming back towards the seat she had vacated. He was looking round, his expression concerned.

'Do you foxtrot?'

The smooth cultured voice shocked her eyes back to the man still holding her imprisoned.

'Yes.' Her reply was automatic. From the corner of her eye she could see Eddie moving along the rows of chairs, looking for her, his hands occupied by two glasses, one of pale ale and one of lemonade shandy.

'Then right-ho!'

The next instant she was whisked onto the dance floor, striving to match the long accomplished steps of her partner as she was whirled this way and that, her supple body bending to the power of this man's will.

She could no longer see Eddie for the twists and turns this dance called for. The lights had dimmed. A spotlight trained on the central faceted crystal globe twisting slowly above the couples sent stars swirling around walls, floor, across the shadowy figures of dancers, glinting off glass jewellery. Langley Makepeace smiled down at her.

'Did you ever tell me your name, little Cinderella?'

'I did. It's Cissy. Cissy Farmer.'

'I shall call you Cinders.'

'No!' She pulled away a little, interrupting the flow of their steps. 'My name is Cissy. I won't answer to anything else.'

In the dim light she heard him chuckle.

'Fine. I promise never to call you anything other than Cissy. That is, if you allow me to know you long enough for an opportunity to call you Cissy.'

'I don't know about that,' she hedged, thinking of Eddie, guilty already that she was abandoning him, and heard Langley chuckle again.

The music ended with a flourish of cymbals and he whirled her round in a finale of twists, flinging her out into a graceful finish.

The lights came up in a blaze, dimming the still revolving globe. Tucking her arm through his, he began to guide her back to his corner. She pulled away.

'I . . . I'd better go back to my seat,' she said hastily. 'Thanks for the dance.'

'My pleasure. I shall escort you there then. Where were you?'

The floor was clearing. Eddie was sitting where he had left her. She could see him easily now and felt terribly exposed.

'I'm with a friend,' she began then hastily altered it. 'Friends.'

Langley gave her a wry grin. 'Later on, then.'

'Yes,' she gasped, and fled.

She told Eddie that she had been paying a visit to the ladies cloakroom. He nodded without comment, handing her her drink. Excuses to Eddie were always easy to make. He was so trusting, always unruffled, seeing nothing untoward in anyone. But Cissy's heart raced, hoping, yet not hoping, Langley would come asking her for another dance, though surely he wouldn't be so indiscreet, seeing her with someone.

Yet there was no escaping that twinge of disappointment when indeed he did not approach her. It was hard not to follow him with her eyes as she glimpsed him among the crowd on the floor, dancing expertly with someone else. Once or twice, dancing with Eddie, they passed close by and she caught the glimmer of his smile in her direction, but she could say farewell to any further meeting with him, that was certain.

Then, as Eddie went for more refreshments to quench their thirsts after a session of hectic jiggling, she saw Langley making towards her as a tango struck up. She held her breath. Oh, heavens! He wasn't about to ask her to dance? She would have to refuse. Oh, cruel, cruel fate!

She noticed then that he wasn't even looking her way. Obviously he had no intention of asking her to dance. Dull anger moved inside her as she watched him draw nearer, apparently to walk right past her. But as he came abreast of her, he paused, looking off into the body of the hall like a spy about to impart some national secret.

'I shall most likely be here next Friday.'

His voice was so quiet she only just heard the words.

With that, he moved off, leaving her gazing after him, her mind in a complete turmoil but her heart already winging its way heavenward. How could he guess that she seldom saw Eddie on Fridays? But then, many a girl stayed at home on a Friday evening to wash her hair and preen herself ready for the weekend ahead. Not all, but many. How very perceptive of him to see that.

Chapter Seven

The half-finished pile of garments on Daisy's bench pushed aside to make it easier to eat lunch, Cissy took a deep breath, and between mouthfuls of bread and cheese, casually mentioned the Friday date.

Daisy stopped chewing to look at her as puzzled as if her friend had announced intentions to enter a lunatic asylum.

'You mean with Eddie? That's not a date. That's going out steady. You don't call that a date.'

'This isn't with Eddie.' She needed very much to tell Daisy about last Saturday. Firstly, because she had to have an ally; secondly, to prove to Daisy, who had not long ago accused her of backing out when it came to action, that she did have the courage to kick over the traces. She had the satisfaction of seeing Daisy's easy expression change to one of consternation.

'You mean someone else? But you're engaged.'

'We've not yet bought the ring.'

'But you can't go out with someone else behind Eddie's back.'

Cissy almost choked on her sandwich. 'Do you think I should tell him then?'

'No! But you won't half be playing with fire. Say if he finds out?'

'He won't find out. It's only for one evening.'

'Yes, but it don't end there, does it?'

Cissy didn't answer and they fell quiet, Daisy munching her lunch as though diplomacy depended on it. Removing the top of her battered vacuum flask she gulped down the tea it held, finding her voice again.

'You ought to think before you go off like that.' She restoppered the flask with a fierce twist of determination while Cissy gazed on her, partly with irritation and partly with satisfaction.

'You're one to talk. Who wanted to leave home last Christmas and go on the stage, then?'

'*I'm* not engaged,' Daisy said acidly.

'Neither am I. Not until we buy the engagement ring, that is.'

She felt suddenly, terribly guilty. Poor Eddie, poor trusting Eddie didn't deserve to be cheated. That was what she was doing – cheating. But how could she pass up such an opportunity?

Cissy swallowed hard on the last of her sandwich. In a way she did love Eddie. She should know by now which side her bread was buttered, yet there was something more than love that kept pulling her away. But what was more than love? Selfishness? Was the need to make something of herself more a pull than the love of someone? She couldn't answer that.

'Anyway,' she said petulantly, crumpling up the empty sandwich bag and dropping it in the bin at her feet among the offcuts of material, 'it's only for one evening.' It made her feel a little better.

'You've not said who the date is,' Daisy reminded, her sandwich bag following Cissy's into the waste bin.

'Just someone I met last week.'

'Who?'

'His name's Langley Makepeace.'

'Ooh, la-di-da! What's he doing with a name like that?'

'Well, I think he lives in west London somewhere.'

'He *is* la-di-da. Good God, Cissy, mind you're not getting out of your depth. You could come a cropper mixing with that sort.'

'I know what I'm doing,' she said peevishly. 'I know his is a different world to mine. I don't expect him to take me off into his world but . . . if only for just one evening it would be nice to have a taste of the one he does come from.'

'Whatever made him pick on you?'

'Don't be nasty!' Cissy shot at her. 'I can conduct myself as good as any of them. That's what I have been taking elocution for. And I know all about deportment and manners and that sort of thing.'

'I'm not being nasty,' Daisy defended, but Cissy wasn't listening, her mind in the clouds now.

'I don't for one minute expect him to ask me to share his life with him,' she repeated. 'But if I don't go on Friday, I'll always be left wondering for the rest of my life whether he might have. It's only for one evening, Eddie need never know. What harm can it do?'

Daisy's shrug spoke volumes, but Cissy ignored it. 'It's wonderful that someone like him has even asked me to meet him.'

Before Daisy could reply, a sharp double clap of the forelady's hands brought the lunch half-hour to an end, and as the power began to wind up, Cissy got up from Daisy's bench and made her way back to her own.

Cissy was losing her nerve. 'Come with me?' she begged, with Friday drawing nearer. Daisy laughed cruelly.

'I'm not playing gooseberry. It's your date.'

'Please, Daisy.'

'You don't have to go.'

'If you won't come with me, then can you do me a favour?'

'That depends.'

'It isn't much. I'll tell my parents I'm going to the pictures with someone from work and as it's across London I might stay the night with her. All you have to do is bear me out if they say anything.'

Daisy's expression was a study. 'You're not thinking of sleeping with this Langley person?'

'Of course not! It's just that if I get home later than usual, I can say I changed my mind about staying and her father or her brother brought me home in a taxi – or something.'

Doubt clouded Daisy's face. 'It's a bit underhanded.'

'Please, Daisy. It's not a lot to ask.'

'I don't know.'

'Oh, Daisy . . .'

'Oh, all right then. But I'm not taking the can back if you do it again.'

'It's just this once.'

There was no risk of Dad finding out. Few ordinary people had a telephone in their homes. The only way he could contact her would be to go there in person and she couldn't see him traipsing halfway across London. If she gave a fictitious address how would he know it wasn't genuine?

Daisy was still concerned. 'You're being deceitful, Cissy, you know that?' But desperation had caught hold of Cissy.

'It'll be fine,' she assured, her fingers crossed behind her back.

Dad, as she had expected, wasn't happy even with the promise of a father seeing her home should she decide not to stay the night. But Mum was more forthcoming.

'So long as her friend's dad sees her 'ome all right.' Nodding her reassurance to Dad that all would be well, he bowed to her judgement.

With her blessing and his dubious agreement, Cissy made for the seclusion of her bedroom to push her dance dress and shoes, make-up and perfume into a bag, and with her best coat and hat over an ordinary dress hurried off.

'I don't perticlerly like 'er being out all night,' were Dad's parting words, but Cissy's heart was soaring as she made her way towards Hammersmith along with the other West End bound.

The place when she arrived was already lively. In the ladies, she changed in one of the toilet cubicles, restuffing the bag with her discarded dress and shoes. Leaning close to an ornate mirror, she put on lipstick and a dash of powder; a touch of rouge, outlined her eyes with a kohl brush, tweeked her already finely shaped eyebrows, patted her shingle into place and applied a splash of Evening in Paris for good measure, wishing it was some Jean Patou creation. But what she could afford had to do.

Satisfied she had done her best with herself, she handed her hat, coat and bag to the cloakroom lady who hung them on a hook. Then, stowing her cloakroom ticket in her handbag, she moved on into the hall, where she was met by the distorted blare of the dance band and an unceasing buzz of talk and laughter. The dance floor was already packed with couples slowly gyrating to the tempo of a painfully dragged out waltz dictated by a half-hidden percussionist. Cissy drew in a deep breath of perfume and cigarette smoke that always sent the blood soaring, and gazed around. It wasn't going to be easy to spot her date in this crush.

Hovering by the door for what seemed an age, she alternately eyed the entrance and the crush of dancers, scanning them as they left the floor with the waltz ending, observing each couple moving back again for a lively one-step. All the time she was growing uncomfortably aware of eyes turned briefly and enquiringly in her direction. She could just imagine their thoughts, those girls who passed by in twos and threes, the couples pausing in their absorption of each other to glance her way, the boys looking for partners, wondering about her. Who was she with? Why was she standing there so long on her own?

The one-step finishing in a crash of cymbals, the floor was again vacated and again filled, this time for a crazy bunny-hop.

Still no sign of him. She was a silly fool. What had she expected? A man like that, with money and parents wallowing in wealth, used to high living – what did he want with her? Most likely he had forgotten about her the moment she was out of sight.

Everything cried out, go home! Be sensible and go home! Yet she couldn't. Not yet. Clinging to her last few shreds of hope, she hung on, looking, waiting, turning her head away should anyone look as if they were approaching to ask her to dance.

She didn't want to dance. Certainly she didn't want to go and sit down – reveal herself the wallflower that she was. There was a lump coming in her throat. The bright lights had begun to grow dangerously misty. None so alone as the lonely in a crowd, came the words in her head. Might as well go home. Yes, go home.

Decision made, she bent her head to fish for her cloakroom ticket, thinking now on what yarn she would spin Mum and Dad at being back so early.

'Cissy?'

She swung round to the light-toned enquiry. And there he was, his grey eyes dramatised by thick dark lashes and eyebrows, his dark hair slicked back and shining with expensive brilliantine. His face radiating affluence, he was looking whimsically down at her.

Cissy felt her own face grow hot, knew it had become bright red as only a fair skin could, and hated this display of embarrassment.

'Oh, it *is* you!' was all she could find to say, adding a further touch of idiosyncrasy: 'You remembered my name.'

'How could I forget it?' The light return made her feel instantly that he was quietly laughing at her. She stood her ground.

'I just assumed you would, that's all.'

The startling grey eyes seemed to hold hers. 'As a matter of fact I've been urging every day along till I could meet you again.'

'That's nice.' God, how stupid that sounded. He was smiling, showing just the edge of white, even teeth.

'I do hope you've not been waiting long. I know it's the woman's prerogative to arrive late. I do apologise.'

How well he spoke, so easily, where she must still watch each unrehearsed word lest it betray her.

'Did you have to come far?' she asked, and again felt angry at her lack of aplomb.

'Belgravia. And you?'

It had been a stupid question – left her wide open. She was flustered, her mind working on where she could pretend to be from. Openly lying didn't come easily and no handy locality came to mind.

Langley Makepeace solved the problem for her, this time with no hint of banter in his tone. 'At a guess, I would say, east London.'

She was defeated, crestfallen. 'What makes you think that?'

'The delightful way you said "my". You speak very well, Cissy, but you have a way of saying "Mie" that says it all, and I loved it. In fact it's what attracted me to you in the first place. That, and your ravishingly pretty face. I needed to know more about you.'

'Is that all you wanted?'

'No. You've been in my head this whole week. And now I'm here, and you're here – what about us using our evening for what it was meant for? They're playing a waltz. Fancy a twirl, then?'

His grammar was so casually full of the errors that would have had Madam Noreah passing out, yet seemed so right on his tongue. She who'd spent hours perfecting her vowels only to have him pick up on the one she'd slipped up on at the first go, she was lacking the one thing he had that she never would have – breeding in the bone, that allowed for sloppy speech and still put him above the life she knew. But at the moment, none of this mattered.

Whisked away in his arms, happiness flooded over her. He didn't care that she was East End. Later she broached the subject again and he laughed, a loud rippling laugh.

'You're not worried about it, are you?'

'I'd rather have been brought up in west London,' she answered as best she could, breathless from the one-step he did so expertly.

'Now that's silly. You mustn't put yourself down, you know. I've great regard for those from the East End. Salt of the earth. You know, I feel I'm beginning to know you very well, Cissy. Hope I get to know you even better and that you feel the same about me. As for origins, if you like, it'll be a secret just between us. I could say you're a foreign princess who I found one day.'

'Don't be silly,' she gasped.

'*Pygmalion*, you know, by George Bernard Shaw.'

'I don't want to be a foreign princess.' She pouted. 'And I don't want you putting it about that I am.'

'Very well, you're plain Cissy Farmer. As a matter of fact it's perfect – its simplicity quite *bon-ton*, don't you think?'

She did, immediately thrilling to the idea.

They danced every one of the next four dances, waltzing, tangoing, one-stepping and shimmying energetically. He had plenty to say, telling her about himself: his father in farming, the family home, as Langley called an obvious mansion in Berkshire, having been in the family for three generations; before that in the dim and distant past there had been a titled ancestor somewhere.

The house in Belgravia was often used for the winter. Not much to do in Berkshire in the winter, he said, the management of which was left to the farm steward and the house was closed, needing just a minimum of staff. The family were back there now, with only he occupying the Belgravia place.

It all sounded so grand, she quelled a little. Langley had attended prep school then public school, then Oxford. Wasn't doing much at the moment, he said – Pater somewhat put out by his lack of interest in a worthwhile career. But why the dickens should he need be? The farm would manage itself when it came to him. With a decent accountant to deal with its running costs, a competent steward, a housekeeper to run the house itself and rents from farm tenants collected regularly, what point was there in *earning* a living?

Cissy, lapping it up, wondered at his interest in her, a girl of council school education, taking elocution lessons at sixpence an hour paid for out of wages as a machinist at Cohens, her father a lighterman, with hardly ever more than two ha'pennies to rub together. Could this really be her – dancing with someone to whom areas like Park Lane and Grosvenor Place were as familiar as Canning Town and East India Dock Road were to her?

'By the way,' he broke off to say, 'not going steady with the chap you were with last week?'

'Oh, no.' How easily she lied. 'We've known each other since we were children. Just a friend. Why?'

'Merely wondering.'

She didn't pursue it. The foxtrot ended, he guided her from the floor, his hand under her elbow. On the perimeter he paused.

'I say, don't you find this place rather a bore? Hardly enough to sustain a whole evening. What d'you say to visiting a little nightclub I know. I've got friends going there. Introduce you to them, what?'

'Where is it?'

'Little place off Cromwell Road. Knightsbridge. The car's nearby. We'd be there in half a tick. What d'you say?'

'I'd love to.' A thrill of nervous anticipation raced through her. How would she be received by his posh friends? But she was sure he'd protect her from any untoward reception they might afford her.

Handing in her cloakroom ticket and collecting the shoes and the dress she had stuffed into the little fabric bag, she met Langley at the exit. His smile did look protective. She'd be all right with him.

Drawing her arm through his, he led her into the April night. The electric street lighting was diffused by the damp mild air and gave her the impression of emerging into some heavenly wonderland. His car was parked some way along the road, a shiny black vehicle from which the lighting bounced and glinted as they approached. Its top could be folded back on fine summer days but at this moment was fully up.

Conducting her to the passenger seat he opened the door for her. Feeling like a queen, she slipped into the seat and watched him close her door and go round to the driver's side to lean in and pull on the starter knob. Going to the front of the vehicle, he gave the engine a brief crank and, as it roared into life, came back to slide in beside her.

'Here we go!' he announced, easing off the brake. Smoothly the car moved forward. 'If you're cold, there's a rug on the back seat.'

'I'm fine!' she yelled, over the rumble of the engine.

'Good!'

He lapsed into silence, concentrating on driving. She watched the shops and houses fly by. It was the first time she had ever sat in a car, much less one moving so fast – twenty-five miles per hour by the big black needle on the indicator – but she wasn't going to tell him that. She just hoped it appeared as if this was nothing at all new to her.

Ten minutes later they were drawing up by a brightly lit electric sign 'The Golden Cockerel' above a dimly lit door. The engine died as the key was turned off and Cissy sat very still as Langley got out and came round to open her door. This was the done thing, she knew, a girl doing nothing until her escort ran to open doors for her. Eddie did the same, of course, but with far less panache, less noticeable.

A doorman in black and gold livery opened the door to them. The interior, small but brightly lit, had a tiny cloakroom like a cubicle, with pink and black drapes. The entire decor was pink and black, very modern in the new cubic design that tended to confuse the vision.

Cissy managed not to blink, acting as though all this was no more than she was used to, as the cloakroom girl took her hat, coat and the bulging, now cheap-looking shoe bag. Beyond a second set of curtains of the same cubic design, dance music could be heard.

Handing in his driving gloves, trilby and white scarf, Langley took her arm and led her through the drapes. Pink was everywhere – varying shades hitting her between the eyes: chairs, tables, carpet around the edge of the small dance floor, the ceiling and the walls, except for embossed figures of crowing cockerels here and there in gold. Even the grand piano on a low dais was pink.

'Ah, there they are!' Langley said, spotting familiar faces seated around a far table. 'Come on, Cissy, I'll introduce you.'

Whisked across the vacated floor, the pianist having finished his number, Cissy found herself before several pairs of enquiring eyes.

'Langley, darling!' gushed a girl, looking up, her dark hair so short as to look like a boy's. Her black dress with tier upon tier of red fringe was definitely silk, her double string of pearls, sea-born.

'Langley, darling, who is it? Do introduce.'

The girl's tawny mascara'd eyes took Cissy in from head to foot.

'This is Cissy Farmer, Margo. Cissy – Margo Fox-Prinshaw.'

A brief nod, the tawny eyes returned to Langley. 'Darling, where did you find her?'

'Nowhere you'd know.'

'Oh, you are a bore!' The painted lips pouted.

'And this is Miles Devlin,' Langley went on with a grin, while Miles, puffing at a cigarette, exclaimed, 'Stunned!'

'And this is Simon Hackett-Claves. And this . . .'

Bombarded by a string of names – Faith Silk, Dickie Verhoeven, Pamela Carstairs, Ginger Bratts, Effie Messenger, Penny Balling-Jones, Paul Marquand – it was hard to memorise any of them.

'And I want no questions asked about Cissy.' Langley said with authority. 'I found her. She's mine.'

Cissy wasn't sure if she cared for that one, but smiled sweetly. It wasn't easy to smile with genuine warmth at any one of them. If the jewellery was real, the smiles she received back were definitely false, these bright young people's minds on the moment – themselves – their own pleasures. She found herself ignored.

'Dickie – it's a tango.' A cigarette in its holder was stubbed out.

'You know I don't tango.'

'Of course you do. Come on!'

'Penny, I want to finish this drink.'

'You haven't time – it'll be finished soon. Besides, you've had enough, don't you think? Come on, Dickie, you old soak!'

Cissy watched the putty-faced Dickie being dragged onto the dance floor, a little unsteadily. The table at which they sat was massed by champagne and cocktail glasses, most of them half empty and rather sticky. Tiny cocktail biscuits littered the pink cloth.

Langley took Cissy's arm, guiding her to an empty chair. 'Let's sit this one out. Have some champagne.'

There was to be more. But this was her first, and it was lovely.

Chapter Eight

Eddie had been in training for a year for the coveted Doggett's Coat and Badge race. All through spring and half the summer, the odd evenings and Sunday mornings rowing strongly and rhythmically up and down the river with his father coaching him had allowed Cissy time to herself; glad, at the same time full of self-reproach for being glad.

It had been unsettling, this conflict of feelings. She had tried not to miss him, for obvious reasons, and felt angry with herself to find that sometimes she did miss him. Being with him so long had become a habit, but recognised as such, it frightened her, knowing the inevitable conclusion to that.

If he were Langley with an exciting life to offer, there'd be no worry. But he wasn't. He was Eddie. Gently offering her a quicksand of a marriage into which she was expected to sink. How could she, even though he stirred something wonderful in her when they were together?

At least his occupation with the race had put off the buying of the engagement ring for a while. They could get engaged any time, but a chance at the Doggetts came only once. He never said that in so many words, of course. For her part she magnanimously told him that she understood – the magnanimity a lie, and lying to Eddie hurt her, he was so gullible, so trusting, and she . . . . She hated herself.

But today, the time to herself must come to an end. Today, Eddie was taking part in his race, when it was over, whether he won or lost, there would be no more days training.

A fine, hot day, the August sun shining down its blessings on the race, all the friends and families of the newly licensed Freemen of the river lined the course from Chelsea Embankment at the approach to the finishing line four and a half miles up the river from the start at London Bridge. As the sweating men, bending over their oars, came into view, each family had begun shouting itself hoarse.

Cissy's own cries of encouragement were drowned by it all. She did want to see Eddie win. She would be proud to see him standing straight and tall as he accepted his rewards. But through it came the knowledge that the evenings of training were past. From now on he would be all hers and she would be all his – for ever and ever.

The leaders of the now well-spaced skiffs came abreast, shooting on towards the finish an eighth of a mile further along, each man pulling strongly, fighting aching, flagging muscles, his eye on his nearest and most dangerous contender, the four hopefuls almost in line with each other.

Mum, in a flowered dress and knitted blue cloche hat, was practically jumping up and down, her bosom bouncing.

'Look – there's Eddie! He's pulling ahead! He's going to win!'

'He's doing well,' Dad said cautiously, eyeing the other skiffs almost alongside that of his future son-in-law. 'Got a way to go yet.'

Eddie's parents were waving their arms in excitement as the two leading craft shot past in a final effort of endurance; first one ahead, then the other, Eddie rowing like a demon. The finish, not half a foot in it.

Eddie was a happy man. He'd come second, but that was enough for him. Bringing his skiff to the bank and leaping on to dry land with a ready hand for the winner, everyone was thumping the heroes' backs, but he hurried, shirt still soaked in perspiration, to where his cluster of supporters stood to catch Cissy to him in triumphant enbrace.

'I did it! I did it, Cissy! I did it!'

'I'm absolutely over the moon.' Her arms came around his neck with genuine pleasure for him, her laughter muffled in his chest. 'But let me breathe, Eddie!'

He too laughed, releasing her as his mother came to kiss him. His father, lean as himself and once just as tall, clutched at his hand and shook it vigorously.

'Well done, son! I'm proud of yer.'

'Yes,' Cissy's mum put in, 'lots of congratulations, Eddie.'

He bent to allow his future mother-in-law to add her congratulatory kiss on the cheek. 'Missed getting me cap and badge, but I didn't dream I'd get anywhere near.'

'You can thank yer dad for that,' Charlie reminded, his deep voice ringing with pride. 'Spendin' all them hours coaching you. You've got 'im ter thank.'

'And well I know it.' Eddie's face glowed with delight as well as from his earlier exertions. He looked across at Cissy. 'But I've got 'er to thank too, for putting up with me being away all of them long evenings, training. Without her understanding, I don't think I'd ever 'ave gone in for it. It's the woman, you know, what helps a man win.'

'Yeah, my Cissy's a good 'un,' Charlie admitted with no small boast, while Cissy blushed at what lay behind her noble generosity. 'But you did it, son.'

Standing back, Cissy noted the pride on her father's face for Eddie, as if Eddie were his own son, which he virtually would be once she and he were married. Next year. Maybe in eight months' time. It would be upon them before they knew it, the date probably firmed by Christmas.

And yet, if she was honest with herself, by next year she might be in a different frame of mind, perhaps she'd love Eddie with all her heart and want to take up the responsibilities of a wife from an ordinary family, all silly adolescent notions put aside.

After all, if she was honest with herself, she must know that her brief escapade with Langley Makepeace was probably coming to an end. She had seen him five times in all, the odd Friday evening when Eddie had been training and she could make her fictitious friend, Olive, available. Not too often of course, in case Dad got suspicious.

Olive had been a godsend and Dad had not once suspected. But soon Olive would disappear – moved away somewhere – for last week Langley had dropped the news that he and his friends would be off to Paris for the autumn, going on to winter in the south of France like migrating birds to play the casinos there and bask in the Mediterranean sun. She should have known anyway that something like that would happen. So it would soon be goodbye to the brief bouts of high life she had enjoyed.

It had all been too good to be true, feeling herself part of the happy band of bright young things. Langley had revelled in her background being kept a secret. To him it was a joke. But he had been attention itself towards her, as if she had indeed been a princess.

In the drawer in her bedroom, beneath her undies, lay a thin gold bangle he'd given to her. She had protested at the time but what was money to him? And it had only been a small one. Naturally she could never wear it, but it would always be a reminder. He'd asked nothing of her in return . . . . Well, he had, but when she'd told him she wasn't that kind of girl, he'd shrugged. She guessed that he got his fun from that tawny-eyed Margo who was always ready to hang on his arm.

She had felt jealous, discarded and betrayed, but then relieved that she hadn't got in too deep. With Langley going off to the Continent with his friends, he'd forget all about her. Just as well then that she hadn't made herself cheap with him – like the cockney girl might.

But if she *had* consented to his request that night several weeks ago, might he have asked her to go with him to Paris? She doubted it.

Following in the rear of the two families now off to the Crown and Anchor for a celebration drink before going on to Eddie's house where a celebration meal would be on hand, Cissy went over the evening when

Langley had kissed her hard on the lips before putting her in the taxi to come home.

'It's late,' he'd whispered, his tone soft and seductive. 'Why not spend the night at my place – go home in the morning? Just say that your friend's father wasn't available to take you home.' He knew about the fictitious Olive of course.

Cissy had bridled, instinct telling her that he could only be after one thing. For an instant he had grown angry, saying she was being a little fool, then just as she was thinking of slapping his face, he'd become protective again. 'You're right, Cissy. You must be thinking all sorts of things of me. I should never have mentioned it.'

But if she had consented to spend the night with him . . .

'All right, ole gel?' Eddie, dropping back, took her arm, bringing her back to the present. 'You looked a bit lost there.'

'I was only thinking,' she said as they trailed after the happy celebrators, but didn't say what, and anyway, he had turned to look at the couple trailing up behind, slowing his pace for them to catch up.

'You all right, Ethel? She all right, Bobby?'

'She's fine. Just got to take things a bit slower, you know.'

'Still a couple of months to go, eh?'

'Yes.' Bobby's face coloured while Ethel, hanging on to his arm like grim death, tightened her lips. Her stomach, well to the fore, almost swamping her small height, spoke volumes, but people would soon forget to count dates. She knew of a couple of other girls around here who had been obliged to marry in a hurry and the regularity of that sort of thing bred disinterest. Her lips tightened nevertheless.

'You two go on,' she said tersely. 'We just fancy taking it easy. Don't want ter 'old you up.'

Her pinched and sour expression was enough of a hint, and without more ado, Eddie strode ahead, bursting with energy as always, obliging Cissy to break into an intermittent trot to keep up with him.

Marriage, Cissy thought, as she strove to keep up with Eddie, had turned Ethel into a real misery guts. Maybe she had expected wonders. But there were no wonders once the excitement of the wedding was over. Just drudgery. Even Bobby's once carefree face had become grave with responsibility. If that was what marriage did for you, you can keep it, came the thought. But she too was committed in a way, wasn't she?

'Cissy – there's a letter fer you.'

The post had come rattling through the letterbox, but as no one had need to write to her, Cissy had ignored it. Now she came downstairs ready for work, her pretty features twisted into a frown of curiosity.

'Who's it from?' she queried, taking the letter Mum handed her.

''Ow should I know? Wouldn't be yer cards, would it?'

'If they handed me my cards,' Cissy said, slitting open the flap of the envelope with her thumb, 'it would be done on the spot. Anyway, they keep a hold on good machinists,' she added, without boast, her thoughts on the sheet of pale green, expensive notepaper. Only one glance was needed to tell her who it was from as she quickly slid it back into its envelope.

'Ain't you going to read it?' asked her mother, craning her neck, her interest pricked.

Cissy tilted the envelope away from the avid gaze. 'It's from a workmate. She left a few weeks ago. I'll read it later.'

'Looks a bit fancy, that paper. Must be doin' well fer herself. That or she's got more money than sense.'

'Probably pinched it from her new employers,' Cissy said. Hurrying back upstairs to the seclusion of her bedroom, thankful that May who shared the room with her had left for work a few moments earlier, so wouldn't be taking her turn to pry, she scanned the short message:

'Haven't seen you for two weeks, Cissy darling, but dying to. How about eight-thirty at the Golden Cockerel, Friday evening? If not, this is to say I'll be leaving for Paris on the 20th August. That's in a fortnight. Must see you before then, I shall be away for a while, more's the pity. For us, that is. Paris for the autumn, and then Biarritz for the winter. Back to Paris for the spring. Won't be back in England before next year, early summer – Paris too hot then. But I need to say goodbye to you, if nothing else. Love and kisses, if only on paper . . . Langley'

It came to her with a terrible jolt as she read it, that she had been just another plaything – an episode in his life which would probably be forgotten the moment he stepped on to the boat for France.

Stepping on to a boat bound for a foreign country . . . something she could only dream about, not even a dream based on fact. She had no idea what it must be like being on a proper passenger boat. She had been across the Thames by the Woolwich ferry many times – ten minutes or so standing shoulder to shoulder if you couldn't get a seat – and on occasion she had been on one of those dirty, smelly, cavernous barges her father drove, and once on a cramped little oily tugboat. But a real ship, even one going only to France – that was well out of the reach of an ordinary working girl's purse.

Maybe on her savings she could, Cissy thought for one wild moment, then sobered quickly. Savings were for more important things – that rainy day – while all he had to do was put his hand in his pocket; he had a *bank* account. She had never been inside a bank, much less have a bank account; the post office savings counter more her mark. He could toss a five-pound note across the counter of Harrods as carelessly as if it were half a crown. She had never even held a five-pound note, much less owned one.

She realised now how silly her hopes had been. How far from his way of life she was. And she had dared to assume she merely had to step across that chasm? There had never been any promise of a future with him, and yet . . . if only . . . oh, if only . . .

A feeling of desperation surged up in her. If she got in touch with him, at least . . . Wonderful hopes began to course again.

During the midday break at Cohens, she made an excuse to Daisy not to have lunch at her bench and hurried out into the sunshine. The Post Office had a telephone box outside it. Reaching it, she fished in her handbag and extracted Langley's letter with his Belgravia telephone number embossed at the top. Giving the number to the operator, she waited with her heart pounding so loud she was sure the operator could hear it.

After a while, a man's light voice enquired in her ear. 'Yes?'

'Langley. It's Cissy.'

'You got my note, then?'

'Yes.'

'And?'

'I'll see you at eight-thirty, if that's all right?'

'Wonderful! I've a lot to tell you.'

'What is it?'

'When I see you. Must rush. 'Bye!'

Daisy looked peeved when she returned, her lunchtime almost over.

'Where were you rushing off to like that?'

'I had to change a pair of stockings before the shop closed for dinner. They had a snag in them.'

'I didn't see any stockings.'

'They were in my bag, that's why.'

The forelady's sharp handclap stopped any further discussion, and Cissy hurried back to her bench for a long afternoon's work, counting the hours until she could see Langley and find out what he had to tell her. It sounded very mysterious, very exciting. She could hardly wait. Thank God it was a Friday. She never saw Eddie on Fridays, supposedly washing her hair, still sticking rigidly to habit.

'This going off to yer friend,' Dad remarked as he came in from work that evening. 'You just watch you don't put that Daisy's nose out of joint, leaving 'er in the lurch for yer new friends. A bit of loyalty wouldn't 'urt. It'd be different if she 'ad a bloke.'

'She's not interested,' Cissy said, coming into the kitchen having dropped her shoe bag with its dance dress behind the hall coat stand for retrieving on her way out. 'She says she has plenty of time to find someone when she's ready.'

'Should be going out with a young man by now,' Mum said, her round face mildly concerned. 'Pretty gel like 'er, the boys should all be flocking around 'er. Look at May, f'rinstance. Fifteen, and already I'm 'aving trouble keeping the boys off 'er. And 'er off the boys, I might add. But that Daisy don't even try to put 'erself out to get a young man. I can't begin to wonder why she don't.'

She wants to better herself, like me, Cissy sympathised covertly with Daisy as she drained her cup of tea. A boyfriend could put paid to all her hopes of singing on the stage. Not that Daisy, for all her earlier bravado, had done much about that. But she still might.

'And another thing,' Dad was going on, opening his *Evening Standard* for a quick pre-dinner glance. ''Ow's Eddie feel about you going off 'alf across London to see friends? Too easy goin', that lad. He ain't goin' off yer? It starts with yer goin' yer separate ways. Don't see no sign yet of that engagement ring 'e was supposed to buy yer.'

Cissy put her cup down sharply, irritated by all the interrogation.

'It costs money, Dad. He's saving hard. And we must have enough for the wedding and a place to live afterwards. Not much left for buying rings and things.'

That was true. But Mum, with that uncanny instinct mothers often have of getting closer to the truth than they imagine, still retained an expression of concern.

She paused in mashing the potatoes in their pot to train her concern upon Cissy.

'A man and a woman in love don't let things like that get in the way of plans. What's 'olding you two up? Like yer dad says, one of you ain't gone cold on the other, 'ave you? Because if so, it won't be fair on either of you. You won't find better than Eddie for an 'usband. And he won't find better than you for a wife, if I say so meself. Either way, one of you is going to 'ave a broken 'eart if anything goes wrong between you. I just pray it don't.'

Cissy let her eyes fall away from her mother's gaze. 'Who says there's anything wrong? Just because we've not yet bought a ring?'

It was with an effort that she brought her gaze back to her mother. 'Look, Mum, I must go.'

There was still suspicion in her mother's eyes. 'Didn't you tell Eddie you was washing your 'air tonight?'

'I did. I will. When I come home.'

'Not goin' ter be late then?' her father said drily.

'Not all that late. I've got to go now.'

Outside at last, Cissy breathed a sigh and put all thoughts of family inquisitions, of Eddie, of love and marriage behind her, eager only to discover what Langley had to tell her that he wouldn't say over the phone. Whatever it was, she intended not to be late back tonight, if only to prove something to her parents and maybe to Eddie, perhaps even to herself.

She found Langley waiting for her outside the nightclub. He was in his car, the engine running as if he'd anticipated the exact moment she would arrive. Cissy felt suddenly quite pampered; quite certain of herself. Eddie would never have yielded to anticipating a thing like that. He believed in two feet kept firmly on the ground, not counting chickens before they hatched, never leaping before looking. There was nothing like that with Langley so accurately judging her turning up on time – in a way it had a feel of romance about it.

On this warm evening with the glow of a fine sunset flooding the sky with gold, the Golden Cockerel's electric sign oddly pale in the luminous light, Langley had the soft top of his car folded back. Just as they did in films, she thought. Yes, it *was* romantic.

He flashed her a smile as she came up to him. 'Hop in!'

'Aren't we going inside?'

'I want to talk to you.'

'Out here? What about?'

'Cissy dear, get in the car and I'll tell you as we drive.'

'Drive? Where are we going?' she asked as she settled into her seat, but he didn't answer, only smiled.

Turning the vehicle round, he headed west – into the sunset, Cissy mused deliciously, reminded of the finale of every Western two-reeler film she had seen.

'Where are we going?' she asked again after a while.

'Chiswick.'

'What's at Chiswick?'

'Peace and quiet.'

'Peace and quiet?' What had he in mind in the peace and quiet of darkness when it came down? She was feeling less certain now. 'Why?'

'We can talk without interruption.'

'What about?'

'Perhaps nothing. Or everything. It will depend on you, my dear.' It was so enigmatically said that she fell silent the rest of the way.

The sun had gone completely as they drew up by the riverside walk at Chiswick. Dusk seemed to Cissy to be descending far too quickly.

The Thames flowed narrower here. Unpolluted by sewage from drains, oil from freighters and tramp steamers, or spillage from wharves, it still retained a lingering essence of the countryside through which it had meandered before reaching this spot. It was quiet too. No lights from office windows, and few from houses; no bridges to be seen, the busy Hammersmith Bridge hidden around the bend of the river to the east and the Chiswick one was around the other bend to the west.

The car engine switched off, Langley made no attempt to get out.

'Is this where we're staying?' Cissy asked. She hadn't known what to expect but had rather imagined there might have been a party going on at some moneyed residence.

'It's quiet here,' he murmured. 'We can talk.'

'Talk about what?'

'About us.'

'What about us?' She was beginning to feel irritated.

He turned to her. 'You know I'm off to Paris in two weeks' time?'

'You told me in your letter.'

'So, what does that mean to you?'

'It means, I suppose, that I won't be seeing you again.' What she had expected, she didn't know, but her heart felt as if it were down in her shoes. 'We've come here so you can say goodbye, I suppose.'

'I've brought you here, Cissy, to ask you to come with me.'

'Come with you?' It was hard to control the pounding of a heart that had suddenly leapt up from its downward trend. Unable to believe what she had heard, she stared at him through the gloom. 'I can't do that. I don't have the same sort of money you have. Margate is more my line.'

There was no preventing the bitterness that crept into her tone. People like him didn't know the half of it, the struggle to save fifty pounds over seven years. What if she did take out her bit of savings? How long would that last? And did she really want to face the baffled looks from those bright, well-heeled, young people when she declined, apparently unreasonably, to buy this or that; do the things they did, and then see the slowly spreading smirks on their faces as the truth dawned?

'I just haven't the money,' she stated flatly. At least she could be honest with Langley. He wouldn't smirk. He didn't.

'What if I provided?' he asked, very quietly.

'You?' She looked up at him with angry pride. 'If you think . . .'

'I didn't mean it to sound like charity. Cissy . . .' He leaned towards her. 'I want you to come with me. Now I have met you, I can't contemplate going without you. I *want* you to come. I'll spend anything on whatever you ask . . . anything to have you come with me.'

'You mean, pay for me? Everything?'

'Yes.'

'That would make me a beggar, Langley.'

'No it wouldn't. You're the girl I've fallen for – head over heels. I couldn't bear the thought of not being with you. Please . . . Cissy darling, I'm not trying to be benevolent or charitable. I don't care. It's us, sharing what

I have. That's what it says in the marriage vows – all my worldly goods. You can't be so proud as to refuse what I want in all heaven to do. Please say you will come, Cissy. Darling Cissy, say you will.'

She had never known him so lacking in self-confidence. Like a small boy pleading for someone to love him. She had never imagined him so vulnerable and wondered if he had been a lonely child. He had never spoken of brothers and sisters; had mentioned inheriting his parents' property in time, so he probably was an only child. But what a sad and lonely life it must have been. Suddenly her heart poured out for him.

Giving herself no time to think clearly as to what she was saying, she blurted out: 'Oh, yes, Langley, I will. I will.'

'Oh, my lovely!' His arms were about her, pulling her towards him. His lips were on hers. He'd kissed her before but never like this. She tasted the sweetness of his breath, even that emitting an essence of wellbeing; sort of scented – like pomade.

His mouth had opened against hers, not like the kisses you saw on the screen but something intimate that she'd never before experienced. His tongue was probing between her closed lips, parting them with strength. It sent shivers of excitement rippling through her and, though she thought this must be not quite the cleanest thing to do, she felt a need to part her own lips. And, oh, Lord, when she did, what a feeling it exploded inside her. Hardly was she aware that his hand was inside her blouse, kneading her breast.

'Oh, oh, oh!' She could hear her voice, smothered by the endless kiss. He was against her, his hand was no longer on her breast but between her thighs, pushing them apart; now inside her cami-knickers, touching bare flesh. Her senses sprang towards that touch, of their own accord, not asking permission . . . 'Oh, Langley!' came a voice that sounded nothing like hers. 'Oh, oh, Langley . . .'

Then quite unexpectedly, the voice cried, 'No! stop it – please!'

Frightened, by him, by herself, by the strength of desire that had surged up inside her, something was prompting her to push him away in a blind panic. She was as out of breath as though she'd been running. Her hand came up and thrust at his face.

'Langley – don't!'

It must have been a painful thrust, for his head jerked back, his exploring hand pulled away. The world for her sprang sharply into focus, the dark edges of the car, his expression seen faintly in the gloom. There was a startled look on his face, one of surprise, anger.

'What the hell do you think you're doing?'

She was crying. She didn't know when she had started crying, but she was, her head bent, tears dropping onto her hands as they hastily smoothed her skirt down.

Chapter Nine

With an air of contentment, Eddie drained the last of the tea in its thick china cup whose chipped rim had been shared by countless other customers during its lifetime.

Most of Mrs Turner's cups were chipped, but her tea was good and strong and welcoming after a long day's work. Gulped down with egg, bacon and sausage, or pie with chips or mash, doorsteps of fresh bread with a dollop of butter, or cheese or corned beef sandwiches cut thick, followed by a wedge of bread pudding or a large helping of apple pie and custard, there was nothing better in this world.

To everyone but Eddie she was Mrs Turner. To him, she was Auntie Lottie – his mother's sister. A widow since 1916, his Uncle Jim having been killed on the Somme, she was a small thin woman who had hardly ever taken half a minute's rest in all her life; to whom trotting was more important than walking, who believed in never doing one thing at a time, more likely to be seen with a mixing spoon in one hand and a paint brush in the other ready to touch up the odd crack or two in her ageing coffee shop.

The coffee shop was at the Blackwall end of Poplar High Street and did a thriving business despite the dereliction of the area. It too had a derelict look about it, but Eddie surmised that had she done it up all posh, most of her rough and ready customers would have been frightened off. Here they felt at home.

She came now to take the bill from one or two men sitting alongside Eddie, but passed him by with an almost imperceptible wink. Later she would probably give him an extra cup of tea, again on the house. If he really insisted upon paying, for the look of the thing, she'd give him a few pence more in his change than was due, despite his protests.

'You shouldn't do this, Auntie,' he told her, keeping his voice down from other customers as he found his attempts to pay his bill on leaving refused yet again.

'Oh, nonsense!' Her gaunt face creased into an affectionate smile. 'After what you do fer me, d'you think I'm goin' ter take money off you? Bet I owe you more'n you could ever owe me, Eddie, me love – the work you've put in 'ere at times.'

'No more'n I should do.' He grinned back.

Being a widow at the mercy of others, so Eddie assumed, she needed a helping hand from time to time. Any moment he had spare, he felt it only right to help keep the place in shipshape order for her – a bit of painting here, a bit of mending there, and now and again some roof repairs. It wasn't a lot, and how could he take money off her for it? It did him good to see her glad of help.

'One day, my dear,' she said to him a few months ago as he washed his hands free of paint with turps and Lifebuoy soap, 'this will all be yours, when I'm gone.'

'For God's sake!' he had burst out, unable to comprehend such a thing as her not being here, unable even to bring himself to say, *You'll live for ever, Auntie*.

She had smiled, the edges of her thin lips gouging into her cheeks.

'I ain't as young as I was,' she had said, patting him on the arm as he dried his hands on a towel. 'Nor none too well, neither.'

'You look all right ter me,' was all he could manage, his lips compressed. And as far as he could see, she did. After all, she was only a couple of years older than his mother, who was forty-six, and that wasn't old enough to be talking about being gone. Except that if he looked a little more closely, she had begun to seem somewhat shrunken. But it was only due to all the work she did. Never gave herself rest, her café dominating her life as any thriving business does its owner.

These last couple of weeks, however, her words seemed to be ringing truer. She didn't trot around the tables as she had once done. Now and again Eddie noticed her thin mouth forming a brief, tight, O-shape, and her right hand would press into her side as though to allay some sharp pain there. Last week he asked her what was the matter.

'Nothink's the matter with me,' she had admonished him.

'You've got a pain in your side, haven't you? You should see a doctor about that, Auntie.'

'I've no time for doctors. Running off to them with a silly twinge. It's just the wind.'

'It could be appendicitis, you know.'

'At my age? Besides, if it was appendicitis, I'd 'ave been flat on me back by now, sick as a dog. It's just a bit of wind. I remember I 'ad it for three weeks when I was a kid. They thought it was appendix then. Me mum took me to the doctor. 'E said wind was what it was, after probin' and pushin' me stomach around. In the end it went away on its own. So I'm not paying no doctor to tell me I've got the wind!'

Eddie had to back down before such intransigence, even though he still felt worried for her health and even though, two weeks later, he still noticed her features tighten momentarily, her body flexing a fraction at the waist every now and again as she served her customers.

It had been taken out of her hands – she would not be going to France with Langley, now knowing what would be expected of her if she did. It had frightened her enough to realise how near she had come to disaster. Perhaps it was all for the best, but it had been awful.

Angry and silent, because he'd obviously been made to look a fool, he had turned the car round and taken her home, leaving her at the end of her road. She told Mum and Dad that the reason she'd come home early was that her friend had been sick all day and couldn't go out; that she thought it best not to stay, and had come home on the train.

She felt miserable all over the weekend. Eddie, totally at a loss to know what was the matter with her, kept trying to cheer her up without once attempting to badger her over the cause of her sulk. He was so kind and thoughtful that it was a relief when Monday came, allowing her to escape back to work.

She told Daisy, however, with whom she shared all her secrets. Daisy was understanding and said perhaps it was all for the best. Cissy had to agree although she didn't want to, and all that day set her face obdurately to the readjustment of her life with Eddie.

Then as she was getting ready for work the following morning the post fluttered through the letterbox, containing another letter addressed to her. The expensive blue envelope could only be from Langley.

'Looks like another one of them fancy letters from that friend what left your firm,' her mother smiled, amused, as she handed it to her.

Cissy put it in her pocket without replying; resisting the temptation to scoot back up to her bedroom to read it, which would have looked very suspicious, and besides, she dared not let herself be late for work and lose half an hour's money by it.

Daisy met her at the bus stop. Finding seats, Daisy gazed avidly over Cissy's arm as the envelope was ripped open and the single blue sheet unfolded to be read.

'Coo!' was all Daisy could say, reading the words with her.

It was full of abject apologies: he didn't know what had got into him; he must have been mad; he had been so overwhelmed by her; he was sorry; could she ever forgive him? He thought of her with the greatest respect. He admired her strength of will, her courage, where he had been a weak fool succumbing to a natural need of her. He'd never do anything like that again without her full consent. He'd wait as long as time itself for that; never again behaving so disrespectfully. He ended by apologising yet again, saying it was her beauty that had overwhelmed him – his ardent apologies in great danger of repeating themselves.

He ended by asking if she would still consider going to Paris with him and their friends . . . she noted it was *their* friends, heaping them with her. He meant what he said – he would pay all her expenses, because he was in love with her.

'Do come, Cissy,' the letter ended. 'I shall have a wretched time without you, my dearest darling.'

Daisy's hazel eyes were round with awe, having scanned everything over Cissy's obliging shoulder.

'Coo!' she said again, stupefied. 'Are you going?'

'I don't know.' Cissy's voice was almost a wail. Her heart seemed to be crying out, urging her to take the enormous step offered to her. Yet how could she? How did one walk along the edge of a chasm, then, without looking, take that step into thin air? What if Langley didn't reach out to catch her as she plummeted down? What if there was no one there at all to break her fall? But that was silly.

'Goodness!' Daisy was saying, her tone envious. 'Fancy him coming it with you like that. Gosh! I wish it was me.'

'I really do love you, Cissy.'

Wary of responding, Cissy stood not looking up into Eddie's ardent handsome face as they said their goodnights.

Wednesday was their local pictures night, the grander West End picture palaces saved for Saturday nights. But the film – *Blood and Sand*, with Rudolf Valentino as a matador whose desire for a local vamp had led to his death in the bullring – had been one Eddie had been waiting for ages to see.

'A damned good film,' he had sighed with satisfaction, as the lights came up and they all stood for the national anthem, vigorously played by the pianist while the photos of King George and Queen Mary came up on the silver screen. 'Good, didn'tcha think?'

She'd echoed that it was, though her heart hadn't been in it. She was not that struck on Valentino, much preferring Raymond Navarra or Douglas Fairbanks.

But it wasn't that which spoiled the film for her so much as her mind having been in a turmoil throughout. It still was. All she could think of was that she was about to break Eddie's heart. How would he take it? Would he grab her in his arms, kiss her savagely, plead with her not to do this thing, or would he, with the shock of it, tell her to go to hell and stalk away to suffer on his own in a corner like a wounded animal?

Either way, she trembled at the prospect of telling him. Even as he spoke these words of love in that way of his, plainly, lacking all the romance she so wanted, she knew she had to say it now and tear both him and herself apart, because – she didn't want to admit it – she did love him. Even as he kissed her, gently – his idea of passion – her veins tingled to the soft touch of those caring lips.

She didn't want her veins to tingle. Without that, she might find it easier to say that she was leaving him to find a life for herself away from here. A life that didn't include him or this place, he and this place were suffocating her.

Yet it was him and his kiss that was suffocating this dream of hers and she could not bring herself to break his heart. At least not with words. It would have to be said by letter. Coward that she was.

'It's been nice tonight,' she said now, wanting only to go indoors and be with her dismal thoughts. She saw his face grow wistful.

'I hate having to say goodnight. I wish we could never have to say goodnight ever again. I wish . . . Oh, Cissy, I wish . . .'

His face closed on hers. His lips felt warm and soft and gentle. Again a tingle stirred deep inside her, not so much in response to the kiss but with love for that rare gentleness that was so much part of him.

Against her lips he whispered: 'When we're married . . . Let's get married soon.'

The spell was shattered. Cissy leaned away. 'We can't afford it,' she managed to say. 'It's going to cost such a lot. We've still got lots more saving to do.'

He was undeterred, pulling her gently back to him. 'I love you for worrying so, Cissy. But we should at least start making proper plans.'

'There's plenty of time. It's not till next spring.'

'But we ain't even set a proper date yet. Me mum's beginning to ask why we ain't. I know your people are beginnin' to wonder and all. We ought to start making a few solid arrangements. The church. The people we're asking. The cars and things. The months go by so quick. Spring'll be on us before we know it, and things 'alf done.

Cissy squirmed in his embrace. 'It'll get done in time. But it's getting late, Eddie. We can't start discussing it all now. I'll see you on Saturday, and we can get down to a real discussion.'

By Saturday there might no longer be need to discuss anything.

He was beaming. Nodding. His handsome face glowing in the faint light of the nearby street lamp, a wavy lock of his fair hair, escaping the clutches of brilliantine, had fallen over his brow giving him a debonairness that momentarily touched her heart. Determination began to waver. What in God's name was she doing?

Again came the vision, as it always did, of a tiny two-up-two-down around the corner from her mum and dad, his mum and dad. She saw herself in a pinny, washing socks and shirts, towels and sheets and then in a tiny kitchen everlastingly cooking evening meals, the same old routine stretching into infinity – all the chances she'd had to sample the richness of life, lost for ever. No!

Something was saying: *this is your last chance. Take it now or be doomed.* Before Saturday, her letter must be on Eddie's doormat. By Saturday she must be gone before he could bring her back to the fold with its consequential imprisonment for life. Yet it was breaking her heart as it would break his. Once away, it would be easier to bear.

Eddie was still beaming. Contemplating Saturday, he was so easy to please; a trait endearing at times, at others, frustrating. Not one for arguing, Cissy knew he wasn't so much concerned about winning or losing an argument as being content to keep his own beliefs while nodding his acquiescence.

She knew too that she was going to have to wait until the very last minute to tell him of her intent. Otherwise he would be straight round, the pain of disbelief weakening those strong features of his, melting her heart, breaking down her resolve. She must word the letter as firmly as possible, give no hint of how he made her feel when he was near her; merely say that she didn't love him, couldn't marry him. Nothing to do with pre-wedding nerves or some other silly notion, but that she did not love him and was going away.

That lie rang like a clarion in her head. She did love him. She did. But to give in now, her dream almost within reach . . .

Sheet after sheet of notepaper was torn up the next day, nothing conveying what she wanted to say. The thought alone of the shock he was to experience almost pulled her resolve to shreds. All she wanted was for it to be all over. And once she was away from here . . .

She didn't realise, but some undefined apprehension had already begun to stir in Eddie. Even as he beamed at her like an idiot, something inside him kept saying, *it won't happen – she'll never marry me.*

Was it fear of marriage? He was sure she loved him. Or was it his own silly self unable to believe that such a wonderful, beautiful girl like Cissy would ever really love him, he with nothing to offer any girl – not even looks?

He needed to get advice. Not his or Cissy's parents. They'd stare at him as if he was mad and tell him he was imagining things. But he was sure he wasn't. He turned instead to his future brother-in-law, Bobby. A married man of only a few months, he might have an answer for this . . . whatever it was that was nagging at him.

Stirring the lukewarm cup of tea Ethel had brought him before huffing off into the kitchen again, her face tight at being told by her husband that Eddie had something private he wanted to speak to him about, Eddie took a deep breath and launched into his worries.

'Me and Cissy,' he began. 'Would you say we was well matched?'

'I would say so,' Bobby said confidently, but Eddie was not at all convinced.

'Trouble is, my idea of enjoyment ain't the sort she particularly enjoys. I'm not a very good dancer. And I'm not one for sitting long hours in the pictures either. Not three times a week. She loves going, and she's a lovely dancer too. Me, I've got two left feet, and that's the truth. I wish I could afford to take 'er to the theatre, perhaps once a week, or to a really nice restaurant, but I can't afford any of that. Not that *and* savin' ter get married. *If* we get married.

Bobby frowned. 'That's a funny thing to say.'

Eddie was still aimlessly stirring his tea, his eyes trained on his cup. 'If it 'as to be said, me and her are as different as chalk and cheese. I love walking. She don't. I love to go rowing on the river, even though it's me job . . . Busman's 'oliday, you might say.' He gave a small laugh, then continued, 'To 'er it's boring.'

'Does she say so?' Bobby's frown had deepened with a sense of something definitely not being right.

'Of course she don't,' Eddie's spoon clinked sharply against the saucer. 'But I know she is. When I take 'er rowing, she goes all quiet and just sits and watches me. She only smiles when I smile at 'er, and I have this awful feeling she's thinking we're going nowhere. I don't mean just boating. I get the same feeling when we go for a walk. I'm not one for strolling aimlessly. I like to get to where I'm going.'

'I thought couples were supposed to stroll.' Bobby's attempted joke didn't even make Eddie's lips twitch. His eyes held a distant look.

'My mother used to tell me that when I was a kid, I'd say, "If we run, it won't be so far to walk!" And I suppose that's how I've always been. I know I tend to take long strides, and Cissy often 'as to trot to keep up with me. I slow down for 'er, but before we know it, I'm off again. And there we are, both out of step, and then she gets annoyed and breaks away from me, and we walk apart. It's not a lot to make a fuss about, yet lately it's seems to me to 'ave become sort of symbolic – the two of us – out of step. You know. As if . . .'

He trailed off, searching for some way to explain how he felt, then began again. 'As if there's such a difference between us – a little thing like us not walking in step. That she feels we ain't . . .'

Again he trailed off, but Bobby began to see what he was trying to say.

Listening to him, it seemed to Bobby that if he had been visited by the sort of premonition Eddie was experiencing, he would never have married Ethel.

The thought came with a bitter surge of regret that their marriage had been a mistake all round. The stunner that Ethel had been before marriage, had afterwards been a real let-down; the sweet thing had become a sour shrew, always moaning about his shortcomings. What had been a delightfully indecisive girl had turned into a carping, mind-changing, misery: 'Why d'you 'ave to do that? Couldn't you do it this way? Can't you ever do it as I want it? Why must I always make all the decisions?' and when he did make them: 'Why couldn't you ask me first? You don't ever consult me, do you?' And so on and so on.

The baby had been a girl. They had hoped for a boy, but where he was content, she, for some unaccountable reason, seemed to blame him for it being a girl – as if he could help that. They had called her Jean.

He hoped their next might be a boy. But after her first experience of childbirth, she had made it loudly plain that she would never go through it again. And to cement that vow, she hadn't allowed him near her since, never letting him forget that it was he who had got her in the family way in the first place, forcing her to marry when she could be having a good time as she put it.

Yes, he could tell Eddie a thing or two about how girls change once they were married, and even though Cissy was his own sister, secretly he felt that Eddie might be in line for a lucky escape.

But he held his peace.

It was not too much of a surprise, therefore, when Eddie knocked on the door of his flat on Saturday morning, a scrunched-up letter in his hand, his face pale as a ghost, his eyes hollow.

Chapter Ten

It was eleven-thirty on Thursday morning, the sun climbing to its zenith made a breeze-ruffled sea glint around the boat like a million diamonds.

Cissy, hatless, in a pale green summer dress and white stockings, reclined in a deckchair on the sun deck listening to the hiss of the ship's bows moving smoothly through the water. Here, out of the breeze, the sun beat down onto her bare arms, a greater warmth than ever one got on the crowded, cold, brown sandy beaches of Margate where the wind came off the sea, damp and salty even on the brightest day. Only half an hour out of Dover but already in this sheltered part of the boat it felt as if she were sailing on a tropical sea. Around her came the laughter of passengers with means, their voices conveying not a care in the world, gay with the comfort money provided.

Cissy narrowed her eyes against the morning glare. Just across the sun deck, Langley was leaning on the rail, arms folded, chatting with Miles Devlin and Effie Messenger. Miles was shortish and sort of podgy. Effie was tallish and extremely thin, with a gaunt face that forbade prettiness. But highly strung and full of go, she was a gas to be with, as Cissy had heard it put, first in with any sort of romp. Already she'd had the hat of one of the crew, snatching it off his head as he went by, throwing it high into the air and squealing with laughter as the wind caught it and sent it spinning overboard. Still laughing, she'd readily offered to pay for the bit of fun, but nothing more was said, as she was one of the more lavish with her money of the first-class paying passengers, and money could speak volumes, Cissy was coming to realise.

Where the rest of Langley's circle of friends were, Cissy had no idea. Most likely in the first-class bar drinking champagne cocktails, she hazarded a guess, but felt too languid to care.

She felt deliciously drowsy. Deliciously . . . already she was picking up the vernacular of those she had been around with just these last few days. Soon she would be indistinguishable from any of them; she might even come to indulge in the same silly high spirits that seemed to bedevil them all. But at this moment she was too indolent to concern herself with that. Far too content, drowsy. Too drowsy even to pinch herself to see if this was indeed she lazing here.

It had been a fairy-tale few days. There had been hardly time to dwell on the consequences of her letter to Eddie, slipped through his letterbox in the early morning light last Saturday, or her letter to her parents left propped up on the kitchen mantelpiece. It seemed so far away now, their world; seemed years away – another life.

She had stolen out of the house around four-thirty that particular morning with little but what she had stood up in: a couple of nightdresses, a change of dress, a second pair of stockings, toothbrush, and a few items of make-up, all packed into the small attaché case from the top shelf of her wardrobe. She also had her birth certificate – Langley had said she would need it to get a passport. Feeling her way about the room she shared with May, dark but for the street lamp down the road, she had prayed not to bumble into something and wake up her sister. Her prayers had been answered – May had slumbered on, undisturbed.

Mum and Dad hadn't stirred either. Cissy knew the routine: Mum up just after five, getting Dad a cup of tea and then doing sandwiches; Dad coming down ten minutes later either to a quick breakfast or else skipping it to have it later in some café near the docks.

But when Cissy had crept out with dawn coming up, looking back for the last time into the gloom of the home she had known since a child, the action produced an unexpectedly empty feeling inside her, all had been quiet but for Dad's faint snoring from upstairs. That in itself heightened the feeling of emptiness and had made her almost want to run back into the house, creep back to bed and forget this madness.

Resolutely, she had closed the door, watching against letting the wood, prone to swelling in the early morning dampness, scrape noisily against the doorjamb. Resolutely, she hoisted her tiny case and her handbag to a firmer grip and turned her face towards the new morning and, hopefully, a different life . . . if Langley's offer was still on.

The first trams started running just after five, the first tube train about the same time. She had reached Liverpool

Street Station as the first workmen's train was emptying out, and had to go with the surge making for the underground Circle Line.

Coming up to street level at Victoria she had made her way to the address on Langley's letter, seeming to walk for ages in the early light of what promised to be a fine day – a good luck sign she had surmised – scrutinising the fine houses set back behind their high ornate railings.

She couldn't remember exactly how she had found it, only able to recall walking up a gravel drive towards the large Georgian-type front door with white portals. Langley's shiny car was sitting in the middle of the drive with the air of a huge sleeping dog; expecting a butler to answer her ring on the electric bell push, she found Langley himself, sleepy-eyed and tousle-haired, clad in a blue silk dressing gown, opening the door to her.

She remembered more vividly his half-hearted welcome and her own embarrassment. She could still feel the sinking sensation seeing his narrow face registering dismay, as it had appeared for that instant. Then he had brightened, became genuinely pleased to see her, and had pulled her into the hall and given her a huge hug, declaring his pleasure that she had decided to come to Paris after all. She knew then that what had looked like dismay had been surprise – nothing more – from a man just awakened from sleep.

He had laughed out loud when she told him she'd brought nothing with her. She hadn't dared tell him that what she owned was too cheap to air. She had, of course, taken out her rainy-day savings on the Friday intending to buy at least a couple of good dresses and maybe a nice hat. She had thought better about affording undies and things that, unseen, could take their chances. But he would not hear a word about using her own money. After coming fully awake and making her a quick breakfast of egg and bacon, he had dragged her out that morning to Kensington High Street, buying her a lovely coat with a huge fox fur collar, a pair of soft leather shoes with Cuban heels and decorated straps, and an exquisite shiny pink straw cloche hat with a deeper pink silk band. 'The rest we'll get in Paris,' he'd said as if it had been arranged months ago. Then he'd taken her off to buy the Channel steamer ticket, all before she had hardly caught her breath.

That evening they had gone to the theatre and afterwards had supper at a glittering restaurant. She remembered second thoughts seeping through her as they returned to his house, her stomach going over and over that all this would have to be paid that night. Not that she'd been terrified of what was expected of her as he conducted her inside, but that this would be her first time ever being made love to. Even Eddie had only ever kissed her, she dying to have him at least fumble inside her blouse. Though he often trembled and seemed on the verge of doing so, he never took that liberty, while she, for all her yearning, hadn't dared to encourage him lest it cement their relationship that little bit too much and entrap her.

In Langley's house she had steeled herself for the unknown; not only that but what he would think of her being so free with herself? But she needn't have worried. Almost as though enjoying playing the gallant gentleman, he had shown her to her room, pecked her goodnight on the cheek, and then retired. In fact, what she remembered most was a sense of deflation as she stood with her back against the closed door, wondering how she could so lack allure that a peck on the cheek had been all she had got.

Her disappointment had finally been dispelled by the room itself. In all her life she'd never seen such a room. Those of the boarding house on holiday at Margate or Ramsgate with her family were often large, but cavernous and sparsely furnished with deal cupboard, dressing table, chair and a sagging iron bedstead with sheets and blankets barely covered by a quilt that had seen more washing than was good for it.

The room Langley had given her had been pure luxury, cream satin everywhere, with drapes and cushions, a delicate cream wardrobe and a dressing table with mirrors. The room had been hers for the next few days until this morning when they had left early – she with even more beautiful clothes and a leather travelling case to put them in. Langley had spared no expense. Had asked nothing of her in return. At least, so far. But eventually he must. Though at the moment it didn't matter.

Sitting in this deckchair, Dover's cliffs being engulfed by a warm sea mist even before they could sink behind the green-white wake of the cross-Channel steamer, she felt content, dreamy, the life she'd known hardly real now. Ahead lay France – Paris. Altogether another world.

Her eyelids felt pleasantly heavy. Above the steady thump of engines, exhilarated chatter and bursts of laughter came and went in waves. Faint tinkling piano music floated from a small piano bar . . . 'When day is done and shadows fall I dream of you . . .'

Lethargic, her eyes only half open, she drew in deep breaths of an assortment of not unpleasant smells and identified each as it came to her; the fresh salt-sea tang; the warm wafting of engine oil; and the acrid soot-bound smell of smoke that had strung itself out from the ship's funnel to hang suspended behind them like a long grey wavering rope across the sea. The cliffs of Dover had quite disappeared.

Floating in her own sea of languor, Cissy closed her eyes and opened them again with a start to the sound of Langley's voice in her ear.

'Come on, lazybones. Some company you are! We're all going to the piano bar for drinks. We'll be docking soon.'

'Soon?' She sat bolt upright. The sun deck, still sunny, was less crowded, and the sun now invaded every part of the deck which had hitherto had shadow in one corner. 'How long have I been here?'

'Best part of the crossing.'

'Why didn't you wake me?'

'You looked so content, asleep. Effie said you looked more like a rag doll. Miles said you looked stunning. I said you looked ravishing – snoring away.'

'Was I *snoring*?'

Langley let out a laugh. 'I'm joking! Come on now, up with you.'

Her hand firmly in his she followed. 'I wasn't snoring, was I?' she begged. A fleeting memory of the last sound she'd heard in a silent house, Dad snoring, appalled her.

'No, of course not,' Langley said.

The piano bar was crowded. The whole group were already there, being jostled about, sipping cocktails and champagne. Cissy had a champagne cocktail bought by Langley after a struggle through a pack of bodies getting last-minute drinks. He had a brandy.

Sipping her drink, Cissy felt wonderful. Four couples. Eight people having a whale of a time – and she was one of them.

With a clanging of bells and roar of engines, the ship's stewards began marshalling passengers towards gangways where the doors would shortly open. Last drinks quickly knocked back and guzzled down, then a mad race to find a porter to handle the baggage, a handsome tip at the ready. Giggling and calling to each other over the jostle as the doors swung back, they spilled out into French sunshine, down the slope of the gangway onto French tarmac.

Cissy stood surrounded by a mound of eight people's baggage, watching Dickie Verhoeven hand a generous tip to their porter who raised a forefinger to his cap in casual nonchalance before examining the size of the tip, then with a satisfied grin departed.

Faith Silk and Effie were sorting out hat boxes and vanity cases, while Pamela Carstairs seemed mesmerised by the opal brooch she was wearing on the loose neck of her white, low-cut cotton dress. Miles and Ginger Bratts were in close discussion over train tickets while Langley went in search of a couple of taxis to take them and their considerable accessories to a hotel for the night before travelling on to Paris by train the following morning.

No one seemed to be taking notice of her. For a moment Cissy felt utterly out of it, ignored. For a moment she was again the Cockney girl whom Langley had first introduced to his circle of fine friends, summed up and dismissed as something quaint. Her only consolation was that Margo Fox-Prinshaw hadn't come, hanging onto Langley's arm, as she would have had she been here, as if she had every right. And perhaps she had. After all, she was Langley's sort. Was she, Cissy Farmer, Langley's sort? Not really. Would she ever be? Had she been brought along only because she was someone different to the rest of them?

She allowed her gaze to wander away, a small hollow pounding inside her chest, then her eyes swung back with an almost abject sense of gratitude as Langley's hand touched her arm. He was back. He had sought her out.

'Good God, Cissy! Still half asleep. Come on, darling, I've found a couple of cabs. A bit decrepit. Lord knows how we're going to get all of us *and* our stuff into them. We'll manage if you four girls can squeeze into one with me and Miles. Ginger and Dickie can go in the other one with the luggage.'

Part of a group again, Cissy sat squashed between the cab door and the three girls. She didn't mind being on the end, and participated in their high-pitched laughter at the flailing arms of a gabbling cabby who seemed at a loss as to how to pack six bodies into his vehicle until given the promise of a huge gratuity.

It now had all the promise of becoming a lot of fun. In her new summer frock, the pretty hat she was wearing, with her fine leather travelling case being bundled with the rest into the second taxi, it was so different to the life she'd left behind. Even the air smelled different: the bitter aroma of freshly ground coffee; the sweet smell of hand-made confectionery and sticky pastries; and something else, something elusive, not exactly perfume – flowers perhaps. There was even a different smell to the taxi, leather rather than London grime, as it rattled its way along the wide promenade flanking the docks, turning off into progressively narrowing cobbled side streets before finally emerging in a substantial promenade with hotels of varying sizes.

'That one!' Langley shouted to the driver, pointing at a hotel further down the street; blue-washed with open pink shutters and pots of red geraniums dangling from white-painted balconies. But at the sight of it, a faint wave of apprehension took hold of Cissy.

'Are we booking rooms for each of us?' she asked amid the almost deafening chatter inside the cab. Silence decended like a curtain. Three pairs of female eyes of varying hues turned themselves upon her. Miles gave a giggle.

'I haven't the faintest!' Effie finally said rather sharply, and turned back to resume the interrupted conversation.

Cissy sat quiet, confused and mortified. She should have laughed, but she didn't. In time she would learn to parry this caustic wit – that was what it was basically – except that it hurt her, so new was she to it. They used it to each other, but she was not yet acclimatised.

The men, of course, were as different as chalk to cheese, pandering to their partners' whims and fancies. Langley did too, but he did it without fawn or favour. Miles, now Miles was a positive groveller, especially where Faith was concerned, and Dickie for all his military affectation, seemed to lose three inches in height when Pamela spoke sharply. Effie of course could demolish any man. Unpretty as she was, there was a certain regality about her that made heads turn, and Cissy had noticed that her partner for this trip was ready to have rings run around him, blushing wildly to his ginger roots every time she touched his hand or leaned confidentially towards him.

The taxi driver was taking his time making it to the hotel Langley had pointed out, getting stuck behind cabs onloading at other hotels. While his fare huffed and puffed at the delay, Cissy thought of Langley. Out of the four, he was the best, and Cissy felt proud. Effie was probably jealous. No doubt that was why she had snapped at her. But Langley was hers. He treated her like royalty – his princess as he still called her. She found herself thinking that she wouldn't mind a bit now if he got her into bed and even began to hope he would.

Then in the very midst of anticipation, Eddie's face leapt into her head, leaving her totally unprepared for the pang that accompanied it. He had never once compromised her as she was sure Langley would sooner or later. With the pang came a rush of conscience. How was Eddie faring? How had he taken her letter? What a silly question. He'd have taken it badly, but what could she do about it now? Nothing.

Pushing conscience away, she lifted her eyes to see Langley looking at her from his seat. His face broke into an understanding smile and as he rose to get out, she saw his eyes flick towards the unsuspecting Effie and back again to her in a mutual conspiracy of ridicule.

Cissy nearly laughed out loud, tension dispersed. The taxi jerked to an erratic halt and those inside made ready to explode out onto the pavement, she with them, Eddie forgotten.

*

'If only we knew where she was. How she is.' Doris sighed as she went about her morning chores like some automaton, trying to hold back her silly tears. She'd been holding them back ever since Cissy's note had been found propped against the clock on the kitchen mantelpiece.

'If only we knew . . .'

'I don't want ter know.' Charlie's tone was hard. 'And if I did, I wouldn't trouble meself ter contact 'er.'

He gave a rumbling cough to disguise the void sitting like a lump of iron inside him and which his tone was in danger of betraying. Part of him wanted to go looking for her, if he knew where to start. The other part – the part she had injured last Saturday morning when she had sneaked off like a low-down thief, not even a goodbye or any sort of explanation or forwarding address – argued that she wasn't worth looking for when she'd walked out as she had. That was the bitterest part, the disowning part.

'All I've done fer 'er . . .' What he wanted to say was all she meant to him, but he didn't '. . . And that's 'ow she be'aves. I tell you this Doris, ole gel, I don't care where she is, but she can bloody well stay there.'

'You can't say that about our own daughter.'

He wasn't listening, railing on to justify himself. 'Fallen in love with someone else? My bloody foot! I'll give 'er fall in love.'

'I only pray she's all right. P'raps she'll come back after a while and tell us she's all right. I won't never be able to rest until she do come back. We ought really to've told the police, but you said . . .'

'She went of 'er own free will,' he cut in savagely. 'I told you, they'll only tell you that themselves, there's nothing they can do.'

'But what if something awful's 'appened to 'er?'

'God knows what Eddie must be feeling right now, poor bugger. All she was to 'im. All 'e was to 'er. That's what I can't forgive. 'Er 'urting 'im. She won't get none better than Eddie, 'ooever this thing is she supposed to 'ave fallen in love with. Fallen in love? I'll give 'im fallen in love if I ever catch 'im. Salt of the earth, Eddie. And this is what she does to 'im. What 'e must be feeling.'

It was the oldest cliche in the world that trouble never comes singly. Cissy's letter still lay in the breast pocket of the old coat Eddie went to work in. Not that he had much heart in work.

It had been read and reread, scrutinised, analysed, for whatever tiniest clue that might hold the reason for her leaving, other than the one she had given: that she had found someone else. There had been no forewarning, no apparent cause as far as he could see, nothing.

He had been determined to comb London to find her. Then the day after Cissy's departure, just as he was about to go looking God knows where for her, had come the second blow – a telegram telling his mother that her sister Lottie had been taken ill.

Aunt Lottie had been taken into the London Hospital where she still lay. She had collapsed with terrible pains while serving her customers. They had called an ambulance which had taken her straight to the hospital. An examination had revealed that she had a . . . his mother had whispered the word cancer as five hundred years ago they might have whispered plague.

Dreadful news that it was, his mother grief-stricken for her sister, it fell to Eddie, instead of going in futile search of Cissy, to spend much of that weekend instead at the hospital with his mother and father. How could he ask them to dwell upon his own problems when theirs and Aunt Lottie's were far more crucial?

Tests revealed a hopeless situation, a growth left too long before being found. There had been a lengthy exploratory operation which the surgeon had closed up again as inoperable. Too late. A matter of weeks – two, maybe three – he came grave-faced to announce to the patient's only sister. Nothing could be done now. It was in God's hands. He was very, very sorry.

The next ten days were spent at Aunt Lottie's bedside at every available moment. His father had to work to keep the money coming into the house. Eddie, needing only to pay his mother for his keep, asked his employers for a bit of time off, unpaid of course, to keep his mother company during her daily vigil at the hospital with no one else to sit beside her, apart from a fleeting visit by a kind customer or two. Aunt Lottie had no children, no husband and no siblings but her sister, and Eddie felt duty bound to let his aunt see that someone else cared. Not that she saw much, lying in drugged stupor.

His employers were obliging. There were many out of work watermen waiting for a few days' work, or even a long three nights without a break, so long as it brought in a bit of money. For Eddie, at least it helped take away some of the loss of Cissy's inexplicable departure.

On the Tuesday of the second week after Cissy's leaving, another telegram arrived. His aunt had passed away in the night – peacefully, it stated. At the hospital they were told that she'd been in no pain, and, a nurse observed with good intention, perhaps it was a mercy she had gone quickly and quietly. No one could dispute that.

It fell to Eddie to notify the Registrar of Births, Marriages and Deaths and find an undertaker, the body lying in the hospital morgue until needed. In all this, Eddie felt the opportunities for going off to search heaven knows where for Cissy were receding further and further. From her there was no word. No word at all.

He went to see her workmate, Daisy Evans, who said she had been just as surprised as he by the suddenness of her friend's going. She said she didn't know who the man was – had never met him. She admitted to having been told his name on one occasion but had completely forgotten it – couldn't begin to think what it was. She also admitted to Cissy's talking about going off to France with him but hadn't believed she'd go that far, and again didn't know where in France she had gone.

'But I wish I had her spirit,' she observed wistfully. 'I've always wanted to go on the stage, you know. One day I will. That's why I went to Madam Noreah's to take singing lessons while Cissy did her elocution. I'm still trying to pluck up the courage to tell my parents I want to leave Cohens and try the stage. I'm sure I could make it. I'm sure.'

Sick at heart after what seemed like hours trying to pump some tiny bit of memory out of Daisy Evans's brain from what Cissy had said to her, Eddie came away just as unclear as he'd been before he went.

Chapter Eleven

'What do we do about the café?' Clara Bennett said, she, her husband Alfred and her son Eddie, sitting in the front room after the last of the few funeral guests had left.

The table still lay spread with the debris of the lunch: a pile of sandwiches curling at the edges, half the fruit cake she'd made, its crumbs littering the paper doily and staining it brown in places, and the half-empty pickle jar. There were several sausage rolls still left too. She had done far too much food for the small gathering there had been.

Quite a few around the graveside though, mostly her poor sister's customers who hadn't come back to the house but respectfully left after the funeral. They had liked her. Clara swallowed back tears.

The day, for September, had been warm and sunny – not quite right really, she thought. Funerals should have properly suitable weather, dull and miserable, sort of compensation for those who have departed this world. Not a fine sunny day with the promise of a wonderful sunset which didn't somehow seem much like any sort of compensation to the poor dear departed no longer able to appreciate such wonders.

'It's bin closed ever since she went into 'ospital,' her husband said, knocking out his pipe on the empty fire grate. 'Might as well stay closed till we 'ear what the solicitors 'ave to say.'

Lottie had left a will. Her only living relatives, being her sister Clara and her nephew Eddie, had been asked to attend the offices of Hodges, Hughes & Hughes, in Commercial Road tomorrow morning at ten. It probably didn't entail much except for the café.

'I mean,' Clara said, 'what if it's willed to me? What'll I do with a café? I ain't got no idea 'ow to run a café.'

'We'll 'ave ter sell it, that's all. If it comes to you, which I expect it will. It might bring in a tidy little sum.'

Clara winced visibly. 'Oh, Alf . . . it sounds so money-grabbin'. I really don't want none of 'er poor money what she worked 'erself into the grave for. I don't want to profit out of me poor sister's death, God bless 'er. I really don't.'

'Who d'you think should 'ave it, then? The cat's 'ome? Look, Clara, she'd've wanted you to 'ave it.'

'What about Eddie, 'ere? Maybe she wanted 'im to 'ave it?'

Alf Bennett rose and put his cold pipe in its rack on the shelf above the fireplace, eased his trouser braces away from his chest with his thick thumbs and stretched his back.

'If it goes to Eddie, then good luck to 'im. 'E needs a bit of luck at this moment – that cow of a Cissy Farmer leavin' 'im in the lurch like that. An' all the weddin' bin thought out, too. You could do with something lucky coming your way, son, and good riddance to bad rubbish is what I say.'

Eddie's lips tightened. He'd listened in silence to the discussion going on over his head, finding no interest in it, no desire to join in, his thoughts centred not on the funeral but on Cissy. He was sick at heart. There seemed little left in life to be happy about with her gone. For her to walk off as she had, she couldn't ever have loved him and the knowledge felt like a physical pain, as though he were being strangled from the inside out. But he wasn't going to rise to his father's besmirching of Cissy. He wasn't going to even mention her.

'I don't want to trade off Aunt Lottie's dying, Dad. If she was to've left anything at all to me, I've got no use fer it. Not now.'

His father gazed down to where Eddie sat on the edge of his chair, leaning forward on his elbows in a sort of gesture of despair.

Eddie was aware of the scrutiny, but what reason was there to lean back like someone with the world at his feet? The only time he felt anywhere near like leaning back in a chair was from sheer exhaustion after a long day working on the river. He hadn't put his heart into his work all that much since Cissy went, yet what little he did do seemed to leave him completely worn out. Without her, nothing was really worth while. Certainly there was nothing to strive for, nothing to make his muscles leap and ripple from the sheer joy of living.

'You can forget about . . .' his father began, then stopped himself, to say instead, 'we'll just wait an' see what your aunt's will 'as ter say, that's all. Weren't much of a life for 'er, workin' all hours God sent without a man at 'er side. Killed 'er in the end. Well, I'm orf ter bed. Up at four tomorrer. We've bin busy lately. Would've bin on a two, three nights stretch 'ad it not been fer the funeral. Got ter make up some time now, two of us bein' orf today, me *and* Eddie. No need fer you ter get up with me tomorrer, Clara. Yer've 'ad a rotten day of it. Sorry about Lottie.'

It seemed to Eddie that he was talking for the sake of it, to fill up the void Eddie's own attitude had provoked. His father's hand came on his shoulder as he passed, and Eddie knew with a pang of gratitude that he was feeling for him, even while against Cissy for her action.

'See yer on the water, son. 'Ave a good sleep.'

To which Eddie nodded wordlessly.

Mr Oliver Hodges laid the stiff, neatly handwritten parchment of his client's last will and testament before Mrs Bennett and her son to see more clearly.

'As you see, my late client has bequeathed her estate to Mr Edward Bennett, your son, apart from two hundred pounds and all her jewellery which she specifically wished you to have, Mrs Bennett. I did beg her at one time to leave a proportionately larger portion of her estate to yourself, her sister, but she said you and your husband would be at a loss what to do with a business. She refused to be swayed, and said it was for the best that it go to her nephew, Edward Bennett, as he is young and would have far more understanding of business. May I offer you my congratulations, Mr Bennett?'

Eddie gave him a look that said he wanted no congratulations, but immediately smiled politely. Solicitors had no tact as far as he could see, though he knew little about them; having never sat in one's office before.

'I didn't expect any of this.'

'I quite understand. A thousand pounds and a going business thrust on one is quite a deal to take in.'

'I never dreamed she was worth so much. I never dreamed she'd leave it to me, lock, stock and barrel.'

'Hardly lock, stock and barrel. Your mother is also included in the will. But I see what you mean.'

'She said once that what she had would be mine. But I really never believed . . .'

Eddie's words failed him as he again focused his eyes on the neat, calligraphic endeavours of some solicitor's clerk by which wills were written. A deep feeling of sadness came over him that he would never again sit in Aunt Lottie's café, have her wink at him as she handed him his egg and sausage, his two slices and tea. The next time he climbed a ladder to paint a ceiling would be for himself. He didn't want to touch another paintbrush on his own account. Poor Aunt Lottie, never to hear her grating voice saying that it was all right, he could keep his money, that he did enough. . . . It was almost too miserable to think about. He swallowed painfully and looked up at the solicitor through suddenly misted eyes, nodding wordlessly.

'You don't 'ave to manage that café,' his mother said, as they left after shaking the solicitor's soft hand.

'I don't want the place anyway,' he told her. 'I think you should take it over, Mum. You and Dad. Dad could get off the river and take things easy. It was always a nice little earner. It must be for Aunt Lottie to've saved all that money.'

'But I don't know nothing about running cafés. I said that before.'

'But you'd learn.'

'And run it down'ill while I am,' she said glumly.

'But you've got it for nothing. Would it matter if you did run it down a bit? It'd soon pick up once you've got the 'ang of it.'

'I couldn't face all them rough watermen what comes in.'

'If Aunt Lottie did it, you can.' He took her arm encouragingly. 'Think about it, Mum. It ain't my sort of life. I like the river too much.'

'What I think you ought ter do is sell it.' She hadn't really been listening. 'With the money you could buy what you often used ter talk about. A tug. You always said you wouldn't ever 'ave enough money fer such an 'ope. Now you 'ave. You could buy yerself a tug and go into the towage business proper. A thousand quid! You could buy two tugs and really do business. You could become a man of real good standing. Someone to look up to and be respected. That'd show that Cissy Farmer. When she comes crying back to you, yer could tell 'er what you think of 'er, and you're a man of means and can 'ave your pick of anyone.'

He didn't want to tell her that he didn't want his pick of anyone. He wanted Cissy. But if he could only show her that he could offer her the world on a plate – his plate, then perhaps she would want him again.

But how could he show her when he had no idea where she was and not the least notion where to look for her?

Daisy was jealous. More, her nose had been put out of joint. All the times she had boasted how she would leave home and go on the stage; the times she'd laughed at Cissy for being weak-kneed and putting obstacles in the way when it came to going off to seek a better life than the one they had. And now it was Cissy who'd done it and she who had been left behind. She almost hated Cissy as she went off to work in the mornings alone, to sit at her bench with some other face across the way in Cissy's place – the job had been filled that very day her note had arrived in old McCreedy's office. It never took long to fill vacancies in the dress-machinist trade.

Daisy consulted Madam Noreah on her chances of finding some sort of opening as a singer. In response, Madam Noreah inhaled deeply.

'My dear, why else have you been coming to me these past two years if not to find the ultimate goal for your excellent voice?' Coming up for breath, she continued, 'There were times I feared you would fall by the wayside as so many of my young pupils do, opting for the easier life of marriage and security, allowing all to go to waste.'

A look of supreme self-satisfaction sent rays across her podgy face and her pregnant-looking bosom rose and fell. She lifted a dramatic hand to embrace the air about her face.

'I never married. My career came first. Always. I had my suitors, you understand. In my youth I was quite fetching, and had men flocking around me, waiting at the stage door with flowers, and wonderful boxes of chocolates, and offers . . . Ah, yes, the offers! Wonderful offers.'

Her pale eyes that had held a faraway look refocused upon Daisy.

'And you, my dear – you will have similar offers . . . As you climb. Ah yes, as you climb. And then . . . Ah, then will your life begin. You *may* marry – in time. Perhaps to some distinguished titled person. Or even to a European count – who knows? And married to such, you may still continue your career. With *your* voice, my dear, as it develops, as it must with dedication, you can scale the very heights. Of course, you must continue your studies – though not under my tuition, I fear.'

She gave a great sigh. 'The time has now come for you to leave me and to move on to those who can teach you far more than I am able. I have felt for some time that you have outgrown my limited abilities to teach you. Now you must spread your wings, my dear, and fly away, or it will be such a waste. Such a cruel waste. Such a sacrilege. I wish you luck and great joy of your talent, dear Daisy. Now go. Go and find yourself, child. Find yourself.'

Exhausted by Madam Noreah's exuberance, as much as the woman was herself, Daisy brought the tone down to earth. 'How do I start?'

Her tutor smiled, utterly undaunted. 'I shall write you a letter of recommendation which you shall take along to the Royal Opera House at Covent Garden. I shall do it this very minute and you must go there as soon as you can. I would waste no time delaying, were I you.'

Enthusiasm bubbling up in the woman like an artesian well, Daisy watched her feverishly seek pen and ink and a sheet of notepaper from the cat-scratched bureau that squatted to one side of the ancient black grand piano. Her podgy hand moved rapidly across the notepaper.

'Ask for Signor Vittorio Citti – an old acquaintance of mine who will be happy to listen to your voice. He will grant you an audition, as a favour to me, and I am sure he will agree that yours is a truly beautiful pure soprano and a promising coloratura.'

Daisy wished she could share the enthusiasm Madam Noreah was displaying. Opera had never been her aim. Something much less heavy would have been more suitable, giving her time to enjoy herself rather than be forever practising scales and the arias which opera demanded. But she held her tongue and took the note Madam Noreah folded into a discoloured white envelope she managed to fish from the bureau.

Armed with her letter of introduction, Daisy went home to face her family with her promising good fortune, expecting disapproval.

Instead, her mother looked awed and said, 'Royal Opera House – well I never!' While her father, not one to bother himself what happened to his children, merely grinned and muttered, 'Bloody load of rubbish if yer arst me.'

It was tantamount to receiving both their blessings, yet it was with misgivings that, in her best dress, coat and hat, she made her way to the address on the letter, the huge, square, dark-bricked edifice of the Royal Opera House standing like a potentate amid the stink of decaying cabbage leaves and rotting vegetables that only the Covent Garden Fruit and Veg Market could create after it was done for the day.

It was surprisingly easy to see Signor Citti. The doorman in his little glass cubicle gave Daisy's note a cursory glance and picked up the phone to speak to someone, repeating the introductory name Daisy had quoted, then directed her to follow the narrow corridor until she came to the last door on the right at the very end, and then to knock on it.

The corridor was a corkscrew of a place, turning left and then left again, finally terminating at a door marked 'Props'. Tapping on the one on her right, as directed, although it had no name, she was bidden by a hoarse voice with a faint Italian accent to enter.

Opening the door cautiously, she found herself looking at a broad-faced man whose wealth of black beard, well splattered with grey, contrasted with his balding head. He looked like the sort of operatic baritone Madam Noreah might once have known very well in their youth, but had, like her, seen the best of his operatic days, possibly following the company these days more in a coaching capacity.

Clad in rust-brown trousers and waistcoat, a striped collarless shirt with a red kerchief at his neck, he beamed at Daisy, advancing upon her with one hand, whose thick fingers carried an assortment of gold rings, held out for the letter she had brought. Still beaming at her, he opened the envelope swiftly, then lowered his somewhat bulging brown eyes to read.

When he lifted them again, his gaze was more businesslike. 'Your tutor writes to say that you possess a remarkable voice.'

'Thank you,' Daisy said, even more nervous than before.

'I should like to hear for-a myself. Please, take off your coat, signorine. I regret there is no piano. I would appreciate to hear a scale. Whichever you choose.'

He listened, bending a critical ear towards her as she complied, still nervous. Listening intently, he moved her voice up through the range so that she was reaching top C, her confidence returning, then requested she sing something easy, something she was familiar with, something she had learned with Madam Noreah.

She chose a short aria from *La Bohème*, but with no accompaniment it lacked magic, at least to her ears. When she had finished, he nodded as though to himself.

'Signorine, you have a nice voice. Attractive. Very pretty . . .'

He broke off to regard her as she stared at him, slowly beginning to comprehend what he was trying to say, the benevolent, almost sad smile he gave her already speaking for him.

'I am sorry. It *is* only . . . a pretty voice. Very attractive. But . . .'

The heavy shoulders shrugged as only an Italian's can – even for a man so ample – full of expression that Daisy now clearly read.

'For opera, a voice must have . . . more – much more! I must tell you, signorine, that I can detect nothing to reassure myself that this voice will ever reach the exactitudes required of an opera singer – not even for chorus. Under rigors as it will have to face, it breaks. There is a weakness. Your tutor was misguided. Your voice, sadly, with all the training, all the coaching it can be given, has no future in opera. I do not say you cannot sing – but in the Royal Opera House? Is not the place. Teatro alla Scala, Weiner Straatsoper, New York Metropolitan Opera House – none of these, my dear signorine, I regret. Your voice, it is not for the great opera houses of the world if that is what you had hoped for. Maybe . . . something less demanding?'

Again he shrugged, his expression sorrowful. He obviously felt he was tearing the heart out of an aspiring singer, sounding her death knell. If only he knew. Even though what he'd said fell like a dull thud on her ears with the aspect of a vague insult, it was what she had half wanted to hear. Madam Noreah had been merely carried away.

'Will I be any good, anywhere?' she asked, her expression sombre. She saw his face brighten with relief.

'In something lighter – why not? It *is* a pleasing voice.'

Getting back into her coat, she gave him a brave smile, taking the thick hand he offered. 'Thank you for telling me the truth.'

'I am sorry,' he said as he followed her to the door and opened it for her, and she was sure she saw the bulbous brown eyes moisten.

Even so, she guessed he had most likely forgotten her by the time she re-entered Covent Garden tube station. But by the time she emerged at Tottenham Court Road, she had definitely forgotten *him*; in her hand a copy of the theatre guide she had picked up at a kiosk in which, by chance, she had noticed that *Rose Marie* showing at Drury Lane Theatre was still open for some auditions for the chorus.

By the time she came out of the stage door several hours later, her excitement almost choked her. Hat and coat off, she'd sung those songs they'd asked for, surprised by the quality of her own voice, as well as by her lack of nerves. She supposed they had all been got rid of while facing the redoubtable Signor Citti. Moreover, she hadn't even dared believe they would want her; had gone in merely on a whim to see what it was like. And now she came out, part of the chorus in a new West End musical! It was hard to believe. But then, had she not been heard by a one-time opera singer who, in his own way, had praised her voice? Praise enough to give her confidence. In time there'd be bigger, more important parts.

Daisy's brown eyes glowed, already seeing her name in lights. From there, who knows? Foreign travel? Might even end up in Paris, where Cissy had said *she* was going. That would make Cissy Farmer look sick, finding her there after running off to France as though she were the only one to do it. Well, she would find out that she wasn't the only one to take that big step into the unknown.

Cissy's first sight of Paris had her completely bowled over. She, who had seen no other city but London, who'd hardly travelled beyond its boundaries apart from odd day trips to Southend or a week in Margate or Ramsgate, now found herself staring at her first ever foreign capital as, with their cases trundled to waiting taxis by a *facteur* (as Langley called the railway porter), she and the others surged from Gare St Lazare railway station, Langley with his arm about her.

The first sound to escape her lips was a sigh, 'Oh-h-h . . .' in her amazement only just avoiding a natural reversion to that old expletive 'Cor!', used before her tutor Madam Noreah had ever got to her.

Langley gave her a smile, rather as though he and not Napoleon had been responsible for the layout of Paris, and his arm tightened about her in a possessive grip. 'I take it you approve, darling.'

'I've never seen anything quite like . . .' Words failed her as her gaze came to rest on a stall directly outside the station, heaped with such banks of flowers. An elderly aproned woman stood bunching a huge mass of them together for a male customer. In London, men on their own would never dream of buying flowers in the street. In the West End of course, but there was always some woman on their arm.

Nearby a policeman in a smart navy blue uniform and pillbox hat, was consulting a notebook, his manner one of calm nonchalance. English bobbies were calm, Cissy reflected, but certainly not nonchalant. It was all so different to England.

But it was the hubbub that struck her the most, swarms of open taxi cabs, honking horns filling the air with continuous noise, yet still failing to drown the sounds of music floating from somewhere. It wasn't barrel organ music as in London or the kerbside drum and cornet blare of ex-servicemen looking for pennies, but a lively accordion which its owner played as though for the sheer joy of it rather than money.

Cissy took a deep breath. Here were those same aromas she'd first noticed on setting foot in France; newly baked bread, freshly ground coffee, flowers. The same hot sunlight poured down from a pearly blue sky to glow upon the grey stone of every building. And what buildings! Every single window had its wrought-iron balcony, not enough to stand on but enough for pots of scarlet geraniums. Even with walls of ageing plaster each building managed to convey a sense of romance.

'It all looks so . . .' Unable to find words, she shook her head in disbelief. Langley laughed.

'Paris will take your breath away, Cissy. She will capture your heart, darling, and you'll never want to leave. That's Paris.'

Seven young people were squashing into one taxi, Miles, fatter than the others, was left to go with the baggage in a second one. Cissy, her blue-grey eyes like saucers at everything she saw from her perch on Langley's lap, marvelled at how they managed not to crash into the hundreds of other cabs in the process.

'Where are we staying?' she managed to ask, without Effie beside her putting her spoke in.

'Montparnasse,' Langley said.

'Where's that?'

He chuckled, vaguely patronisingly. 'We'll be there soon, darling. Meanwhile you just enjoy the sights. We're turning into Boulevard Haussman. This is where I'll take you shopping, here and Rue de Rivoli and Rue Royale. There's the Opera.' He gave a flourish towards its domed grandeur as they circled round it into what he said was Avenue de L'Opera, from there pointing out one impressive building after another like a paid tour guide.

How well he pronounced those French names, Cissy thought, drinking in every one and wondering if she'd ever learn French enough to make him proud of her.

'They call the area where we will be living the Quarter,' he explained. 'Loads of Americans go there. Artists live there. Gertrude Stein, Ezra Pound, Ernest Hemingway. You'll see them all.'

She had heard of the first two – vaguely. Writers, poets, something like that. The third name didn't ring familiar.

'Who's Ernest Hemingway?' she asked.

'My God!' Effie beside her burst out, as if to say doesn't she know anything? Her painted eyes raised heavenward.

'A new writer,' Langley said quickly, leaning forward a fraction to give Effie a straight glance. The movement made Cissy feel suddenly, wonderfully, protected. 'Talented, though. He'll be famous one day, but lots of people have probably not yet heard that much of him. Don't you agree, *Effie,* darling?' he added pointedly.

Effie's red lips opened to retort, but there came a piercing yell from Faith, scrunched against Miles.

'Oh! Oh! Oh, I have cramp in my foot!' The moment of tension was broken. 'Dickie – get off it!'

'I'm not on your silly foot,' protested Dickie. 'Your shoes are too tight. You're always getting cramp because you wear them too tight.'

'You had your foot on it.' Faith had her foot in the air, shoeless, and was rubbing it desperately. 'Oh, oh,' she sighed, the pain fading.

'My foot wasn't anywhere near yours.'

'It was!' Ths small round face, beautifully made-up, was filled with pique. 'It's a good job you moved when you did, or I'd have had to throw myself out of this cab with the pain. I'd have landed in the road and most probably been run over! All because you weren't caring how much room you were taking. How would you have felt then?'

'Simply ghastly, darling!'

'So I should think.'

Cissy smiled at the disruption, already dissipating. Wonderful to be part of it all: the brief squabbles, the sharp little disputes; the shrill laughter, the excitement of silly capers; the contentment of lolling at the end of the day, the apparently profound observations idly murmured, no one truly listening; finally going wearily off to bed in whatever hotel they'd stayed – four rooms, four couples.

She had been so nervous as Langley closed their door on the others. There had been a large four-poster bed towards which he had taken her, sitting her down gently. Standing in front of her he had removed his bow tie and slipped out of his jacket, leisurely, easily, all the time smiling reassurance at her as though none of this was new to him. But it had been new to her.

Not trusting herself to speak, aware that what was happening was what had been expected of her all along and that she had known all along what to expect, her heart thumping heavily, she'd had no idea how she was meant to conduct herself. The most vivid thing she now recalled was herself praying that he wouldn't see just how uncertain she'd been on how to conduct herself.

He had bent, kissed her lightly on the lips. His, just a little cool, had sent something almost like an electric shock through her, making her draw in her breath sharply. As his hands began easing her loose-fitting summer dress over her head, she'd even been prompted to automatically shift her weight from the bed to let it slide upward. His hands around her back had slipped the hooks of her brassiere, and released of their fashionable flattening restriction, her small tight breasts had leapt at him in such a way that her first instinct had been to hide them with her hands. But he had gently laid her back onto the counterpane, his body on hers, his lips growing firm. Camiknicks slipped down over her ankles, she'd lain beneath him, oddly surprised that she was naked.

Her first time – it would never be forgotten. Fear – that would never be forgotten either. But then came such a feeling, apprehension smoothed away by such a sensation she could never have described.

There had been a moment when her mind had cried, what if I get pregnant? But in the midst of arousing her to a pitch when all thought of such things had been swept aside, he'd turned sharply away leaving her momentarily bewildered as he appeared occupied by something she couldn't see. When he had turned back to her, it was as though the small interruption had never been, but she knew immediately the reason of his turning away from her. Knowing herself protected, loving him for his care of her, the rest had been wonderful. Afterwards, she had slept in his arms, slept soundly, and the following morning with the sunshine streaming through lacy curtains to light the whole room with misty glitter, he'd made love to her again.

On the train to Paris, they had all had separate sleeping berths, but she was now established in everyone's eyes as Langley's partner, as Effie was Dickie Verhoevan's, Pamela was Ginger's, and Faith was Miles's.

And now they were rattling along boulevards and across the wide Pont Neuf with its views of the Notre Dame on her left, through narrow cobbled streets of romantic, flaking-walled houses, even here every window had its low wrought-iron railing and glowing geraniums, soon to be tumbling out of the taxi at whatever address she was being taken to, there to share Langley's bed, she hoped, for ever.

Chapter Twelve

Eddie stood on the tug *London Enterprise* as she rocked gently on a slack tide. The tug, Clyde-built, a bit battered from her fifteen years service, and a bit on the light side too at 95 tons, was going to take more of a bite out of his inheritance than he'd have liked. All he hoped was that he'd be able to recoup some of his outlay with work before the craft began eating into the remainder of his money with maintenance and other expenses.

He'd been over her with a fine-tooth comb, taken her for a run up the river, but could find nothing radically wrong with her, apart from a certain amount of rust and a boiler that needed a bit of going over in the not too distant future, but hopefully not a refit which would make this less of a good deal than it first seemed.

The owner who had had her for some ten years, had perhaps not been as gentle with her as he might, by the look of her, but on the whole she appeared moderately sound if Eddie had read between the lines of the marine survey report, all survey reports by tradition making a craft look worse than she was.

Standing on deck with her owner, a Mr Glover, an old salt on the brink of retiring, Eddie knew by now that this unpretentious-looking tug was as much as he could afford if he wanted to start up business with a bit of capital left for hidden expenditure. He was beginning to feel excited, but he kept his face expressionless. The owner, on the other hand, was certainly no poker player, his need to sell showing plainly, causing Eddie to wonder what the man knew that he didn't.

'Twelve 'undred,' the man said. 'Can't let 'er go fer less.'

He had already come down from fifteen – a somewhat ambitious price, Eddie thought, considering her condition. Eddie had shaken his head, his first offer of nine hundred pounds being all he felt he dared afford, which was still a lot of money to him. He now let his gaze sweep the deck from stem to stern, pursing his lips dubiously in a time-honoured manner. One part of him wanted the owner to drop his price to that first offer, but if truth be known, the other part of him didn't. If the man stood his ground, then he'd feel much more certain of the tug's worth. If the man dropped his price too readily, then would come the nagging question, what was wrong with the thing? Yet he couldn't come anywhere near meeting that first asking price. He tried one more time.

'Cash,' he reminded. 'No hanging around for loans to be granted – that sort of thing. But I can't go much beyond my first offer.'

The man's lips tightened, even though his eyes, sharpened by years of gazing at horizons, glittered, Eddie interpreted, with fear of standing his ground too firmly and maybe losing a potential buyer. Seeing it, Eddie was beset by another doubt. Had other buyers turned the craft down, seeing faults he was missing and was he the idiot the man had seen coming?

His expression impassive, he watched the other's begin to register obstinacy, and felt more heartened – even more heartened as the man's tone, for all his obduracy, began to betray a hint of pleading.

'An' I can't come down any more neither, Mr Bennett. As I told yer, I 'ave ter retire. I don't wan'ter, but I 'ave ter. Me 'ealth, y'see. But I can't let 'er go fer nuffink. I've got ter live.'

Eddie nodded. An old waterman, age nudging him off the river that had been his life. It was sad in its way. It came to them all in time. Even so, the stubborn effort to bargain convinced him that he was on to a good thing after all, but it was worth standing his ground.

'I suppose I could go to a thousand. But that 'as to be my very last offer, Mr Glover. And as I said, cash on the nail.'

The man's features contorted as he gnawed his lips for so long that Eddie had the feeling he was trying to eat through them. The crinkled brow finally folded into even deeper creases of defeat.

'All right, then. I'll 'ave ter take it. Done!'

The leathery, wrinkled features retained their dejected expression as the man spat on his hand and held it out. Eddie likewise spat on his and clasped the offered paw, wishing now that he had gone up to only nine hundred and fifty instead of the thousand.

All that remained was the signing over of the papers over a pint in the nearest pub. It had been a good deal, he was sure of it. The owner of a tug, and barring a quick overhaul and a slap of paint, he was in business. A one-man band of a business, he'd be competing with the big companies for work. It was a risk he was prepared for, risk his only panacea to the nagging constant of Cissy.

Elation managed to stay with him as he drank down the pint he had bought, but the moment they parted company to go their separate ways, it faded like the sun going behind a cloud; in its place, the despondency that had hardly left him these four months.

It was his dad's badgering that had finally made him put to use the money left him. For months there had seemed no point bothering now Cissy wasn't here. At night his chest would feel as though it had a ton of bricks on it. He would awake each dark autumn morning with such a depth of despair that his first word of the day was 'Shit . . .' spoken aloud and venomously, a cry for relief but more like a death wail. His first thought each morning, and his last one at night was of her. And if sleep did obliterate her image for a while, it only needed him to wake up to have her dancing there in his head again. In the empty life Cissy had left him, buying the tug had been the only bit of relief, but now the business settled, the old void returned worse than ever. Yet he had to push himself onward in the hope, always the hope, that she would return some day. He had to have something to offer her when that day came. He'd never lose sight of that.

He renamed the tug *Cicely*, after Cissy. His father said he was a bloody fool doing that, childish; told him to pull himself together.

'Time goes on,' he comforted, which to Eddie wasn't that greatly comforting. 'You'll forget all about 'er after a while. After a while, son, you'll meet someone else just as good as 'er, an' get married.'

But he would never get married. If Cissy never came back, he would remain as he was, unmarried to the end of his days. And his new tug, *Cicely*, would be his reminder of that – in the face of all those who thought he was being a bloody fool, and childish.

For Daisy things were going splendidly. Spring 1926 with *Rose Marie* still playing to packed houses, she was relishing every second of it. Of course it was hard work. Of course it left her tired after two shows a day. But what a wonderful tiredness.

All the family had been to watch her, straining for a glimpse of her among the Indian maidens forming the chorus. Mum and Dad were so proud of her they had seen it three times, once on complimentary tickets and twice paying for themselves – the second time meaning Mum had to hock her best teaset to buy the tickets. Daisy would have like to have paid for them, but the salary for her few moments on stage wasn't all that much. Still, one had to start somewhere and her hope of going further was stimulating and certainly better than dressmaking at Cohens.

She often thought of those days when she and Cissy would sit at one another's bench to eat their sandwiches; the evenings they would go up the West End. Now she was working in a West End theatre and Cissy was in Paris; had been to Biarritz for the winter, she'd sent her a postcard from there, and her last letter once more bore a Paris address.

That old boyfriend of hers, Eddie Bennett, had come when she had still been at Cohens last autumn, asking if she knew where Cissy was. It had left her feeling pulled both ways and terribly guilty. She had mentioned Paris but hadn't given him Cissy's address, nor intended to, because Cissy's letters all sounded so tremendously happy.

Biarritz had been heavenly. Lounging in deckchairs, the sun beating down on bare arms and legs, making it hard to remember it was winter. Cissy's thoughts had often wandered to what it must be like in London. Rain, wind, fog, snow, and even on a clear day, the frost hanging on.

She had been sorry to leave when they had all decided it was time to return to Paris.

'We'll go back next winter, my darling, you can be sure of that,' Langley had soothed, as she craned her neck round for a last lingering look at the craggy Basque coast as the long train snaked on into the pine forests of the Landes.

Now they were all back in Paris to pick up where they had left off: resuming the unending round of dining elegantly at Maxim's, Escargot-Montorgeuil, Lucas Carton, Ritz; and less elegantly – in fact spilling over with high spirits – at the Coupole, the Dome with its jazz band upstairs and its jazz-age wallpaper downstairs; La Boeuf where they played jazz into the early hours; the Select which stayed open all night and Falstaffs that sold a drink with a kick enough to see its patrons wanting to climb lamp-posts as they left; and of course, the Jockey Club where the Americans were apt to gather. There were a thousand and one places to enjoy oneself, and yes, Paris in its way was quite as heavenly as Biarritz in its way, where one danced all night and slept all day and had seen its famous wonders so many times they'd all become boring.

'How long will we be staying here now?' she asked, as she unpacked in their apartment before going off to La Rotonde for a snack.

He paused in the act of draping one of his vacation jackets, a blue and fawn striped jacket, over a coat hanger in his wardrobe. 'How long did you *want* to stay?'

She was taken by surprise. 'As long as you, I expect.'

'Ah, yes.' He paused to regard her. 'You weren't thinking of going back to England soon?'

Alarm overcame her as she stared back into that, she felt, purposely enigmatic face. Sometimes he could look like this, and sometimes in the midst of her happiest moment, there would come a fear that he was tiring of her, though she would rather have died than let him see her fear. Now she laughed, the tinkling laugh he often remarked on as delicious, hoping it didn't strike him as false.

'Why should I want to go back to England?'

'We'll have to go back eventually.'

Cissy's face brightened. The word 'we' made all the difference between heaven and hell for her. 'Not yet, though?' she queried, relieved.

He gave a casual chuckle and went back to hanging things on rails. 'No, not yet. I was thinking, we might stay the summer and autumn and then all pop off down to the Med for the winter. What d'you say?'

Cissy let the sandals she was holding clatter onto the floorboards. 'Oh, darling! It'd be just divine! Oh, can we?'

'Why not? Of course it's early days yet and we might have a change of companions by then. Effie and Dickie plan to go back home around June. Effie had a letter from Margo saying she's coming over. Not sure it's with anyone, but she'll have Effie and Dickie's apartment.'

A stab of jealousy shot through Cissy. Margo Fox-Prinshaw, the dark-haired girl who'd looked so certain of Langley that first time she'd met her. As if she was his. Had there once been something between them and was he indeed tiring of her and fancying Margo Fox-Prinshaw again? Suddenly the sunshine beyond their small window didn't seem so bright.

'Would she come here on her own?'

'She knows how to look after herself.' Langley seemed unusually interested in folding up one of his used shirts. There *was* something.

'Oh, she could always do that,' Cissy said acidly, and had him glance at her, grinning, the blue of his eyes accentuated by the dark lashes, adopting a knowing, teasing look.

'You're not jealous, are you?'

Cissy pouted. 'Why should I be jealous?'

'Because she was once my girlfriend, you know.'

'I had guessed as much.' Cissy forced herself to shrug, blinking away the tears already stinging her eyes. 'If you want her to be that again, I can always go home.'

Langley didn't reply. The shirt he had been so carefully folding, he laid back onto the bed, smoothing it with exaggerated care. His silence could only mean one thing, she was sure. Then just as she was becoming convinced of that, he straightened up, and coming towards her, took her gently by the arms, bringing her towards him.

'You're a silly little fool, Cissy. Don't you realise, you're the one I asked to come here with me. D'you think I'd bring you all the way here, give you everything you want if I fancied her over you? It was over long ago with her. Silly, silly darling . . .'

His lips found hers, pressing their need of her with a slow yet deliberate insistence. Unable to help herself, Cissy responded, the last of her tears dampening his cheeks as he bore her slowly down on the bed between the cases and scattered paraphernalia of unpacking, her tears drying and forgotten as he made love to her.

It was no pleasure to Eddie that business was managing to do better than he'd first expected. Time and again he told himself that with Cissy at his side there would have been nothing they couldn't have achieved together. As it was, he was merely going through the motions of making a go of it. Yet it seemed to make a go of itself, despite him.

Hardly had the *Cicely* been licked into a shape, when two salvage operations came, one after the other. In both cases he had been on the spot – in a thick February fog a Spanish vessel grounded in the Lower Hope towed off successfully, his and two other tugs got her off, and a week later, again in fog, a freighter had gone ashore on the east coast, he again being on hand. His share of the salvage agreement in each case combined to almost cover what he'd laid out on the *Cicely*.

A fortnight later came another lucrative salvage job. What he had expected to take years to recuperate on his outlay had taken a month. With more than enough to pay for the work on the *Cicely*'s boilers, the scraping off of rust and repainting, he had a trim-looking vessel and even showed a profit. Moreover, the salvage jobs had got him known enough to be given work over some of the bigger companies. It was more likely he was a fraction cheaper, but they had proved his worth.

By March he was toying with the idea of plunging in on the strength of what he was earning to try to procure a loan for a second tug – to go into business properly. In time he would get himself an office from which to operate instead of the corner of his bedroom at home. His father looked worried when he outlined his plans.

'You go easy, lad. Overstretching yerself, yer could come a cropper an' lose everything.'

'I know what I'm doing,' he countered.

But his father was a sceptical man, had been out of work too often in his life to go seeing it through rose-tinted spectacles, despite the café that Eddie had insisted his mother try to run. She had promptly insisted he get an agent to sell it, saying she didn't fancy being worried to death by things like running cafés. With everyone in agreement it had finally been sold, Eddie insisting she take half the money which she did begrudgingly, saying that it would be there if ever he needed it. She hadn't spent a penny of her six hundred, just as she hadn't spent any of the two hundred her sister had left her. 'It'll be for a rainy day,' she'd stated, but in her view it hadn't yet been rainy enough. He had agreed with her – business could be a headache at his time of life. With a younger man just starting out, it was different. But young men were headstrong, apt to get carried away.

'You'd do well ter sit down and do a few sums,' he said now to Eddie. 'If yer do get a second tug, who's goin' ter skipper it? You'll 'ave ter pay someone. And you'll 'ave ter make sure he knows 'is job. That means paying 'im a bit more. If you 'it 'ard times, who's goin' ter buy the tug back orf you? 'Ard times can come out of the blue.'

Eddie was alive to that. Anything could come out of the blue. Had it not been like that with Cissy – one day talking of marriage, the next, gone? Yes, he knew how suddenly things came out of the blue.

Thrusting aside that dismal memory, he concentrated on how best to avoid taking someone on and paying them wages – if of course he could get a mortgage to buy a second tug, which he rather doubted anyway. He had no collateral but for the tug he owned. If he couldn't meet the repayments and had to sell the only tug that was his . . .

'What I need,' he said, 'is for someone to go into partnership with me.' A working partner bringing in his share of money.

'I wouldn't trust partners,' his dad growled.

That was true. Better someone you know. His eyes growing bright and hopeful, Eddie gazed at his father. 'You've driven tugs half your life as well as lighters. You know the river inside out. Would you come in with me?'

'You want me to put yer mother's bit of money in your business?'

'That wasn't what I meant.'

'I know, son. But ain't I a bit old to start goin' into business?'

'Old? You're not fifty yet. But once you've got your own business, no one can give you the push, pension you off when they think you are too old to work.'

'You can just as likely get the push in your own business, lad. When work drops off. When you get in debt and 'ave ter sell up.'

The enthusiasm fading from Eddie's eyes, he nodded. 'You're right, Dad. I can't ask Mum to risk her nest egg, can I? Sorry, Dad, I got a bit carried away there.'

'That's all right, son.' His father's lean hand came upon his shoulder. 'I wasn't saying I wouldn't. Yer mum'll 'ave to be asked what she thinks. I know what she'll say. She'll say she'd rather lend the money to you than get upset worrying about business.'

'I don't want her to lend me anything,' Eddie burst out. 'It was just a thought, that's all.'

'A good thought. The more I think about it, the more I like it. But you 'ave to realise, it *is* a risk. And I don't intend to use any of her money, you understand, son? It 'as ter be paid back to 'er as soon as possible. It's just a loan. No interest of course. That way any bank loan you get won't kill yer with the interest they ask. But it'll all 'ave to be thought out carefully, gone into properly.'

Eddie could have kissed him, but he merely pumped his father's hand knowing they were more than just father and son but partners in business, working together between them to bring in the profits . . . God grant there'd be profits. But the way he felt at this moment, how could there not be? His father, who he would come more and more to call by his Christian name Alfred, or Alf as he was more usually known, was a seasoned, no-nonsense waterman. He knew the river like the back of his hand and could stand up to any man. Yes, he and Alf would make a formidable team. It was all so exciting.

Thinking about it, he forgot to think about Cissy for six whole hours.

His father proved to have a natural flair for business. Alf Bennett, with his length of time on the river as well as his weight of years affording him respect, was seen as a tough man who knew his stuff, whereas Eddie, for all his determination – that given time would rival his father's – had a hidden soft centre that, coupled with youth, was in some eyes not up to the hard dealings of the towage business.

Almost immediately the partnership was formed, their luck seemed to take off to even greater heights, the first in the form of another tug which they finally got for a relatively silly price.

From the quayside, they regarded the vessel with a sceptical but calculating gaze, the name *Cosmo* was barely distinguishable for red rust.

'It'll go for scrap, that one,' whispered Alf, out of the hovering owner's hearing. 'He'll get next to nothing for it and he knows it. Could offer him a silly price, see what comes out of it.'

The owner moved towards them, noting the interest. 'Nice little craft,' he announced. 'Goin' cheap.'

'How much?' Alf spoke up, his deep voice commanding.

'Just under a thousand. She's as sound as a bell.'

'Rust bucket,' Alf said bluntly. The man gave him a hurt look.

'Just needs a coat of paint, no more'n that. Rest of 'er's good as new. I might go a bit lower, I suppose.'

'Five 'undred?' Alf smiled affably.

Eddie held his breath. Silly prices were one thing, but five hundred – it was a ridiculous offer. But he knew better than to contradict his partner in front of someone else, making them both look amateurs. As he had expected, the vendor looked affronted.

'I should cocoa! If you're gonna talk daft, I got no time!'

'Fine with me,' Alf said, and touching Eddie's arm, led him away.

'What're you doing, Dad?' Eddie hissed as they moved off. 'What happened to bargaining?'

His father was walking slowly, not allowing too much distance to develop between them and the man. 'Bargaining? It ain't worth the rust it's got on it. If he don't bite, we ain't lost nothing. If he does, then we've got ourselves another vessel and it ain't cost us an arm an' a leg.'

Before Eddie could argue or agree, there came a shout from behind. ' 'Arf a mo!'

Alf paused and looked back over his shoulder. 'Whatcha want?'

'Don't go orf 'alf-cocked. 'Ow much did yer say?'

'Five 'undred.'

'I can go down ter eight, maybe.'

'Ain't worth it,' Alf called back. 'D'you think it's worth it?' he addressed Eddie.

Eddie picked up on his dad's cue. 'Ain't worth 'alf that. No.'

The man was coming towards them. 'You ain't even looked 'er over. Looks is deceptive. Take her fer a run up the river. I guarantee she'll perform well . . . for what I'm askin' for 'er. I 'ad a marine survey done on 'er.'

'How long ago was that, then?'

'This year.'

'Bent, I bet,' Alf whispered from the corner of his mouth to Eddie. Aloud, he said, 'If we take 'er up the river, how far d'you think she'll go?'

The man hesitated. 'I admit there is a bit of work to do on 'er.'

'As I thought. 'Fraid we're wastin' yer time, mate. Sorry but she don't look worth four 'undred as she is. You'd just about get that for scrap. Tell yer what, we'll take 'er, five 'undred, no more, and give 'er a short run to see how she handles.'

The man gave a yelp as though his toe had been trodden on by an elephant. 'Go on, yer bastards! Sod orf! I don't deal wiv crooks!'

This time, both men stood their ground in silent accordance, both looking erudite, watching the man switch his eyes several times from them to his rusting hulk and back again, his expression desperate.

Half an hour later, Eddie and his father sat together in the pub hoping against hope that they had done the right thing, the so-called satisfactory test run having exposed all the faults imaginable.

'Five hundred!' Eddie gasped, fearing to think how much getting the vessel into shape was going to cost. At least there would be no bank loan at a crippling interest, his mum sighing as she handed over most of her nest egg on an agreement to pay her back with a bit extra.

It took three months hard work getting the *Cosmo* into decent repair, much of the cost of that luckily being derived from regular towage work with the *Cicely*. Though their second tug was never to be a good-looking vessel, she did prove herself a workhorse, her engines, when finally working without breaking down every other day, were far more powerful than the CICELY's.

The two tugs found plenty of work: taking down the stevedores who handled the high explosives for the PLA at Hole Haven; repositioning seagoing vessels who'd dragged their anchor or had no facilities for raising steam after being laid up, the help of a tug being far more economical; at Corytown oil depot shoving awkward vessels across its short jetty, one tug ahead, one astern; standing by to ease the big passenger ships gently to the landing stage and off again out into the main stream, needing usually only one tug, maybe two if the wind was driving the liner towards the stage; and there were still a hundred and one smaller jobs, dock work, taking a ship through the Old Entrance to Tilbury Dock, towing lighters, full and empty.

Eddie's hope was to procure an agreement to escort the big incoming liners up to Tilbury, but usually the big companies like Wilkins had this. Maybe in time. And one day, if Cissy ever came back, he would have a company as large as any of them to offer her. Such dreams . . .

'Miss Evans?'

The fat man stood barring her way as she made with the rest of the chorus towards the dressing rooms.

Daisy paused, seeing the flash of small teeth bared in a smile, was immediately put on guard. 'Yes?'

'I am sorry to stop you . . .' The voice bore a French accent. 'I 'ave been watching you with interest from where I 'ave been sitting in the theatre. I introduce myself . . . Monsieur Maurice Graude . . .' His bow possessed a peculiarly French gracefulness, despite his bulk.

'I am seeking for a troupe of good dancers to take to France, to Paree, and I wonder, Miss Evans, 'ave you ever considered to work in France, in Paree? If you 'ave, 'ere is my card . . .'

With a flourish, a fawn-coloured card was extracted from a wallet taken out of his breast pocket to be put into her extended hand. 'If you find yourself interested in work in Paree, you will contact me at that address. Already I 'ave five girls. I need six, and you will make an excellent six. If I do not 'ear from you, Miss Evans, I shall look for some other one to take your place. I 'ope you avail yourself of the offer, so for now – *au revoir*, mademoiselle.'

For a moment dumbfounded, Daisy watched him incline his head once more, but as he turned away, she galvanised into life.

'Mr . . .'

'Graude.' He smiled his small-toothed smile.

'Mr Graude, I don't do Folies Bergère stuff.'

'Stuff.' He mulled the word over as if it amused him, the smile broadening. 'Ah, *oui*, stuff. No, mademoiselle. This engagement is for – for a – what you say – a musical. It is at the Chatelet. It is a fine large theatre. The musical is *Pauvre Ma'amoiselle* – it will run for many weeks, months. It will be very successful, I think. For you, together with five other English girls, a good place in the chorus. After that . . .'

He gave a huge shrug of his shoulders as though to say she could reach unscaled heights should she wish to.

Daisy's brown eyes glowed. 'Can I let you know soon?'

'By tomorrow morning. *Oui*?'

'Yes,' she breathed. She was on her way. To Paris. She wondered if she might bump into Cissy there. What a surprise that would be.

Chapter Thirteen

The whole country had come out in support of the miners in a nationwide general strike. Nothing moved: buses stood empty in their depots, trains in their sidings; services became non-existent with streets uncleaned, dustbins unemptied, milk and bread and coal undelivered; offices closed, and a brick through the window of any shop employing outside labour to keep it open.

On the Thames, while the larger tug companies had hardly any of their fleet working, with only a few of their men willing to handle them, the smaller companies had no such problems, apart from an immediate hunt to get coal which became in short supply almost overnight with nothing being delivered to the yards from the pits. Some of the big companies took their tugs across the North Sea to Flushing in the Netherlands for their coal, but those like Eddie and his father, being small concerns, had to get theirs where they could.

At least with so few tugs on the river, there was plenty of work. There were also risks. The strikers, seeing the tugs as an essential service threatening to undermine their cause, were ready to do battle with anyone, employee or owner, who dared take their vessels out to the big ships lying idle with no one to handle or offload. Even with the navy doing what it could to protect the tugs, there were fights.

The strike was in its seventh day when Eddie found Bobby Farmer, Cissy's brother, sitting indolently in a coffee shop, sporting a black eye. He grinned, delicately touching the spot when Eddie enquired about it.

'Bit of trouble down at the docks. They've brought the army out. The bloody army, mind you! Like we was the enemy. It's gettin' beyond a joke. Then of course I went and said the wrong thing, didn't I?'

He gave a rueful grimace. 'I went and said I know the miners are 'aving a rough time of it. They've got my sympathy. But we ain't nothing to do with mining. My life's on the river and going on strike fer miners 'alf across the country, ain't going ter put bread on my table or pay me rent. And this could go on fer months. What d'we all do when we ain't got a crust to give our kids? Mind, I'm not fer breaking a strike when it's a good cause. And I admit this one's a good cause. It must be, to 'ave the ole country come out on strike . . .'

He paused to take a gulp of his tea, wincing at the effort to get his lips around the cup. He put it down.

'But I can air me views, can't I? Trouble was, what with troops being there an' all to rile 'em up even more, someone didn't see eye to eye with me. So he thumped me in one of 'em instead. That was as we was 'aving a bit of a clash with some of them troops. Turned into a real bloody fight 'ere and there. Might not've 'appened except for them bringing out the bloody army. They're still up there now, at the East India Docks – trucks an' soldiers, all done up in tin 'elmets and bloody gas capes, and rifles. Like a second world war's broken out. Christ knows who they think they're going ter shoot with them rifles of theirs.'

'You should've kept your nose clean,' Eddie advised as he sipped his scalding coffee. 'Kept your mouth shut.'

Bobby laughed. 'Yeah, I should've. But it was worse than that. My Ethel weren't none too pleased, seeing me black eye. I told her I'd caught me eye on the safety bar of the bus I was comin' home on as it stopped suddenly. She was all sympathy at first, then she suddenly said, "There's a strike on. There ain't no buses running." Gawd, she didn't 'alf 'it the ceiling, 'cos she knew then I'd been in a fight. I really thought she was goin' ter black me other one.'

Eddie smiled appropriately, but while Bobby had gone on about him and Ethel, Eddie's thoughts had lingered on Cissy and the opportunity given for him to ask about her. He did so, but received a sad negative headshake.

'Not a whisper.'

'Nothing at all?' It was hard to credit she still hadn't been in touch with her family. On the odd occasions he'd run into Bobby, the reply was ever the same. 'Not a whisper.'

'Hasn't no one even tried to find her?' he continued, but Bobby as on other occasions looked grim.

'Like I said, 'er dad won't let any of us even mention 'er name. I don't understand it, Eddie, he's the nicest, amiablest, easy-going bloke anyone could wish ter meet. But on this, it's like trying ter punch yer way through a brick wall, to get 'im to come round. Though I tell a lie when I said we 'aven't 'eard. She sent us a Christmas card. It came from a place called Biarritz in France, but there wasn't no proper address on it. Dad threw it straight on the fire when 'e saw it. Made Mum cry, though she didn't make much fuss – just turned away. But I saw tears on her cheeks.'

'What's the rest of your family say?'

'The boys . . . you know kids. Harry don't properly understand and Sidney – he's fourteen now – more interested in 'is mates and don't care. May – she misses Cissy. But then, she's all boys. Got no time.'

'And you?' Eddie's heart was racing hopefully. A Christmas card – it had to be a start. 'Ever thought of trying to trace her yourself?'

'I've got other worries.' The laugh sounded a little bitter.

'But she's your sister,' he persisted. 'Biarritz, you said?'

'I've got me troubles, Eddie.'

'*What* troubles?'

'Ethel.' Bobby's eyes had grown strangely hollow. He bit his lips for a moment, then, his voice dropping: 'I 'ave ter tell someone or I'll explode. Y'see, me an' Ethel . . . We – well, we don't get on that good. She don't 'ave anything to do with me . . . you know, *that way*. Not since the baby was born. She blames me for it being a gel. She blames me fer her 'aving it. She blames me fer . . . blames me fer everything. Fer not loving 'er, she says, for the life we've got. Fer everything.'

'I'm sorry,' was all Eddie could say, trying hard not to let his mind wander to the more urgent matter of

Cissy. Everyone had their troubles. He hadn't meant the conversation to go this way.

'It's not just that.' Bobby leant forward. 'Eddie, can you keep something to yerself?'

'Of course.'

'Well, it's . . . I've gorn an' met someone else. Her people 'ave a fish shop across the river. Good bit of fish an' chips they do there, and I often went in when I was over that side. Well, me an' 'er . . . you can guess the rest. We've been goin' out together, secretly, fer about six months. Now she's pregnant, and I don't know what to do.'

Eddie nodded sympathetically. There was nothing *he* could do, no advice he could or wanted to give. All he wanted was news of Cissy.

The little biplane stood on the tarmac, its propeller whirling fast enough to be just a silvery circular blue. Everything looked terribly flimsy, the struts between the wings so thin, like string, the wings themselves shuddering. The whole plane shuddering. Cissy felt her bones melting.

'I can't, Langley. I can't get in that thing!'

'I've never, never known such a baby!' came Effie's high-pitched voice behind her.

Effie, clad in a leather jacket and jodhpurs, sheepskin-lined helmet and huge goggles, the brown tones set off by a long, bright pink gauzy scarf, had just been up in the thing, shrieking with delight behind Ginger who'd held a full pilot's licence for two years. Pamela and Faith had both been up and returned to earth raving about the experience.

Ginger was standing in front of Cissy, grinning. 'It's as safe as houses. I promise on my honour not to go too high or loop the loop.'

Langley's arm pressed hers reassuringly. 'Go on, darling. Take the plunge. It'll be all right. Go and have fun.'

'Oh, do go on, Cissy darling!' echoed Effie. 'Take the plunge and have fun and Langley will be so tremendously proud of you. You will be tremendously proud of her, won't you, Langley?'

He shook his head indulgently, chuckling at her caustic witticism while Cissy smouldered. Effie was going back to England next week, and good riddance. Margo coming out could never be as awful as her; Margo, from what Cissy remembered, was an intense sort of person – a femme fatale, but now she had lost her menace. Langley had been so ardent in his lovemaking of late and had bought Cissy so many lovely things, it seemed that no one could ever threaten this relationship now.

She let him guide her to the noisy plane as it stood juddering on the tarmac. Donned in a warm jacket and leather helmet similar to Effie's but without the gaudy pink scarf, she pulled the goggles down over her eyes as Ginger eased himself with accustomed agility into the front cockpit, leaving Langley to help her climb into the cramped rear one.

Langley stood back, shouting above the growing roar of the engine. 'You're going to love it!'

She read his lips rather than heard him and gave a nervous wave, feeling she really ought to be hanging on to the sides of the cockpit in case she fell out, the strap around her seeming far too inadequate.

This summer in Paris, she had felt so reckless, tearing off in fast open cars, often sitting on the rear of the back seat; in Biarritz she'd stood in a speedboat, bumping alarmingly up and down over the waves with spray dashing her face; she'd been to the top of the Eiffel Tower and leaned precariously out over the highest parapet for a bet of a rope of seed pearls belonging to Pamela, relying only on Langley to keep a tight hold of her while the city below seemed to swing around her.

Everything adventurous, she felt nothing could frighten her again. But this was something different – nothing solid between the floor of the cockpit and the world a thousand feet below.

She saw Ginger's thumbs go up, signalling take-off. The tiny plane roared into life; began to move forward, to gather speed. Soon the tarmac was speeding past, faster than any car, the aircraft shuddering as though it would snap in two. Faster, faster. Suddenly the juddering ceased, the ground dropped away. Cissy gasped, her breath drawn into her lungs almost involuntarily. She held it, eyes shut. She felt she was leaning backwards, even before the plane began to climb.

The wind was rushing past her ears. The engine didn't sound quite so loud, though still loud enough, still roaring at full throttle. Opening her eyes, she glanced over the side to see how high they were. It was the worst thing she could have done. She had somehow imagined to see the ground about as far away as it had been from the Eiffel Tower. It wasn't. It was miles below her. The tower had at least been her terra firma. Here there was none.

'Oh, Ginger!'

But they were levelling out. The terrifying sound of the engine was moderating to a droning sort of whine; the wind in her face felt comforting, its rushing in her ears quite steady. It brought a sudden feeling of exhilaration. The world below didn't seem to matter any more. She was in safe hands. Ginger had a full pilot's licence.

'Oh, Ginger,' she sighed, ecstatic, adoring the world from above. Who would have thought two years ago that she would be flying high in the sky in a plane hired especially for her and her friends . . . yes, friends – even Effie from this height. Even Margo.

'Cissy!'

Cissy swung round at the call. She had been out shopping for shoes and had bought a hat instead, a deep cloche, cream-coloured, with a tiny brim covered with fawn applique. It had cost the earth, but Langley had given her his chequebook and said to use what she wanted.

It was a wonderful feeling, he was so generous. He behaved as if they were engaged, although he hadn't bought an engagement ring as such – two rings, but not for that hand yet. Whenever they made love, he'd speak to her like a man speaking to a fiancée, and though not making plans for the future, talked of being together always. He treated her so protectively, even when making love, except for one time a couple of months ago when he hadn't been so careful, but so wonderful, she hadn't thought at the time. When she did, she'd been terrified. But her periods appeared as if nothing had happened.

When she told him of her fright, he had resumed his caution, saying they couldn't have anything like that happen. She understood. The way he spoke sometimes, she knew one day they'd be married, she would be proudly introduced to his parents and her life would be settled and wealthy as his wife. If she did fall pregnant, they'd marry just that bit sooner. Though his insistence on being careful after that scare had saddened her a little because she would have felt so proud carrying his child knowing she would be his wife, she forgave his not being keen for anything to happen outside marriage; loved his sometimes old-fashioned views.

Cissy stretched her neck to see who had called her and watched the figure come hurrying towards her, arm raised, hand waving frantically. On recognition her heart missed a beat with disbelief.

Daisy, as large as life, in a frilly pink jabot blouse, a cluster of artificial carnations in the lapel of her black jacket, and the shortest of white pleated skirts, rushed up with a ready embrace.

'I bet you're surprised. Fancy seeing me, eh?'

Cissy extricated herself. 'What are you doing here?'

'I'm living here. In Paris.' Beneath the brim of her pink hat, her brown eyes danced. 'Oh, Cissy, I've got such a lot to tell you. Can we go somewhere for a coffee and a good chat? Do you mind?'

'No, not at all.' She felt stupefied by Daisy's sudden appearance. 'There's a place just round the corner.'

Over coffee and gateau with Daisy smoking a cigarette in a green Bakelite holder the whole time, she related all that had happened to her since Cissy's leaving: the Covent Garden audition, the one at Drury Lane, the stars she'd met and the talent scout who'd got her a prominent part in the chorus here in Paris, the Chatelet.

'I didn't hear anything more for months,' she regaled. 'I thought he'd forgotten all about it, or that it was merely one of those fairy tales some of them spin you. Then suddenly . . . well, here I am. I've been here about a month. Fancy not bumping into you before now.'

Cissy, still slightly over-awed at Daisy's being here, listened happily enough until she mentioned it being exactly a year since Eddie Bennett had gone to Cohens to ask if she knew where Cissy was.

'I told you all about that in one of my letters,' Daisy continued, daintily removing a smear of gateau from her upper lip with a middle finger and studying the cream on it before sucking it clean with a small kissing sound and wiping the finger on a napkin. 'It don't seem all that time ago. So much has happened. I just didn't know what to say to him. It was awful, having to tell lies. Well, not exactly lies. I didn't even know then where you were except that you'd said you were going to Paris. But when I did get your address, I certainly wasn't going to pass it on to him – not unless you wanted me to. Well, I told you about it in my letter, didn't I?'

As Cissy nodded, Daisy took a deep intake of breath and cigarette smoke. 'You didn't tell him though, did you?'

Cissy shook her head, and Daisy ploughed on. 'Well, I expect you're nicely settled now with your . . . what's his name, the one you came out with?'

'Langley.'

'Yes.' Daisy swallowed the last of her gateau and drank the last of the coffee in her cup. Laying her second cigarette in its holder on the glass ashtray, she lifted the slim silver coffee pot, holding it poised. 'More coffee, Cissy? There's some left.'

'No, I don't think so. I'll have to be on my way.'

The coffee pot was replaced. 'And so must I. Have to get back for the first house this afternoon. It's all go. But I do love it. I love it here.' She stubbed the cigarette out in its ashtray, removing the burnt end and popping the holder into her handbag. 'I'll get the bill. My treat. Look, can we meet next Saturday morning? It'd be lovely having someone I know in Paris. There are the other few girls in the show who're English, but there's nothing like being with an old friend, is there? Shall we meet?'

Cissy smiled happily. 'I don't see why not.'

The bill paid, addresses exchanged, they walked out into the August sunshine, and, pecking each other's cheeks, went their separate ways.

Meeting Daisy had been as wonderful as it had been unexpected and, she realised only after she returned to have lunch with Langley, Margo and the friend Margo had brought out with her, a Percy Mildenhall, it was also an enjoyable change from the affected chatter she had become used to this past year.

For some odd reason, she didn't tell Langley about Daisy. If anyone had asked her why, she couldn't have told them when she wasn't even sure herself. But something inside her made her feel that it was not a matter she wanted to share with him. Maybe because it might diminish her in his eyes or he might laugh. She didn't know.

In early November, with Paris skies becoming as dull as London ones, they began talking of trying Venice where the legendary Adriatic sea lapped warm against the discoloured bases of treasured buildings and the sky, hopefully, would remain blue and hot.

Yet somehow, Cissy did not feel the excitement and elation of last year when they had gone to Biarritz. She told herself it was because she'd probably grown blasé to all the high living, swanning it up at Le Mans or being silly on some chateau terrace, shooting at bits of fine china. She told herself the journey to Venice would be tiresome, those around her just a little boring. But it was really the idea of leaving Daisy. These last two months had been so enjoyable, not having to put on airs with Daisy. Nothing like an old friend . . . her words that first time they met. But it was more than that – it was a breath of fresh air being as she used to be, and oh, so pleasant – making her realise that this last year she had been just playing a part, not true to herself at all.

Now she was off again, living it up, playing a part again. It was sad saying goodbye to Daisy but she would see her when she returned. Daisy would be staying in Paris for a long time. She had met someone. His name was Theodore Helgott. She called him Teddy, and sometimes affectionately 'my German'. Cissy met him once and was taken by his soft brown though somewhat worldly eyes, his open smile and charming manners. He was a small handsome man of about forty, eighteen years Daisy's senior. But she was so obviously in love, and told Cissy every last detail of his life story.

He had been born in Dusseldorf, his father a financier of some sort. He never knew his mother who had died giving birth to him and had been brought up by servants. He was seven when his father married someone whom he did business with. She was Christian, but his father had never been that concerned with his Jewish faith anyway. When he was eleven his father had died too, and after two years his stepmother married back into her own faith. So, neither one thing nor the other, with a stepmother who understandably had no real motherly affection for him, he was left to his own devices and at fifteen left home to make a life for himself. Ending up in Paris, he had done very well, something in finance dealing in investments, so Cissy gleaned, for Daisy said it was too involved for her. At least, Cissy thought as she listened to the history of Herr Theodore Helgott, if Daisy did end up marrying him, she would want for nothing.

So, leaving Daisy to her German, Cissy departed with her own clique to Biarritz – despite what Langley had said about Venice, after a lot of debate and argument, it was Biarritz again, because Margo hadn't been for two years and wanted to renew her acquaintance with it, and Margo, being Margo, got her way. It was the playground of the rich after all, and as Margo said, why go off exploring the unknown when all you want is to be somewhere where other fashionable people know you?

Cissy didn't mind too much. It would still be warm and romantic and perhaps all that warmth and romance would prompt Langley to propose marriage this year. She hoped so, they'd been together long enough.

But she was destined to go on hoping. Every time he made love to her, she expected a proposal to follow. She hinted, but he hadn't picked up on it. She baulked at hinting too strongly and perhaps that was why he hadn't. Making love never seemed quite the right time, strangely enough, to mention marriage. Other times, there was too much going on to turn his mind in that direction. But he would propose eventually.

At the moment he seemed content with their present arrangement, revelling in his role of introducing her again to all the pleasures Biarritz had to offer and delighting in her more gauche moments, as she tried hard to play tennis as skilfully as the others who had been playing it all their lives.

Langley of course was an expert tennis player, his lithe frame strikingly handsome in well-pressed, gleaming white ducks and white shirt with a neat striped tie. His game was graceful yet full of power and he was always laughing, that light chuckle of his echoing across the courts, when he bettered an opponent.

This year too he had finally taught Cissy to swim – at least, she could float and flail her arms enough to move herself forward through the water. He'd laugh at her, his own strokes perfect in every way. But whether swimming or not, she loved the bathing dresses that hugged her figure and, as she remembered from jumping up and down in the freezing summer North Sea at Margate, didn't sag or stretch with the weight of water.

But whatever they were doing, be it splashing in the warm gentle ocean in a well-fitting bathing dress and swimming cap, lounging on hot, motorcar-lined beaches beneath the shallow sloping Basque cliffs, or pecking at a crisp salad and lobster lunch, a floral wrap draped over her bathing dress, later to be swapped for the little black crêpe de chine number with gauzy godets and handkerchief points, Egyptian-style jewellery, a sequined petalled hat and tango shoes with cross-over laces and silk flesh-coloured stockings, for an evening of dancing or gaming,

Cissy was still new enough to this life to see herself time and time again with an outsider's eye, comparing herself to that person of yesterday.

She was still conscious of being thrilled at sitting on the back of speeding sport cars, in a fine check jacket and skirt, light jersey wool jumper, scarf and expensive hat, while people like Margo and Faith and Pamela took it all for granted, and always would. How could she take it all for granted when she had known the ordinary side of life? She still remembered carefully counting shillings in order to buy a halfway decent pair of shoes or to keep up her elocution lessons, foregoing tram fares to do so and begrudging every rainy day that forced her to spend out on public transport rather than walk.

She vividly recalled her days at Cohens with a resultant low sensation in the stomach. Then her mind would wander to the simple pleasures of weekend freedom, strolling in the park with Eddie, going to the cinema with him, her mind conjuring up a picture of herself sitting at one end of a rowing boat while he was at the other, rowing mightily, his lean muscles rippling under a well-worn, striped shirt and his smile . . .

No, she would not acknowledge the feelings the memory of his smile brought – feelings of longing she'd rather not have.

Chapter Fourteen

'Langley, I've something to tell you!' She was excited. He would be so pleased, and so proud of her.

They were back in Paris – had arrived about the middle of April, the most delightful month to be in Paris. Cissy had returned to find Daisy had married her German and was now living in beautiful apartments not far from the Auteuil racetrack. She and Cissy had met twice in that time, Daisy looking marvellous and happy, no longer struggling to make a living with a chorus.

It was now May. The twenty-first of May 1927 – an auspicious day during which endless streams of chara-bancs and motorcars had been heading for Le Bourget airfield from all directions since mid-afternoon. They had all come to watch Charles Lindbergh land from his non-stop solo flight from New York. He had already been in the air some thirty-three hours and not a wink of sleep. How could he, flying out there all alone? It was now ten-twenty at night and still no sign of the tiny plane – the *Spirit of St Louis*. Tension that for the past hour had been gripping the crowds clustered on the dark field, except for some floodlights, was slowly mounting. The wireless had reported sightings but no one was sure where Lindbergh was now and if he was still safe, or how safely he'd land on this field now teaming with humanity.

Cissy tugged at Langley's arm. 'Did you hear what I said, darling? I've something important to tell you.'

'Not now!' He shook his arm free of her grip and pointed towards the western sky still with its faintest traces of twilight. 'Look! There she is!'

Every eye in their group followed his pointing finger. A tiny moving speck of light had appeared, growing more discernible with each second. Everywhere people were beginning to point. Excitement grew more frantic as the sound of the tiny monoplane's engine was heard, getting steadily louder. People were clambering on to the roofs of cars to see better. Langley grabbed Cissy and began hoisting her up on to the roof of the nearest unattended vehicle. Climbing up beside her, he held her tightly around the waist to steady her as she teetered uncertainly.

'God! What a thing! History in the making!'

Cheering rose up in a sustained roar from every throat as the plane began making its gliding descent, engine purring, the landing strip hastily vacated by the hordes of onlookers.

'God – what I wouldn't give to be him!' Langley shouted above the final roar of the engine and the welcoming burst of cheering as the plane touched down, ran a few yards to a stop, the engine coughing and dying away.

The crowd surged forward as the hero emerged from the cockpit, his hand held up in a salute to them all. Reporters had already surrounded him, bulbs flashing as photo after photo was taken for their papers; notaries, VIPs, friends of the hero, all were there up the front, the rest, the eager onlookers, held back by a line of grinning policemen.

Cissy had put aside her news for the present. Ecstatic as any here, she shrieked and waved and stretched her neck for a better glimpse of Lindbergh's lanky figure as he leapt nimbly down from the aeroplane.

'History, yes!' she yelled to Langley's remarks.

To think she was actually here, seeing it all first hand instead of on the cinema newsreels later. News – history being made, here in front of her. And when the excitement finally died down she'd tell Langley of her own bit of news, equally as important, equally as exciting – that come December, Langley would be a father. The thought brought a wonderful thrill fluttering through her.

Cissy, her skin, tanned by Biarritz sunshine, emphasising her fair hair, pale blue, printed chiffon dress and sequined jacket, looked and felt stunning as she walked into the sedate party on Langley's arm.

There hadn't been time to tell him her news with so much going on: Lindbergh's arrival; drinks in a small secluded but wildly expensive bar afterwards with everyone talking at once; hurrying home to prepare for this party to which Langley and company had somehow managed to get invited, Margo Fox-Prinshaw's people being known in high circles.

All the names that mattered were there, all hoping Lindbergh might put in an appearance later if not too tired. The large third floor hotel room was a continuous hubbub of unbroken conversation, interspersed with bursts of laughter against a background of forks clattering on plates while silent waiters with trays of golden champagne in wide glasses eased smoothly between the knots of people. In a far corner a piano played 'The Man I Love' – Cissy could just make out the tune.

'Over there!' Margo's husky voice rose above the din. Margo, bare-backed in ivory georgette and a dozen barbaric gold bangles, began shouldering her way through the squash of the famous as though they were mere commonality, the rest of her group in tow. Langley hung back, his hand pressing itself over Cissy's threaded through his arm.

'Let her get on with it.' He smiled, his smile thrilling her to the core as it always did. 'We'll get ourselves a drink. Go out on the balcony, though I suspect it's as crowded out there as it is in here. We could perch on the parapet and look over the city.'

Cissy laughed. If he knew her condition, he wouldn't let her anywhere near the parapet. Time enough to tell him when they got home, most probably in the early hours, going on to a nightclub first.

'Oh, God, there you are!' Margo was beside them, a drink already in her hand. She hooked her arm through Langley's as she seemed to love to do, had made a point of doing it ever since coming to France, dragging his hand away from where it lay on Cissy's. Her grey eyes, heavily made up with kohl, gazed up into his, almost adoringly after a quick glance at Cissy, Cissy felt sure, to see if she was noticing.

'Haven't you a drink yet, you poor old thing? What *have* you been doing? We've found a nice little corner by the piano. Do come along, darling.'

Dragged through the crowd, she still holding his arm, while Cissy hanging on to the other was all but pulled along, the trio met up with the others where Margo said they were.

'Langley, darling, you and I will go and get ourselves a glass of champagne each. We'll bring you one, Cissy. Be back in two ticks.'

Cissy's heart plummeted as she watched them go. She'd been so happy a moment ago. Now as she peeked between the gaps in the close-packed elegance of evening wear she could see the two of them by the buffet table. Margo popped a delicacy into Langley's mouth. He was smiling, chewing, sipping his drink, and Margo stretched her face up to him and kissed him on the lips. What was worse was that he didn't draw back. He was still smiling as Margo took her lips away from his.

A great wave of jealousy and dismay was washing through Cissy's chest as they remained lingering by the buffet, herself utterly forgotten. They were talking, their backs to her. Were they discussing her? He seemed content to have Margo entice him away. And why not? Margo had known him longer. She had probably enticed him many times before, before Cissy had come on the scene – had probably enticed him into her bed before now. Just a flick of her finger was all she needed, with her grey, kohl-rimmed eyes and her golden hair and every fibre of her fantastic figure proclaiming a knowledge of the world Cissy would never have.

Cissy felt sick visualising the two of them in bed, rolling over each other, legs entwined, naked, the climax. . . . She wanted to vomit, the vision was so clear. Around her the rest of her friends were chatting as though nothing untoward had passed between those by the buffet. They hadn't even noticed that she had dropped out of the conversation, had in fact not even taken part in it.

She saw the pair finally turn from the table. They were coming back. Langley had two glasses of champagne. Margo with her arm linked possessively and confidently through his, Cissy wondered, vindictively, how he managed not to spill the drink when he was so encumbered by that bitch's arm.

She didn't smile as she was handed her glass, and knew her lower lip was pouting. Her throat was tight and it was difficult to keep her eyes from gathering excess moisture.

'Are you all right, Cissy?'

'I'm fine.

Margo was now talking to Miles, Faith, Ginger and Pamela, one slim hand supporting a bare elbow, her glass delicately balanced in the other. As her eyes, glancing sideways, met Cissy's, those bright red lips quirked at the corners in a taunting smile. Seeing her standing there with those crafty grey eyes slewing her way, and that assured smile of hers, Cissy wanted to go over and hit her. The words formed in her head: *You think you can take him from me. Well, just you try.*

But she wasn't sure she could stop her. Margo had a fearful ability to twist men around her little finger, including Langley, as she had just shown. She'd exercised that ability several times in Biarritz but it wasn't because she wanted him, or she'd have persisted. It was no more than showing people like Cissy that they had no hold over their man if Margo so chose.

'You don't look fine, my sweet.' Langley's reply brought her back to him. He was frowning, apparently at a loss to understand what had got into her – as if he didn't know.

'I told you, I'm fine,' she snapped, then in case he moved angrily away, perhaps to seek Margo again, hastily modulated her tone. 'I feel a little tired perhaps. All the excitement today.'

'Oh.' The tone sounded vaguely irritated. Was he looking for an excuse to be angry with her and justifiably go off with Margo?

She hastily shook off the feeling. He wouldn't have bothered to ask her how she felt if he intended any intrigue with Margo, would he? She looked quickly towards her rival. Margo was no longer looking at her, but at Langley. And there was a smile, suggestive of a knowing wink. Langley returned the smile.

'Do you want to go home?'

'Home?' There was a childish second of panic, visualising herself rejected, sent back to England. The fear must have shown for he gave her a questioning look.

'Aren't you feeling well? We could leave here now, if you want. I'm not much bothered. These parties can get awfully dull. Do you want to go, darling?'

How could she have been so silly? Suddenly life was joyful again. Margo meant nothing. She needed to be pitied really. Half the time unable to hang on to a man for looking around for other conquests, poor Percy Mildenhall whom she had brought with her to Paris, used merely as a stopgap.

Cissy noticed Percy standing on the sideline like a lanky question mark, looking on as Margo laid a flirtatious hand on Miles's arm. Faith was looking dark and Cissy knew just how she was feeling. Percy too. Both of them unsure, sensing danger. But Langley was safe from Margo's intrigues, and so was she. Tonight she would tell him about the baby. That would cement their relationship through which even Margo would not be able to hack her way.

It was next morning before she told him. They had come home earlier than everyone else, she suspected because Langley wanted desperately to make love after having seen her so fraught by something that still escaped him. He made love with his usual sustained urgency, bringing her to such prolonged heights of delight in her own climax that anything as mundane as even the news of her pregnancy was out of place.

These days, expertly counting her safe times, he knew when there was no need to take precautions as once he'd done, the result being a wonderful sense of freedom. Her falling pregnant had happened during one of those times when he had miscalculated, but it didn't matter. He'd be the first to acknowledge that it had to happen sometime.

'You remember I had some news to tell you?' she asked, after Ginger had gone back to his own apartment having popped in to borrow a spot of jam for the croissants he and Pamela were having for breakfast.

Langley, still in his dressing gown, stopped drinking his coffee to look at her. 'You did mention wanting to tell me something yesterday.'

'I know. And it's the most wonderful news. I'm pregnant, Langley.' His eyes had become fixed on hers. The light in them seemed to flicker. 'You're going to be a father,' she hurried on.

His gaze hadn't changed. 'I'm sorry?'

'I bet you're not!' She laughed gaily. 'I'm going to have a baby – *your* baby. Isn't it wonderful, darling?'

Langley looked at her a while longer, then dropped his gaze to put his cup gently back on its saucer. 'You can't be pregnant.'

'I am.' Men never understood how things like this happened; were always amazed when they were told, as if it had nothing to do with making love but more with some great miracle beyond their abilities.

'I am, Langley,' she persisted.

He was still contemplating his coffee cup as though it held the answer. 'How do you know?'

'You know how regular I am. You could set your watch by me. Well, last month I missed, and I've missed again this month. Besides, I feel somehow different. And yesterday morning I was sick. Quite suddenly and for no reason.'

She knew about that from her mother having been pregnant with Harry – remembered her running to the sink shutting the kitchen door behind her so no one would come in, and the sound of retching, and then her mother emerging, looking relieved and saying how she hated the sick end of pregnancy. That's how she knew. She had been thirteen then, old enough to take note. Dad had looked at Mum when she told him just as Langley was looking at her now – somewhat mystified, shocked, even dismayed. But he'd been pleased after he'd got over the surprise. And so would Langley.

'I'm definitely pregnant,' she said happily, new confidence coming upon her as she'd never had before. She laughed gaily. 'Well, say something!'

'You'll have to get rid of it,' he said quietly.

Cissy stared at him, not comprehending, the remnants of laughter frozen on her lips; still fixed there as she asked, 'Langley, what do you mean?'

'I mean get rid of it.'

'But I'm pregnant. Don't you . . .?'

'Exactly. That's the last thing we wanted to happen.'

'How can you say that? I thought you'd want us to . . . How can you say that? Langley, look at me!'

She watched him comply and wished he hadn't. The look in his eyes was enough to stop the blood in her veins. Now he rose, throwing his napkin down on the little round marble-topped table they always breakfasted on.

'How could you let yourself get pregnant?'

'How could I ...? Langley, you were there too. You knew the risks we were taking when we . . . You didn't seem to mind. I thought you hoped that at some time . . . Oh, God, darling, I thought you'd be so pleased.'

'Pleased! I'm devastated. What'll my people say?'

'We could get married before anyone suspects. I'm only a couple of months, and no one would ever know.'

'I've never mentioned marriage to you.'

'I know, darling, but I thought . . .'

'Then you thought wrong, didn't you, *darling*.' It wasn't the way he would normally call her that. There was no tenderness in it, only fear and sarcasm and – dear God, was it loathing?

'You said you loved me!'

'I've said I love you to lots of girls. Oh, you're the first I've been with for so long. And I do love you. But marriage . . . Christ! Haven't you realised that when I finally settle down, it will have to be with someone of my own class? How could I take *you* home to meet my people? They'd wipe their hands of me. They'd cut off my allowance until I got rid of you.' He grew suddenly tender, relaxing, came round the table towards her. 'I thought you understood that, Cissy. I thought you always understood. Now come here, you silly little thing, and we'll discuss this like sensible . . .'

'No!' Hastily she backed away, making him halt where she had been a moment before. 'No, I don't want you to cuddle me. You've just told me to get rid of my baby . . . our baby.'

'That's what I said.' His eyes had again grown hard. 'If you want me to put it bluntly, if you want us to carry on together, you've got to get rid of that thing inside you. Otherwise . . .'

'Otherwise – what?'

'Otherwise, we must call it a day. I'll pay for the abortion. But if you really intend to go through with this – stupidity – I'll pay your fare home. Back to England.'

'No, you don't mean that. Where would I go?'

'Home to your people, I suppose.'

'I can't go back to them!' Her voice was a wail for pity, for his understanding, but his expression hadn't changed.

'Then you'll have to do what you like. But we can't stay together – not now, not unless you get yourself seen to. Honestly, darling, God knows where you got the idea of marriage.'

He stalked past her. 'I'm going out for a while, Cissy. Think about what I've said. And when I come back and you feel more rational, we'll talk.'

She stood listening to him in the bathroom, following his movements as he washed, shaved, combed and smoothed his dark hair with expensive brilliantine; her mind following him into the bedroom where he took off his dressing gown to put on his clothes. She was still standing where he'd left her as he came out of the bedroom, neatly dressed in dark trousers, shirt and tie, light sports jacket and holding a straw boater.

He paused, gently regarding her. 'I know it's a bit of a shock for you, Cissy, my darling – as it was for me. I didn't think you'd be so silly as to let yourself get in that state. But now you have, you do need some time to think – to see my side of it. Once this business is out of the way, we can go on as before. We've been happy together and there's no reason why we can't go on being happy. Good job you told me when you did. And don't be frightened, Cissy, my sweet thing. It'll be easy to get rid of it, being so early. It's nothing. Just a small snip or something and you'll be your old self again. This happened to me once before, and she was as right as rain a few days afterwards. And we'll get the best person we can find. As you know from what I've paid for you so far, money's no object. You'll be quite safe.'

Paid for her? She felt, suddenly, like a prostitute. She didn't move as he came over to peck her cheek; didn't move as he went out the door cheerfully telling her to be good, he already over the shock, the problem for him solved. In fact she could feel nothing, think of nothing except that she had been paid for.

Chapter Fifteen

In the lovely carpeted oatmeal and fawn salon of her fine apartments, Daisy stalked about, stopping occasionally to regard Cissy with pity and shake her head angrily as Cissy unfolded her tale.

'What are you going to do now?'

'I don't know.'

It had been all so awful. A nightmare, and like a nightmare, even now, unreal. Yet it had been real. She had sat waiting for Langley's return, unable to believe what he'd said, all the while trying to convince herself that it had all been a mistake, that when he came back everything would be all right – that it had been the shock that had made him act so.

When he did return, she actually did think nothing had changed. He had been nice, no doubt sure that she would bow to his wishes, saying he was ready to discuss it rationally. But she hadn't been able to discuss anything rationally – not the way he referred to the operation as if what she carried was a piece of butcher's meat. As she dissolved into tears by the table, he'd lost his temper; had pulled some money from his wallet, throwing it down in front of her saying she could do what she liked with it – take herself back home or get an abortion – but that either way, he was returning to England, with Margo.

All the time she had been waiting for him to come back, praying everything would reconcile itself, he'd been in Margo's apartment, in her bed making love to her, already divorcing himself of Cissy and the problem she had presented him with.

Devastated, half-suffocated by weeping, and unable to think, she'd watched him scribble an address which he said tersely was the name of an expensive and highly recommended clinic – he didn't want any back-street damage on his conscience, he added – and dropped it fluttering on top of the wad of notes.

For a while he'd stood looking at her, his expression softening with something like nostalgia or regret, but when she continued her unabated weeping, the expression had hardened again and he had turned abruptly and stalked out, leaving her alone to pack and leave as he had asked.

After that, everything had been a blur. She hadn't been at all sure where she had gone or what she had done until she had got herself here to Daisy's home.

All this she explained between fresh bouts of gulping sobs while Daisy listened, growing more livid as the tale unfolded. Now she stood in front of Cissy, her oval face tight with anger for her friend.

'Show me the address of this clinic.'

Cissy looked up, alarmed. 'Not you too, Daisy? Do *you* really think I should get rid of it?'

Daisy sat down on the sofa beside her. 'Surely you can't want it, Cissy? Not after the way he's behaved? He's been a beast, but for your own sake, you're going to have to do something.'

'I loved him, Daisy. I did love him. I still do.'

Daisy's hand was smoothing hers. 'Are you sure?'

'I wouldn't feel like this if I didn't. I don't know what to do. It was what he did. The way he put the money down on the table as if . . . as if I was a common prostitute he'd picked up off the streets. I never once dreamt that was all I was to him. But that's all I am really.'

'Don't be silly.' Daisy put an arm around her. 'Don't let him get you thinking things like that. You were genuinely in love. It's he who's been shameful, leading you on because it suited him, even though he bought you this and that. But then he's got money to throw around, I expect, coming from Daddy, never having to work for it. Now my Teddy had to work to get where he is. He's a genuinely wonderful man . . .'

But Cissy wasn't listening. 'I couldn't believe he'd be like that. When he came back and asked me if I'd thought things over, he was so calm and I thought it was just one of those tiffs we've had before, and everything was all right again. But when he started saying that we couldn't carry on, because I was unreliable, I knew . . . I knew then . . .'

Overcome by the distress of those last few hours, she broke into a fresh spasm of weeping. It had all been so sordid. The way he'd said he didn't care if she had the baby or not, or what she did with the money, so long as she was out of his life. He'd brought up Margo and said that unlike little fools from the slums who knew no better than to get pregnant, thinking they could trap a man in to marrying them, Margo knew the rules and understood that going to bed a few times with a fellow did not automatically guarantee marriage which, in the best circles, was properly arranged, certainly not with Cissy's sort; that sowing wild oats was something understood by everyone who is anyone.

'Well, I don't understand it,' she told Daisy between strangled sobs. 'And I don't want to. Us, Daisy, we may come from poor families, but they're good people. They're not hypocrites like those with so much money they don't know what to do with it, except throw it about on high living and drink, smoking hashish and marijuana and having sex with each other at the drop of a hat, and leading people like me on.'

'But you knew the sort of life you were getting into when you left home. You knew you would be sharing his bed and that eventually an accident could happen. You couldn't *not* have realised what sort of capers those sort of people get up to. Everyone knows what they're like.'

'But I thought . . . I thought it was different with me and Langley. He always made it seem different, always so considerate, talking about our life together.'

'Until it came to facing the music.'

'I know I've been stupid. I really thought he loved me. I really thought . . .'

Breaking into sobs again, it was some time before she could go on.

'I made a fool of myself, pleading with him. I knew I was degrading myself, but I couldn't help it. He said I was behaving like a cheap little slut and it nauseated him. That's when he started to count out the money and write that name on a piece of paper and said he never wanted to see me again. I couldn't believe he could be so hard and unfeeling. He'd always been so sweet and so caring, and we'd had such wonderful times together.'

'What did you do with the money?' Daisy asked, practical in the face of Cissy's tears.

'I left it where it was on the table.'

'You did what?' Daisy leaned away from her in astonishment.

'I couldn't touch it. When he told me to pack my things and said that everything he'd given me was mine to keep, I picked up the money and threw it at him and told him he could keep his stinking money.' Another sob broke from her. 'He laughed, Daisy. He laughed. He just laughed, and then he gave me a strange look and walked out, leaving it all on the floor. He said that he didn't want to see me there when he got back and if I had any sense in my head I would pick it all up, because he would burn it if I didn't.'

'And you left it all on the floor? Oh, Cissy, you idiot!'

'I was going to. Then I thought I'd burn it for him instead, and then take lots of aspirins and kill myself.'

Daisy's arm tightened about her. 'But you didn't. And you didn't burn the money either, did you? Say you didn't burn it, Cissy.'

'I meant to. I really didn't know what I wanted to do, so I just picked it all up and went and packed up all my things and left. I didn't know where to go or what to do. I know I wandered around for hours until I got tired. I kept looking at the address of the clinic he'd given me. I think I nearly went there, but somehow, I – I couldn't. I don't know why. I don't want the baby. How would I ever cope? Yet I couldn't do what he asked. I remember thinking that I'd be grovelling like a little slave doing what he wanted me to do. I've been doing that all along, Daisy – all these months. That's all I've been – his slave and plaything. And it hurts, Daisy. It hurts so much. And to think I gave up everything for him. Eddie, my family, my life back home, and for what? For nothing. Now I can't even go back home, to Eddie or my family. What am I going to do, Daisy? I'd be better off dead.'

Daisy held her as she wept into her shoulder. 'How much did he give you, Cissy?'

Stemming her tears, dragging the sleeve of her fine angora coat across her tear-laden eyes, Cissy fished into her handbag and brought out a thick wad of crumpled notes, handing it to Daisy without looking at it. The very sight of it would have started her off weeping again.

Her head bent low, hands screwed into loose fists against her face, she didn't look as Daisy began counting. Only when she heard her gasp did she look up. The money lay in two piles on the low onyx coffee table in front of them, in five-hundred and one-thousand franc notes.

'Cissy! There must be . . .' she made a second hasty calculation. 'In English money there must be nearly eight hundred pounds. Good Lord! What sort of clinic did he have in mind? You could go ten times over!'

Despite herself, Cissy smiled through her tears at the way Daisy was wont to overemphasise. She hadn't changed. But the idea of going even once made the marrow in her bones freeze, the humiliation of creeping into the place, being stared at, looked over, examined, her knowledge of French limited as she submitted herself to some po-faced French doctor's probing, the pitiful results of all that probing being taken away in a bedpan by an equally po-faced French nurse. No, she couldn't face that, couldn't face the thought of seeing herself a murderer, the bloody remains of her stupidity born away like so much offal.

'I can't . . . I can't go through that.' She was in Daisy's arms, her words pouring out almost inarticulate. 'So much money to do that – it makes doing it even more wicked. I'm taking his money just to kill . . . It's wrong when it's my fault. Poor little thing didn't ask for . . .'

Daisy's hand was soothing her back. 'There, there. It's all right. You don't have to get rid of it, you know.'

'And if I don't? How can I bring up a child all on my own in a foreign country? I can't even speak French enough to . . .'

Daisy held her a little way away, gazing into her wretched tear-stained face. 'I know you feel you can't go home. But I think you should.'

'Oh, no!' The tears were drying. She sniffed back the remnants of her weakness, a determination she wouldn't have believed she possessed beginning to take its place. 'I couldn't face them, not now. I've been a fool, thoughtless and selfish.' The tears had dispersed, leaving her quite cold and immune to all that her future might hold. 'I'm not going back to have the door slammed in my face. I'm not going to give anyone that satisfaction. I've decided, Daisy. I'm going to keep this baby. I think I'll open up a shop somewhere and keep us both.'

'A shop?'

'Something. I don't know.'

'But a shop? A business? What do you know about business?'

The question sobered her. Yes, what did she know? No one in her family had ever had a business. She hadn't the faintest knowledge of business. Yet she must do something. She straightened up.

'I don't know yet. I don't know how I'll manage on my own. But I will. I will, somehow.'

Daisy seemed to be lost in thought. 'You don't have to be on your own. You've got me, Cissy. What're friends for, if not to help?'

'How can *you* help me?' Cissy said, her haughtiness unintentional.

Daisy didn't flinch. 'Well, if you really are intent on keeping this baby, there's a home for you here. God knows, the place is big enough. There's plenty of room for a dozen people.'

Again Cissy smiled. Daisy and her exaggeration. She remembered how they had made such plans to leave home. In the end it had been her to go first, with Daisy following after. And now they were both here – friends still. And it was such a depth of relief knowing they were.

Thoughts of Langley still hurt like a knife wound, the love she thought she'd had for him still too painful, too real to shrug off, and she knew that were he to ask, she'd go back to him immediately like the silly fool she was. But he wouldn't ask. That was obvious now. She had been just a passing thing, and no doubt he and Margo were laughing over her this very minute. That vision was the worst hurt.

'What about your husband?' she asked lamely, in an attempt to push the dismal thoughts from her. 'Won't he object?'

'Teddy? He'd be only too happy. He'd even help you to get started up in something. He's that kind of person. You know, compassionate.'

The apparently unintentional comparison between Daisy's and her own recent relationship brought a pang of jealousy which, in spite of Daisy's offers of help that Cissy had no option but to accept, stirred in her something nearer to hatred that Daisy should be so happy with her man while she was forced to accept handouts. She had no one else to turn to, nothing to look forward to but the birth of the baby of someone who no longer wanted her. For a moment she hated everyone – Daisy, that loyal loving husband of hers, the perfidious Langley, she knew that now, and his baby . . .

The hatred stopped in its tracks. She wanted the baby. Not just to show him that she wouldn't do just what he expected. Not just to keep his money and make a life for herself to prove that no matter what his opinion of her she was her own woman, but that she actually *wanted* the baby. As if approving, pride flowed up like a living thing inside her.

Daisy was waiting for Theodore as he came in, hardly giving him time to lay down his case and pour a drink before embarking on Cissy and her predicament, Cissy by that time was safely installed in a bedroom.

'So you see I had to put her up for a while. And Lord knows we've room enough here for her to stay until she gets herself sorted out.'

Her aim was not to make it seem an indefinite thing, but Theodore was his usual benign self, happy to lend a helping hand, and of course there was room enough in this huge five-bedroomed apartment.

'God forbid I should deny a woman alone in Paris a roof over her head,' he vowed in his faintly guttural English. Even in French, which he spoke quite a lot with Daisy so that she could learn the language, there was still that German hardness overlaying the softer French which impeded rather than helped her to speak it as she should.

'The poor young woman,' he went on, after hearing the whole story, 'I wonder should you send to her family a letter to inform them where she is? It must be for them very worrying to not know this.'

'I'm not sure. It could set the cat among the pigeons, interfering and telling them. On the other hand they must be worried not knowing where she is.'

His dark eyebrows drew together. 'It would be a kindness to them to know, but as you say to interfere is to set a cat among the pigeons. Such a clatter would they make flying up to dislodge the peace of mind of her family. You are right, Daisy. Best I think to let the sleeping cat lie for a while.'

Daisy suppressed a grin. She loved this German of hers, not only for his ease in understanding another's point of view, but for his odd misquotations of sayings that came naturally by to her, and yet making them sound wise and logical. Loving him, she deeply pitied Cissy her loss. To think that at one time she had been so jealous of her. Instantly mortified by her own self-satisfaction, which no true friend should give houseroom to when another is in trouble, she scourged herself with genuine sorrow for Cissy. If there was any help she could give, she would bend over backwards to do it, no matter if it meant turning her home upside down. Yet for all her good intentions, an inner voice kept coming back: there but for the grace of God . . .

But for Teddy, she too could have come very unstuck in this lovely, captivating, dangerous city. Her mind flicked back to that week just before meeting him, her heart being stolen away as Cissy's had – in her case by a casually handsome, rakish jazz-band singer. Flattered by his attentions as he offered her the moon, she had, innocently, nearly reached out for it as he had urged and, like Cissy, had not known how very far away that moon was and the danger of overstretching for it.

Just in time Teddy had come along, offering stability, wealth, love and loyalty, his gentle companionship that following week eradicating the smooth jazz-band singer from her mind.

Yes, she had been indeed fortunate to escape the trap into which Cissy had fallen – with no Theodore Helgott to rescue her. And by that token she sternly pushed aside all feelings of smugness in the face of her friend's misfortune.

Had Eddie been on hand, he might have been to Cissy what Teddy had been to her. But Cissy had actually left Eddie for that suave, pampered ladykiller, so there really was no comparison, and of course, as Teddy had agreed, it would set cats among pigeons by interfering and letting her people know of her whereabouts without consulting her first. Later perhaps, but not yet. Not with Cissy pregnant and all.

*

Bobby Farmer, hunched over a pint in the Prince of Orange, had been bemoaning his lot to Eddie and Eddie's father for half an hour.

'I don't know what I'm going ter do. No use tryin' ter talk to me mum and dad about something like this. They've 'ad enough with Cissy going off the rails without me addin' to it all. I can't say anything to Ethel's people neither. They're dead against me.'

Listening, Eddie felt he couldn't care less about Bobby's entanglement with this girl who'd had his baby, his head filled with the ring of Cissy's name on her brother's lips a moment before as Bobby moaned how he wished she were here to talk to and give him advice. No one could have wished her here more than Eddie himself.

'Has she never got in touch with you since that last Christmas?' he asked suddenly and saw Bobby's expression go blank, his train of thought interrupted.

'Who?'

'Your sister.'

'May?'

'No . . . er, Cissy.' The name came awkwardly to Eddie, aware of his father's disparaging glance at his alluding to her.

'Oh . . . No, not since that Christmas we got that card. Wasn't no card this year. I often wonder . . . But as I was saying, I couldn't go on leading a double life. It wasn't fair to Ethel, and it was killin' me. She – Vera, that is – the one who's had my baby, knows about Ethel, but Ethel didn't know about her until last week. I mean, Vera's baby's more'n six months old now. I couldn't keep it to meself any longer.'

'You know what you are, don't yer?' put in Alf Bennett, draining his pint. 'You're a bloody fool, and that's putting it mildly.'

'Yeah,' Bobby said dismally. 'If I could only turn the clock back.'

If only I could too, thought Eddie, feeling equally as dismal.

'So what're you goin' ter do?' asked Alf.

Bobby shrugged. 'I don't know. Fat's really in the fire now.'

'I reckon you'd 'ave ter divorce. If you're unhappy with your Ethel and she's miserable with you, then you two are best done with it all, and you'll 'ave to marry this, what's-her-name. Mind you, divorce, even if there's a guilty party, could take two years or more.'

'It ain't as simple as that. I can't leave Ethel and our own kid to fend for themselves. But I don't want to leave Vera in the lurch with hers. I'm at me wits' end.'

Bobby had thought about it long and hard these last monhs, but there was still no answer. What hurt most was the way Ethel kept going on about his family, as if they were dirt.

'I should've known,' she'd said in her fury. 'I should've been warned when you got me pregnant what you was like. It's in the blood if you ask me. Your sister's no better than she ought to be, running off and leaving that poor Eddie like she did. And your other sister, May, she ain't none too fussy about the blokes she goes out with either. And that brother of yours, Sidney – hardly been in work since he left school last year. Didn't want to go on the river like you an' his dad. Oh no, wants to go his own way, and always out of work. A fine bloody family to go turning up their noses at the likes of my folks for being dockers. Well, my family do have some respect for themselves. And don't you think I'm goin' ter move over for your tart and 'er baby, Bobby Farmer.'

At the kitchen table, Bobby had sat slumped and sullen with no defence for himself or his family against Ethel's flagellant tongue, knowing himself entirely at fault but silently praying she would soon exhaust herself. But she'd had plenty more to say.

'I bet you think you're a real stallion. Me 'ere with your kid, and that tart over the river with yer other. And 'ow many more I don't know about, eh? In the blood, that's what it is. A real chip off the old block. Cissy gone off to Lord knows where, prostituting herself all around France I don't doubt, most likely carting around someone's bastard. And that Eddie Bennett, the silly sod, still moping after her after two years or more, working himself to death for his business, dreaming of the day he'll meet 'er again. I know. Some 'opes, that!

'And that's another thing – made a proper success of it. Him and his father rolling in it. And where've you got, you feckless bugger? Still a bloody lighterman, working fer others, in and out of work, grovelling around fer jobs when Eddie Bennett what ain't even got a wife to support can make his way in the world. And all you can do is get some trollop in the family way and sod how I feel.'

It had been no use telling her that work was becoming increasingly harder to get. All he could do was sit there as she'd railed on, his family's good name laid in the mud, his sister lambasted, and Eddie lampooned for a simpleton for clinging to her memory. But that part he didn't speak of to Eddie.

Chapter Sixteen

'I think I would like to sell hats,' Cissy said, giving Daisy and Theodore a hesitant smile to cement the statement.

It was perhaps the first time in six months, since Langley's departure in fact, that she'd been halfway able to make any proper decision of her own and feel easy in her mind about it.

After the first days of weeping she had withdrawn into herself, on the surface trying to behave normally in their presence because it would have looked churlish not to after all they had done for her, opening up their home as they had. But she had felt more lonely in their company than if she had indeed been alone. In the isolation of her own bedroom she had felt bitter, her heart filled with empty hatred of Langley, for his careless outrageous disregard of what he had done, hating even more the knowledge that were he to come asking forgiveness and for her to return to him, she'd still forgive and return.

Those following months her heart ached for him even as it hated him. But slowly, as with all wounds that must heal unless worried by a desire to be kept open, the hurt diminished little by little. It did not go away entirely; the scar, red and angry, would take far longer to fade to the white line that could be forgotten most of the time, noticed only on the odd occasion, the wound distantly remembered as if happening to another. It had yet to reach that stage, but was diminished enough to now and again allow her a moment of lighter spirit.

It was one of these moments now, as she sat at the dining table in the Helgotts' gold and brown *salle à manger*. The meal on this November evening had been largely ignored in the interest of Cissy's future. Now, the art deco table lamps and wall lamps had been switched on to glow upon a wealth of Lalique glassware, gold and brown walls and the brown gauze curtains at the tall windows that were not yet drawn against the twilight. The last lingering arc of luminescence, which Theodore said was called *dammerschein* in German, throwing an unreal light over all three people, they were again engaged in the debate that had been discussed on and off these six months on how best Cissy might use her money for her future when finally able to go her own way.

Not that either had ever hinted she should. It worried her that they were so patient, never betraying any weariness of her being here. Daisy's husband, mostly at his office, had little need to see her and she kept to her room as much as possible in the evenings so as not to infringe on his privacy when he came home. Daisy enjoyed having someone to talk to and shop with and was always saying how she would miss her when she finally went her own way, which in itself spoke of an eventual and understood termination to her stay here, although it was accepted that this wouldn't be for a while yet.

It had been taken for granted that she wouldn't find herself a job until well after the baby was born, but now, her middle swollen and heavy with only four weeks to go to the event, talk of what she would do when all was back to normal had become a nightly discussion.

'It's going to have to be a shop of some sort,' Daisy had sparked off this evening's dinner debate. 'That's all I can think of.'

'I don't know the first thing about running a shop,' Cissy hedged, but Theodore had been a calming influence as always.

'Dear woman, it is a matter of common sense and a natural ability to sell. Also to buy. Wisely. Any *dummkopf* can buy. But in buying and knowing how to sell at a good profit what is bought, that is the part that matters. If you should wish, I will advice give you at any time. I will charge nothing. Ha! Ha!'

His sharp raucous laugh made his listener jump, but Cissy smiled her gratitude of the offer. She knew herself in safe hands with these people, but more and more she looked forward to the day when she could finally go her own way. All the time she dallied here her money was dwindling, no matter how frugal she tried to be.

'I don't think I would like a shop here in Paris,' she said. 'I'm still not good enough at French to get by trying to sell things.'

Theodore gave another explosive laugh. 'Practise it every moment you have. By the time you are ready, you can sell to the sharpest Frenchwoman. Am I not proof? I came to this country a foreigner, and here have made my fortune. Although times I have when I wish very much to go back to Germany, to Dusseldorf, to see my father's grave, and when the time comes for me to die, to be buried beside him . . .'

'Teddy!' Daisy's face was a picture of fear. 'Don't talk like that!'

He leaned across the table and patted her rigid hand. 'Not for many long years yet, *mein liebling*. Not for many long years. Together we grow old. But there – we get off the subject. Cissy, my dear young woman, why so especially do you want to sell hats?'

Cissy played with her sweet. 'Like Daisy said, I can't think of anything else. I don't want to go back to dress-making. I did it before I came to Paris. In a factory. It's drudgery, and I'm sick of it.'

'There are too many dressmakers, anyway, in Paris,' Daisy said.

'On the other hand,' Theodore said, 'it is what you know. What do you know of selling hats?'

'*Women's* hats,' Daisy put in quickly. 'Cissy is acquainted with the height of fashion, and she knows what we want.'

'Knowing, selling . . .' Theodore gave an expressive shrug. 'There is a difference.'

'She could get a job in a ladies hat shop until she knows a bit more about all that. And, of course, the sooner she starts . . .

'She must wait until the suckling of her child is completed.'

'Yes, of course.'

'And who is to look after the child when she begins to work?'

'I will.'

'You?'

'Why not?' Daisy giggled. 'It'll give me some experience for when I have my own babies.'

'Which I hope soon if God is willing,' Theodore said fervently, his dark eyes filling with a loving light.

Daisy gazed back at them. 'I hope so too. But until then, I could look after it for Cissy. I'd love that. I'm sure it's the best idea?'

'You are, of course, right.' His proud expression deepened to be matched by Daisy's own as she clasped his hand across the table.

'Of course I'm right. It'll give her a chance to sort things out.'

Excluded from all this talk about her future, Cissy looked from one to the other. The way they consulted together like two happy children making plans; the way their faces softened in response to each other's ideas; the adoration glowing in Theodore's eyes and the certainty of being adored shining in Daisy's; her heart seemed like a brick beneath her ribs. Who'd ever want to love her, a child at her side as proof of her tarnished state? She had been out of her mind to continue with this pregnancy. Langley had been right all along. It wouldn't have been such a terrible thing to have terminated it, an operation so small it would hardly have been remembered, and she would still have been his. In time, perhaps, his high ideals about marriage might have modified to embrace her. She would never know.

She wanted to burst into tears, to cry out that she didn't care what they proposed as to the direction her life would take, it was all pointless, all a waste. But she didn't. She just sat listening to her life being discussed, and whatever the decision she would abide by it.

*

The first twinge was felt as she got into the taxi to go shopping with Daisy. Huddled into her coat against a brief snow flurry, she ignored it, putting it down to the way she was holding herself against the cold.

She shouldn't have been going out, but being closeted in the flat for two weeks awaiting the now well-overdue birth – Daisy had heard it said that the first were often late coming, or maybe Cissy had miscalculated somehow – Daisy suggested a short shopping trip might help brush away the cobwebs if nothing else. But mostly Daisy wanted to Christmas shop.

Disdaining to take the Metro, in case anything happened while they were on it, she said, but in truth she'd so gone up in the world that she disliked her once sole means of travel, a taxi had been ordered, with expense no object, to take them directly to a few of those fine fashionable shops in Boulevard Haussman. Cissy couldn't help a tinge of bitterness that Daisy could afford to ignore public transport these days where she herself now had to watch every centime.

It was the same with clothes: Daisy, wearing the height of fashion that showed up her remarkably slim figure, wearied of a new dress or shoes within a couple of weeks, while Cissy, hers fast growing outdated, remembered that only months ago she too would toss aside hardly worn garments as carelessly as Daisy now did. No doubt she would be wearing the same things a year, maybe two years from now, the money Langley had given her needing to be hung on to for far more important things. She couldn't help feeling a little jealous of Daisy, and a little wistful for what might have been.

And where would she have been now had she and Langley remained together? Still slim and desirable, the baby she now carried a long forgotten incident, she'd have not even paused to recall it. Doing all the things she used to do, crazily dancing to some blaring jazz band, returning still somewhat intoxicated in the grey dawn to their art deco decorated apartments, a slightly worn dress tossed aside, another to be bought sometime that afternoon, together with a fabulous, wildly exotic bottle of Jean Patou perfume; Biarritz for the winter; Venice perhaps, or the Côte d'Azure. Was Langley there now, at one of those resorts, his arm around Margo? Maybe in bed with her. Or perhaps with some other girl by now, that girl exquisitely dressed and perfumed as she Cissy had once been. Instead here she was . . .

It was all so degrading. She no longer enjoyed shopping with Daisy, not because of her swollen waistline, but because she knew what would happen – what always happened when they went shopping together. Daisy would see something that might suit her friend, and as Cissy hung back knowing she must not be extravagant with what Langley had left her, which even as she watched was fast dwindling merely on living, Daisy would eagerly get it for her – nothing vastly expensive because even she knew when generosity became vulgarity, but even the smallest gift was an embarrassment to someone afraid to spend much-needed money so as to appear equally as lavish. Even this taxi. As usual Daisy had refused Cissy's part of the fare, and so in her innocence unwittingly belittling her by another fine degree.

It was in the taxi just after passing over the Pont de la Concorde into the great square whose vast proportions always made Cissy's eyes feel vaguely out of focus, that the pain caught her again. Not too bad to make a fuss about, but this time an alarm bell did begin to ring.

'Oh . . . Daisy . . . We've got to go back home!'

'But we're . . .' But one glance at her tense expression was enough for Daisy to forgo all thoughts of that new gown she'd set her heart on for Christmas, only three days away. Disappointment showed on her face but in an instant she was leaning forward commanding the taxi driver to turn his vehicle swiftly around the ornate fountains and central obelisk of the busy Place de la Concorde and head for home as fast as traffic allowed.

'It's got to be a boy,' Daisy said as she sat on the edge of a tall-backed chair in the waiting room of the private convent-run hospital. 'Her going nearly three weeks over her time, and it taking so long to come now – it has to be. They say boys are lazy.'

Theodore nodded wordlessly. He didn't look comfortable here, looked as though he'd much rather be at his office desk, but Christmas Eve, he'd closed the office early, as was expected. Now he paced the floor of the cold, neat little waiting room looking decidedly out of place.

'It can't be much longer,' Daisy said, for need of something better to say, though she was seldom stumped. Having got going again, she wasn't now. 'Fifteen hours. Mind you, she didn't have all that much pain to start with, did she? Hardly any really. I mean, after the taxi dropped us up at home, there was nothing – not until this morning. And I was sitting at her bedside and she was chirpy enough then. It didn't really start until a few hours ago.

I just hope it doesn't go on too long, for her sake. It's nearly midnight. Nearly Christmas Day. Wouldn't it be funny if it's born on Christmas Day? I wish something would happen.'

As if in answer, the door opened to admit a sister in a starched shell-like cap with flaring white wings and a stiff blue and white uniform, her scrubbed face as radiant as if she were a relative.

'You are the friends of Mademoiselle Farmer?' she enquired in rapid French. 'You will be pleased to know that the child has been born safely. It is a girl. Both the mother and the child are very well.'

'Oh, *merci*!' Daisy said excitedly, and went on in halting French to ask when they could see them. She was told Cissy was sleeping but they were welcome to come back in the morning, and if they would like to see the child it was in the crèche where they could peep at it through the glass partition. It was a very modern hospital. Babies were taken from their mothers immediately after birth so that the weary mother could rest.

'Ah . . . she's lovely, perfect,' Daisy sighed, maternal instincts flooding out of her. She felt Theodore's strong hand tighten across her shoulder.

'Please God, ours may be as perfect.'

'And as beautiful. But us two are quite nice-looking people. We're bound to have beautiful children.'

'Please God,' he said.

Cissy was sitting up in bed, her baby in its crib beside her, as her two visitors approached. The look of relief on her face that they were the first in was apparent even as they entered the ward.

Daisy had begged to be let into the small ward a few minutes before the main inrush of fathers and adoring relatives; spinning a yarn to the stone-faced sister in charge as to how the mother and her fiancé had been due to marry, but that he had been killed in a tragic accident, leaving the mother alone and unmarried and with child. She'd stressed the poor girl's suffering, having been so in love and now so alone in the world, and that, but for the grace of God, any girl could be left as she had been left.

Hoping to crack the woman's sense of the practical and appeal to any romance she might have in her, Daisy had sighed that it would be a kindness to the distressed mother if her visitors could be allowed in that little bit earlier so that she would not have to sit alone while other fathers came to see their wives.

She had put it so poignantly, so convincingly, that the cold face took on a slight flush and the stonework metamorphosed to sympathetic putty. The doors had been opened a fraction unto them three minutes before the official time, much to the many frowns and asides of those left waiting in the cold corridor.

In a way it wasn't all lies. It would have been distressing for Cissy to see husbands coming in to cuddle their wives and admire what they had sired, while she lay alone, conscious of her own isolation and the enquiring eyes turning in her direction as to why no husband was leaning over her. Cissy and Theodore were able to surround her, not so much to protect her from those curious glances but so that she would not have to notice them.

Daisy bent over the scrap in its crib, lifting back the frilled cap to see better. 'She's gorgeous, Cissy! She's like you. I'm so glad. How do you feel?' She straightened up to regard the mother.

Cissy smiled wanly. 'Like I've been pulled through a hedge backwards.'

'I bet you do,' Daisy said as Theodore frowned his incomprehension of the statement.

'Backwards, through a hedge?' he echoed.

'It's a saying. I'll explain it to you later.' She turned back to Cissy. 'You look well. Congratulations, darling. I bet you're relieved it's all over.'

Cissy gave a faint shrug. For hours yesterday all she could think about was that she had been a damned fool. To go through all this for another man's child – a man who had walked out on her. At some insane moment at the height of her labour had come the thought that when this was over, she would take the baby to a quiet place on the Seine and in the darkness of night beneath the shadow of one of its ponts, drop the alien body into the dark waters. Then it would be all over. But as the tiny scrap was placed into her arms, faintly bluish, with a streak of blood across its little nose and cheek, her heart swelled with love and pride and the knowledge that this little life had come out of her – nothing to do with him, and no one could take it away from her. To think that she could have had such a thought made her shudder, even as she shrugged so offhandedly.

'Aren't you thrilled?'

Yes, she was. And Langley could go and boil his head. Suddenly she wanted nothing to do with him. Suddenly she knew what she wanted from life. She'd get on, make a success of it, be her own person, bring up her daughter and give her the best that money could buy. And to hell with men and love and shame. She would seek a position in a shop, a small shop, learn what there was to learn and then she would make her own way in the world. But how lovely it would have been if everything could have been normal – a good husband, a supportive family to come and admire her achievement, a nice little house not far away from them – rather like her brother Bobby had, like her sister May would one day have, like she would have had with Eddie Bennett. She wondered briefly where he was and how he was and what he was doing, then dismissed it to watch Daisy lift her baby from its hospital crib.

'What're you going to call her?'

'I don't know.'

Daisy frowned, gently rocking the sleepy form. 'It's Christmas Day. How about Noelle? It sounds very French. Being born in France too. What about Noelle Louise – doesn't that sound beautiful?'

Certain of her decision as Cissy smiled agreement, so far having no name in mind for her new daughter, Daisy dropped a kiss upon the tiny smooth cheek. 'And we will be Noelle Louise's godparents,' she added defiantly as a sister came and took the baby from her to put it back firmly in its crib – hospital regulations – tightly tucking it in like some Russian doll.

Her days revolved around Noelle and nothing else. She would sit for hours watching the little hands jerking happily, those large blue eyes darting about with such knowing looks as if in recognition of some previous life. Little sounds of ecstacy would issue forth from those puckered rosy red lips, and Cissy would feel her heart give little skips at almost each sound, rejoicing in the soft feel of those tiny hands.

Amid the luxurious surroundings of Daisy's home, the radio playing softly, she felt safer than she ever had since coming to France, even with Langley. But Langley was becoming an ever more distant shadow – an episode she'd rather not remember. More clearly she remembered her times with Eddie, but then that memory would make her heart plummet so that she quickly turned her thoughts away from it. Yet she couldn't escape a wish that she could go home, pick up the pieces, begin again. That, of course, was out of the question. Even if she could be sure of forgiveness from everyone, Eddie, her family, pride would not have let her go crawling back seeking it. She told herself that she was happier here, just her and Noelle, Daisy and Theodore, and as they expressed no desire to see her gone, she felt she was content.

Winter gave way to spring. Trees lining the boulevards of Paris budded into leaf and then into blossom. Parisians cast off the heavier of their garments and colour came back to the city in the shape of bright dresses and lightweight hats, this year with broader brims, and gaiety grew more abundant, for even in winter it never truly departed as it might have done in sombre London. Music always present, summer or winter, became even more light-hearted, and flower stalls became even more full of blossom, parks and open spaces more full of people and lovers – especially lovers.

Daisy did her best to get Cissy to go out, but it was like hitting her head against a brick wall, even though Cissy seemed happy.

'I'm content enough staying here with Noelle.'

'But we can take her out with us. She's not going to catch cold or anything with the weather so lovely and warm – if that's what you're worrying about.'

'I know, but you don't need me hanging around.'

'For goodness sake! I love us going shopping together. Like we did last year.'

'But it won't be the same for you, me pushing a pram around.'

'I don't mind.'

'No, I'm happy here.'

Daisy gave up.

Theodore got tickets for the theatre, for each of them.

'It will be nice for you to come out with us for an evening.'

Cissy's alarm was overt. 'What about Noelle?'

'For that evening we will get a nurse for her.'

'I couldn't leave her with a *stranger*.'

'We'll be getting one from a reputable agency,' Daisy said a little irritably, but Cissy shook her head.

'I don't want to be a nuisance. You and Theodore go on your own. You don't see each other enough as it is with your work taking up all your time, Theodore. You two go. I'm quite happy here. Honestly.'

'You're getting to be a recluse, Cissy. You used to be so lively, but you're growing into a real misery.'

'I'm not,' Cissy defended. 'I just want to be with Noelle.'

'That's what I mean,' Daisy said pointedly, and left it at that.

Chapter Seventeen

Daisy had been as happy about Noelle's birth as if it had been her own baby; without thinking she'd said she couldn't wait to tell her parents all about it. But Cissy had sworn her to silence.

'It'll get back to my family. You know how things spread. It won't take them long to find out where I am. I don't want the upset of being badgered to go back to them and be looked down on. I mean what I say, Daisy. Don't tell anyone.'

Daisy had shrugged, nodded her acquiescence and in her letters to her family did her best to avoid reference to the baby. It wasn't easy. Her natural excitement bubbling over, many times she'd have to scrap a whole sheet when something had slipped in quite unnoticed about the little things the baby did. Especially now. Noelle was six months old, growing more interesting each day, and as the months went by Daisy felt herself beginning to grow increasingly broody for a baby of her own.

She told Theodore. He said, 'Then we should begin seriously for a family,' but so far nothing had happened.

Still, she consoled herself, not everyone fell at the drop of a hat. Meanwhile, she'd soon be looking after Noelle on her own. Although Cissy was trying to cling on to breastfeeding which kept Noelle bound to her, her milk was beginning to dry up. The time was approaching when the baby could be left in her charge while Cissy began to look for work.

So looking forward to the prospect, hardly able to wait for Cissy to get started, keeping her vow of secrecy became even harder when, before the event bound her to childminding, she took an opportunity to visit her family in England.

It was only her second visit since her marriage. The first had been a couple of months after the wedding and Teddy had come with her. They had already met him at the wedding itself, he paying for their trip. They'd been most appreciative of his generosity and had taken to him immediately, particularly having seen how comfortably he could keep their daughter – done well for herself as the saying went – even if he was Jewish and German and had a funny foreign accent, having money covered a lot of sins, so Daisy thought, slantingly amused at their motive as she saw it.

Cissy wasn't too pleased by this present need to go visiting across the Channel. 'It is only for a week?' she wanted to be reassured.

'One week,' Daisy promised. It was surprising how so lacking in self-confidence Cissy had become. Too much reliance on others, that was her trouble. There was a time when Cissy had been the one to lead, calling the tune; and when she'd met that Langley, had suffered no compunction about letting Eddie down. She had no doubt that Cissy had been to the very fore with her society friends at Biarritz and elsewhere. Now here she was, shivering in her shoes about being left on her own to cope for one week. How on earth would she ever manage the business she was so intent on if this was how she behaved?

'Teddy will be around,' she reassured. 'He'll keep you company. And it *is* only a week.'

'I never know what to say to him,' Cissy pouted. This was something Daisy had never realised. 'I'll just be glad when you get back.'

'Give me a chance,' Daisy laughed. 'I haven't even gone yet.'

It was wonderful seeing her parents after so long. Talk about the fatted calf – her mother at the stove making probably the best meals she'd cooked in her life, relations turning up to see her, a party on the Saturday in her honour, bombarded by endless questions. How was she? How did she like living in France? How was her husband doing? Theodore, wasn't it? And what was her peculiar married name again – Halfgot? Helgott, she corrected. Was it German then? Of course it was German. But isn't he Jewish too? Did she light those candles on Friday nights and did they observe the Jewish Sabbath? No, she didn't light candles, she told them. Teddy hadn't practised his religion for years, just as lots of other people don't practise theirs. Oh, Teddy – was that what she called him? It sounded quite English really.

Daisy suffered it all with a smile, only too happy to be home for a while. Eager to tell everyone about her life, her lovely home, her marvellous Paris shopping sprees, she let slip the lots of money her generous husband made – information that instantly reaped slewed looks and a hasty change of topic, indicative, she sensed, of jealousy and accusations of boasting. She learned to keep accounts of her spending to herself except that her mother was so over the moon about her Daisy 'landing on her feet so to speak' it just invited more slanted looks and very readable changes of topic.

'It's a big flat you got then,' her mother said as she dished up the Sunday dinner.

'They're called apartments. And yes, Mum, it's quite spacious.'

Her mum, dishing up the greens on to plates of roast lamb, baked potatoes and Yorkshire pudding, looked at her. 'I bet it feels a bit empty at times, just you and Teddy there? When do you two plan to start a family then? Babies are a blessing when they come along. Help to fill up an empty home.'

'We'll get around to it when we're ready,' Daisy said, passing her a plate for her Aunt Maud.

'You should. Time goes too quick. Before you know it, it's almost too late. And you don't want to be too old before you start. Come on, sit up to the table, love.'

She and Dad, her aunt and uncle and Mum sat themselves down to eat, Mum passing the gravy round in its dish – a special Sunday tradition; the rest of the week gravy got poured over each plate of potatoes, meat and greens *before* being brought to the table.

'And Teddy's that much older than you, luv,' Mum took up her point again, spooning mint sauce over her lamb. 'What I mean is, if you two don't start thinking about it soon, he'll be too old to be a father. I mean to say, you not needing to work, don't it get lonely for you in your big fla . . . apartment?'

'Oh, I'm never lonely,' Daisy defended, cutting into a slice of her roast lamb with real gusto, her mind on that first succulent taste. It was nice to get back to good old English cooking after the continental stuff they were always eating, Teddy was fond of his French and German food. 'Not with Cissy and the baby there and it's going to be a real joy for me looking after her when . . .' She stopped forking up her piece of lamb, her head still down but her eyes furtive, aware that her mother had also stopped eating.

'Baby? What baby?'

'Oh . . .' Daisy thought quickly. 'I sometimes give eye to . . .'

'You said something about Cissy? You don't mean Cissy Farmer what you used to go around with – the one what you used to work with? Not 'er? Didn't she go to France too? And she's got a baby? So she got married then? Do 'er and 'er 'usband live with you as well?'

'Nice to see a place full of young people,' Aunt Maud said through a mouthful of Yorkshire pudding.

Daisy was flustered, looking for a reply, but her dad intervened, obviously aware of her confusion.

'Ain't no 'usband around if you ask me. Ain't married, is she?'

'Well . . .' There was no thought of eating for the moment. She put down her knife and fork and stared helplessly at her parents. 'Look, it's supposed to be a secret. Cissy doesn't want me to tell anyone. She doesn't want her family to know anything about her.'

'Don't tell us the poor girl got into trouble,' quavered her aunt, her small mouth with its faint moustache on the upper lip forming an 'O' shape, while her uncle carried on ploughing into his food. It was none of his business.

'Of course she 'as.' Daisy's father, usually so indolent about the silly problems of womenfolk, was suddenly intent. 'And you're over there, 'arbouring 'er?'

'I'm not harbouring anyone, Dad. She's not a criminal. She's someone who's been badly let down. Her . . . her husband-to-be jilted her.' She decided on the spur of the moment to keep to a similar story to the one she'd told at the hospital when Cissy's baby had been born. 'He let her down and left her to have her baby all on her own. I had to take her in.'

'Of course you had to, luv.' Her mother laid an understanding hand on her arm. 'It'd be like you to help a friend in need. But don't her family know nuthink about it?'

'No. And she doesn't want them to know. So, please, Mum, keep it to yourself.'

Warming to the tale, she let it all unfold throughout dinner, like one of those wandering storytellers of old who would go from village to village long before anyone could read or write, taking pleasure from the oohs and ahs it drew. It certainly was a burden off her own shoulders after so long having to keep it out of her letters.

'But it *mustn't* go any further,' she cautioned when the tale was done. 'For Cissy's sake. She's my best friend. Promise now.'

'Well, I never,' sighed her mother, getting up to dish up the apple tart and custard to round off Sunday dinner. 'Of course, I'll promise. Won't we, Dick?' and as her husband shrugged, having already put silly women's gossip out of his mind, thus liable to say nothing, she added, 'We won't tell a soul,' her eyes wandering to her sister who nodded vigorously and brother-in-law who made no response, already buried in the more urgent business of eating his afters.

'Not a soul, we won't.'

Daisy wasn't so sure and wished she hadn't been quite so candid. It must have seemed such an unusual story that relayed to even the most innocuous listener in time it was bound to filter through to those concerned. It only needed her mother to go boasting about the grand life her daughter was leading in Paris with her wealthy husband, adding the bit about her daughter's generosity to a friend in need in order to open up a way of mentioning how opulent her Paris apartment was.

She could just see the direction her mother's thoughts could take. A casual remark to a neighbour or two – no harm in that? Living here in Plaistow, Cissy Farmer's people living in Canning Town, the busy Barking Road and East India Dock Road dividing them, it was as good a barrier as the Grand Canyon, neither borough with any excuse to bother the other.

But what if one of her mother's neighbours had a relative living in Canning Town who might know the Farmers? If it got out, how could she ever face Cissy again? She'd been so carried away she'd given none of this a thought.

Daisy's imagination knew no bounds and tormented her for weeks after coming home, waiting for a letter to arrive from the Farmers, or worse still, a ring of the bell to her apartment and a voice asking for Cissy Farmer.

A month passed. Two months. No letters, no unwanted callers. Daisy relaxed. At her persuasion, Cissy began looking for employment, doing the rounds, reluctantly leaving Noelle to her care.

Finding a job in a modiste or a boutique or even a mercerie – in England a common haberdasher's – was proving more difficult than she or Cissy had imagined.

'I've no qualifications, no experience,' Cissy bemoaned, relaying what she had been told. 'No one wants me. I can't speak French well enough for them.'

'Give it time,' Daisy consoled. 'You've only just started. Someone is bound to take you on eventually.'

It was cold comfort and Cissy grimaced. 'I've got to get something. The money Langley gave me is running out quicker than I ever thought it would, just on keeping me and Noelle.'

If it was a hint for her to waive the measly 'rent' as they termed it, which Cissy had insisted in the first place she took, Daisy almost succumbed, but there was a principle here, and Cissy had been spending her money on other things, personal things, clothing, bon-bons, make-up, records which she had taken to playing over and over on Daisy's new fine lacquered radiogram, and a dozen other personal indulgences. The nominal rent she handed over was the least of her outgoings.

Daisy said nothing, but Cissy was already off on another tack.

'I've been thinking, Daisy, why don't I buy a shop anyway and put in an assistant who knows the ropes to run it for me? That way I won't have to learn it myself. There are lots of shopkeepers like that.'

'That is not a good idea,' said Theodore when Daisy told him. 'It is known that employees will diddle . . . is that the word, my dear, diddle? Will diddle their employers right, left and centre.'

He was proud of the colloquialisms he had picked up from her over the twenty months of their marriage, airing them as often as possible, gratified to see her smile at this one as he enlarged on his advice.

'She would be a fool to embark on such a venture. I will tell her no, she must not go down that road.'

He sat down to explain it to Cissy, patiently, in the face of her constant distraction with Noelle's needs to be changed, to be given a rusk to suck, to have her little hands and face wiped afterwards, and to be settled down in her cot for a nap. The folly of her good idea finally getting through to her, Cissy was impelled to resign herself to going out yet again to look for a suitable position.

It was another five months before anything came along. In December, staff, any staff, were urgently needed for the Christmas rush and she was at last taken on by a small boutique on the outer perimeter of Paris. It was a start and served to supplement her fast-decreasing resources.

It was the hardest thing she felt she had ever done, taking herself off to work that first day, knowing too that she was only on probation until Christmas was over.

She hadn't worked since leaving Cohens. Then she had been young and carefree. She'd had Daisy working with her. She'd also been in England. But here, all on her own in strange employment, in what was suddenly a strange country for all she'd been here three years, her whole body was shaking as she entered the rather old-fashioned boutique. She felt entirely alone. Not only that, but leaving Noelle to Daisy had been the greatest wrench she had ever imagined, greater even than when Langley had gone.

Terrified perhaps for the first time in her life, sick at heart at having to leave Noelle, those deep blue eyes wide with questions at her leaving still etched on her very soul, she stood watching her new employer come towards her.

Madame Flavigny had interviewed her prior to this, but this second meeting was no easier than the first. She was a thin, narrow-faced, middle-aged, formidable woman in sombre black but for several long strings of deep red garnets over her flat bodice. She wore long earrings and the hem of her dress only just cleared her ankles, far longer than the new fashion of hems again below the knee, conveying an impression that hers had never been any shorter than it was now. Slightly greying, but once jet-black hair scraped back from the forehead into a bun, pince-nez clenched a narrow nose over which she peered at Cissy.

Facing this intrepid-looking woman in the quiet interior of this her domain, Cissy took a deep breath and swallowed hard.

'*Je m'appelle* . . . Medemoiselle Farmer,' she faltered, saw the thin lips tighten at her accent. There came a curt nod before turning away, a forefinger crooked over her sharp little black shoulders for her to follow.

'*Veuillez passer par ici*, Mademoiselle.'

Cissy shivered at this her first introduction to her place of work, saw before her a life of bowing and scraping, learning nothing, going nowhere. She wanted to turn and run, to go home – not to Daisy's but really home, to have her mother cuddle her, to see her father smiling at her, to feel Eddie's comforting arm around her waist, but she could only follow as she had been bidden. Oh, God, what a fool she was!

Chapter Eighteen

Madame Flavigny glared over her pince-nez at Cissy. 'With a customer, you will not gaze elsewhere, Mademoiselle Farmer, as though you have no interest in her. From now on you will concentrate your whole attention solely upon my customers and nothing else. Do you understand what I am saying?'

Abashed, Cissy nodded. It wasn't easy to follow Madame Flavigny's terse French when she was angry, but she grasped that in her effort to get the gist of what her customer had been asking – a customer who had immediately gone to complain to the proprieter of the inattentiveness of her staff – she had indeed looked away, but only to see if a clue might present itself as to what the woman required.

Most of her customers she understood. Hearing her English accent, many would out of kindness speak a little slower for her benefit and some seemed to enjoy the experience of being attended by an English woman. Others, however, beset by centuries of resentment of anything English, by tradition deriding their cousins across the Channel, seemed to Cissy to take a delight in speaking even faster so that she must pinpoint all her concentration on what they wanted so as not to provoke Madame Flavigny's displeasure by mistaking what was being asked of her. It seemed no matter what she did it was always wrong.

As months went by she was beginning to comprehend even the fastest talker, with of course the odd hiccup, as now. But try as she might, her accent remained as strong as ever, and this was another bone of contention with some of them.

'This is impossible!' observed one particularly awkward customer, loud enough for the whole shop to hear, when Cissy had been there for just over four months. 'What pleasure is there when being attended to, having to be addressed in such discourteous, crude terms? Where is the proprietor? Why are we being asked to put up with such service?'

Madame Flavigny, with a hard glance towards Cissy, had taken the woman aside, speaking in low urgent tones with a flourish of gestures, the customer nodding and shrugging until served by Madame herself had finally left the premises duly satisfied with a triumphant smirk at the mortified assistant.

'If you cannot speak civilly to my customers,' Madame Flavigny told her afterwards, 'then you had better not speak at all. Merely nod and say as little as possible. Meanwhile, Mademoiselle Farmer, I would advise you to concern yourself more upon learning to speak our language properly during your leisure moments than flitting about enjoying yourself. If you cannot or will not improve yourself, I shall have to dispense with your services.'

Taking the hint, Cissy applied herself to getting her tongue around those French 'r's and correcting her vowel sounds. But it was so hard. There were still those customers whose naturally short tempers or whose day had been less than happy gave them cause to vent themselves upon her as an excuse to let off steam.

'I don't think I can take it much longer,' she told Daisy at the end of June. 'I almost wish she would sack me. Except that I come cheap.'

'What would you do for another job?' Daisy asked, her mind more on pretending to walk a fluffy toy dog for eighteen-month-old Noelle's amusement, while Cissy looked on, her daughter so wrapped up with her friend that Daisy might have been her mother rather than she.

Working six days a week, crowding onto an omnibus or flocking into the Metro for home each evening, seeing so little of Noelle and seeing her turn more and more towards Daisy because she wasn't there, for how much longer could it go on? There was no likelihood of her being shown how a shop was run, being treated more like a general dogsbody. She had gleaned some idea on her own, but she wasn't so sure she would ever make a success of running a shop here in Paris.

'You had enough trouble finding that job,' Daisy continued. 'I'd stick with what you've got.' She wriggled the fluffy toy in Noelle's face. Cissy's heart ached hearing the resultant giddy laugh. 'Apart from that, you haven't got such a bad life here, have you? We do try to make you as happy as possible, me and Teddy.'

'I know you do,' Cissy said, watching her daughter. 'I'm grateful.'

'You don't have to be grateful. I *like* you being here. Me looking after Noelle. Without you both it would be so quiet here. I miss us not going shopping during the week as we used to, of course. Still, I do have Noelle, don't I? I daren't think what I'd do without her.'

Cissy looked sharply at her. She was lately beginning to say things like this in a yearning tone as if she had a wish for a child of her own. She had never said it outright and even scoffed at the idea of being saddled with a family, saying there was lots of time for that. Yet it sometimes sounded when she spoke of Noelle as if she was almost laying claim to her and as though she were filling some need.

'I'll have to leave here one day,' Cissy said now in a strange urge to test her. 'I can't go on living here indefinitely.'

Her test was proving positive. Daisy's brown eyes grew fractionally alarmed. 'You're going to find it hard going to work with her around.'

'I'm going to have to face it sooner or later.'

'Yes, but . . .' Daisy relaxed visibly as if convinced of the weight of her next words. 'Not for ages yet. You couldn't go out at weekends living on your own. And you couldn't afford a nurse for her. Pity you haven't made any friends where you work. Though we do try to make life interesting for you here, don't we?'

It wasn't easy to make friends. At the boutique there was just her and a middle-aged cashier, seemingly chained to her high stool behind the railed cash desk. But Theodore saw to it that she was seldom left out if they went to the theatre, a nurse hired to look after Noelle. Last Saturday, they had visited the Theatre l'Apollo to see the show entitled *Au Temps des Valses* – in London, it was called *Bitter Sweet*. The songs of course were in French: '*Je Vous Reverrai*' – 'I'll See You Again', and '*Abandonnee*' – 'Kiss Me'. Just as lovely to hear, except that her eyes had filled with tears of nostalgia for the dear old London days, listening to reviews and musicals from up in the gods, all she and Daisy could afford then, but such happy days they had been.

On Sundays if the weather was fine, all three, with little Noelle, would eat out, stroll in the Tuileries or by the banks of the Seine; wander around the flea market fingering second-hand and antique wares. Sometimes they would go for a spin into the countryside in Teddy's German Daimler, maybe just to nearby Auteuil racetrack for the steeplechasing where he'd buy them champagne. Sipping hers, Cissy would recall when she had taken such things for granted instead of feeling a hanger-on.

On these occasions, yearning for what had been, became something of an obsession, as did dreaming of great success perhaps in the fashion business. They were just dreams; her dwindling savings viewed with alarm these days. One needed lots more than she had to get started. Theodore might have agreed to help finance her had she asked, but she wasn't prepared to go cap in hand to anyone. But they did torment her so, those dreams, just as her old memories taunted her. Yet she wanted them to taunt and torment – a way of keeping her up to scratch, she supposed.

It was on a whim of recreating those days of opulence the following evening that, instead of going to the Metro after a long day serving customers, she diverted to go and take a peek at the last of the afternoon shoppers in the Rue de Rivoli.

Every shop window looked like a stage in the golden light of the long summer evening, rich women were loading the back of their cars with bright and beautiful parcels and boxes. She knew the drill well: tonight on a man's arm, they would go on to the opera, or to the theatre, maybe to a private bar or a teeming jazz club, a group of black jazz musicians playing the night away – no work for society women to get up for in the morning – while they drank cocktails. Ah, those lovely cocktails.

Langley once told her how the name had come about: a farmer having lost his best fighting cock said whoever found it would have the hand of his daughter in marriage. A toast was drunk to a soldier who had found it, but the girl confused by his good looks mixed up the drinks producing a concoction as motley as the cock's tail, hence cocktail.

Remembering the story she suddenly saw Langley in her mind and the life that could never be hers again. Sick at heart, she turned and ran down the Metro and all the way home, mostly to try to eradicate his face from her mind, or because of it, kept thinking how crucial it had become that she must either get her own shop or else live the rest of her life as nothing more than a shop assistant.

Reaching home, neatly sidestepping an enquiring Daisy as to why she was late, Daisy already giving Noelle her supper, she made for her room to think her thoughts out more clearly before returning to eat her own supper, Daisy by then too occupied with Theodore to ask where she had been.

Her thoughts didn't take long to analyse. With every month that went by, the money was being eaten into – clothes for Noelle, growing so fast, and clothes for herself. The 1929 fashion had come in this summer with hems below the knee again, flowing lines, busts making a gentle reappearance, waists returning, hats with ever larger brims. The shapeless Charleston dress of the last couple of years was gone for good, making last year's clothes already out of date. Still fashion-conscious despite her reduced circumstances, Cissy felt it acutely. She'd have to look chic managing her own shop. But a complete new wardrobe cost money. There must be no more delay or there'd be nothing left to start a shop with. And she was so sick of working for a carping, ungrateful employer.

'I've made up my mind,' she told a concerned Theodore and Daisy when she came to the table. 'If I don't do it now, I never will. So I've decided. I can't see it working here, though. I'd have to compete with Parisians and they've got a head start over me. So I think it might be better for me to go back and start up business in London.'

Theodore regarded her anxiously. 'If you should need advice, you cannot reach us quickly from London. Is it not impractical?'

'And what about Noelle?' Daisy put in, her voice tinged with panic. 'She's used to being here. To uproot her. You'll have your work cut out finding premises *and* looking after her. You've nowhere to live for a start. And we won't be there to help out.'

This dampened her immediate enthusiasm. 'I suppose I could go on my own for a week or so to look for something suitable, and then send for her. Would it be asking too much of you, giving eye to her without me being here?' The moment she said it, she regretted it as relief lit Daisy's face like a bright beam.

'Of course it wouldn't. I'd be only too glad. But you are sure you know what you're doing?'

'I've no option. I have to try before all my money disappears.'

There was a little under six hundred pounds left from what Langley had given her. Working these last nine months had kept it from eroding even further, but down payment on shop accommodation and a couple of rooms to live in would take a great chunk out of it. And there'd still be stock to get. It could leave her stony broke if money didn't come in straight away.

Theodore must have read her thoughts, his handsome sallow face concerned. 'And should you fail? It is so easy – far easier than you would think – for a business to fail, over little things, unforeseen things. And you can so quickly have no money left. But to remember one thing, my dear. If this should happen, which God forbid, we are always here. Money I can find to help you – not to start another business, of course. For if one business fails, another will also, a small proof of unsound business mind. But help there will always be from myself and Daisy should you be in need. No obligation to you at all.'

Tears formed in Cissy's eyes, touched by the warmth and generosity. She swallowed them back before making a fool of herself and smiled bravely. 'Thank you,

Theodore. I intend to make a go of this. But I really do want to thank you . . . thank you both, for everything.'

'Ach!' He shrugged self-consciously, perhaps the only time she had ever seen him do so, as Daisy got up and came around the table to hug her.

'Don't worry, Cissy. Noelle will be fine with me, and before you know it, you'll be on your feet, up and running, and you can come and get her. We might even come over ourselves and see how you are getting on. Oh, Cissy, good luck. Lots and lots of luck.'

She left for England at the beginning of September, her heart full of strange discomfort, a mingling of fear of the future, of sadness at leaving Daisy who had become more like a sister than a friend and an even deeper sadness at having to leave her daughter behind, if only for a few weeks. There was also a pent-up sense of excitement at going back to London, coupled with a certain amount of trepidation knowing her family would be not far away and the likelihood of bumping into them. What would she do if that happened? What would she say? But worse, what if they turned away from her, crossed to the other side of the road to avoid her? She didn't know if they had ever forgiven her, couldn't blame them for not doing so. She saw now the wrong she had done – had seen it for a long time but it had been too late to make amends. And if they had been ready to forgive, would they now, seeing the baby? Evidence of her bad life, as they would see it.

That last night, Theodore opened a bottle of champagne to give a toast to her future success. When Noelle had been put to bed, Cissy had sat telling her a bedtime story until her eyelids closed; for a long while afterwards had stayed just looking at her. The weeks before she would see her again loomed like a lifetime, a gulf, but she had to bear it.

She kissed her, sleeping, the dark eyelashes lying gently on the soft cheeks, the mouth a rosebud, relaxed in sleep. Her child. If hearts break, it felt then that hers was being torn to pieces. It was harder wrenching herself away in the quiet stillness of her daughter's room than ever it was the following morning with everyone talking at once. Daisy kissing her, Theodore warmly shaking her hand and that one last cuddle for Noelle before handing her back to Daisy.

Going up the gangway of the cross-Channel steamer, turning again and again to wave, careless of getting in other passengers' way, her eyes trained on the small figure of Noelle, her heart breaking anew, it felt more as though she were going to Australia for ever and ever than merely to England, twenty miles across a strip of water.

The steamer pulled away, she waved until the three figures merged with all the other figures. She watched, straining her eyes at the diminishing docks of Calais becoming a bluish blur indistinguishable from the rest of the French coastline, the coast itself finally lost from view in the faint midday mist over the sea. Finally, with nothing more to see, she turned to seek somewhere to sit.

She thought of that other trip across the Channel, going to France, then an adventure, a bubbling of excitement, so sure of herself, of her life with Langley, surrounded by his friends – yes, *his* friends, not hers. Now she was going back, alone. She couldn't remember ever feeling so alone. Huddled in a chair she watched the sea, the midday haze lying grey upon it so that there seemed no horizon, the sun having to struggle to get through, an orbless light, nothing more, and for all the air was warm, Cissy shivered.

Eddie had three tugs now, business going well these last three years, so well it sometimes took his breath away.

Sitting in his office during a rare quieter moment, Eddie smiled grimly thinking how much he could have offered Cissy had she stayed with him. He still thought of her from time to time and it still hurt when he did, but as with most things the edges had blunted a little, worn by the passing of time.

He and Alf, his father, seldom went on the tugs now. Their work was in their office, over a Millwall warehouse: one cluttered room, a reception area, a gents toilet, a ladies one for a typist-cum-receptionist and a filing clerk. Alf was happy enough, feeling the need to sit back at his age, but Eddie sometimes pined for the estuary breeze on his face, the salty tang of the sea flowing up past Southend, that morning cuppa in the wheelhouse, the bump of a tug's bow nudging against a big ship's hull, the feel of a hawser on his palms. He had others to manage the tugs while he sat here dictating letters to a typist not long out of high school and still hesitant with her shorthand, or negotiated with clients on the phone until his ear felt like a ripe tomato. But sometimes he could make his escape, go up along the river for a few miles, savouring memories of the old days on the Thames. It always struck him as odd that where he'd once dreamed of owning a business, doing nothing but sit in a warm office on wet days, now that he had all that, it felt that something had been lost along the way; a feeling of indifference to what he'd achieved that seemed all wrong when he recalled those dreams.

There had been little time just lately to go dreaming up along the river. Work was pouring in, charter work, his tugs towing the big lighters containing the spoil from the Tilbury Docks for the Dutch reclamation scheme on the marshes, an ongoing job bringing in substantial fees; helping to manoeuvre the big boats through dock entrances, salvage accounting for a good income too, he was even toying with the idea of a fourth tug – a real fleet – in time a business every bit as big as Watkins Ltd.

Bobby Farmer worked for him now, a godsend, worked flat out, doing all the overtime he could get. From what he said, he and Ethel lived a precarious married life. She hadn't consented to a divorce and still clung to him like the proverbial shit to a blanket. Not only did he have to keep her and his daughter, but he also felt obliged to send some of his earnings to support his bastard across the river; to keep the mother quiet, Eddie assumed, sending the money through the post hoping she might one day get married to someone and release him from his debt. It was plain that Bobby had no love for the boy; had never seen him and called him a little bloodsucker. Yet his own daughter Jean whom he could hardly provide for after supporting a love child, he doted on, Eddie thought, probably compensating for a nagging, unloving wife.

He stopped doodling on his blotting pad as the phone jangled. It was his marine insurance company about the present cover on the *Cicely*, now that she'd had a refit. The phone replaced, another ring, this time an agent – a firm wishing to charter a tug to assist in several days submarine cable-laying off Lowestoft. Another call, a tug to take up scrap from an obsolete warship being broken up: £60 a day here. OK, fine. Meantime, the salvage money was coming in, Eddie could see his business leaping from strength to strength; the purchase of another tug was a distinct possibility. He already had his eye on one, a good vessel, practically new. He'd see about it next week. It was October 1929, in two months, 1930, a new era. Nothing could stop him now.

Something could, though he and thousands like him that October didn't realise it. Three weeks into October, a drama began unfolding in New York's financial market, a bull market, which had speculators rushing to make quick profits from industrial stocks which were more than doubling in value. Banks were lending out billions of dollars to brokers trading on the New York Stock Market. Then suddenly the bottom dropped out, rocking financiers with a quake destined to send tremors around the world. The *Brooklyn Daily Eagle* bore headlines: 'Wall St in Panic as Stocks Crash.'

In London, Eddie, who didn't take the *Brooklyn Daily Eagle,* read it in the London papers only after he'd put a down payment on his fourth tug. Even then he and his father didn't realise the repercussions the rush to sell shares would have on his business.

Cissy gazed around the empty shop. It probably wasn't as bad as it looked. Clear away all the debris, the splintered wooden boxes, the scattered and screwed-up sheets of newspaper, the old broken chair in one corner, the bundle of old rags in the other and the stack of unusable shelving. The ceiling and dirty blue walls repainted, a few renovated counters put in with the minimum of expense, she hoped, nice drapes, cheap but cheerful and before you know it . . .

At first it had been hopeless finding premises. There were places, but all in the wrong areas. Her dream of a nice little boutique in the West End with Madame Fermier painted above it to add a touch of French, she perhaps lapsing into French to her customers to overawe them as they entered her bright but tasteful premises, had faded weeks ago. There was no way in which she could afford anything near the West End, and she had finally settled for this place in Bethnal Green Road – a nice wide road with lots of shoppers even if it was tatty, with paper flying about all over the place with every slight puff of wind. In a week or two she would be trading, she hoped, and then she'd be able to send for Noelle.

There had been no hope of going back for Noelle. Last week, hot on the heels of her letter saying she had put a down payment on this place, Daisy came over to visit, bringing Noelle with her. But seeing the state of the premises, the peeling wallpaper of the two rooms and kitchen above it, the lack of decent toilet facilities, Daisy was appalled.

'You can't bring her up here! Good God, Cissy, she'll catch all sorts of germs and things. She's never been used to this . . . this . . . squalor. Oh, Cissy, I shall have to take her back with me for a few weeks more. You have to get sorted out before she can come here, you must know that.'

Of course she knew it. But she did so want Noelle with her and her heart plummeted even as she acknowledged that she knew it was true.

'You'll come over again, though, won't you.' she questioned urgently as Daisy made ready to leave the next morning after a miserable night spent trying to fit her and Noelle into her one bedroom, the two of them sharing her single bed while she slept in the sagging armchair that went with the rented accommodation.

Daisy had given the box-like living room a dubious look. 'It's not the most savoury place to bring a child. Not only that, but I daren't ask Teddy to pay for another trip over. Things aren't what they were. I've never known anything to change so drastically for us.'

'How do you mean?' Cissy said, alarmed.

'Since that Wall Street business,' she explained, as together they went downstairs towards the shop for Daisy to take her leave. 'Teddy's finding it hard. He lost a good deal of investments over that. Thank God he had the luck to sell quite a lot of his shares just before it happened. More luck than we imagined at the time. He had some big deal or other, you see. He needed to cash in a lot of shares and things – I don't understand it that much – but I don't know where we'd be now if circumstances hadn't made him do it when he did. We're the lucky ones. The papers say some investors hanged themselves or jumped off high buildings in New York. Literally thousands have lost whole fortunes, have nothing left – not a bean. I saw a picture in one of the American papers showing someone trying to sell a Daimler for just a hundred dollars. Can you imagine? And he still apparently couldn't get anyone to buy it. Isn't it just terrible to come down to that?

'But now, of course, Teddy's having to work much harder and keep his head screwed on the right way.

Businesses need finance but they're having to tighten their belts. And so is he. He's worried about taking chances, the climate being what it is now. No one's got any money. Strange how it suddenly disappeared like that. *Someone* must have it all. I thought it would all blow over by now, after three months. But it just keeps getting worse. So I can't really keep popping over.'

Cissy glowered. After all, Noelle was *her* child. 'I'd come there if I didn't have to get this place in order.'

'Will you be able to cope?' Daisy asked, watching the two-year-old Noelle toddling around amid the rubbish on the floor. 'There's a lot to be done here. Have you got enough money left for it?'

'I'll manage,' Cissy said tersely. Daisy hadn't seen the light.

Daisy nodded. 'I wish we could pay for you to come over, but as I said, funds are a bit tight at present.'

Cissy remained silent. So much for the help Theodore had offered whenever she might need it.

'And anyway,' Daisy prattled on, 'you've got your work cut out here for a while, haven't you? Perhaps later on when you're settled and the money starts coming in.'

'And Noelle?'

'I don't mind looking after her for as long as you want. She's no trouble. I'm sure things will settle themselves, and then when you've got this place nice and shipshape and you're up and running, she'll be able to settle down here. She goes to kindergarten a couple of times a week now, you know. Didn't I tell you in my last letter? She started at the local *école* which has a sort of créche attached for little ones her age. She's already beginning to pick up French.'

It was like listening to a mother singing the praises of her daughter and Cissy wanted suddenly to scream at her that she was the mother, not Daisy. But Daisy seemed so blithe about it all, and she had been a great help in times of need, so how could she jump down her throat now? She was tired, that was all, worn out by searching for somewhere to live, to trade; most of the time thoroughly despondent, unable to think straight. And now she'd found something it was like some sort of reaction had set in, making her more downhearted than exhilarated. It wasn't Daisy's fault.

'I'll see her soon then.' She smiled, leaned forward and kissed Noelle. 'I'll see you in a little while, my love,' and was startled by Noelle leaning away from her as if a stranger had kissed her.

Chapter Nineteen

'Miss Farmer, isn't it?'

On her way along Bethnal Green Road in search of a brief lunchtime snack, Cissy turned sharply, instantly on the alert at the sound of her name called. Her eyes grew guarded as the full figure bore down upon her through the spring sunshine like a ship in full sail, except that it was attired in rusty black despite the fine weather.

Collecting herself, Cissy managed a smile but Madam Noreah was already on course for a joyful reunion, as she took a deep preparatory breath her immense bosom swelled to even greater size.

'My goodness, what a surprise seeing you, my dear. I said to myself when I noticed you on the other side of the road, "That must be young Miss Farmer, whom I used to teach elocution." But how you've changed, my dear. It must be . . . why, several years since I last saw you. After all this time. How are you, my dear?'

'I'm . . . fine, thank you,' Cissy stuttered, non-committal.

'How nice. Where have you been keeping yourself? I remember you left my lessons so suddenly. I did wonder what had happened, but the young lady who used to come with you to my lessons – Daisy something, wasn't it? such a lovely singing voice she had – said you had gone abroad suddenly. I hoped it was for something nice rather than nasty. She left too, you know. To seek success with opera, but I heard she went in the chorus of some musical or other. Such a pity. Such a waste of talent. But there . . . How very fashionable you look. You must have been successful in life after all. Are you here on a visit?'

'No.' Forced into a reply, Cissy just hoped she could sidestep the woman and be away with the minimum of explanation.

'Oh, you are here permanently. What are you doing with yourself these days?'

'I . . . Please excuse me, Madam Noreah. I have to be on my way. I'm late for an appointment. It was nice to have met you again. I'm sorry it has to be so brief a meeting.'

The large face, even more flabby than she remembered, beamed at her, Cissy's excuses not even scoring a glancing blow. 'I'm so glad you still speak beautifully – that you have not forgotten all I tried to impress upon you. One feels quite gratified to know one's efforts have been rewarded. I do so trust it stood you in good stead, my dear. By your appearance . . .' she surveyed Cissy's light blue dress and smart jacket, painfully bought with a little of her fast-vanishing money. 'I would say it has. Indeed so.'

Cissy resigned herself to being polite until she could decently make her escape. 'Are you still teaching, Madam Noreah?' Best to keep off the subject of herself.

The heavy features sagged a little. She looked old and sad. 'Alas, no. It became too much for me, my dear. One reaches a stage . . .' There was a huge sigh, the vast pregnant-looking bosom heaving beneath the ancient voluminous black coat. 'I had to abandon my poor cats, you know. A very kind neighbour promised to look after some of them, and I found homes for three more, but the rest, the cats' home, I'm afraid. I dread to visualise their fate. But I am consoled that I did my best for them while they lived, and many of them were, I think, approaching their time to leave this mortal coil, as the Bard would say. I have one now, to keep me company, a young creature I suspect will outlast me . . .'

'Oh, Madam Noreah!' Cissy cried in real emotion, but the elderly woman smiled.

'I am quite content as things stand. One cannot go on for ever, and my *health* remains good. It is but the ravages of time that plague us who have grown old. I can view my life with some satisfaction.'

Now was time to make her escape as a sixth sense began to denote the conversation threatening to return to herself. 'I really do have to go, Madam Noreah,' she exclaimed. 'I shall be so late.'

'Of course, my dear.' Madam Noreah came out of her reverie. 'I mustn't stop you.'

'It *was* nice meeting you.'

'Yes, indeed. And mutually so. Well, goodbye, my dear. We may meet again. Who knows.'

'Who knows,' Cissy echoed, grateful to be off. 'Goodbye, then.'

'Goodbye, my dear. And be happy.'

Smiling her own good wishes, Cissy went her way, but on a whim turned to glance back at the ample figure before the lunchtime crowds swallowed it up. She saw an old woman who in her day had enjoyed a full life, if not in fine operatic parts, then with opera's celebrities, rubbing shoulders with them at opera houses, parties; no doubt once a vital young woman with peaches and cream complexion and vibrant shining hair (what colour, Cissy could not begin to know) and a bounce in her step, now reduced to a black-clad figure with bulging chest, hair grey rats' tails. Her lonely life was now no more than scrapbooks, faded photo albums and a jumble of fuzzy memories. But she had her cat.

Feeling strangely sad, Cissy watched her go. Such an ending to all that life – it could come to anyone. The thought brought a disquieting shiver which she hurriedly shrugged off – too close to home – and she turned abruptly away, heading towards the little Jewish shop that did those delicious hot salt beef sandwiches. A couple of those would soon dispel that last dismal thought.

Nibbling her sandwich between sips of tea at the back of her shop, she thought again of Madam Noreah and hoped that the chance meeting would go no further. If news of her reached her family's ears – but that was silly. Who would her old elocution teacher ever meet who would remotely know Cissy Farmer? Nor had she given Madam Noreah any clue as to where she lived. She was safe enough.

Brushing away the crumbs and finishing her last drop of tea, she got up and went back into the shop – she had dispensed with the word boutique, no one in England quite knowing what it meant, and simply called it The

Haberdashery Shop – to turn the 'Closed' notice around to 'Open' and unlock the door for afternoon customers.

After her initial efforts these past couple of months trying to entice ordinary East End housewives, or even shop girls, into thinking Paris fashion, she finally realised the error of her ways. Young women working in the West End shopped in the West End and nowhere else, and the ordinary housewife sought more serviceable hats than the stunning ones Cissy had been displaying in her window. In fact such hats merely frightened off the ordinary housewife. Paris fashion hats were ignored.

Slowly she'd been forced to lower her sights, removing her two fine jardinieres of flowers in her window and the half-dozen tastefully arranged Parisian hats on the stands the jardinieres framed. Instead she hung a dozen plain serviceable hats on hooks, giving over the rest of the window to things people around here would buy: scarves, gloves, socks, stockings, handkerchieves; knitting wool, knitting needles and patterns; crochet cotton, crochet hooks and patterns.

Inside she rearranged the counters and shelves more modestly to hold humbler displays. In truth it was now a wool shop cum haberdasher's and customers began coming in. There were always women who needed to mend and knit and darn, with a bit of cotton crochet thrown in to brighten up an impoverished home. She began to show a profit, though nothing like the one she'd first visualised so confidently. If the tiny profit kept the wolf from the door it certainly didn't swell her savings or even help decorate the upstairs accommodation as she'd have liked; certainly it didn't allow for trips over to Paris to see her daughter, and that was the worst of it.

Daisy had paid another visit last month but after a good sit-down discussion, Cissy had agreed to her taking Noelle back with her 'just for a little while longer', as Daisy put it.

Madam Noreah took it on herself to pay her old neighbour a visit, the one who had kindly taken in some of her cats, just to see if she had kept her promise to give eye to them, the poor strays.

She was gratified to see that she had, although, unlike in her day, they were fed outside and occupied a somewhat tumbledown shed in the back yard.

'At least they're out of the rain,' the woman defended, as she and Madam Noreah sat at the kitchen table over a cup of tea and, after her visitor had given a little sigh, went on to ask how she was faring.

'I get by,' Madam Noreah told her with a small shrug of her black cotton-draped shoulders, the hot August sunshine making no difference to her penchant for black. 'It is a struggle making do on what little savings I have. I am glad of my pension, small as it is.'

Her neighbour nodded, watching her own accent in the face of those beautifully rounded vowels so at odds with the shapeless black figure, scuffed handbag, tatty hat and unkempt, dusty grey hair of her visitor.

'Don't you miss giving lessons? I expect the money came in handy.'

'It did indeed. But I cannot sustain it now. Age, you know.'

'I remember your pupils coming and going. That piano of yours going it, and them scales they used to sing. Went on for hours, it did. But of course, I didn't mind really. D'you ever see any of your old pupils these days?'

'Alas no. Young people forget. It is as though a tutor ceases to be once the lessons are done, the time gone by, the pupil grown. Though I did bump into one young woman, a pupil of mine, in Bethnal Green Road. Some two months ago, or was it three? Time has no meaning when there is nothing to fill one's day. It was so gratifying to discover that what I had taught her at the time had been an asset to her, her diction still perfect.'

'Who'd that be then?' asked her neighbour, gulping her tea.

'A Miss Farmer. Lived in Canning Town, but eventually went to live in France, so I was told at the time by her friend – another pupil. To have a pupil of mine who had done so well for herself in a foreign country is most gratifying. She has returned to England and was looking very prosperous when I met her.'

'I've got a sister in Canning Town – Ruscoe Road. You'd think this Farmer pupil you had would've found lessons nearer where she lived.'

'I pride myself that my pupils considered it worth their while to travel any distance to me,' Madam Noreah put in, irked that her talents were in question. Her cup and saucer back onto the table, she made ready to take her leave. She had only come to satisfy herself that the welfare of her little strays was not in jeopardy, not to discuss her business. She didn't think she'd be paying her former neighbour a second visit.

Intrigued by one of Madam Noreah's pupils from Canning Town having done so well as to live in France, the neighbour mentioned it to her sister a month later in passing, her vernacular more comfortable with her sister than it had been with Madam Fanny Adams as she scathingly called her.

'Farmer?' echoed her sister, immediately attentive. 'Would that be Cissy Farmer? 'Er what went off to go abroad, walked out I was told, wivvout a word to 'er mum an' dad. Just walked out. I wouldn't 'ave known about them except it was talked about in the shop up the corner at the time. They tried to keep it quiet, but you know what people are like. Bit of good gossip. I wonder if they're still livin' there?'

The telephone on Eddie's desk rang. His father sighed and got up to go over to the vacant desk. Eddie was skippering one of the tugs himself these days, things getting tighter by the minute. World depression was biting everyone since the Wall Street affair last year. The fourth tug they'd bought that very week had sold at a loss; they were now seriously thinking of getting rid of another one, leaving just two. They'd had to let its skipper go, he taking it with a look of bleak desperation on his face – with over two million unemployed now, there were no jobs to be had.

Eddie skippered now. Even though it would have saved another wage, Alf felt himself too old to go back on the river, contending with its tides and currents and God knows what else. He felt too old for a lot of things lately. He wasn't old by any standard, just that he couldn't stop worrying where the business would end up, and that was enough to make anyone feel old.

He worried too about this pain in his chest when doing anything strenuous after resting. Indigestion maybe. On the other hand . . . He'd have to see the quack at some time, see what it really was. Probably the worry of the business, every penny sunk into it and less and less work coming in. Getting him down that's what it was.

Eddie didn't help. This question of getting rid of that third tug; Alf felt it should be the *Cicely*. She'd soon be needing new engines and a big hull overhaul, but with no money, it was out of the question.

'She's not powerful enough for big jobs,' he'd argued, but Eddie wouldn't hear of getting rid of her.

'I just need to see the bank,' he'd said. 'They'd give us a loan on security of the other two. No trouble.' He wouldn't hear Alf's solid argument that loans have to be paid back, and from what?

He clung to the *Cicely* as though she were that Farmer girl herself after whom he'd named her, the silly bugger. Still hankering after her, he was hanging on to some floating tub past her working days.

'Throwing good money after bad, better she went for scrap,' Alf had told him and had watched the look on his face as though a mother had been told to give away her baby. He manned that tub all the time now, hanging on to it like it was a lover, really acting like some silly sod, and that was putting it mildly.

Reaching across the desk for the jangling telephone, his thoughts still on his foolish son, he announced: 'Bennett's Towage Company!'

'Mr Bennett? It's Bobby Farmer. Is Eddie there?'

'No. Sorry.' They had laid Bobby off in the early part of the year. It had been hard to do, the man needing to keep working, like them all. Eddie had felt guilty about it but it had been imperative to lay off several at the time.

Of necessity, Bobby being extra to their needs had sadly been one of them. Keep only who you could afford was today's motto. 'Can I give him a message?'

There was a long pause, then, 'Look, Mr Bennett, I'm not sure if I should really speak to him. I've been worrying about it and I know I should at least say something. But now I'm not sure.'

'What is it you don't want to speak to him about?' Alf felt a grin come into his tone, but Bobby's remained deadly serious.

'It's like this. My mother met someone when she was out shopping the other day. I don't know how true this is, but I still think Eddie ought to know – if *you* think he should, of course.'

'What should he know?' Bobby was being silly and Alf was getting rattled.

'It's this woman me mum met. She said my sister – you know, Cissy – she was seen in Bethnal Green Road, a couple of months back, I think.'

'A couple of months?'

'Me mum's only just 'eard. Someone told this woman that Cissy is living there. Me mum's really upset.'

'So you thought you'd upset my Eddie too.'

'I just thought . . .'

'Look 'ere,' Alf cut in, his amusement long disappeared. 'It's been over between them two for a long time. It's all done and finished with and I don't want 'im upset all over again. I think it's best he don't know anything about what your mother was told.'

'But that's what's worrying me, Mr Bennett. He'll know sooner or later and when he finds out that I knew, that everyone knows except 'im . . . Well, it just ain't fair. I think he should be given the benefit of knowin' before everyone else. I was worried about being the first one to tell 'im and I'm glad it was you answered the phone. I've got a clear conscience now. So, if it's all right with you, Mr Bennett, I'll leave it to you to tell 'im, shall I? If you think it's right. Sorry to've rung to tell you. I 'ope it was okay? No jobs going, I suppose?'

No, sadly there weren't any jobs going. Alf put the phone down rather too sharply and sat staring at its black bulk on the desk as though it might tell him what to do now, the brow of his narrow, weather-worn face creased in dilemma, Bobby's parting plea for a job occupying not the tiniest corner of his mind.

Eddie came into the office around seven that evening looking weary, up since four-thirty that morning; dark starting work, dark finishing.

'How'd it go today?' were Alf's first words, testing the air.

Eddie grinned, dropping his cap and choker on the desk top and himself in the well-worn swivel chair which until lately had been his domain, twisting it round to look up at his father.

'Bit of a heavy day, but a bit of luck too, thanks to the weather.'

A force seven had been blowing all day, driving low grey clouds and squally rain before it, the river choppy as the North Sea, though Alf saw very little of it from the filmy yellowing windows of the office, thanking his lucky stars on a day like this that he was warm and dry.

On the *Cicely* Eddie would have had a hard day, him as skipper, his crew, mate, engineer, fireman, and a lad doing all the mundane work as well as making tea – buckets of tea to cheer them all up, huddled in the cabin between jobs, out of the rain. Still, despite the filthy weather, Eddie did look pleased with himself.

'What bit of luck?' Alf prompted.

'Salvage.'

All ears now, his father saw a ray of hope glinting on Bennett's Towage Company's horizon. 'How big?'

'Big enough. Freighter in collision with another ship. Ruddy great hole in her side. We got a rope to 'er and towed 'er ashore at Bugsby Hole. Stayed and pumped 'er out till the PLA came and took over.'

His father's eyes dubious now. 'She took it okay, the *Cicely*?'

'Why not? She's a good workhorse despite what you think of her. She responded well today.'

There was no quenching Eddie's triumph, his pride, and something as near to love as a man might show the woman of his dreams. Seeing it, Alf frowned. Still associating his first ever tug with a continuing hope of one day claiming Cissy Farmer for his own. The dilemma came back to him – should he tell Eddie about her brother's phone call? He decided not, at least not yet – not while Eddie was looking so mighty pleased with himself.

Cissy was no good for him. He'd be better off without her. Even so, as Bobby had said, he'd find out eventually. But there was time enough to tell him. Meanwhile, giving it a few weeks, he would hike down to Bethnal Green and do a bit of reconnoitering. And depending upon what he found, then would be the time to tell Eddie what he had heard.

*

By mid-November, nothing had been heard. Alf breathed a sigh of relief, glad that he'd said nothing to Eddie. It had probably been just a rumour anyway. But he was still determined to find out for himself.

It was nearly Christmas before he finally got round to taking himself to Bethnal Green. There was too much else on his mind, Eddie was talking again of getting the *Cicely* up to scratch on the salvage reward she'd made – it was all Alf could do to stop him spending it all in one go.

The money had been a godsend. No need to go cap in hand to banks. The Dutchman had been carrying cargo worth some three hundred thousand pounds. The reward had come to around two and a half thousand, enough to get all three tugs in good order, pay three crews' wages for a few months, plus a good cut for each of the *Cicely*'s crew, the largest to the engineer, then the mate, the fireman, and finally the deck boy. It did Alf's heart good to see that young lad's face as he received his six pounds ten shillings – a fortune compared to his weekly wage of one pound ten shillings, and enough, the boy had announced happily, to buy the bike he'd always wanted. As well as all that, the office lighting and heating bills and a little of the rent had been taken care of for a while and there was still something left in the bank.

Eddie's answer to his father's argument that doing up the *Cicely* was just making a silk purse from a sow's ear, was that winter might see more salvage jobs as good as that. It took quite a few heated arguments to explain that with the Depression still biting hard, every tug owner large or small on the lookout for work, he was counting chickens too soon.

By mid-December Eddie had settled down a little, allowing Alf to think once more about finding out if Cissy Farmer really was living in Bethnal Green. If she was, then she had to be down on her beam ends in some squalid rooming house. Why else would she come back to England if she wasn't broke? No doubt she'd been let down by whoever she'd gone off with. It served her bloody well right as far as Alf was concerned. But he didn't only want to find her in order to gloat, but to warn her against any possible thought of coming whining back to Eddie in hope of him baling her out, which Eddie would do at the drop of a hat, even now, if his father knew him – the silly sod.

In a biting wind on the Saturday afternoon prior to Christmas, leaving Eddie to mind the shop as it were, he took a tuppenny tram ride and with his long spare frame huddled inside his overcoat, began the long walk from the Victoria Park end of the road to the Shoreditch end. He passed shops with sprinkling of Christmas decorations in their windows; busy stalls under whose flapping canvas awnings acetylene lamps hissed and swayed in the cold wind, casting wavering stark-white light over shoppers and stallholders; varying smells – the stale-blood whiff of meat and chickens out on counters for half a day, the salt tang of fish, the sharp one of oranges and apples and the warm sugary smell of toffee kneaded by hand, stretched to unbelievable lengths on hooks and twisted together into colourful sticks ready for cutting with huge scissors into pillow-like lumps ready for sale. There was the savoury aroma of cooked pies, pork dripping, saveloys and meat faggots from the pork butcher's on the corner of Wilmot Street. And all to the hubbub of everyone out doing last minute shopping for the weekend.

How he expected to find Cissy Farmer was anyone's guess. Odder things happen, he told himself, though by the time he'd gone halfway, he had begun to question what he was doing. Then a name over a small green and white painted shop made him pause: Fermier Paris Fashions half-obliterated while beneath, in more positive lettering, The Haberdashery Shop. Why he should connect this with the name Farmer he wasn't sure, but he peered in through the door. The interior was bright against the dark outside, and the shop was busy. But he supposed women would always haunt shops selling knitting wool. Nothing to do with Cissy Farmer.

He chuckled to himself at the thought that it could ever be. A slim young woman had come to the counter to help a customer select some skeins of blue wool. Holding them up to the light for the customer to better judge, her face flooded by light turned towards him.

She hadn't noticed him standing there beyond the ring of brightness but to him that face under the light was clearly recognisable. Smiling and prosperous, that face was enjoying a good trade. A bolt of disbelief and anger snatched at his chest. Prosperous. The woman who'd walked out on his son had done well for herself, while Eddie had spent his time struggling, watching a business he'd worked so hard to make a go of slowly spiralling downward, despite their salvage money those couple of months back.

He could hardly breathe for anger. It actually hurt, his arm a heavy ache. Blasted indigestion. In his hurry to be away from the office he had bolted the fish and chips Eddie had brought in with him.

He stood there, his fury hardly to be borne, ready to stride into the shop to confront her. But something more urgent was replacing fury. The cold biting into his chest, he'd seek shelter for a moment or two from the painfully bitter wind, then return to face her. He went on a few yards, felt himself begin to stagger and then to pitch forward with the increased pain, had a vague impression of people coming to his aid . . .

Chapter Twenty

Eddie sat in his office. He'd had to get out of the house, leaving his mother with his father's relations – all the kin she had in the world and they merely in-laws. If only she'd been able to have more children. It would have been a comfort to her. But even he, her only child, was no comfort, running out like he had when she most needed him. But he'd had to get away for an hour or two.

Now, in the darkened office, the moon glinting off the black river to throw a thin pale light across the ceiling, he sat almost savouring the empty sensation of knowing his father was no longer here.

All over Christmas they had sat by his side in the London Hospital, gazing at his quiet grey face and closed eyes, then at the bare cream walls of the ward and the half-drawn green curtains around the bed while doctors and nurses came and went. Once or twice his eyes opened. Recognising his loved ones, the lips twitched faintly. On one occasion he had spoken, his deep voice rasping, a whisper. Eddie and his mother had simultaneously bent forward to catch the words . . .

'Cissy . . . Bethnal Green . . .'

Nothing more had passed his father's lips and on Boxing Day he had passed quietly away.

It was only now that Eddie thought again of the rasped whisper. To the very last his father had thought of him, his happiness, a wish for it, that one day he would find it – God bless him . . .

Tears filled Eddie's eyes, and in the loneliness of his office, he bent his head into his arm on the desk where his father would usually have sat, and gave himself up to the emptiness inside him.

In her little living room above the shop, Cissy sat re-reading Daisy's letter that had come with her Christmas card. It was New Year's Eve, the shop shut that little bit earlier, but no one about to celebrate this last day of 1930 as yet. After a dinner of whatever had been left from Christmas, the food stretched to last all week, the stew of chicken bones and giblets getting thinner and thinner with more vegetables being added, the last bit of Christmas pudding with custard and what was left of any nuts there had been, the streets would soon come alive with people going off to parties, to relations, or to renew acquaintance with parents and family they'd seen only the week before. For her there would be no family to celebrate with.

Cissy lifted her eyes from the letter to glance towards the scuffed oak sideboard at the tiny card from Noelle that had been included in Daisy's card, the words 'Happy Christmas, Mummy', written in Daisy's hand, though there had been three elongated, uneven, very shaky Xs – her daughter's personal kisses to her. Not that they could mean much to a little girl who had seen her mother only twice this year.

Cissy let her thoughts dwell on her daughter. At least she called Daisy auntie and not mummy. She called *her* mummy, but what did the name mean to her? What was in a name? It was feelings that counted; love and affection, and that she must show her Auntie Daisy more than her, being constantly with her.

The last time Daisy had come over, Noelle had clung to her, holding her hand, hanging back from any move Cissy made towards her. She had allowed herself to be sat on her lap but after a while had wriggled off and gone to play on the other side of the tiny living room. They had taken a bus ride up West and had gone to Hyde Park for her to play, and it was plain the child had been happy feeding the ducks and swans on the Serpentine with the bread Cissy had brought along, running back to her for more: 'More, Mummy! More b'ead, Mummy!' as though she really did understand what mummy meant in that sense of belonging.

But when they had arrived back home, she had once again hung back from any contact with Cissy, quietly leaning against Daisy as though for protection.

It had been an entirely wrong move to come back to England without her, she knew that now, whatever Daisy might say about unwholesome surroundings and lack of constant attention with her having to work all the time. She could of course demand her back any time she wanted, but she knew it would be considered senseless. Yet the longer she left it, the harder it would become to ask for her back. Yet again, Daisy was right – what did she have to offer her?

To give her her due, Daisy wrote every two weeks, usually enclosing photos of Noelle, photos that always made Cissy's heart die a little to see how fast she was growing, how lovely, how happy.

Strangely enough, when she was working down in the shop, she hardly thought of her and often found it hard to believe she was a mother. Her life was so solo, it often felt strange to think that one day she would have her daughter here and couldn't imagine how her life would be then.

Cissy bent her head to read on. She had read the letter through the moment it had arrived, but with her simple meal for one eaten, a couple of sausages, baked beans and mashed potato, and the couple of dishes washed up, there was little else to do.

Daisy's other news these days tended to be a little glum. It seemed unfair, she wrote: people read in the newspapers how terrible unemployment was in America, England, Germany – especially in Germany – but apart from French newspapers, there was little said about how badly France was doing. As if other countries apart from those three hardly existed. Reading it, Cissy couldn't help feeling how continental Daisy had become; hardly ever a sigh for England and her old life. But then, why should she? She was happy with her life, with her Theodore, with Noelle.

Perhaps not so happy, though. The letter, like her others, bemoaned the lack of a child of her own, said they were trying hard but still nothing had happened. Teddy, she said, didn't seem as disappointed as her, but he had his own troubles. His business wasn't at all buoyant these days and he was feeling very down; he had found a sudden yearning to go back to Germany, constantly sighing for his homeland, Depression or no Depression. He seemed so unsettled now in France and said he'd feel more at home with his own countrymen – kept talking of visiting his father's grave and putting a stone on it, the way Jewish people did on their loved ones' graves. 'A bit morbid if you ask me,' Daisy wrote, 'after all these years not bothering.' But she did fancy the idea of going to live in Germany. 'I've never been anywhere except France,' she continued. 'I'd like to see more of the Continent, and Teddy says once we're settled in Dusseldorf, we might have a holiday in Austria or Switzerland, but that depends on how his business picks up of course.'

And take Noelle with them, Cissy thought bitterly, lifting her eyes from Daisy's exuberant pen. Her daughter would share this New Year's Eve with them as she had shared every other one. Noelle should be with her – just the two of them here together. But what chance had she? Life was all skimp and scrape, the last of her savings gone into her shop and little of the profits she had hoped for coming in.

Such were the dreams of the dreamers, she thought bitterly as she poured herself a small measure of whisky saved from a half-bottle she had been hanging on to for months for this evening. No matter how down on one's luck, the New Year had to be toasted with something in the hope for better times, even by those celebrating on their own and with little to show for all their hard work, like herself.

Every day she had to watch people looking at her window, debating if their money would stretch to that nice hat, those warm gloves, that fine wool scarf. But if they came in it was for a box of pins or a spool of cotton. That sort of thing brought in small profit, her initial stock of fashionable hats gathering dust at the rear of the shop and her hopes of bringing Noelle back or even visiting her as far away as ever.

Her only consolation had been sending her Christmas present to her, a big fluffy teddy bear for which she hadn't begrudged dipping into what little profit she had made this year. All her money seemed to be going on sending little gifts for Noelle so she would be constantly reminded of her mother, the rest on keeping up her own appearance. Looking at her, people saw a successful woman, but appearances were deceptive. If only they knew how she watched every window-shopper.

Christmas shoppers, of course, were an exception, but she was acutely aware of the wrong impression it gave everyone, as though she were rolling in dough. After the holidays, with another long year of belt-tightening ahead, it would be back to seeing them gazing longingly into shop windows, pinched faces reflecting the wish that there was money enough to buy even the cheapest of luxuries. These days there was seldom enough to buy essentials. It reflected on the shop owner too. On everyone. In some ways she could count herself lucky she supposed, but it still didn't enable her to bring Noelle back here, not yet.

Placing her drink on the sideboard ready for midnight, she turned on the knob of the oval-topped, fret-fronted wireless bought second-hand. As soft dance-band music issued forth, she sank into her armchair by the coal fire letting the soothing rhythm of music wash over her, and wondered what Daisy and Theodore would be doing tonight. Were they staying quietly at home, Noelle already in bed, leaving them to see the old year out, or had they engaged a nurse for her while they went out on the town to mix with the crowds making merry in Paris? Once she had been part of all that. But that was all over now . . .

She awoke with a start, almost on instinct that the New Year must be nigh. Outside her window she could hear East Londoners making ready in their own way: slurred singing, girls squealing, young boys calling cheekily to them; across the road in one of the flats above the shops a party was going on, the sash window up, despite the cold night air, to let out some of the heat and fug of close-packed bodies all smoking and drinking; old tunes thumped out of a piano, raucous voices singing away to them.

The strokes of 1931 made themselves heard on Cissy's wireless set. She got up and picked up her whisky from the sideboard in readiness, counted the strokes: one, two, three, four. 'Fer the Sake of Ole Lang Syne' rising from every throat beyond her window within her hearing.

She followed them in her head: 'Should old acquaintance be forgot.'

Oh, my little girl . . . She felt a traitor, her child left behind in her own selfish need to prove herself. This year – this new year she vowed to have her back, Daisy's views of unsavoury conditions or not.

Oh, Daisy . . . her truest friend. How could she bear her a grudge just because she seemed to be taking more care of Noelle than she could herself? If Langley had been here . . .

Oh, Langley – where was he now? Where were all the friends he had introduced her to? But she didn't care about them. They were nothing – shadows of a distant past.

Five, six, seven. She remembered instead the old friends she had once known, good friends, girls at school, at work, boyfriends, long since married she expected. And her family – Mum, Dad, Bobby, May . . . all of them.

Eight, nine, ten. And then there was Eddie. Suddenly she wanted Eddie so much. Suddenly she felt lonely, so alone. On the spur of the moment she reached out towards the wireless set, with a sharp twist of her wrist switched off the last two strokes. Going to the sink in the corner of her neat but basic living room, she tipped the untouched whisky into it. Leaving the empty glass on the wooden draining board, she went into her bedroom, flinging off her clothes and scrambling into her nightdress.

The bed creaked as she got in to pull the quilt over her ears to shut out the singing, the last good wishes in the street below, the cries of goodnight. ' 'Night, Marie! 'Night, Dan! 'Night, Violet! See you in the morning, Alice! 'Appy New Year! Yeah, 'Appy New Year!'

Cissy closed her eyes and prayed for sleep.

Every morning at crack of dawn Bobby trudged off through all weathers, unable to afford bus fares, bound for the lighterage pool in hope of an employer giving out a bit of work.

Today, after braving the February sleet, he stood watching the clerk as a leopard watches its prey, his eyes widening as the man reached out to answer the phone's first urgent summons, every muscle tensed to spring to action as the receiver was replaced. How many wanted? The clerk surveyed the tight knot of hopefuls, called out that Bollins wanted men – two only – banana boat at Wilson's Wharf. Bedlam broke out. The crowd of men surged forward, voices and arms raised, hands waving frantically for the job that meant the difference between a family eating and starving, the difference between the relief on a wife's face and pinched resignation of another empty table tomorrow.

They all knew it, were all desperate for the chance to work – there might be no other today. Every day it was a free fight to get it. This morning was no exception. Bobby shouldered with the rest, but many had gathered at the pool before him, early arrivals, could have even been waiting since the small hours for the gates to open at seven, though in this bone-chilling weather, he doubted it. Excitement died to a low mumble as the two lucky ones, triumph and anticipation on their grey faces, shouldered their way out, making for Wilson's Wharf.

Bobby watched them go and watched a few of the despondents ease out, too tired and fed up to wait. There were two options now, trudge back home or stay here, hoping something else would come up. It could be a futile wait, the damp air eating into the shed and himself as he waited the hours away. Or he could give up now, go home and at least get warm. But if he missed a chance of work, there'd be Ethel to face.

He decided to hang on for a couple of hours more, his broad face stubborn with his refusal to give in, but growing colder by the hour, finally even his resolve began to waver. Ebb tide, there'd be no more ships to come up, even humble jobs like dredging, freighting sludge down to the estuary in drop-bottom hoppers, all taken. Men would work on them for as long as they were wanted, winching up the huge doors after fifty tons of cold wet mud had slurped down like thick porridge. It was a filthy cold job in this weather and with just straight pay at the end of it no doubt; didn't matter how many hours a man worked, employers were less generous with overtime these days when there were so many waiting to take over, men grateful for what they could get. It made an employer greedy when work was like looking for gold dust. Nothing more would come in now. Bobby turned away from the dwindling group.

He couldn't face going home just yet, Ethel's nagging driving him silly, always the same if no work had come his way: how did he think she was going to feed the three of them, him, her and little Jean, if he didn't bring in any wages? As if mass unemployment was his fault. No, he couldn't face her, so he went round to his parents' place instead.

In the warmth of Mum's kitchen he sat over a cup of tea with his father. Fifty now, his father was more or less unwanted, younger men chosen to work, if at all, by employers. Whenever Bobby visited, his father always looked the same – dispirited and at a loss what to do with himself. He'd never had a hobby, always been too busy on the river. Now there was nothing to take up his idle hours.

But Sidney was a young man and he was out of work too. Harry, coming up to fourteen, had nothing to look forward to either at the end of his last term at school. May at twenty still had a job, doing what Cissy used to do, machining. Not much of that, *and* she was on short time, her employer having managed to keep on his best girls in case things got better. She was almost the sole breadwinner these days, so there was no money for herself and she seldom went out except to hang around on street corners wishing some boy, hopefully in work, might snatch her up and marry her. But there were few of them, even though she was pretty enough for anyone to want to snatch up.

'Do Ethel know you're here?' Doris asked, her small face ruddy from making toast by the fire for her family's midday meal. She began to spread the toast with plum jam. No point putting margarine on as well, which could be saved for another day. Jam tasted quite nice on its own sinking into the toast without a barrier of margarine.

Bobby waved away the slice she put before him. 'No thanks, Mum. I'm having something to eat when I get home. I'll be going soon.'

'You should've gone straight there, Bobby. Not going 'ome, she'll be wondering if you got yourself a bit of work.'

'Well, I didn't, and I don't fancy 'er going on at me because I didn't. I just wanted to pop in 'ere first for a break.'

'Bloody cold out there today,' Charlie put in gruffly. 'Meself, I don't see no point catchin' me death waiting around the pool for nothing.' He seemed so despondent, Bobby looked at him encouragingly.

'It'll get better in time. Soon. You wait.'

'Bin waitin' fer a year. It's just gettin' worse.'

'What you got for dinner tonight, then?' Bobby quickly changed the subject, looking up at his mother as he pushed away the plate she was still trying to offer him.

'Honestly, Mum, I 'ad a decent breakfast this morning. I ain't hungry.'

She smiled, relented, and put the slice on his father's plate. 'Dinner? We've got a nice bit of scrag. Well, we 'ad it yesterday and I've put the bones back and a few more veg. And for afters, a bit of suet pudding. Well, we had some of it yesterday. What's left is nice fried in a bit of marg, and we can put jam on it.'

'Sounds good.'

'And what've you got tonight?'

Bobby gave a wry grin. 'Bread an' grumble, I reckon. Ethel's gonna give me the length of 'er tongue when I get 'ome. It's a wonder her mouth don't ache sometimes.'

'She ain't so bad, Bobby. We've got 'ard times. Any woman would moan over it now and again.'

'Now and again!' He gave a low bitter chuckle, but something made him think of Cissy. She had always been so lively. Even when he and she did have their differences, as all brothers and sisters do, she had not been one for holding a grudge, not like Ethel and her never-ending nag, nag, nag. Except that something must have been gnawing at Cissy that day she had upped and walked out, and no word since. Going off with some man? There had to be more to it than that. And then last October someone telling Mum that she'd been seen locally, Cissy still hadn't contacted any of them.

May, on short time, had come round one afternoon just after that to tell him what Mum had heard. He'd had no work that day and Ethel in one of her tantrums had snatched up Jean and gone off round to her mother's to work it off on her. With her out of the way, May had felt it opportune to air her concern about Dad having put his foot down upon any effort to go in search of Cissy, even though she was so near.

'She must've really hurt Dad, going away like she did,' May had said. 'He won't let Mum talk about her, go and find her or have any dealings with her at all. Mum understands how he feels, but it has upset her terrible, as you can well imagine.'

She had told him not to say anything to Ethel about it, as it would be all around the neighbourhood. 'You know what Ethel's like.' Yes, he knew well what Ethel was like. 'And if it got back to Dad's ears, I'd really be in hot water. And I don't think it would help one bit for any of us to go looking for her. I'd like to, but it could cause an awful lot of trouble if any of us did that behind Dad's back. As nice as he is, I don't want to get into his bad books – not over someone that walked out on all of us like that. I'm not really sure I can forgive her. At least she's near home now and it's really up to her what she does. She's grown up enough to make her own life. I've told you because you're the only one of us what didn't know yet.'

He had honoured her confidence, apart from telling Eddie's father. He knew then that he'd been wrong, but it couldn't have got to Eddie's ears after all because nothing had come of it. Perhaps it had all been for the best. And then Eddie's father had died, which made it seem all for the best. He'd have liked to go and find her for himself, out of curiosity, but, as May had said, it could cause more trouble. Anyway, it was none of his business. He and Cissy had grown miles apart – brothers and sisters didn't always keep close together as books and films would have it. Yet at this moment he was again curious. Odd to think of her so near and yet no contact made.

Forgetting Dad was sitting there, the thought was out of his mouth before he could stop it. He could have bitten off his tongue.

There was a moment of profound silence, his father's broad face looked as though it had turned to stone in the act of chewing his toast, and when his mother finally spoke, her voice was unnaturally brittle, as though she had rehearsed the words just for this occasion and for her husband's ears.

'I don't want nothing to do with it. She's gone 'er own way, that's all I know an' all I want to know.'

'But she's near here.' He should have shut his silly mouth there and then, but he couldn't, not now he'd started it. 'She's probably too proud to come creeping back.'

'Proud?' The word broke from his father's lips as though he had spat, and little half-masticated crumbs of toast shot onto the tablecloth. 'What call's she got to be proud? A tart!'

'No, Dad, you're wrong. Cissy wasn't no tart . . .'

'Bobby . . .' The pleading cry from his mother stopped him. 'Bobby, it's 'ard for us. We didn't ask to be treated like she treated me an' your dad. It 'urt us both. She's made 'er bed.'

He was about to argue but the expression on both their faces was not to be borne. He couldn't add to their agony with more argument. All he said was, 'Eddie don't know, does he?' very softly.

Doris shook her head. Her voice trembled. 'I don't think so.'

'He should be told she's around 'ere, at least so he can make up his mind what to do.'

Neither of them answered. His father went back to eating his toast and his mother bent her head to pour another cup of tea, now somewhat less than lukewarm and well stewed. Normally she would have made fresh had she needed it, and no one needed any more, but she poured herself one anyway, added a touch of condensed milk and began to sip the half-cold bitter stuff, a far-away look on her face.

Bobby made his farewell soon afterwards. He had made up his mind. He would tell Eddie Bennett about Cissy. Whether it was kind or not, he wasn't certain. But it was right that the man should know, or so he thought. He should have told him long ago.

Chapter Twenty-One

Eddie's brown eyes were dark with reproach and disbelief, certainly not with the excitement Bobby had expected to see there.

'So that's what he meant,' Eddie heard him whisper to himself.

Filled now with guilt at having burdened this man with what he had thought would be helpful news, Bobby looked away, not understanding or wanting to question the remark.

Eddie sat at the desk twiddling a pencil between his long strong fingers with a delicate manipulation, his eyes still on his visitor. 'When did you say you told my father?'

'Around October, November, not long after me mum 'eard it.'

'He never told me.'

'I'm sorry, I thought he would. But I'm not surprised he didn't. I wondered when I phoned whether I was doing the right thing. I admit I was relieved when it was your dad I spoke to and not you. By the way, I was sorry to hear about him. He was no age really to . . .'

His condolence was waved away. Eddie put the pencil down and got up to walk about the office with its two narrow dingy windows looking out onto the Thames just visible between a couple of other warehouses on the wharf. He stopped pacing suddenly and turned to face Bobby.

'This person who told your mother . . . did she say where she'd seen her – Cissy?'

'All I know is, someone told her, and someone told them that her old elocution teacher bumped into 'er in Bethnal Green Road. The old teacher seemed to think she was living somewhere in that area, not far from where she met 'er.'

'What made her think that?'

Bobby looked anxious. 'I don't know. I only know what me mum said.' He waited for some reaction, but Eddie had turned away, his attention apparently taken by the filmy view through the window. He stood there so long, saying nothing, that Bobby finally rose. It was all getting rather embarrassing and now he wanted to be away.

'Look, Eddie . . . I only came because I took it your dad couldn't have passed on me message. I thought, if he'd told you, you'd 'ave been round to us before now to find out a lot more about it.'

'Yeah,' came the distracted reply. Bobby fidgeted.

'Look, I've got to go.'

'Yeah,' Eddie said again. He seemed miles away, in a world of his own. Leaving him still standing gazing out of the window onto the strip of Thames between the warehouses, Bobby let himself out.

*

In the wide Bethnal Green Road, buzzing with traffic and Saturday shoppers, littered with rubbish carelessly dropped, filled by shouts of stallholders, while the heat of an afternoon May sun wafted up in waves from the pavement, and poured down to penetrate the shoulders of his best blue suit, Eddie stood uncertain which direction to take.

She could be living in any one of these turnings off the main road, down any alley, above any shop. All he could do was walk up and down in hope that he might see her going along. He had been doing that for four hours. His feet in best shoes, tight from lack of use, had begun to ache. He was hot and bothered and hungry, the succulent smells from cafés and butchers' shops heightened. It had been a stupid move, a wasted effort. Dad would have called him a silly sod, and he'd be right.

It had taken the best part of a month to make up his mind to come here. So many obstacles standing in his way: the worry of a business not going as it should; his own apathy, still there over the death of his father, even after five months, fighting to overcome it and run the business efficiently. Then there was his mother. Bereaved and needing a shoulder to lean on – after their initial promises to keep an eye on her, that they would be there if she wanted for anything, Dad's people had melted away like butter on the tongue. It was left to him to support her, do what he could for her. There was little coming in from the business to keep himself much less supplement her ridiculous widow's pension. Dad having sunk most of her nest egg in the tug business, now not even bumping along the ground, he could only do his best for her with what little he had. His mind was more taken up with all that rather than going hunting for Cissy, he told himself.

Even though she was reputed to be in England, there was no proof that she was still here. Even if she was, would she thank him for coming looking for her? She'd made her choice long ago. She wouldn't want him coming round now, interfering in her life. If she had wanted him, she would have sought him out. All this was reason enough. But the one true reason, one he tried to evade most of the time, was that if he did find her, what had he to offer? All those dreams of one day laying a thriving business at her feet – phuh!

Eddie gave a small explosive sound of self-derision. He had nothing – was back to that one original tug now, the *Cicely*, nicely equipped and willing to work, but competing with big companies that could still survive the Depression – all he'd built up was slowly going downhill. It was true what they said – money came to money, the moment it began to dwindle less and less money came in. He was slowly grinding to a halt. So here he was, a man with no set idea, trying to find someone who might not even be here, and if she was, how could he in his poor financial state ever dare to dream of claiming her back?

He began to move on, without purpose, unaware he was following the path his father had taken five months before. He too noted the sign above one particular shop selling knitting wool, patterns and such, and wondered for a moment. But in his case, with the sinking but still bright sun directly in his eyes, it wasn't possible to pierce the shop's comparatively darker interior. Besides, it was six o'clock and the shop was closed. There was nothing to make him pause and he walked on.

Reaching Shoreditch, his feet weary and nothing achieved, his only thought was to hop on a bus home. At the appropriate stop he settled himself to waiting the ten minutes for the next one. He was hungry but there was no question of spending good money in a café when there was a lovingly cooked tea at home. Expecting him when she saw him, taking it that he'd been working late as he often did, his mother would have kept something hot for him, a marvel with the meanest food.

Cursing the lengthening wait, he looked across at the stop on the opposite side where buses bore people into the City. It had been a long time since he'd gone into the West End; he had no reason to and it would be a long time probably before he ever did. A knot of hopefuls stood there by the red flag-shaped sign on its pole like patient cattle, just as those on his side were doing. Yet another person joined them, settling with her weight on one leg more than the other, hip pushed out, gloved hands clasped loosely, an envelope handbag securely held against her by one arm. With nothing much else to do, Eddie let his gaze wander idly over the slim-fitting black suit, the tiny black and white hat with a pencil feather and a short veil set jauntily on her head, the high-heeled shoes completing the elegant look of her. She had such fair hair too, softly waved . . .

A shock like a discharge of electricity shot through him. Was his vulnerable state playing tricks with him? It was her. It was Cissy. He could be wrong . . . It might not be her. But already he was halfway across the road, dodging the traffic. From the corner of his eye he saw the bus looming that would take her away from him. It towered as he made a leap for the kerb. It was closer than he had thought.

He heard the deep-seated screech of brakes, the driver's incensed yell, 'You silly born bugger!' But he was on the pavement, thrusting his way through those jostling to board, ignoring the angry driver.

'Cissy! Cissy!'

Her foot on the running board, she turned, looked over his head.

'Cissy!'

Her scan came down to his level and she saw him. Her face blanching, she remained statue-like, one foot still on the running board, one hand gripping the central steel safety pole. People were pushing past her.

'Come on!' came the conductor's irritable command, seeing a pile-up of passengers. 'Come on . . . On or off?'

Struggling with those late arrivals hurrying to board, Eddie pushed further towards her.

'Stop bloody shovin', mate. Give the women a chance, will yuh?'

This from an older bonneted woman in a threadbare coat, but he hardly noticed. Cissy was getting down from the bus, and that was all that mattered.

Cissy was in his arms, the last of the passengers had boarded the bus. The bus was pulling away. But Cissy was in his arms.

For a while neither said anything, merely held each other as though frightened that, should they let go, the moment would prove to be no more than an illusion and each would be alone.

It was Eddie who spoke first. 'I've been searching. I didn't know where you were. I was told you were home, but I didn't know where.'

At the sound of his voice, Cissy leaned away from him. They hadn't kissed, yet she leaned away as if they had and she hadn't expected it. Her eyes were wide and clearest blue as they stared into his in wavering uncertainty.

'Oh, Eddie . . . I didn't want you to find me.'

It was his turn to look uncertain. 'Why?'

'Because . . . because I left you. I went away.'

'But you came back, didn't you? You should've come to me.'

Her face had grown hard. 'What, to ask for forgiveness?'

'No.'

'I didn't . . . I don't expect you to forgive me. I never wrote to you or contacted you.'

'You didn't contact your family either. I think they were hurt.'

Now she hung her head, letting go of him. 'I imagine they were. I don't expect them to forgive me. Why should I expect you to?'

'Because . . .' He reached out and with a finger beneath her chin, lifted it so that she was made to look up at him. 'Because I love you. I ain't ever stopped loving you, and there's nothing to forgive.'

'But you must have been hurt by what I did.'

'Yes. And I went on hurting. Until today, seeing you. It's all gone and all that's left is what was always there inside me. Loving you . . . No, Cissy . . .' He pulled her face back as she made to shrug away from his hold. 'No, you hear me out. You've 'ad your turn. Now I want mine. I know you was bowled over by this bloke what 'ad more to give you than I ever could. And I couldn't blame you. Just that I was the one left – the one what 'ad all the pain of losing you. But I worked. Christ, Cissy,

I worked so bloody 'ard, so that when you finally came back – and I was always sure you would, because them sort of blokes don't last – I'd 'ave something to offer you. Until eighteen months ago, I 'ad a lot to offer you. A bloody good business. I could've got us a damn fine house to live in, out of London, and you'd 'ave wanted for nothing. Cissy . . .'

He tried to pull her towards him but when she remained rigid, he stopped trying. It struck her then that he was so much older, far more mature than the man she had walked out on. He seemed as though that come what may, he would always be in control.

'But now I've found you,' he continued, his tone low and hollow, 'I can't offer you what I'd once hoped to any more. The Depression's hit me like it's hit everyone.'

He began to tell her about his towage business, but paused, aware of more people beginning to gather for the next bus.

'We can't talk here. Let's go somewhere for a cuppa.'

As she nodded, he threaded her arm through his as though it was the most natural thing in the world to do and guided her away. She thought suddenly of how Langley would do that, then hurriedly dismissed him. That was another world, a world gone for ever. And now she didn't want it back, ever, surprising herself that she didn't. She was home.

Standing beside Eddie in the waning light, she waited for the door to open to his knock. Nothing had changed in four years, still the dirty brown brick, the flat-faced windows, the peeling green paintwork, still the same lace curtains or at least a similar pattern.

Nothing in the street had changed. The only change was in herself, remembering the wide Paris boulevards, the quaint cobbled back-streets where even the most humble dwelling fired the romantic spirit. Now living in the wide and busy if dirty and littered Bethnal Green Road, by comparison these streets, away from the hustle and bustle of main road shops, had an air of neglect and disillusionment.

She shivered slightly as she waited for someone to answer Eddie's knock. 'What if they close the door in our faces?' she asked.

He smiled down at her and she felt the reassuring pressure of his hand in hers. 'They won't close the door in my face.'

He looked up expectantly as someone fumbled with the catch on the far side. Cissy drew in a deep breath as the door was opened wide, the enquiring smile of her mother greeting her.

Seeing Cissy, the smile faded. Obviously she had expected someone else, a neighbour perhaps. Now there was only guarded surprise and shock.

'Hello, Mum,' she began, but a warning pressure of Eddie's hand stopped her.

'Mrs Farmer, I've something I've got to tell you. Can we come in for a moment or two?'

The round faded blue eyes wavered. 'Well . . . I don't know.'

A man's voice came from within, deep and full. Cissy recognised it as her father's. 'Who is it?'

'It's . . . no one, dear,' her mother called back, and Cissy felt the words bite into her. But Eddie was talking quickly.

'We do need to talk to you, Mrs Farmer. Most seriously.'

She hesitated, finally opened the door a little wider. 'You'd best come in a moment, then,' she said, at the same time throwing a hasty look left and right along the street. To Cissy it seemed as though she were admitting a fugitive from prison.

They followed her into the narrow passage, but there she stopped them. 'You wait 'ere a moment. I've got to tell your . . . I've got to tell 'im you're 'ere.'

The hesitation in naming her father for what he was to her didn't escape Cissy. She caught her lower lip between her teeth and held back the cry to be welcomed, forgiven. She stood very still beside Eddie as her mother went into the room, closing the door behind her, leaving them to wait in the dim passageway with its tiny hallstand full of coats and its slightly pockmarked mirror. She said nothing, could find nothing to say, even to Eddie.

Beyond the door, her father's voice rose, the words coming plainly. 'Tell 'er to bugger off. I don't want ter see 'er.'

And then her mother. 'But she's got Eddie with her.'

'She can 'ave the good God Himself with 'er. I ain't seeing 'er.'

Eddie let go her hand. 'Wait here,' he ordered, and before she could say anything, he had opened the door to the front room and was inside, leaving her alone. Her heart thumping wildly, feeling suddenly sick, Cissy listened, half expecting him to be bundled bodily out.

'Mr Farmer. You know me. You've never 'ad any quarrel with me.'

'Not till now. What you brought 'er 'ere for?'

'I met her today. We've 'ad a long talk, me and Cissy. I won't go into lots of detail, Mr Farmer, but I'm ready to forgive 'er. You might say she made a fool of herself, and she's had a nasty lesson. She was young and silly going off like that and she knows it. But now she's come back and wants to make amends. And, as I said, I've forgiven 'er and I'm ready to welcome 'er back – take 'er back.'

'Then more bloody fool you.' Listening at the door the harshness in her father's tone made Cissy jump, but Eddie's voice remained steady.

'If I'm a bloody fool, Mr Farmer, I'll be the first to say so. Maybe I am, but it ain't for you to judge if I should 'ave her back or not. And if *I* can, then I'm asking you to try and do the same.'

'Not if I live ter be 'undred years old. I won't ever forgive 'er for what she put me and 'er mum through. Put years on 'er mum, she did, and for that I won't ever forgive 'er.'

In all this, her mother hadn't spoken. Cissy hoped she might run to her defence, but there had been no sound from her. Even her mother wasn't prepared to speak up for her.

'She's your daughter, Mr Farmer.'

'She ain't no daughter of mine. Never will be again. And you can tell 'er that yourself, though I've no doubt she's 'earing every word through that door.'

In response, Cissy leapt back as though her father could actually see her. But though she stood with her back to the passage wall, the thin wood of the door let through every word as clear as if it wasn't there at all. Eddie's voice rang out.

'It makes no matter, Mr Farmer. I 'aven't told Cissy yet, but I intend to marry 'er, if she'll 'ave me. Way things are at present, I ain't got a lot to offer 'er – not what I once 'oped I would. But there's never any standing still altogether and in time things might change and get better. I 'ope they do. But I ain't waiting for 'em. If she's willing to take me as I am, then I'm 'ere for her. And it would be nice, Mr Farmer, if you was 'ere for 'er too. But if you ain't then it won't make no difference to me. It might to 'er, but then she'll 'ave me to fight for 'er, won't she?'

There came a coughing growl from her father. 'I suppose you think by sayin' that, we'll be forced to come to yer weddin'.'

But Cissy was already fighting to calm the rapid beating inside her breast. He had asked her to marry him, or had from a distance. It was enough.

'Oh, yes, yes,' she whispered. She felt hardly able to breathe. She wanted to rush in and throw herself into Eddie's arms. But she had to remain calm, had to control herself. Eddie was talking, his voice low.

'No, I don't expect you to come. And I do understand. I might've felt the same in your place, Mr Farmer. But I'm 'ere, and I intend to ask her to be my wife. We'll get married quietly – if she'll 'ave me – and we'll get on with our lives, and you'll get on with yours, and I don't suppose much'll be changed by it, do you?'

It sounded to Cissy as though he were saying that if every creature on the earth died tomorrow, it would still go on spinning, and still look the same from out there in space. It was a silly thought and suddenly it made her want to cry.

That was how she was as Eddie came out of the room, her face buried in her hands, no longer feeling the chic young woman he'd met a couple of hours ago, more a little girl hunched over with sorrow as well as happiness, and unable to differentiate between the two. It was to her as if the world, or at least everyone in it, was indeed threatening to come to an end, and that she and Eddie would be the only ones left to struggle alone.

His voice came softly to her, somewhat far away. 'Cissy, are you all right?'

She nodded into her covering hands. 'I just feel . . . overwhelmed, sad, happy . . . I don't know what I feel.'

The door had opened again. Cissy looked up. It was her mother.

'Cissy,' she whispered. 'I ain't forgiving you entirely. Not as quick as all that. You caused this family a lot of 'urt and 'eartache, and it ain't a thing to get over lightly, but what I'm saying is I know what Eddie's talkin' about, and if you two are going to marry, then I want to give me blessing. Things is very 'ard these days and Lord knows you'll 'ave a lot to cope with, but you'll manage, the pair of you. All's well what ends well, so they say, and though blessings ain't much, I can at least give 'em to you both. In time your dad'll come round if I know 'im. Ain't one to 'old a grudge when there's no grudge to 'old. He's really a decent sort, your dad.'

In seconds, Cissy was in her arms, sobbing. 'I know. I know he is.'

'Now you give me your address,' Doris said, as she held her daughter gently. 'And I'll come and see you.'

*

As they left, bubbles of excitement were already surging up inside her. It didn't matter any more what Dad felt about her, how bitterly he had renounced her – all she could think of was whether to gasp out her acceptance breathlessly on the very brink of Eddie asking, or whether she should bridle a little so as not to make herself look too eager. But he didn't ask. He said little except that he was taking her to see his mother, having mentioned on the way to her parents' home his father's death, waving away her instant condolences almost brusquely.

She supposed that being taken to see his mother might be considered a proposal of sorts and she assumed that this was all she could expect, remembering the cautious, practical man Eddie had always been. But how she wished it could have been more the romantic one she'd have liked. Disappointment swept over her in waves which she tried hard to ignore as they reached his home, even though he smiled fondly down at her.

Meeting him this evening – a mere three hours ago, for all it now seemed like ages ago – the first heart-crushing rush of joy issuing from that amazing meeting now past, he was treating her as casually as if they had been reunited months ago and had settled down to routine. Nor was it as if she had never met his mother before. It was all so deflating, that lovely bubbling excitement dissipated, her arm through his, yet she feeling oddly distanced by it all. Even making conversation was becoming hard, not knowing what to say to him, she trying to keep in step with him, the old problem.

'It's been so long since I saw your mum,' she said, more to fill a hiatus, instantly ruing the remark that emphasised her long absence, but he didn't seem bothered by it for he had already forgiven her. He had said as much to her father.

All he said was, 'She'll be so glad you and me are together again.' He seemed to assume that he had proposed to her face to face, in the recognised way, and that she had said yes, again in the conventional way. Of course she would have said yes, but it would have been nice to have had the opportunity to say it, not just have it taken for granted. She felt a little irritated by it.

In this frame of mind, she accepted Mrs Bennett's warm, if verging on the stoic, greeting, her recent bereavement and the sad timing of her son's news bravely held at bay as Eddie announced, 'Me and Cissy's going to get married, Mum,' – news that would have so pleased his father – Cissy could see it behind the smile, and squirmed as the pale hazel eyes, brimming, looked from one to the other.

'Oh, Eddie, I'm so pleased for you – pleased for you both.' Her arms out to him, she hugged him to her, then came and kissed Cissy. 'I always hoped, you know. I was so sorry how things turned out. But everything's all right again, and I do wish you both every 'appiness.'

Eddie was smiling proudly. He had his arm about Cissy. She was his and he was pleased with himself, pleased with her. His world had come together after all his heartache, and so had hers. Yet he still hadn't proposed properly. He probably never would, and though some of the romance had been lost by it, she felt it had to be enough. Romance – that sweeping off the feet romance – had no substance to it, had it? A whispering of lovely words, were they ever reliable? She knew by bitter experience, didn't she, that they were not. Better, wasn't it, to have lasting love starting quietly than being swept off one's feet to last only months? Yet, it would have been nice to have been asked.

While her son devoured the tea she'd had waiting for him, stretching sausages and mashed potato to provide for Cissy, Mrs Bennett talked non-stop: how had Eddie's day been, and what a coincidence it was the two of them meeting like that, and what was her shop like and what sort of things was she selling? She would pop down Bethnal Green Road and buy some wool or something from her – as if that sufficed to help Cissy's business. She submitted to the woman's questions with no observations of her own, noted with a stab of conscience how she kept well away from any mention of her being abroad, conversation kept strictly to a lighter side.

'And when do you two plan the wedding for?'

Eddie looked over the moon. 'It'll be a quiet one, I expect. We ain't had no time to talk about it properly, but we'll be doing that soon enough.' He turned towards Cissy. 'After we've finished tea, I could take you and show you my office. We could do a bit of serious talking there.'

While Mrs Bennett smiled her approval, he studied Cissy's face for her agreement, which she gave with a nod, after which he fell to downing his portion of the rice pudding his mother had baked.

His office wasn't large. Cluttered and, she imagined, somewhat dark during the day with the window, inaccessible from the outside, a dirty brown from not having been cleaned in years, there were faint odours of fish and cattle cake and dozens of others from surrounding wharves. The light switched on, she stood in the centre of the room, having been conducted through the small outer office where his secretary had left her typewriter protected by such a tatty dust cover that Cissy hazarded the machine beneath had to be second-hand.

'It's not much,' he said ruefully, seeing her slow survey of the room. 'We were going to move offices a couple of years ago when things were better than they are now.'

'We?' she queried absently.

'Me and Dad. We was in partnership – until he died.'

'Oh yes, I'm sorry.'

'One of those things.'

'How did you come to start up this business?' she asked, hurriedly changing the subject. His shrug had told her he didn't want to talk about his father's death. They must have been so close, she thought, and felt a small tug of envy and of regret that she had not been there when he probably most needed her.

'I had a bit of a windfall. An inheritance – couple of months after you left.' The remark sounded pointed, and again came the twinge of guilt. She was quite prepared for him to follow it up with another that had she been there, he might have been well able to match the enticement offered by the man she had gone off with. But he said no more, except to give a short account of how he'd come into the money.

'So this is it,' he concluded, again ruefully, this time conveying the impression that she could back out if she wanted.

Cissy turned to look at him and knew now that if he had nothing but the clothes he stood up in and was up to his eyes in debt, it was him she wanted and no one else. Suddenly she was in his arms.

'It doesn't matter, Eddie. We can make a go of it – you with this and me with my shop. Neither of us is making much money, but we could pool our resources. We can make a go of things.'

'I reckon we could,' he began, but she had lifted her face to kiss him. She felt the warm lips on hers, knew again the tingle that used to surge through her at his touch all those years ago.

A need was gripping them both, their lips parting and hungry, her hands behind his neck so that he would not let go of her. But his arms held her, one hand moving round to knead her breast as together they rocked, moved, strove to draw ever nearer to each other. With only one other way to be even closer, each knew that this, their first time ever, would make them one, the dingy little office becoming a magic shady dell for making love in.

But first, he must prepare the place. Reluctantly he let his hold on her fall away, enough to remove his coat and to lay it on the floor with a sort of nest-building instinct, while she, her heart beating with heavy expectant thuds against her ribs, watched the meticulous preparation. So absorbed he was in ensuring her comfort that she found her love for him bursting out of her.

Nest completed, he lay her down and with careful fingers undid her suit, her blouse, the side zip of her skirt, not once looking at her, but concentrating deeply on what he was doing, and that so slowly, she wanted to help. It wasn't so much he taking his time as time being taken. Even as she slipped her skirt off for him he watched only with reverence; neither self-conscious nor self-assured, but seemingly humbled by this moment, special to them both.

Carefully, he lay on top of her. The warmth of his flesh touching her thighs made her arch convulsively towards him and he moved into her with slow rhythmic pulses, bringing them together. Not a word had been said. Words would have broken the mystery of it, the very act of his love was enough.

When it was over, and they lay in each other's arms on his coat, Cissy felt she had never known such contentment. He hadn't brought her to any raging climax, yet it had been a coupling like no other she had known, sweet and gentle and caring. That was Eddie. She felt at this moment that should he never bring her to her climax, it would still be enough that he make love to her for the rest of their lives. Better than the mad thrashing of limbs, the panting for even more heights of orgasmic excitement that she'd experienced with Langley Makepeace, this was all she would ever want.

Slowly she sat up, it dawning on her that Eddie still hadn't asked her to her face if she would marry him, her only knowledge of it had come through hearing him express it to others – his mother, her father – a second-hand proposal. The thought prompted a small unexpected stab of resentment, unwarranted, she knew, because if he hadn't loved her he'd never have made love to her, yet rancour was there nevertheless.

At her movement he too sat up, his brown eyes full of contentment. For a moment longer they gazed into hers, but grew faintly bewildered seeing something there he could not define. Then as he slowly read the message they held, the bewilderment cleared and he smiled.

'Cissy, there's something I haven't done,' he said quietly, his low voice muffled by the dingy little office.

'I've not asked you properly if you would marry me. Would you like to?'

For a moment she didn't reply, then the inanity of the request hit her. What a time to ask. She felt laughter bubble up, bursting out in peal after peal of convulsive joy. Seconds later he too had joined in, the office ringing to their united laughter. How she loved this man to whom she clung, laughing. Why had she not realised it years ago?

Chapter Twenty-Two

She still hadn't told Eddie about her daughter. She shuddered to think how he'd take it. How did one start on a thing like that? He should have been told the very day they met, but it hadn't seemed appropriate then. It stood to reason, though, that the longer the delay the harder it would be. He would have to know sometime rather than find out when Daisy came over to the wedding, for she had to ask Daisy.

They still corresponded regularly and frequently, Daisy with all Noelle's recent doings, and she with endless accounts of Eddie and the wedding arrangements.

Oddly enough, now that she had Eddie to think about, fretting for Noelle had grown considerably less. Sometimes she'd forget about her for days on end and then feel uncomfortably guilty that she had, that as a mother she ought to be pining for her return constantly. She made an effort to retain that longing, even welcoming that old prickle of jealousy when Daisy wrote ever more possessively about Noelle.

Of course Eddie must be told. But the weeks were going by, the wedding was only a month away – August – at her own request a registry office affair with which Eddie was happy, not being particularly given to religion. He hadn't been inside a church for years other than for the odd friend's wedding and more recently his father's funeral which had shaken him anyway, enough that he wouldn't be disposed to reawakening the memory by marrying in church.

It was all arranged. For their honeymoon they'd be going down to Bournemouth for a couple of days – all they could afford. There was his business and her shop to consider. For the time being they'd have her rented little flat, his mother stoically accepting the arrangement which would leave her entirely on her own. He had promised to pop in every day for half an hour, hoping that would help a little to ease the wrench of his leaving, but he had his own life to lead, his own marriage to care for. Cissy felt sad for her, the poignant offer of part of her two-bedroomed home for the newly-weds had to be refused for there would be only the one room for them and they wouldn't have their privacy. Cissy needed to be near her shop to open each morning, and though Eddie would have to go off to his office, there was no sense in them both going off in different directions when she was already there above her shop. So Mrs Bennett would have to let her son go and face up to being alone as best she could. Cissy steeled herself against too much pity in the light that she too had been forced into loneliness in the past and at this very moment did not have her child with her – worse still, could not even talk about her, as yet.

The brief list of guests being made out highlighted that vividly. Daisy and Theodore wouldn't be overjoyed if she were to leave out their precious little Noelle. She was sure Daisy had begun to look upon her as her very own.

As time went on, it had become ever more apparent that Daisy, still without a child of her own, was turning more and more to Noelle to take the place of the one she so wanted and still couldn't have. It could be read between the lines of her every letter.

Sometimes Cissy wondered if it wouldn't be better to leave things as they stood. Would it really be kind to any of them for her to demand Noelle back? Eddie, trusting, innocent Eddie, put through the trauma of knowing that there had been a child – a bastard – from her alliance with Langley Makepeace? Did he deserve that, after all that had transpired these last couple of months? Cissy was in particular fear of his reaction, worried that at the last moment she would find herself rejected, alone again, and this time with no one to bale her out. Eddie was her salvation and she loved him so very much, the thought of his walking away from her was something not to be borne.

They made love on a regular basis now – in the comfort of her flat, away from everyone, as though they were already married. Life was so sweet. Why disrupt it now over a child she hardly knew? Noelle was her own flesh and blood and yet she knew so little, saw so little of her, it was as though that episode in her life had been a dream. After all, she was happy with Eddie and he was innocently unaware of any existing child; Noelle seemed contented with her 'auntie', and Daisy was as happy as any loving mother. So why rock the boat?

Even so, the nagging knowledge persisted that secrets were only in existence to reveal themselves at the most inopportune moment, their sole design to put a spoke in the wheels of happiness.

Then came a letter from Daisy to make her wonder if she really did need to tell him after all, that it might be as well to let sleeping offpsring lie. Strange, she thought as she read, how circumstances can alter cases.

Theodore had his arms around his wife, feeling her sobbing resounding right through his narrow chest.

'I didn't deserve this,' she sobbed. 'I'd always hoped.'

'It is not the end of the world, beloved,' he murmured, his face in her dark tousled hair. 'Our love will strengthen us and will bring us more closely together to face this sad business.'

He had tried not to sound complacent or resigned, but Daisy raised her face to his, features contorted with grief. 'It's all right for you! You're a man, you don't have to suffer the stigma or the ache of knowing you can't have a child.'

'It is as sorrowful for me as it is for you. All my life have I thought to be a father one day. But now it seems God has decreed otherwise. Who are we to protest against that? Remember, my dear, there is still our Noelle.'

'She's not *our* Noelle.'

He frowned. 'Ah, sometimes I forget.'

Tears ran freely down her cheeks. 'Cissy could easily write one day, out of the blue, asking for her back. She's getting married soon, and she's bound to. There's nothing to stop her. Noelle's not *ours*. And soon she won't even *be* with us. I don't think I could bear her not being here. And me unable to have children . . . Oh, Teddy!' She dropped her face to his chest again. 'I don't know what I'll do if she writes asking for her back.'

Theodore thought for a moment, one slim hand patting his wife's shaking shoulders almost in rhythm with his thoughts. 'There are good doctors in Germany. I have never felt trust in those here. They have aloofness with foreigners that I have my doubts of them. I should feel more comfortable with those in my own country who I am sure would go into greater investigation with your case. And also I have a desire to return to my homeland. With the financial depression we are having, I do not feel as well as I should feel – not so alert in my dealings. I am certain that my health is a little ailing and I have a great enticement to see my father's grave before it is too late.'

Now Daisy lifted her head to stare up at him in alarm. She even moved back from him for a better look. It was late in the evening. He had not long come home from his office and she had noticed then how strained he looked. Little Noelle had been crying as he entered, the apartment ringing to her yells as Daisy rocked her. Three years old and wanting to run everywhere instead of walk, she had caught her temple painfully on the corner of the heavy walnut dining table. Theodore had let his briefcase fall to the ground as he hurried to help console her, rubbing at the hurt place until her crying had been reduced to quiet intermittent sobs. Now with her tucked safely in her bed after a drink of warm milk, having refused to eat anything, their own supper still to be dished up, he looked tired and, dare she say, ill.

For a long time his struggle against the times had been slowly defeating him. He had not been made poor by any means. Companies still needed to borrow money. But they were more discerning, tetchy, baulking against the customary pound of flesh all financiers required as of right, where once they would have paid up without the bat of an accountant's eyelid. It all served to press down upon him.

'See your father's grave?' she echoed fearfully. 'What for? There's nothing wrong with you, is there?'

'I am just tired, *mein liebling*. Perhaps in Germany I will relax.'

'The Depression's as bad there as it is anywhere. Worse. Germany's in a terrible state. It's got the worst unemployment of anywhere.'

'We shall not go immediately.' He smiled. 'By next year the world will have recovered a little and my country will see better times.'

He leaned towards her. 'I should very much like to go home, Daisy. I am becoming so homesick of late. You will not be disappointed with my homeland. She is beautiful. Her people are good, clean and precise in all they do, self-respecting and generous, are not of such easy nonchalance as here. You will like them, I am sure. The people are very . . . like the British in manner. You will feel at home, I know.'

She was beginning to get over the initial shock of the news that the hospital had given her this afternoon following a lengthy, sometimes delayed series of tests on her continued inability to conceive. Drying her tears she decided that hospitals were not always right. This one's approach to her problem had been, to say the least, lackadaisical. She would bide her time, and when she and Teddy eventually went to live in Germany, have more tests, proper tests done, and maybe by next year . . .

But if they too found her unable to have children, she had Noelle, who was now like her own child. She prayed constantly that now Cissy had someone else to love and care for, she might let her stay here. More than likely Cissy would have children from her marriage, so what would she want with a love child who only held memories for her of a man who had so cruelly let her down?

Feeling slightly better and more optimistic, Daisy sat down at the lovely bureau in their beautiful bedroom and wrote to Cissy on the declining state of their finances, of Teddy's fancy to go to Germany, of the sorry news so far about her failure to conceive and ending with a request that she continue to look after Noelle for a while longer; being that the wedding was so near, Noelle might disrupt the arrangements.

Reading it, Cissy felt fate had taken a hand, and that perhaps it wouldn't really be the wisest thing to tell Eddie about her child yet.

'I think you ought to let bygones be bygones, Charlie.'

Doris stood over her husband, the dress she had got from a stall in Petticoat Lane this Sunday morning, a nice pink and white print, dangling from her hand after May had altered it for her.

She, May and Cissy had been on a shopping spree for wedding stuff yesterday and had really scoured the lane, each of them pleased with what they'd come home with. May, as Cissy's bridesmaid, had found something suitable in yellow taffeta in one of the nicer Jewish shops. Cissy had found a lovely wedding dress in the same shop, white satin with a small cape, and had gone somewhere else for her tiny headdress of wax orange blossom and short veil.

'She's always had good taste,' Doris observed, after she'd departed to her flat. 'She and Eddie will make a lovely couple next Saturday.'

But Charlie didn't share her sentiments. 'Got a cheek, marrying in white. What's virgin about 'er, I ask yer, after what she's done?'

With Eddie claiming Cissy for his wife, he'd had to form a reluctant truce. Not much he could do about it really, but he felt deep inside that he could never truly forgive her for what she'd done even if Eddie had; less, knowing what he and Doris did, Doris'd sworn him to secrecy. 'It's her business and no one else's,' she had said firmly. 'If she wants to tell 'im about the baby, then it's for 'er and not us to let 'im know. She'll do it when she thinks the time's ripe.'

'She ain't being fair to 'im,' Charlie had complained, rightly so, he felt. 'I won't let the cat out of the bag, but when 'e does find out, I wouldn't want ter be in 'er shoes. Too nice a bloke to 'ave the wool pulled over 'is eyes. But you watch out, my gel, like all nice quiet blokes, there can be an 'idden temper underneath.'

'Then you leave 'is 'idden temper to 'im,' was all she said as she went off to try on her altered dress.

Cissy's secret was indeed known only to her parents and they had kept it well. They hadn't even told May or Bobby, and for that she was profoundly grateful to them both – more than they would ever realise, more than words could ever say.

Her only concern was Daisy and Theodore. How would they introduce Noelle? If they brought her, that was. She had a feeling that Daisy would do the right thing by her, leave the child behind in the care of a hired nurse, which they still seemed able to afford despite Daisy's bemoaning her lot these days.

From the old longing to see her daughter, Cissy now found herself hoping they wouldn't bring her. One thing she knew, she could trust Daisy implicitly to keep her secret. Her whole world now revolving around Eddie she surprised even herself that her motherly love could all but disappear. If that was the case, arrangements could be made for Daisy to keep her, foster her, perhaps one day adopt her. Eddie may never need to know and her dread of the consequences of his knowing began to fade. Daisy would be over the moon, she was sure.

The wedding day, from seeming so long away in May, had galloped up to them with such increasing speed that it set Cissy into a panic that she wouldn't have everything ready for the day. Two days to go, the food for the wedding breakfast prepared by both mothers, Eddie footing the bill for what had been bought, the reception to be held in his office of all places, the largest accommodation for two dozen people. His mother's home wasn't half big enough, and her father, although having come to terms with her, still wasn't disposed to those terms enough to allow his house to be invaded by her wedding guests.

*

'How does it look?'

Cissy watched her sister's critical gaze as she stood in front of the mirror in her parents' bedroom, another begrudging concession from Dad that she could get married from here.

He would give her away. She overheard him say to Mum, 'She didn't need me giving 'er away last time she left 'ome.' And her mother's short shrift. 'It's tradition, Charlie, so shut up about it!'

She wasn't going to have her eldest daughter's wedding day spoiled by sour faces. She had forgiven her long ago.

May regarded the dress, leaning back on her heels where she had been stitching up the slightly drooping sides – cheap dress, Cissy thought with a pang of wistfulness. Had she married Langley Makepeace, hers would have been the wedding of the year in a gown that was the height of fashion and a string of bridesmaids, a reception to beat all receptions, press photographers from the papers and afterwards a beautiful country house to live in. But she wasn't marrying Langley Makepeace with his comfortable inheritance. She was marrying Eddie Bennett, with both of them struggling to keep their respective, slowly downward-spiralling businesses from coming to a bump at the bottom if the country didn't pick up soon. Quickly she shrugged off the vague feeling of bitterness and sudden panic that had gripped her. Eddie loved her and she him.

'It looks a lot better now,' May was saying. 'In fact, Cissy, you look a wow. Let's get your headdress on. We've got to be at the registry office in twenty minutes.'

Twenty minutes. In twenty-five minutes she'd be Mrs Eddie Bennett. It sounded truly wonderful. What was more, she was carrying Eddie's child, she was sure. She had missed last month's period and this one was already a week late. But this time she was getting married. That was for certain. In twenty minutes. Cissy's heart sang with prayers of thanks to a God she hadn't thought of since praying for help after Langley had thrown money at her and walked out telling her not to be there when he returned.

If she was pregnant, and there was no reason why she shouldn't be, she had a gift to give her husband that could match no other.

The car had returned from dropping the rest of the family at the registry office, this its third trip. Two cars had been out of the question. Dad was unable to pay for a thing for his daughter, so she had put her hand in her own pocket for it. With a last minute prink of her dress and picking up her small shop-bought spray of three creamy roses and a trail of fern, nothing too elaborate or expensive, she came down the stairs. May followed behind in her frilled primose dress and a tiny posy of sweet peas made by an aunt from her own window box. Dad was at the bottom in his best suit – one Cissy faintly recognised with a pang of sadness as being the same that had been hanging in his wardrobe the day she had left home. Out of work, there was no thought of buying another, even for this special day.

'Ready, Dad?'

He gave a curt nod. Only his eyes, not quite as round and blue as they'd once been, age creeping up on him, betrayed him in a begrudging glow of pride. Though she noticed it, it didn't compensate for the curt nod. His refusal to answer in words was hurtful. But she smiled it away, following him to the waiting car. He hadn't even taken her arm.

The registry office was crowded. Surprise at the sight of so many, every chair occupied, and even more standing at the back so that the doors couldn't be properly shut, took away the trial of coming here beside her silent father.

As she paused prior to making her entrance for a last-minute arranging of her dress, Cissy peered in through the half-open door which someone was trying vainly to hold closed, hoping to discover who they all were. Surely she hadn't invited this many, but before she could focus, the door was opened for her and at a signal, she took Dad's arm whether he liked it or not, and came in, May holding the door open for her before following.

Eddie was already to one side, waiting for her. He looked so very handsome as he glanced round, the smile he gave her remarkably steady for someone about to be married. He stepped across to stand beside her, and she felt her love flood over her like a warm wave.

Side by side they approached the registrar's table. The registrar, giving each a stiff smile, began the formalities in a businesslike tone. In no time at all it was over, leaving Cissy dazed by the swiftness of it all – married, the signing done, everyone hurried out for confetti and good wishes to be showered over the happy pair, a few lucky enough to have cameras ushering them into line, each focusing with an eye jammed against their box-shaped contraption. Dazed, she smiled for them and they looked into each other's eyes for them. She had never been so happy; could hardly wait to be off on their honeymoon, alone with him. But there was the reception to get through first, the good wishes to be given, the food to be devoured, goodbyes to be said. And then, ah . . .

At the door of Eddie's office, they stood with their families, Eddie's mother looking pitifully alone among them, to receive their guests. Before long the office was full of people, many of whom she didn't recognise.

'Who are they all?' she hissed.

Eddie grinned. 'Friends. Blokes on the river. They clubbed together to buy us a wedding present. Couldn't leave 'em out.'

She smiled, shook hands as each one came in, men and their wives, not looking as prosperous as they once had in her dad's day when work on the water brought in good pay.

'We haven't got enough to feed them all,' she whispered slantwise, as in dismay she watched the room fill.

Again Eddie grinned. 'They've brought their own, mostly. They said they would.'

Sure enough, Eddie's desk, pushed back to the wall beside the filing cabinet, the surfaces covered with cloths and the food their parents had already made, began to fill with offerings of cold sausages, small wedges of cheddar cheese, pickled onions, gherkins, savaloys and little homemade cakes. There were even a couple of cherished bottles of gin, probably nicked at one time or other, going to join the bottles of beer and glasses set out on the desk in the tiny reception office. The two shelves above the desk displaying what wedding presents they had received, still wrapped in cheap gift paper or the paper bags in which they'd been purchased.

The lights on, although it was still daylight, the room was soon filling with a fug of pipe and cigarette smoke, a buzz of voices, and music from the old gramophone one of Eddie's guests had lugged up the narrow stairs. Being kissed and congratulated, Cissy looked around. There were far more people she didn't know than family, but she felt suddenly elated. She had a well-attended wedding, she had a lovely steady man for a husband, her parents had forgiven her and had come to see her married, what more could she want?

Daisy and Theodore had arrived the night before and taken a room at some hotel. Cissy was relieved to see that her daughter had been left behind, though Daisy had asked as a favour that her mother and father be invited. As a wonderful and trusted friend over the past years, how could she say no? Daisy had brought such a lovely wedding present – a full dinner and tea service, far too lovely to use. Unintentionally, it reminded her how changed their roles were, Daisy still able to afford such things despite the times, while she herself continued to struggle to keep herself looking respectable, every last penny of Langley's money sunk into her shop. But there were thousands far worse off, with nothing to ease their misery. If the worst came to the worst she could always sell her business and live on the proceeds. Many had nothing.

The cake had been cut and distributed, the table was looking as though an army of voracious rats had marched across it, the first waltz – 'I'll Be Loving You, Always' – was ceremoniously danced by the happy couple and the bottles of drinks in the dingy outer office were already half empty, the effects showing in flushed faces. It was the most wonderful party she could ever imagine. She hadn't seen much of Eddie, everyone insisting on commandeering their separate attention. She saw him now, through the tight-packed throng in the dingy little office, talking to Daisy's parents, and she turned away, smiling happily.

Mrs Evans, a small, pretty if slightly tubby figure next to her large beefy husband, stared up at Eddie, her round, downy face ready to break into smiles at the first word said to her.

'We just wanted to offer our congratulations,' she chirped and gave her husband a nudge. 'Didn't we, Dick?'

Prompted, her husband brought his gaze away from the filmy office window to say, 'Yeah, we did,' before returning to stare into the middle distance.

In comparison with her, his heavy features and jutting lower lip gave all the appearance of indolence and lack of interest in conversation. It was easy to see who their bubbly daughter took after. Eddie glimpsed Daisy across the room clinging to her German husband's arm and could hear her high giddy laugh from here.

'You 'ad a lovely day for it – the wedding,' Mrs Evans was saying. 'It could've easily been raining, but it didn't, did it, Dick? I said, didn't I, Dick – they're a lucky pair to 'ave nice weather. It's nice for you too, ain't it, 'aving a ready-made family? But I suppose you will be 'aving little'uns of yer own eventually, won't you?'

Eddie's wandering attention had become riveted on her, his brows knitting together in confusion. 'I'm sorry, Mrs Evans, little'uns of whose own?'

'Why yours. As well as Cissy's.'

'Cissy's?' His frown deepened. 'I don't understand. Cissy's what?'

The round face had begun to glow, a flush spreading slowly across the downy cheeks. 'Oh, I . . . I must've made a mistake. Got confused . . . with someone else.'

Eddie felt his face tighten. She wasn't confusing him with anyone else, he was sure. Little cogs were turning in his head, notches slipping one into the other to set strange wheels of thought in motion to form something he didn't want to acknowledge.

'No, Mrs Evans.' His voice grated upon his own ears. 'I don't think so. What *about* Cissy?'

'It's . . . nothing. Honest.' Stammering, she backed away, clutching at her husband's arm, pulling him protesting with her. 'Anyway, it's time we went. I'll tell Daisy we're going. We've 'ad a lovely time. And thanks fer inviting us.'

Before he could persist, the Evanses were pushing across the room like people swimming against the tide; a few words hastily mouthed at Daisy, who shot a look in his direction. Eddie could see it all; saw Daisy's teeth catch at her bottom lip, and then she turned on her mother, her face contorted, her words obviously whispered being hissed at her, her hands gesticulating in a secretive way. He watched her bend a little to peck her mother's cheek leaving the two to trail out. For a second Daisy turned again to Eddie, saw him still watching and turned away quickly.

From now on, Eddie felt a compulsion to watch. No longer enjoying his wedding, he was a spy watching everyone, every move anyone made, quick to read something into anything: the way Cissy looked across at him, was that a sly glance? Did she carry a secret? Why that frown on her father's face? Did he know something more about his daughter? Was that why he'd been so slow to forgive her? And her mother, attentive and keeping closer to her – what had Cissy shared with her that she hadn't shared with him, now her husband? And Bobby, standing there with his sulky wife, what had he said to Eddie's own father who had died with the secret still locked away? Every fibre of him tried to believe that he'd misinterpreted Daisy's mother's embarrassment, yet common sense said that her slip of the tongue and clumsy attempt to cover it up could point only to one thing. For his own peace of mind he must have this out with Cissy at the first chance he got.

Yet in the end, fearing what he might discover, he said nothing. What the ear doesn't hear . . . He did not want his heart to grieve, so he said nothing. And Cissy, who was so much in love with him, suspected nothing, gave herself to him completely that night and every night of the honeymoon, helping him willingly when he remained limp, putting his failure down to marital nerves, knowing how successful had been their premarital love and on the way home telling him excitedly that she thought she was already a couple of months pregnant.

He thought he made a decent job of looking joyful about her news as he wondered if she had once just as excitedly told someone else of a pregnancy. And the baby, where was it now? Did Daisy Evans have it – Cissy's long-standing friend who still lived in Paris? That could be why Mrs Evans had become flustered in nearly letting the cat out of the bag. And what of Cissy? Did she love the child if what he imagined was true? Why hadn't she told him – again if what he was imagining was true?

'As well as Cissy's . . .' The remark bounced around in his head; haunting him for months afterwards, but he never asked, and as Cissy's stomach began to grow, pride in what they had made together clouded out the vision of what her life had been before. He was to be a father and the past must be put aside. It didn't, shouldn't matter.

But sometimes, in the dead of night when he couldn't sleep . . .

Chapter Twenty-Three

The past was behind her. Cissy was happy, her worries over, except of course about the lack of money – but that was universal. The important thing was, they were together – she was carrying Eddie's child inside her. For that alone, she felt moments of ecstatic happiness.

He should have been the same, and he was happy about her pregnancy, but for the most part he seemed to have grown moody, lost in a world of his own sometimes. Probably over his tug business, she assumed and shrugged it off, vowing to help should he decide to share any worry with her. It was hard graft nowadays. He would come home tired and tetchy – so unlike the Eddie she had known before they had married.

It must be money, it bothered them all. If only she could do more in her shop – entice more customers – perhaps then he wouldn't look so dismal, wouldn't be so worried about the future with a little one on the way.

She invested a small portion of her meagre profit having some handbills made, to be posted through letter-boxes in the area. She didn't tell Eddie. In his present mood he would have called it a waste of time. He was forever criticising the things she tried to do, or so it seemed to her. He was so down, and these days it was well known that once a person became down, they stayed down, became despondent and then indolent, accepting their lot. She didn't want that to happen to Eddie. At least the handbills would draw the curiosity of a few more customers to see what she had to sell. The trouble was, who would want to be attended by someone with a stomach way out in front? Very few women worked after marriage. Those that did were frowned on, seen as not quite decent. True this was her own business, but to be seen heavily pregnant and working was just not done. She would be pitied, seen to be someone in dire straits. And nothing served more to put a customer off buying than some proprietress showing herself to be in dire straits by working in her condition.

'Eddie, what are we going to do about the shop?' she asked him just before Christmas.

Sitting by the fire, the standard lamp behind her for light, she was sorting through some trade magazines. This was her busiest time. She had been quite pleased with her modest increase in sales, though after the New Year it would dwindle away again to its normal trade, which wasn't as she had once hoped it would be.

Eddie looked up from his *Evening Standard*. The light shone directly on his face emphasising his disinterest. 'Don't know. It's your shop.'

His reply was short and terse, almost impatient. It was so unlike him. He hadn't even asked what she meant, but she brushed it aside and began explaining without being prompted.

'It's just that I'm six months now. I'm getting too big to be seen in there. Customers are looking. I often notice them frowning. It's not good for trade. They look almost sorry for me.'

Eddie remained looking at her. He knew what she meant. There was nothing worse than appearing to be grovelling cap in hand to procure a deal. He knew all about that. Made sure he wore his best bib and tucker to the office – had to look smart so that anyone meeting him would hopefully see a prosperous man and put business his way. But it wasn't easy when he was often in his old clothes skippering the *Cicely*, loathe to pay out on a full crew. He felt for Cissy. At the same time, back came the old thoughts. They made his reply sharp.

'My advice'd be to sell up,' he said at last, returning to his newspaper. 'Not as if it brings in that much, way things are. Could be more handy what you get for it. It's just advice, the way I see it, that's all. It's your money to do what you like with.'

Cissy looked as if she'd been stung. 'Sell? I couldn't do that. We need what the shop brings in. Even if it isn't much, it's regular. If I sold up, the money would be gone within a year. And if times don't get any better, what'll we live on then?'

'You mean I can't provide.' He kept his eyes on his newspaper.

'No, I don't mean that. I mean . . . it must help. In the times we are living in, every little helps. It must do.'

He was still giving the paper all his attention, his head down. 'It won't 'elp us fer much longer, will it?'

He knew it sounded more like an accusation than a statement, but he couldn't moderate it. 'If yer want to keep the place and can't manage it yerself, you've got ter find someone to look after it for you. That costs money. We ain't got money. Not from what I provide.'

The second connotation could not be overlooked this time. Cissy had caught it. She leaned towards him. 'Darling, I'm not trying to put you down. I don't mean you can't provide for us. I just want to help.'

Now he looked at her, the newspaper rustling noisily as he lay it down sharply on his lap. 'Putting someone in while you 'ave the baby, is goin' ter be more trouble than it's worth. It'll more likely be a bloody great weight round our necks.'

Cissy winced visibly. 'Eddie, don't swear. You never used to. What have I done? You seem so surly. You've been surly ever since . . . ever since we got married, and I don't know what's wrong.'

How could he tell her? How could he ever broach the subject now? It should have been done at the time, clearing the air for better or worse. Too late now. He must live with it, try to get over it. But it was hard. He loved her, yet he couldn't get over her deception. Deception that he supposed was still being continued. If one day, she came to him and said, Eddie, I've something I have to tell you, he would forgive her with all his heart. But until then . . .

'Nothing's the matter,' he answered her now, and saw her frown.

'It's the times we're living in. Things will get better. They must. This depression can't go on forever.'

'Maybe not.' He picked up his paper, went back to it again. 'When d'you reckon on giving up bein' in the shop?'

'I don't know. I can manage until the New Year. It's getting busier with Christmas only a couple of weeks off and finding someone now just would be silly. I know how to keep customers buying. After that . . .'

'After that, we'll be paying someone else,' he finished sourly, looking up to see her grimace again and that lost, confused look that was often on her face these days.

'What *is* the matter, Eddie? Is it your business – worrying you – is that it?'

'No more than usual.'

'But . . . but you used to be so lively – so cheerful. You were always cheerful when I first knew you.'

'Then I must've changed. Settled down.'

'No, it's more than that. What's worrying you, darling?'

'Darling!' He couldn't help the word bursting forth, steeped in sarcasm, unlike him. 'What the bloody 'ell's "darling"? You sound like one of them bloody silly flappers you went off with. Can't you forget hobnobbing with the idle rich? I'm a bit of a come-down for you after them, ain't I?'

Cissy stood up sharply, the pile of knitting catalogues she had been thumbing through sliding to the floor in an untidy jumble.

'Why are you being so nasty? I've done nothing to you, Eddie. I don't consider you a come-down. I love you. I love what you are. You can't be jealous of something that doesn't even mean anything to me any more. I know I was silly in those days. But I'm older now. I've got over all that. I'm a wife now, and soon to be a mother . . .' He saw her blanch angrily at his sudden caustic laugh, but she ploughed on. 'I have responsibilities now and if we can both pull together, things will turn out all right.

But sometimes you seem to be trying to block me – in every way. I'm doing my best for us, Eddie.'

'And *my* best ain't good enough for you, is that it?'

He almost added, if that's the case go back to your fancy boyfriend – the one what gave you a baby. But he caught himself in time, instead he got up, dropping his paper on the chair behind him. 'I'm tired. I need an early night. I think I'll 'ave a wash and go to bed.'

Cissy sat down again. 'I'll follow in a minute,' she said limply, but he didn't reply as he went out to the tiny kitchen to wash.

Christmas was spent quietly, with his mother. The first anniversary of his father's death, how could they not be with her? But Cissy hated every minute, having to endure the renewed grieving, though she understood.

'This time last year,' Mrs Bennett sighed, as she dished up a small chicken, all she could afford, though Cissy and Eddie had helped her out with some of the fare. 'I 'ad my poor Alf with me this time last year. No one could've guessed within days he'd be taken.'

As they sat themselves down at the table, Eddie went and put his arms about her.

'I miss 'im too, Mum.' His brown eyes swam with tears, managing not to let them spill over onto his cheeks.

Mrs Bennett wiped her eyes and stoically motioned her son back to his place. 'We mustn't let it spoil our Christmas dinner. But I think it'd be nice to say a little prayer for 'im, don't you?'

'That would be nice, Mum,' Eddie said, sitting down.

Together the three bent their heads over their plates, their hands loosely clasped.

'Dear God,' intoned Mrs Bennett, taking the initiative as the wife of the deceased. 'Let us be truly thankful for what we're about to receive, and bless my dear Alf, Eddie's father, in 'eaven.' She looked up quickly. 'He will be in 'eaven – 'e was a good man. Never did no one any wrong.'

Eddie ran a hand across his nose, sniffing. Cissy watched them both from under her brows, feeling for her husband in his loss.

'A good businessman, was your father,' Mrs Bennett continued. 'If things 'ad been different, and if that money we got from my poor sister 'ad been at the start of his life, he'd've done really well. But that's 'ow it goes for the likes of us – always too late. Not that I wish my poor sister gone earlier than she did. A dear friend to me, she was, and I miss 'er too. Dear God, bless 'er too. We miss 'er as well as my poor Alf.'

Cissy assumed she was determined to put a downer on the whole of their Christmas, remembering her Alf and her sister, the dear departeds, but Mrs Bennett finally came to herself with a deep brave sigh. 'Well, we mustn't let our dinners get cold. My Alf wouldn't've wanted that.'

'No,' Eddie enjoined and after another brief sniff to rid himself of grief and memories of better times, fell to eating what had been put before him.

Even so, it was a dismal day, inside and out. Cissy longed for the summer and warm sunny weather, longed for March and for her baby to be born, longed for tomorrow, Boxing Day with her family, Mrs Bennett having been persuaded to come with them to help alleviate her sense of loss at this her saddest time of the year and for many years to come.

Compared to her gloomy home with just one piece of holly over the mantel mirror, Mum's was an Aladdin's cave – decorations from a dozen past Christmases regularly brought down from the attic. This year, put up by May, who had a boyfriend now who had helped her. Usually a small new garland would be added each year, perhaps an old and tatty one discarded, the collection growing steadily in its box. But not this year. No money to squander on inessential bits and pieces.

Little money or not, unemployment or not, this was Christmas – misery and festivity had no part with each other. Conversation was batted back and forth. Cheap, but nicely made food – Mum had always been good at making something out of nothing when feeding her own. Cissy knew full well that in her condition she would end up with heartburn, eating so much pastry, cheap and cheerful but light, with the meagrest filling of mincemeat or sausage, the leftovers of cold pork with pickles and Christmas pudding afterwards – no money for rich Christmas cakes, pudding did well enough cold, cut into slices.

The main meal around midday was usually eaten in a rush so as to get to the London Palladium. It was a tradition with her family as far back as Cissy could remember, they would pack themselves off as soon after dinner as possible for the afternoon matinee of whatever pantomime was showing. It didn't matter that everyone had seen most of them several times before, they were always different, always exciting, a different well-known actress playing principal boy, a popular male comedian playing the dame in outrageously coloured dress and striped stockings. There were always new songs taught to the audience so they could join in. With spectacular flying ballets and fairies galore, who cared if the thread of the original tale was completely lost? It was tremendous fun and afterwards they'd come home to settle down by the fireside and finish up whatever was left over from the Boxing Day dinner, rejuvenated by two and a half hours of sheer silliness.

This year it was different. They were not going to a pantomime. Partly because there were no children except for Bobby and Ethel's and anyway, Ethel, not feeling disposed to carting off up West after a big meal, had decided to go home, dragging her protesting husband with her. And partly because no one felt like paying hard-saved Boxing Day money just to act the fool. They went instead to Drury Lane for a bit of culture, entertained in the meantime by endless buskers as they stood in line for the gods – the cheapest top balcony seats – for the new musical *Cavalcade* that had been raved about since October.

Cissy enjoyed it immensely, the first time she'd been anywhere nice since her marriage. Eddie seemed to like it, though he said little about it, while his mother said she couldn't understand it.

'It wasn't a proper musical, was it?' she said as they came out. 'Not like the musicals I've bin used to. Bit too 'ighbrow for me.'

Cissy's parents had loved it. The sheer magnificent pageantry of it, filling everyone with hope of better times around the corner if the whole country pulled together, had made them come over all patriotic. After all Britain had survived wars and far worse times; the last war had been the worst anyone could ever have gone through.

Things must get better soon – the menfolk back in full employment, money in the purse, more food on the table. Her parents wouldn't stop talking about it.

May had loved it purely because she was in love with Noel Coward as well as her current boyfriend Lenny, and anything Noel Coward produced or played in was meat and drink to her. She had all his songs, buying sixpenny copies of sheet music, painfully picking out the notes on a friend's piano, not having one herself.

Harry at fourteen had been bored, except when what seemed to him like hundreds of scarlet or khaki-clad soldiers were seen marching past along the back of the stage. Otherwise he complained endlessly about not being taken to see a pantomime which wasn't fair.

Sidney, now sixteen, hadn't gone. More interested in a girl he had his eye on he'd been rewarded by her interest in him and had taken her out instead.

'I thought it was very enjoyable,' Cissy's mother said when they got back home. Immediately setting about making a cup of tea for everyone, she looked refreshed, her rounded face, of late fraught with anxiety and drawn with care, tonight more brisk and younger-looking, more optimistic. Even her father, sitting chatting to Eddie and herself as if she had never left home, bore an air of optimism, and though it probably wouldn't last long, Cissy suspected, to her it had been the best Boxing Day ever, and she was looking forward to 1932 and her new baby.

Her mind was made up. She wrote to Daisy to explain how well she and Eddie had settled down together, that he still knew nothing about Noelle and was thrilled to bits about becoming a father.

'So there's really no need to go rocking the boat, if you see what I mean,' she wrote blithely. 'I know how much you love Noelle. On the other hand, I seem to be seeing less and less of her. And what with the baby coming, I was wondering, if you agree, Daisy, wouldn't it be best to let things stand as they are? To be honest, I often don't feel at all like her mother. I'm sure you are more a mother to her than I'll ever be. If you were to continue raising her, she'll never have to suffer any confusion should she be told when she is older that I'm really her mother. That is if you need to tell her at all. What's the point of upsetting her – and Eddie? I'll wait to hear what you think, Daisy. I know you love her dearly and it would be a wrench for you to part with her. And I know Theodore loves her too.'

She wrote a lot more besides: about her life and money worries; how she hoped that between them, she and Eddie would eventually make a go of things; said she was wonderfully happy, though she was careful to make no mention of Eddie's strange new moods. After all, why give Daisy, who never failed to laud her Theodore's attributes, the chance to crow sympathy for her?

Mrs Bennett stood pouring the tea for her son and daughter-in-law on their regular Sunday afternoon visit, her gaze riveted purposefully on what she was doing though she was addressing Cissy.

'I've bin thinking, dear, ain't it time you packed up in that shop of yours? I was wond'ring – save paying some-one to look after it for you, I could give eye to it. Just until the little one's born and you're on yer feet again.'

Cissy and Eddie exchanged glances of amazement. This woman, still sighing after her Alf and conveying the impression of total inability to ever cope alone, was now offering to run a shop. Unbelievable.

'After all,' she continued as she handed Cissy a brimming cup of extremely weak brew, 'you're two months off 'aving the baby. You can't go on working. Look at the size of you.'

Eddie, still startled, studied his mother's pinched face as she handed him his tea. 'But when you had a chance to manage Aunt Lottie's café, you wouldn't do it. You shied away – said you'd no idea how to.'

'That was then,' she said as she sat down with her own cup, pushing a round paper packet towards the two of them. 'Biscuit?'

Both shook their heads, trying to probe the reasoning.

'Yes, that was then,' she picked up, 'when I didn't need to. Your poor father was bringing in good wages and it all seemed such an extra 'eadache then. This is different. It won't be for ever an' I could 'elp you both out. Like I said, just till you're on your feet again, Cissy. I mean, you've got ter be sensible. You don't want ter give up a nice little goldmine like that. One day when things get better, you'll be glad of it. It could make you a mint, that place – when things get better.'

Everywhere people were saying: when things get better and that it can't go on for ever. Optimism, a small seed fighting to take root, to push upwards towards some dimly imagined light despite all the signs pointing to dark days for a long time yet. The problem was that should the tiny seed of hope fail to germinate quickly enough, it would wither and die, all the old despair, the pessimism, returning worse than before. At this moment, however, Mrs Bennett was full of optimism for the future, which was so unlike her since her bereavement.

'And when . . .' she didn't say if, 'Eddie's business picks up again with better times, you two could be rolling in it.' Her eyes shone with an unconcealed cunning light. 'And if I can 'elp you two through your bad times, you can 'elp me when I'm old and you're rich.'

Eddie burst out laughing. 'Rich! Oh, Mum, I can't see that ever 'appening.'

Cissy wasn't laughing. 'I can. Your mum's right, Eddie. She'd be a wonderful help. I could do with it right now. And who knows what the future might hold.' She turned to her mother-in-law. 'Thank you, Mum, I'll be so very grateful to take up your offer.'

'It'd give me something to do,' her mother-in-law returned briskly, her expression so set that it bordered on comical. 'It's about time I stopped grievin' over my poor Alf. Though I do miss 'im so.'

There was a proviso to the offer that Cissy hadn't reckoned on. At Mrs Bennett's suggestion that it would be more convenient, she moved herself in with them – for the time being as she said – she and Cissy sharing the double bed and Eddie consigned to the couch. 'Only until the baby's born,' she explained, but Cissy had begun to wonder.

Not only that, but Mrs Bennett wasn't Cissy. Cissy knew without questioning that it was her own business sense and natural charm that had been her selling point. Mrs Bennett as an elderly woman and, despite her previous resolve, exuding sadness, repelled rather than attracted the customers. Nor was she always sure what she was doing, often requiring Cissy with her stomach grossly out in front to waddle down the narrow, wooden and rickety outside stairs to the yard in all weathers and in through the shop's back door to give advice.

Of course the woman's heart had been in the right place when she had offered her help, but anyone could see that she had taken on more than she was capable of and that she did not enjoy it, perhaps even regretted having been so generous. Having offered, she braved the ordeal as best she could, but it did reflect on her service to her customers.

In the background Cissy, unable to show herself, seethed as Mrs Bennett gave wrong change, kept customers waiting and infuriated them as she searched frantically through odd piles of knitting patterns for the one they had selected, finally having to hurry up the outside stairs to ask, pleading and panicking, if there was some other pile she couldn't find. She often left customers alone in the shop, at liberty to help themselves without paying, the temptation in this day and age of need too great for even the most honest to resist.

The shop grew emptier. Mrs Bennett grew more tired as the last two months dragged on by and would flop into a chair at the end of the day while Cissy, guilty and anxious to make amends, constantly willed the day forward when her baby would be born.

Chapter Twenty-Four

'Eddie!'

She had got out of bed as quietly as she could, so as not to disturb her mother-in-law, and crept into the front room where Eddie was in a deep sleep, curled up in a most uncomfortable manner, the eiderdown that had belonged to his parents, half on the floor, the pillow askew.

She gave his shoulder a small shake. 'Eddie. Get up, darling – I think I've started.'

'Yeah, started,' he mumbled, his sleep disturbed, then came fully awake, sitting up staring at her. 'You've started? Are you sure?'

'I'm very sure.'

'Yes, I suppose you would be,' he said, but stopped sharp as though he had caught himself saying something he shouldn't. Leaping out of bed, he took her by the shoulders, his tone moderating to one of concern. 'Stay here. I'll go and tell the doctor. What time is it?'

'Two o'clock,' she whispered. 'Or thereabouts.'

'Where's Mum?'

'Asleep. I tried not to disturb her.'

He was struggling out of pyjamas and into his clothes. 'Go and wake her up. You'll need her with you while I'm gone. Though I'll only be a couple of ticks.'

Doctor Fisher, tall, lean and balding, resided and practised over a shop several doors down. She knew Eddie would be back as quickly as he had predicted, their doctor telephoning from there for an ambulance, Cissy having been booked in at the London Hospital.

Out into the chilly March morning half an hour later, Cissy dressed and guided downstairs to the waiting ambulance by her mother-in-law, Eddie was the picture of concern.

All three sitting together as the vehicle made its way through the deserted, rain-flecked streets, he fretted at the vehicle's almost leisurely pace as Cissy's pains came and went at least four times in his estimation.

The ambulance man with them grinned at his chafing. 'Plenty of time, mate. Her first, is it?'

'No . . . er, yes.' He caught himself in time, shot Cissy a look but she was occupied by another spasm. But what if she had caught some small significance in that slip of the tongue?

He was still squirming when the vehicle drew to a stop and Cissy was assisted down by two nurses who had come out to receive her. He watched her being conducted through the hospital doors, a nurse on either side helping her shuffling gait, the trio already laughing at a quip from one of the nurses about her cup of cocoa having had to be left and that some people do pick their times! He felt reprieved. Cissy couldn't have heard.

'No need to wait, Mr Bennett,' a nurse – he thought a staff nurse, though he wasn't familiar with uniforms – came back to tell him after Cissy had been taken off to be examined somewhere in the depths of the hospital. She smiled encouragement at him and his mother. 'Nothing will happen for hours. Your wife is in good hands, Mr Bennett. Come back around midday and wait in reception. You will most likely find yourself a father by then. The second usually comes into the world a lot faster than the first.'

'The second?' He was aware of his mother gazing at the woman as though she were an imbecile. 'No, dear, this is 'er first. They ain't been married 'ardly a year.'

The staff nurse gave her a smile that said truth will out but she was loath to be the bearer of it. 'According to our examination, this isn't . . .'

Eddie was pulling his mother away. 'It's all right, nurse. We do understand. We'll come back in the morning.' He all but dragged his confused and protesting mother to the entrance.

It was a tight-lipped woman who saw him off to the hospital next morning, her excuse that Thursday with half-day closing necessitated her being in the shop to deal with morning customers – true, though not imperative. So he went alone. He went late. By that time Cissy was asleep after the birth of a son three hours before. The staff nurse had been right. It had come quickly. After all, it was her second child.

He sat beside her in the long twenty-bedded ward, watching her sleeping. Other mothers sat in their beds cuddling their newborn and chatting, the ward was filled with a buzz of conversation. Bedpans clattered distantly, trolleys soughed softly on the ward's grey linoleum, the air rustled to the starched progress of a passing nurse, but he felt apart from it all, sitting there torn between contrasting sensations: tenderness, hurt, sorrow for the lie she'd been living; anger against it; pride in his new son and her achievement; and a profound sense of disillusionment that someone before him had put his seed into her. Did she still love that person? All the time he had made love to her, had she been thinking of that other one, comparing them, sighing for him even as he, Eddie, thrilled to those sighs?

A nurse came cradling a small bundle, put it into the tiny crib beside the bed with its basic hospital trimmings, and smiled down at Eddie. 'Congratulations, Mr Bennett. He is a lovely baby. What're you going to call him? Or haven't you settled on a name yet?'

'Not yet.' His own smile was stiff and the nurse, suspecting she was intruding, left in an indiscreet rustle of uniform, as Cissy stirred, opened her eyes and smiled at her husband for his approval.

Cissy, still bleary from the small amount of gas she'd been given to alleviate some of the birth pains, bore a look of utter happiness.

'D'you like him?' she mumbled. Eddie nodded, taking the hand she held out to him.

'I've hardly seen him,' she continued blissfully. 'They took him away so quickly. But he's ours now, darling. Our first child.'

It was a simple statement, one to make any father proud. But in its very simplicity it screamed, lie! '*My* first,' he wanted to yell at her. 'But your second.'

Cissy was frowning at him. 'What's the matter, darling? If you're worried about me, I'm fine. It wasn't half as bad as I'd imagined. Oh, it was hard work, but it was so quick.' She was growing stronger by the minute, her face glowing. 'He came out like a little wet rabbit. It was such a wonderful feeling. A boy. It's just what we both wanted, wasn't it? What shall we call him?'

Eddie was hardly listening. Tell me, his heart was imploring her. Tell me about the other one, how it all came about. Tell me, and I'll love you to the end of time and forget all about that other life of yours. Only, tell me, please! He wanted to shake it out of her, but she was still frowning, perplexed, so he smiled down at her instead.

It was impossible to sleep. Pictures and voices marched through his head every time he closed his eyes; Cissy, happy if sleepy, asking him what they should call the baby – she had settled on Edward after him. He'd nodded in agreement, wondering what name she'd settled on for the other child she'd had. Had it been a boy or a girl? Pictures floated against his eyelids, of her being made love to by someone else; of her and her friend Daisy bringing up the child, playing with it, making plans for it.

Tossing and turning he tried to think of other things, but it was hopeless. In the end he got up and made a cup of tea, in the process disturbing his mother who got up too.

'If only she'd tell me, right out,' he sighed, as in the small cold hours they sat opposite each other at the small dining table beside the sofa he used as a bed. His mother suddenly reached out and took his hand.

'You've got to face 'er with it.' He tried to avoid her intense regard, but she held him with her earnestness.

'What 'appened with her was before you and 'er met again. She was free to do what she pleased. It wasn't right, and far be it from me to condemn your own wife to your face, but two wrongs don't make a right. I don't say I forgive 'er but I do pity 'er for what 'appened. It can 'appen to any gel.'

'Only those who go looking for it,' he put in sourly.

'Any gel what thinks she's in love,' she persisted. 'Or in the clutches of some 'eartless swine what makes her think she's in love. I thought about it a lot yesterday, Eddie, and I reckon that we shouldn't judge what we don't know. I think the past should be put behind the pair of you, or it'll muck up yer marriage. Forgive 'er, Eddie. That's my advice.'

Eddie studied his rapidly cooling tea. 'I don't want to face her with it. All I want is for her to come to me and say that our son ain't the only baby she's 'ad. All the time she keeps it to 'erself, she's lying. All I want is 'er to tell me, herself. But I ain't goin' ter *make* 'er tell me. If she don't tell me 'erself – if she's living a lie – then this ain't no marriage, nor ever will be. She's got to come to me of 'er own free will. Otherwise it don't mean nothing.'

His mother let go his hand and took a sip of tea. 'I can't 'elp you there, luv. I can't see no way out of what you're wanting.'

After she had gone back to bed, her older body unused to the burning of midnight oil, claiming the stronger need to sleep, Eddie sat on in the glare of the central electric light, always more stark in the small silent hours, and stared into space, his brain churning over a mass of unformed thoughts.

But after a day or so, something constructive had come out of the muddle in his mind. His mother was right – she was never going to tell him. It was too much to hope for. And so he would tell her. Far better out in the open than bottling up in unspoken resentment maybe. In this he was resolved.

Before that, however, he had to be sure and not go accusing her on the back of half truths. He would write to Daisy. With the truth she might in some way alleviate the pressures building up inside him.

Two days before Cissy and her baby son were due to come home, while his mother was down in the shop, Eddie went to the drawer that was Cissy's. There had to be a letter somewhere from her friend which would give the address. He found a pile of letters stuffed at the back of the drawer, neatly pinned together minus their envelopes for room, each one from Daisy.

There, like some sneak thief, he sat on the edge of the bed reading account after account of a beloved daughter. Words written as though endeavouring to console a bereaved parent. They spoke so plainly of a mother whose love for her absent daughter had torn at her heart that it tore at his too, and sent waves of pity flying towards her. How had she borne it? How could he hate her, so broken by that estrangement?

There were several tiny pictures, stark in black and white: Noelle at eighteen months he judged, in a high chair, sunshine streaming in at a window. Her prettiness clutched at him with something very near to pain. She bore no resemblance to her mother as he could see, pretty as Cissy was. She had to take after the father, obviously handsome – unlike himself. A wreath of hatred for the unknown man coiled itself around inside him. How could Cissy love someone like himself after that? In his mind he saw the handsome couple they must have made.

Unfolding yet another letter, he studied the picture – one of the child taken in a garden setting surrounded by toys; another, a little older in a snowy park playing with a middle-aged man in a fur-collared coat and a fedora hat, he looked like Daisy's German husband; yet another, older still, the rosebud lips open in a smile, cuddling her foster mother as though she were her true mother.

Unable to help himself, he began to read the letter accompanying the photograph, the date well over a year before:

'Cissy, dear, give it time. I know how you are feeling. I find it bad enough yearning *for a child of my own. But you having to leave Noelle behind, and knowing how that beast of a man left you, I know how much it must hurt. All I can say is times will get better for you, I know they will, and before you know it you'll be sending for her . . .'*

Eddie's eyes misted. Such pain, and such pain too from the foster mother who was finding more and more love for a child not her own.

Putting it aside, Eddie selected the most recent one, lying on top of the rest, dated only a few weeks ago:

'Dear Cissy – I'm overjoyed. I've felt for a long time that you and Noelle were drifting apart. I mean you don't often see her now. But I never dared expect to hear you say I could take her on as though she were

mine. Of course I shall bring her up with all the love I'd give to my own child, if I had one. I don't think I'll ever be able to have children. There seems to be no reason for it, but some of us aren't blessed that way. Though Teddy says when we go to live in Germany, which will be at the end of this year, he will arrange for all the tests to be done again, the hospitals in Germany being the most efficient in the world, even if it costs all he has – and as you know, we're not as well off as we once were. This Depression seems to be hanging on for ever. Things must alter soon. But Teddy says it will be better for us once we get to Dusseldorf – I'll send you the address when we get there. He loves Noelle too, like she was his own daughter. She calls him Papa now, or Vater which is German for father. He is teaching her German. She already speaks French now she mixes with other children. She's very bright, you know. I know how you fretted for her at one time and I understood, but now you've got Eddie and the baby'll be here soon – to tell the truth, I'd be devastated parting with Noelle now, she's like my own child to me. And I'm so absolutely thrilled you've come to a decision about letting her go to me. I know you've done the right thing . . .'

Where Eddie had felt pity, a readiness to understand, now there was anger, returning with renewed vigor. Cissy was still acting out her lie, to the extent of forsaking her own daughter. That she'd loved Noelle once there was no denying by the tone of Daisy's letters, yet now here she was ready to give her away. It vaguely occurred to him that it was being done for love for him, that he should be overwhelmed by the sacrifice, but it struck him so unnatural and monstrous, that he clouded his vision to that initial thought, saw instead someone clinging to the first straw that had come her way, him, even though that straw was soggy and in danger of sinking. Was that all he was to her, just something to cling to with her business floundering? Had she ever loved him? He wanted to weep. Instead he clenched his teeth and folded the letter slowly, putting the letters and photographs into their right places, and pulling Cissy's undies over them, closed the drawer.

When Cissy came home, happy and bubbly, her son in her arms, he had already drawn a line under his resolve to tell her what he knew. Since reading her letters, he no longer wanted her to break down and confess all as it were. He wanted to hear nothing of her pain, the anguish she might have suffered throughout those lonely years, how she had been forsaken by a man she had trusted and, he had no doubt, loved, of having to sacrifice her daughter to another's care while she tried to make a decent home for her. If he had been asked to listen to it all, he felt he might have throttled her. All he wanted was to go on with his life as though he had no knowledge of any of it, even though it was all but breaking his heart.

With his new resolve, he even managed to smile at her as she came home with their son.

Mrs Bennett regarded her son as he prepared for work. Five in the morning but already past dawn, being only just the other side of the longest day of the year.

Eddie started early, doing all he could to keep work coming in, he did a lot of the paperwork himself now, only just able to afford a girl part-time; sometimes having to go out and slog long hours on the *Cicely* to save paying a skipper, the old tug coaxed every inch of the way upstream and down, sometimes not coming home until after midnight if work had come his way. It was such a pity. He'd always been a hard worker, dedicated, and a darn good tugman, and he deserved better.

He seemed so down these days. A wife and baby to feed now, yet he was still looked on as fortunate by others, not only being in work but having a business, even though that business was floundering with next to nothing coming in. Still owing money to the bank to keep him going, them breathing down his neck every so often, people didn't realise there was as much pressure on him as those out of work. There was the *Cicely* to be maintained, a crew to be paid, his office lighting and heating to be paid, a girl to do his paperwork if only part-time, and a dozen other things. He could give up the office premises perhaps, and work from home to save money, but how could you meet prospective clients in the back room of a poky little flat above a shop and still give confidence of a thriving business? It was true what they said: once you're down, no one wants to pick you up. Well, that's how it seemed to her. And all the time she watched her son silently bearing his burden, keeping his worries to himself, not even sharing them with his wife. Mrs Bennett felt her heart go out to him as she removed his empty cereal bowl and his teacup to wash up.

She always got up with him, making breakfast and a sandwich or two to take with him for midday. She didn't mind. It compensated for what he was doing for her, and she was always up early.

Cissy was still sleeping. Eddie wanted it that way. She had been up for much of the night as Edward was restless. She would awake shortly, wash and dress little Edward, give him his feed, then put him down and open up the shop.

For the first few weeks after Edward was born, Cissy had pottered around a little, but had soon begun to take over again. Not that Mrs Bennett minded. She had hated serving in that shop, glad to take a back seat. And it wasn't that Cissy was ungrateful for all she'd done. But it did leave a funny feeling having to hand over the reins after all she had been doing. If anyone had asked her what she felt, she couldn't have said, except that it was a funny feeling. It would soon be time she went home. And anyway, she couldn't go on doing Eddie out of his bed, could she? No, she could see the light was flickering.

She was happy with the arrangements they'd been discussing last weekend. In a couple of weeks she would go back home and come over each day to look after Edward while Cissy was in the shop, where she apparently couldn't wait to be. She'd get the last workman's tram from Canning Town to Shoreditch, then a bus along Bethnal Green Road. Eddie would provide her fare and she'd have her meals here. It would keep her busy, stop her fretting for Alf, save her money on food, and she much preferred looking after the baby than tending that terrifying shop. In fact she couldn't wait to have Edward in her care. Her only treasured grandchild, who wouldn't be? The sweet little love.

'I'm really looking forward to our new arrangements, Eddie,' she said as she packed his sandwiches.

He was about ready to leave. He stood looking at her. 'Are you sure it'll be all right, Mum? I know you agreed, but . . .'

'Of course it's all right,' she said quickly, handing him his packet of sandwiches and the flask of tea.

He eyed her uncertainly. 'It's not like it's just round the corner. There's all that travelling, you gettin' up so early, and you're not as young as you was.'

'It'll be the making of me.' She smiled. 'Now off you go.'

'You've done so much for us.' He stood his ground. 'It feels like we're turning you out after all you've done.'

'You ain't turning me out. I can't go on for ever taking your bed. No, luv, it'll give me something to get up in the mornings for, coming over 'ere to give eye to the baby. I can be near and watch 'im grow. Not all grans can say that. You'll never know what a tonic to me it'll be looking after 'im – so like his grandad.'

'If you're sure we ain't making a convenience of you, Mum.'

'Of course you ain't. I'm only too 'appy. Now go on.'

She bustled him out, then after the door to the street had closed on Eddie, went down to the tiny back kitchen behind the shop and came up with fresh tea all to herself before going to wake Cissy.

Sipping the hot brew, sitting at the dining table in the temporary quietness of the living room, she smiled contemplatively. It was true what she'd said, they'd never know that even at his tender age, Edward was going to be good for her, would give her something far greater in return for that which she was doing for him.

And so it did. The strength she gained from looking after him grew steadily, like someone fast recovering from some illness. As the days slid into weeks, she rose to each day with renewed vigor, eager to be off, leaving her house around eight with a new spring in her step, clambering aboard the last workman's, swaying to the tram's jolting, along with office and factory girls still in jobs, feeling as young as them; no longer found herself mourning for Alf quite as regularly as she had. Of course, she could not help thinking from time to time that had he been here to see his grandson, he'd have been so proud, and she would shed a little tear at the oddest of times for what might have been.

The baby looked so much like him, even at this age. When he grew up, Eddie would take him into his business and he would become strong and sinewy like his father, like Alf had been. Take Edward into the business? That was if there was any business to take him into.

Eddie hadn't been able to make a go of it at all since his father had died. Sometimes she would look at him and feel it was killing him, bit by bit. Worry over a business had no right to make a man look as Eddie looked. But there was nothing she could do to help, except take care of Edward for him while he and Cissy worked to make ends meet, and just hope they would finally rise up out of the financial rut that this country's never-ending crisis seemed to be digging for them, for everyone. Where it would all end, she sometimes dreaded to think.

Closing the door behind him, Eddie walked swiftly, his stride long, his haversack bumping against his hip. At this time of year dawn had a special feeling to it, a clarity that was all its own and he took deep fortifying breaths of its freshness, filling his lungs.

Bethnal Green Road was deserted, quiet, inviting time to think. Once he gained Commercial Street, things would come alive, trams rattling and whining, early morning lorries rumbling, bikes – droves of them – weaving in and out of traffic, avoiding tram lines sunk into the road like small curving ravines, bells tinkling, riders chatting as they peddled. There would be a flock of workmen around his stop, all at the ready to push and shove to get on when the tram arrived. Until then, he savoured the quietness of the morning.

But that led to thinking, and thinking these days was disastrous, leading to worrying about business, the little it brought in, and in turn to thinking about Cissy.

He didn't want to think of Cissy. He concentrated his thoughts on little Edward, for a moment smiled to himself. The lad was growing so fast, so robust, it was amazing, magical, how he had changed in three months from the little scrap of helplessness he'd been, to a sturdy-fleshed, arm-flailing little person who already knew his own mind.

Eddie felt his chest swell with pride in his achievement. Edward looked so like Dad . . . he no longer thought of his father as Alf. Those days had gone. No longer here, his father was Dad and would remain so to him to the end of memory. But thinking of him brought pain and he hastily dragged his mind away to turn it again to little Edward, soon to be demanding his morning feed from Cissy. But he didn't want to think of her, so he turned his mind back again to business.

Today he was going straight onto his tug. Joan, the girl who did his typing and paperwork part-time, would be in today. She would let herself in with a key, a reliable, trustworthy girl; she'd catch up with any work from the day before yesterday, take phone messages and leave them for him when he came in around seven or eight this evening to catch up with anything that might need doing, he finally going home around nine.

It wasn't the most satisfactory way to carry on a business and he could sense as well as see it going down and down, very slowly, like a feather or a leaf that had fallen off a tree being wafted up and down here and there by odd upcurrents of air yet always lessening the distance between itself and the ground. It had a dream-like quality to it, and sometimes he felt that if only he could take a sledgehammer to the whole thing, break it physically, or catch that leaf and pull it to the ground in one jerk, this nagging waiting for things to run themselves down would come to an end. He would be bankrupt and have to join the endless dole queue with others, relying on someone else to give handouts. In a way, left to fate, it seemed easier to bear. But he knew this was foolish thinking; that he would go on struggling until he, that leaf, came to rest among all the other fallen leaves to rot away, dreaming of how things might have been.

It was having to fight for the money to pay bills, to pay wages, that was killing. He badly needed a proper crew instead of the bare three of them – Pete Robertson his engineer, Jack Stoker his fireman, and himself, skipper. They pulled together as best they could, took turns with duties fit only for a tea-boy, and made their own tea. They understood, sympathised and were grateful to have a job. But for him it was chaos. What he needed was a mate who could take over the skippering when he himself was needed in the office, but as it stood at present, there was not enough money coming in to pay a mate's wage full-time. It was always a dilemma: save on crew and not get a job done properly, or pay out and gamble that work would come in enough to compensate for the outlay.

Cissy on the other hand had been finding the going a little easier lately, so she said; even suggesting, as she totted up her takings last week, that it might be the start of better times and if it carried on like that they might begin putting something from the shop into the towage side to help kick it back into life. As if she thought that without her help he'd sink without trace. He was not prepared to stoop to handouts. It was her money – even though she used it to buy food, clothes, things like that. She could plough whatever was left back into her shop. He'd take care of his own end. He wouldn't touch her money, not with a bargepole, he wouldn't. It had been got from that one she'd been with in France, that he had gleaned from one of her letters, and he wanted none of it. He'd struggle or go under before taking a penny of hers to bolster the business he'd built.

He turned into the main road to be met head on by its bustle, and made towards the swaying mob all trying at once to board the tram that would take him to Stepney. No time now to think; fight for a seat or stand strap-hanging. The conductor squeezed between passengers taking fares, giving out tickets, little faded green oblong things, the machine pinging like mad – anyone looking at this crush wouldn't think that there was massive unemployment across the land. The air reeked of tobacco smoke and someone's breath in your face, while on rainy days the dank odour of wet jackets and caps pervaded. And all the time the tram filled with the deep, hollow booming of men's voices chatting about football, the wife, the boss, the state of affairs.

Off the tram, Eddie walked briskly through Rotherhithe Tunnel to Bellamy's Wharf where his crew of two were waiting for him. Instantly he felt his spirits rise. Nothing better than being on the river, and being master of your own decisions; working a vessel up or down river, its engines pounding under your feet, the power behind the noisy, cranking, clacking machinery towing a string of laden barges or nudging a big ship into a dock or to a wharf as a crew worked together like the parts of a well-oiled engine.

Together they walked through the wharf, the roadsman waiting to pick them up in his boat to take them to where the *Cicely* had been moored the night before. A quick brew-up, and off to the first job of the day. Eddie, his eyes keen, set on the moment – up through the bridges, in the bridge-hole the tug's engines compressing eardrums, the roaring rush of displaced water, then coming out the other side, engine quietening to almost nothing after the noise.

During these moments he no longer felt bowed down by business worry; did not think of Cissy and the lie she still lived with him or even of his baby son. He was on the river. Nothing existed beyond the job ahead, the water beneath his tug's hull. He was on the river. He was in his element.

Chapter Twenty-Five

'You know, Mum, I'm beginning to think marriage is a killer of any loving relationship,' Cissy sighed, her gaze following the groups of schoolboy football enthusiasts running about the playing fields, their shirts smudges of blues, reds and greens, their figures made small by distance, like their shouts of encouragement to each other. The football season was just starting and they were making the most of it on this the first Sunday morning in September.

Cissy and her mother had taken to a regular wander on Sunday mornings to the recreation ground near to where her parents lived. It was pleasant sitting on the weather-worn, penknife-scratched bench for the sun's warmth to pour down on them and do them a bit of good.

Cissy dropped her gaze to Edward's pram to assure herself that he was not lying in direct sunlight which it was said could give babies a permanent squint. The September sun lower in the sky now could find its way under a pram hood too easily.

'I thought we would go on being so deeply in love with each other, but it all seems to have gone out of the window. Something has gone out of it – I don't know what, and it worries me. I'm still so much in love with him, but he doesn't want to know. All he does when he's home is drool over Edward or read the papers and go to sleep.'

'Well, he does work hard, I expect.' Doris bent to readjust the pram's covers a little. A slightly chilly breeze had sprung up after such a lovely warm start to the morning and over to the west the sky had turned a little greyish with a haze of thin, she suspected but hoped not, rain-bearing clouds.

'Even so, Mum, I feel I'm just part of the furniture. He doesn't even seem interested when I try to tell him about the shop. I'm sure we're doing a little better these days.'

'I'm glad to 'ear that, dear. I get so worried for you and Eddie.'

'Does Dad get worried?' She didn't miss the oblique look her mother shot at her.

'Oh, yes.' The reply far too hastily said.

'What's he say?' she tested, aware of tension still between them.

'Not a lot. 'E don't say much these days about anythink.' Doris straightened up from the pram. 'I worry about your dad, Cissy. Been drawing into 'imself for a couple of years now.'

'But he still hasn't forgiven me, has he?'

'Good Lord, Cissy, that's bin over and done with fer ages. It was got over the moment you and Eddie got married.'

'Sometimes I'm not so sure – at least not with Dad. I never realised how much I hurt him, you know. I wish I could do something to bring back how it used to be, when he used to laugh with me and *at* me. He never laughs now – not at me.'

'It's not you, Cissy, luv. He don't laugh at no one. It's 'avin' no work and not able to get any – not at 'is age. They want younger men – if they ever want anyone at all. But 'e ain't that old.'

Again came a sidelong glance. 'I was wonderin', Cissy . . . Do Eddie ever 'ave any need fer 'elp on his tug? Your dad did quite a bit of towing in 'is time. He do know what he's doing. He's always bin a good waterman. Always dedicated to 'is work, 'e was. Never once shirked or caused trouble, and everyone looked up to 'im in 'is day. Still got it in 'im, if only someone'd give 'im a chance.'

It sounded so like a character reference tinged with pleading that Cissy felt herself squirm with embarrassment. All she could mumble was: 'I don't know if he wants anyone, Mum. I could ask him . . .'

'Oh, no! Don't go asking 'im outright. I don't want 'im to think I was beggin'. And I don't want yer dad to know what I said either. I just thought your Eddie might be needin' someone.'

'I know.' Cissy gave her a comforting smile. 'I could put it in a round-about way so Eddie doesn't feel obligated and if there is any chance . . . He'll keep an ear to the ground for Dad. But at the moment, he's struggling along with a crew of three, and that includes himself. He's even had to do without a mate. It's hard going. They don't even have a lad on board. I think they all muck in as best they can.'

'Yer dad could do odd jobs . . .' The words were seared off as if they had burned her tongue, her mother's round face reddening as she heard herself pleading on behalf of her husband for a job, any job, even to offering him on a level with a tea-boy. It was degrading and they both knew it. Cissy could have burst into tears for her.

If he had heard them discussing him just then, he would have died from humiliation. He would, Cissy truly believed, have died rather than sink to what Mum was suggesting – most certainly would never have looked her in the eyes again. After all the respect he had known as a Freeman of the Thames, who would dare ask him to sink to doing the job a deck-boy would do, making tea, taking on all the dirty tasks? Dad was still clinging to his self-respect in the eyes of his family if no one else – no, she wouldn't deign to insult him with dregs when what he needed was a long draught of hope.

The look of horror on her face had not gone unnoticed by her mother whose lips tightened, making something more out of it merely, Cissy imagined, to cover her own tracks.

'It was just a thought,' she said sharply annoyed. 'Forget it.'

'I want to help you and Dad.' It was Cissy who was now doing the pleading, making a bad job of it, and she saw the lips compress still more.

'I'm sorry we're a burden to you, Cissy.' The paper bag that had held a couple of apples scrunched harshly and suddenly between her mother's hands.

'Don't be angry, Mum,' Cissy pleaded. 'I didn't mean to make it sound like that.'

'If only I knew where to turn. But I don't. Your sister May's out of work now. And 'er bloke too. A nice boy. They've started courtin' serious, but what 'opes have they got of getting married with not a penny to bless themselves with? And Bobby – I don't know 'ow he's managing. Spends hours down at the gates, just 'oping for the odd job to be 'anded out. It's criminal. It's beggin', that's what it is. And then to 'ave you look at me like that because I asked . . .'

'I didn't mean to!' Cissy broke in desperately. 'I'd do anything for you and Dad. I've not forgotten how you got him to forgive me for leaving home the way I did. If I could compensate for my stupidity – if I could take those years back, I would. I want to do all I can to make amends. I want to help you both but I don't want you to think I'm imposing on you or being patronising.'

'I don't understand them long words, Cissy. It was learning words like that what gave you big ideas so you went off to find what you didn't think you could get 'ere. Well, you found out, didn't you? I'm not blaming you for wanting somethin' better than we could ever give you, but it was the way you did it, and . . .'

'You still can't forgive me. Even you. So it's obvious Dad hasn't.'

Doris began neatly folding the empty apple bag with exaggerated care, putting it back in her large black handbag. She didn't look at her daughter. 'As I've said before, it was over long ago.'

But not forgotten, Cissy thought, watching her mother's exercise with the paper-bag folding, a silent censure if ever there was one.

Her mother leaned forward to put the dummy back into Edward's mouth as he began to whimper. 'Gettin' near 'is feeding time, I reckon.' She tenderly regarded the baby. 'Getting a bit chilly too. It looks like rain over there. You coming back for a cuppa before you go on 'ome?'

She appeared to have recovered from her moment of pique and Cissy nodded, getting up from the bench, drawing Edward's blankets up over him. 'It's on my way home. I might as well say hello to Dad.'

'More likely Eddie's just worried about 'is business,' Doris said out of the blue as they moved off towards home, startling Cissy. 'You worrying about marriage not being all 'earts an' flowers any more,' she elucidated. 'It do 'appen. Kids come along, jobs take an upper hand – if there's any, that is. Wife looking after little 'uns, 'usband trying to be a decent breadwinner. No one can go on for ever like they was a couple of lovesick youngsters. It ain't natural and it ain't convenient. No work'd ever get done if we carried on like we did before we was married.'

'I suppose so,' Cissy said glumly, gazing into the pram. 'But with us it just seems there's something in the way, and I don't know what.'

'It's just nature.' Her mother smiled, and dismissed the subject.

'It is settled at last. Christmas we will move to Germany.'

Theodore sat in his button-backed black leather easy chair, the one he used for thinking in when not at his bureau in his study in their fine apartment on Avenue du Mal Lyantey overlooking the Auteuil racetrack.

He and Daisy had returned from yet another fruitless consultation over her continuing childless state.

Although he would still do all he could for her, he had more or less become resigned to the idea of never becoming a parent. She hadn't. And now her sweet brown eyes were full of tears and his own heart wept for her sorrow, watching her pacing, pacing, pacing his small red-carpeted study. How elegant she looked in that slim woollen dress with its Peter Pan collar. A dress to suit a figure unmarred by childbearing. But so much happier would she be were it a sack of a thing to disguise a bulging waistline.

'We will go to Dusseldorf,' he furthered. 'I will find a good house and we will obtain for you a good specialist on problems of women.'

'I can't ask you to keep putting yourself out for me, Teddy,' she sighed, still pacing. 'Spending out good money taking me to Germany, just because of my selfish needs.'

He put out a slim sallow hand and caught hers, bringing her gently to a halt. 'It is my selfish needs too, my love. I am getting tired, tired of my long exile, which is self-imposed. I had intended to be in France for just a little while, after which, my fortune made, I intended to return to my homeland and boast of the wealth I had made here. My wealth I made, but I grew also older and set in my ways. Why bother to go back home? Would my stepmother, if still alive, care what I had made? No. So I stayed. But now the time has come . . .'

She leapt at him as he paused, her arms going round him. 'You're not ill, Teddy? You're not ill, are you?'

'Of course I am not ill.' He eased her rigid embrace. 'I am weary – of France. I yearn now for my own country, my homeland, *mein heimat*. I need to converse again with others in *Deutsch* and hear it spoken to me. I am homesick, Daisy. After all these years, I am homesick.'

'God, I thought . . .' She shifted herself more comfortably on to his lap. 'I remember once you talking about visiting your father's grave. "When the time comes," you said. It frightened me then. And hearing you just now, I thought such thoughts. I suddenly felt so awfully frightened. I really thought . . .' She couldn't go on and nestled her head against his chest.

He smiled down at her, pulling his head back to gaze into her face. 'The time *has* come, my dear. But not for what you think. We go now to Germany and I will enjoy to renew all my memories of my childhood and feel young again. In Germany, revitalised, I will live another fifty years or more.'

Now she laughed. 'That'd make you ninety-six – almost one hundred.'

'I intend to live to one hundred,' he announced emphatically and kissed her.

Germany was all he said it would be. Taking a two-week trip on his own first of all, he found them a lovely old house, black and white with gables and windowboxes that in the spring and summer would be bright with flowers of all colours.

Tired as she was from days of packing, the journey by car three weeks later, their belongings and furniture going on ahead in a van, Daisy could hardly contain herself from going completely hysterical with delight at the sight of the house he had chosen for them. Some ten kilometres from Dusseldorf – his office would be in the centre of Dusseldorf itself – it was situated in a pretty little village called Kaiserwerth.

Her joyful squeals echoed through the house as she raced up the dark polished wood stairs to visit each of the three bedrooms, peering first from one bedroom window onto the loveliest little square she had even seen, despite the winter-bared trees around it and a powdering of overnight snow; then from another to glimpse a church spire which Teddy told her belonged to St Suidbert; a third window onto nothing but treetops going mistily and silently into the wintery distance.

'Oh, Teddy, it's wonderful,' her voice echoed back down the stairs. 'It's so beautiful . . . The scenery, the outlook – oh, I love it! I'm going to be so happy here.'

He smiled quietly, little Noelle's hand in his, taking pleasure from her wild exuberance, and waited. It wasn't a long wait. In seconds Daisy was tripping back downstairs to embrace him, before making more exhilarated rounds of the downstairs area – sitting room, living room, spacious German kitchen with a huge black range and hooks for hanging sides of bacon and 'things' as she squealed out, coming back to grab Noelle up in her arms for a specially conducted tour, particularly the room that would be hers. Most of the house was already furnished on his orders, prompting Daisy to stop in her tracks, to look at him with mingled anxiety and adoration.

'Oh, Teddy! All this just for me? It must have cost the earth! You said you weren't doing as well as you once did. Can we afford it?'

'It has been done,' he slowly smiled at her concern. 'It is paid for, so do not worry, my dear.'

But she was already off again, the four-year-old but petite Noelle in her arms, light as a feather in her continued excitement.

In the master bedroom Teddy had installed a four-poster at the foot of which he'd had placed an antique ottoman. There by the window was a delightful dressing table, draped in the same colour pink as the drapes at two tiny diamond-paned casement windows, the wallpaper was all tiny pink flowers and the mirrors in the wardrobes gave the room such proportions that Daisy gasped, gasped too at the central white fluffy carpet covering the woodblock flooring.

Noelle's bedroom was done out in pale green; wouldn't have been Daisy's most favoured choice but Teddy had explained that the weather could get very warm in summer, so facing south, the room would appear cooler she supposed.

The third smaller room was mostly white, already optimistically papered with designs of toys and animals. Daisy had already paused at this room on her first tour around the second floor and for a moment her hand had flown to her heart, her voice silenced briefly, her love flowing out to her husband and his certain belief that once in Germany she would bear him a child.

When she finally came downstairs again with Noelle beside her, she kissed him. 'Thank you,' she said, and having interpreted that pause in her first moments of excitement, he understood implicitly what she was referring to.

'I'm selling the *Cicely*.' Eddie could hardly bring himself to say the name. Cissy had known for a long time that he'd named the boat for her.

She looked up, startled, from dishing up his evening meal. 'She's all you've got. How can you . . .'

'I've decided she's more trouble than she's worth. I've decided to get something I can rely on.' It was almost as if he were referring to her, but she of course had no idea.

'You can't afford it.' She stood with the gravy spoon paused over his sausage toad, her blue eyes wide with horror. 'It's coming up to Christmas and we can hardly afford to have a decent one, without us spending out changing tugs.'

'I'm going to 'ave to. There's one going that I've got my eye on, but I've got to sell one to buy one.'

'But not this time of year, Eddie. And you love the *Cicely*.'

'Ain't no such thing as love in business.' His voice sounded harsh even to his ears. 'In times like these, ain't no room for sentiment. I'm getting rid of 'er and taking up this offer. Harrisons are cutting down on their men and they're selling off some of their fleet.'

'Of course,' she sighed sadly, understanding now. 'It's horrible, the state the country's in, unemployment going up and up. Even big firms like Harrisons cutting back.'

He ignored the sadness. 'I'm gettin' in quick and taking up the offer while it's going.

'It'll cost far more than you'll get for the *Cicely*. Have you a buyer for her?'

She still spoke so nicely. He thought she might have lost some of that posh accent by now, but she hadn't. Almost as though she thought herself a cut above all those around here, a cut above him. He took a vaguely vicious delight in his next words.

'I'm letting 'er go for scrap.'

'Scrap! You'll get next to nothing for her.'

'Better than shoving 'er up and down river like I'm doing now.'

'But even that's better than sending her for scrap.'

'I've made up me mind.'

'But you're going to have to borrow on top of everything else. I can't see the banks helping you. We've got no collateral without the *Cicely*. And you're not going to one of those sharks to get what it's going to cost you. Eddie, we can't afford it! We can't afford to take chances like this. We'll be getting in over our heads.'

He stood up sharply. 'I'll decide what we can afford and what we can't.'

Cissy dropped the gravy spoon noisily onto his plate, glaring at him. 'You're being silly, Eddie. How can we live? There's no money coming in as it is – well, hardly enough. The lease on the shop expires next year and the rent's bound to go up. We're just about breaking even, what with giving your mother something for coming over here each day to look after Edward. And though I don't begrudge her, it still all adds up. Don't you see, until the tug you're talking so grandly of buying begins to pay for itself, we're going to have to rely only on what our shop brings in.'

He shook his head at her. 'Your shop. Not mine.'

'Ours! How can you talk like that? What we both bring in is to keep the three of us. I thought we shared our responsibilities. It's not *my* shop – it's *ours.*'

They stood glaring at each other. Her eyes were swimming with tears and he wanted suddenly to clutch her to him, the feeling consuming him. To hell with the past. The only person he was wounding was himself – confusing her, yes, but wounding himself, for she had no idea why he was as he was. Yet he couldn't forget that she was still living her lie with him. Two years and still not a word about her daughter. He hated her for it, like a pain. Swinging away from her, leaving his dinner untouched, he went and grabbed his coat from the dark little passage to take himself off into the damp night to walk off that hatred like a pain. He would return later, calmed.

By the time he got up for work next morning, it had abated, leaving in its place a dull ache of despondency that always followed these bouts. They were becoming ever more frequent and they frightened him. It was not Cissy he hated so much but what she was doing, doing to him.

Four-thirty and pitch dark in January, she and the baby had hours before they'd get up. She thought he let her sleep on out of kindness to her, having no idea it was so that he would not have to speak to her in the mornings, the time when his hurt was at its strongest. He was not at his best in the morning, and he was afraid that one day he'd let it show and out it would all come, that simmering grievance. Then what would become of their marriage? She thought he still loved her. He *did* still love her. It was just that . . . but why go over and over it in his mind? It solved nothing.

Sawing himself a couple of doorsteps, spreading them with margarine and jam and pressing them together to make a sandwich to stuff into a paper bag, his Thermos filled with tea, milk, sugar, he pushed the lot into his small haversack and quietly let himself out.

Joan, his typist, would come in around eight-thirty to do whatever there was to be done. Today he was going straight to the *Cicely*, where he had her moored off Gravesend.

Counting himself, she had a full crew at the moment on the strength of a good week's towage last week and a promising start to this week as well; 1933 might be the beginning of better things, but he allowed himself to be only cautiously optimistic.

Today he and Tom Ainsworth, another struggling one-man band like himself, were bringing a coaster up from the Medway around the Isle of Grain to Tilbury, but what worried him was the hard easterly wind this morning and too much swell for comfort.

He said so to Tom, but Tom needed the work as much as he did.

'Nothin' ter worry about, Ed, a little breeze like this. I've brung a big'un up river in worse'n this.'

'Not around the Isle of Grain. You're dealin' with the estuary, not bloody Blackwall point. A swell like this . . .'

'It'll be all right, I tell yer,' the other one cut in confidently.

But it wasn't all right. Whatever happened, it seemed to happen in seconds, a chain of circumstances he should have predicted but didn't. Somehow in a huge swell the *Cicely* got herself at right angles to the ship and was pulled round. The ship seemed to surge forward suddenly and the *Cicely* caught the full wash off the propellers. Before Eddie had time to think, his tug had capsized, throwing the lot of them into the water.

He had a glimpse of Tom's heavy horrified face on the other tug as he went overboard. Then the water closed over his head, obliterating all sight of the world above it. He seemed to go down for ever, seemed to have no way of coming up, though which way was up he had no idea. Bubbles were surging around him, dragging at him, there was a heavy pounding in his ears – the coaster's propellers thumping, churning the water or only his heart thumping? He didn't know, except that it felt unbearable. He found himself fighting the drag of the propellers, his lungs bursting, the pounding becoming deafening. Then his muscles grew slack and useless, the thumping slid away into blackness leaving him no longer aware of anything, floating, half in and half out on the swell but he was no longer aware of that either.

Cissy screamed.

'Where is he? I have to see him!'

The policemen had hold of her drooping body, supporting her. 'It's all right, Mrs Bennett. We're taking you there now. Is there anyone can give eye to your boy?'

'Neighbours,' she said weakly. 'Has anyone told his mother?'

'Someone's round there now. She'll be at the hospital. Now, what neighbour?'

'Anyone. Only hurry, please. I've got to be with him.'

'Of course. Right now.'

Led down to the waiting police car, she let herself be helped in while another policeman stayed behind to lock up her shop for her and find the neighbour willing to watch the baby while its mother was away.

By the time Cissy reached the Southend hospital where they had taken Eddie, she had gathered her wits a little. The trauma of the shock still lingered, the policemen, their faces grave, entering her shop, taking her aside – something every waterman's or seaman's wife dreaded;

the words accident, capsized, sweeping over her like a great wave.

Hardly able to comprehend what was being said to her, her mind had conjured up only visions of Eddie's body floating face down in the Thames; all the stories she'd heard of how it claimed victims, took them down to roll them around, nine days or so later to release its hold on them to fetch up in some backwater along with rubbish, old bottles, driftwood. All she could see was Eddie's bloated body turning slowly, slowly in that quiet dirty water to be discovered by some lighterman's lad or a group of children playing on the bankside.

She had only gradually become aware of someone saying her husband was in hospital; had been lucky, saved by someone named Tom Ainsworth while the other three of the crew had not yet been recovered. Dimly, she had heard that she was being taken to the hospital if she were up to it, she by then weak and faint from what she had been imagining.

The sight of Eddie came as a shock. She had expected to find him sickly faced, unconscious. Instead he was sitting up in the bed, though his expression was glum.

'We've lost 'er,' his first words. No greeting, no reassurance that he was fine or whatever – just, 'We've lost 'er.'

Dazed, Cissy sank down on the chair placed ready for her at his bedside. 'Lost who?'

'The tug. She went down. Like a lead weight. I've got nothing now.' He looked as though he were about to cry. Cissy took his hand, it felt cold, the slim, strong fingers slack.

'It could have been you, darling. Those poor men, but it could have been you too. Who cares about the tug?'

He wasn't listening. 'There's the insurance, but I owe the bank. They'll take most of that with no boat as security. And I've still got to pay off the rest of the year's insurance premium.'

She couldn't help it. She felt suddenly angry. He had hardly looked at her. She might as well not be here. He seemed utterly unmoved that she had been through hell earlier on, believing the worst and coming here to express her immense relief, her joy for his safety when he could have been lost to her for ever. And yet all he was worried about was the damned tug.

'You were going to let her go for scrap for next to nothing anyway. So what's the difference, you sending her for scrap or her sinking?'

'I don't know.' He sounded lost. He still wasn't looking at her, seemed as though he hardly knew she was there. 'The way I feel at this moment, I don't care. I've got past caring. It's all a bloody rotten farce anyway – life . . . marriage . . .' He gave a shuddering sigh. 'Love.'

He leaned forward and she caught him as his head touched against her shoulder. Her arms around him, his body shaking, racked by silent grief, she rocked him gently, the despondency in his voice draining away her anger. And now she was crying too, sending up damp prayers of thanks that he had been saved.

Chapter Twenty-Six

By Christmas they had settled in, Noelle was delighted with the first fall of snow. The Christmas carols drifting from St Suidbert sung in German sounded so much more lovely, people in the square greeting each other, candles in all the windows and, from the local inn, loud and lively singing every night.

'They know how to celebrate the festive season,' Daisy said, overcome by it all, and had Theodore look at her with a bemused expression as if to say, what is so strange about that?

She hadn't had time yet to meet those of the village, except for two who had come to the door with welcome cakes but as she'd been in the bath at the time, they had given them to Theodore and left without her seeing them. But it didn't matter. She would meet them in due course once she was proficient enough in German to converse with her neighbours. She was studying very hard. After all, this was to be her home. When writing to her parents, she could add that she now spoke German as well as French. She could just hear her mother saying as she read: 'Fancy, now!'

Theodore seemed rejuvenated. A new man, he took her out and about showing off his country. They went out several times to restaurants over the festive season. Everyone was so sociable, whole families going together to eating places. On these occasions, Noelle was left with a young woman Teddy had found in the village. Coming twice a week, Alda, a chubby, rosy-cheeked girl of seventeen, also kept the house scrupulously tidy leaving Daisy to cook, wash and iron. As yet Daisy hadn't had much to do with her, her German so rapid and she had no English at all so Daisy could only just make her needs understood with a lot of comic gesticulating that made Alda smile, but then the girl was always smiling, never frowned, the easiest-going person Daisy had ever met.

January was white and crisp. Towards the end of the month, the snow was deep but the road meticulously cleared, Theodore took them to Altstadt, the part of Dusseldorf where he had been brought up as a child. His early memories must have been happy ones, she thought as she watched him gazing reflectively about him at the narrow cobbled streets and tall narrow four-storey houses, each washed a different pastel colour, like rows of cachou sweets. Some were topped with curved façades. Others had steep roofs with windows set in them standing proud, their window frames elaborately carved. It was a place to make anyone feel happy. She could understand how he felt.

With a sort of inherent pride, he took them to see the market place with its equestrian statue of Jan Wellem, the city's ruler from 1679 to 1716, who, Teddy added, had improved the city's trade so greatly that it became one of Germany's most important industrial towns.

'It was Jan Wellem who built our first synagogue here,' Teddy said with such pride to his tone that Daisy looked at him sharply, for the first time realising that for all he did not practise his religion, it was nevertheless engrained deep into his soul from generations past.

For a moment she felt suddenly excluded. Unable to help it, she found herself saying: 'Come on, Teddy, I think Noelle's getting a bit bored.' Noelle was indeed tugging at her hand, smelling some sweet cakes being made nearby.

'Can I have a cake, Auntie – can I?' Daisy insisted she called her auntie, despite that Teddy was *Vater* to her rather than *Onkel* which he disliked, laughing that in a way it made him feel old, an old chap.

Almost reluctantly, he smiled that lovely slow smile of his. 'Of course,' he said, coming back to the present.

They spent the rest of the day down by the Rhine and, despite the cold, Theodore made snowballs to throw at Noelle which she threw back, her efforts resulting in their disintegrating into powder the moment they left her small hand, making her squeal with frustration.

On the way home they had coffee and cake in a small restaurant. Daisy, who under Teddy's tuition found learning to read German far easier than speaking it, took one of the newspapers folded over in racks for people to read as they drank; with an effort made out that President Paul von Hindenberg had given the chancellorship to Adolf Hitler whose party had won nearly twelve million votes in the recent elections. It seemed deadly dull and not worth reading, politics were bad enough – in German they were utterly boring.

But it said that a great torchlit procession was to be held in Berlin in celebration of the post and she found herself wishing she could be there to see it. Berlin of course was too far away for it to be considered, so she settled herself to trying to decipher a brief account of Amy Johnson's round trip from London to Capetown and back in her Gypsy Moth aeroplane. The rest of the news concerned something about South Africa quitting the Gold Standard, whatever that meant, but as that was again politics, she turned to the fashion pages instead. At least she could look at the pictures without fighting with the words.

Theodore too had been scanning the main news in the paper he had selected. She noticed afterwards that he went very quiet and decided he must be again thinking of his old home. He had been quiet then for a time. So she left him in peace to think his thoughts.

Noelle tucked up in bed after supper, a little German fairy story told to her by Teddy, which he said his father had told him as a child, Daisy took herself upstairs for a hot bath. Nothing could be more delicious, she thought lying there soaking, enveloped in steam, than a hot bath after a winter's day. Afterwards, in her nightie and dressing gown, wet hair wrapped in a warm towel, she made for her and Teddy's bedroom, the all-enveloping warmth from the kitchen range reaching even up there, and sat down by her dressing table to write a reply to Cissy's latest letter, already one week old.

It wasn't going to be easy. Cissy's letter had been disturbing. Her first thought had been to give what comforting words she could in the face of her terrible tidings. But suddenly she had a better idea.

Putting aside paper and pen, she grabbed Cissy's letter and raced downstairs, her slippers flapping eagerly on the polished wood. Teddy was sitting in his armchair smoking his pipe, his gentle deep brown eyes contemplating the fire now blazing in the grate, even brighter for the cold outside, while the slow sweet strains of Brahms' German Requiem wafted softly from the radiogram.

Slimly handsome for a man of forty-six, beneath almost black hair his pale narrow face with its strong nose and firm but gentle lips looked so deep in thought that Daisy knew she was disturbing him. But unable to stop her own headlong rush, she had already done so, his pensive expression transformed to one of concern.

'Gently, *lieberling*! You will fall.'

She ignored the warning. 'I've just had a thought. You know Cissy's husband lost his tug and he's having some sort of trouble with his insurance or something?'

'So I understand.'

'And you know his bank loaned him money on the security of his tug? Cissy's explained some of it here.' She waved the letter in the air. 'I don't think she understands it any more than I do, but it looks like they insisted he had a policy or something to cover the loan, well now he hasn't got the boat. He's been paid out by the insurance but he's still got to pay the premium for the rest of the year and the bank wants its money back too. Something like that. But what it means is he'll be in the clear paying back with the insurance money, but he hasn't got a bean now to buy another boat to keep him in business. All that work and now he's got nothing.'

She stopped for a second, out of breath from running and talking, for a deep intake of air to refill her lungs, and went on.

'I was wondering, Teddy, he's got nothing now.'

'His wife has her shop.'

'We can't expect her to look after the three of them – her, him and their baby – on what that brings in.'

'Many others must do so.'

'I know, but banks and things – they're always after their pound of flesh . . .' She ignored the quirky ironic smile he gave at that. He had read his Shakespeare too. 'But I was wondering if you were to lend . . . well, Cissy is almost family, isn't she, so Eddie is as well, and she's been so wonderful letting me carry on taking care of Noelle. I love Noelle so much, I can't thank her enough for . . .'

'One moment, please.' Theodore lifted a narrow hand to stop the flow of words. 'I am in the business of lending money, yes. But it is a business, my dear, not a charity.'

Daisy's face fell. Dumbstruck, she stared at him, saw a face gone tight and cold, almost cruelly efficient. She had never seen this side of him before – the hard, calculating side that he kept in his office, the face he presented to his clients. She could hardly believe it and now she realised that before coming home he would put away that face and bring out the one he reserved for her, the mild, loving one. And she had always thought the only face he'd ever had had been the kind and loving one. It was like being told a lie.

Confused by it, all she could say was, 'Charity begins at home, Teddy, darling,' and saw him smile at her, slowly, sorrowfully, back to the man she knew.

'Were I to begin lending money to all my friends, for nothing, I shall end up as poor as they.'

Daisy's own eyes grew hard now. Two could play his game. 'Do you ever give when professional bodies ask you for charity for some cause or other?'

'Of course.'

'Then what's the difference between them and Cissy?' she burst out, suddenly vehement. 'You get nothing back from giving to charity except the satisfaction of giving. At least Eddie will pay you back in time, and if you want interest, I'm sure he'd agree to that, though I think it would be charitable not to charge my closest friend's husband what the banks charge, or more. You were charitable enough to take Cissy *in* when she needed help. I'm not asking you *not* to expect anything out of it. I know you run a business but I just thought you'd be kinder to him than some cold-blooded banks who probably wouldn't even consider him now.'

'Because, my dear, they know him for a bad risk.'

'And what if he is?' she shot back at him, his calm argument in the face of her anger riling her. 'He'll be as honourable as he can under the circumstances. As for bad risk, but for the grace of God . . . And it wasn't because he couldn't manage his business. The tug sank. And he needs to keep his family's head above water *now* – not later. If you could just be nice, for my sake, for Cissy's.' She was pleading now. 'If you could just help him out, tide him over for the time being until he's back on his feet again. Oh, please, Teddy! If Cissy has to sell her shop, they'll have nothing. And all the good you did letting her stay here that time will be wasted.'

For a moment he looked at her as she fell silent, standing before him, her chest heaving, her argument exhausted. Then getting up, he went to the radiogram and lifted the arm from Brahms' German Requiem which had long since come to an end. Gently lifting the record off the turntable he carefully put it in its sleeve, putting the sleeve in the cupboard rack underneath, everything done with utmost deliberation. Closing the cupboard doors, he came back and sat down. All this while Daisy waited and watched, for the first time in her life feeling real anger mounting towards him.

'I will think about it,' he said, but she wasn't quite yet done.

'Teddy . . . ' Her tone was businesslike, as cold as his had been. She came and sat stiffly on the arm of his chair, towering over him. 'Teddy, I can't see us ever having children. Not now. But we do still have Cissy's daughter. She even spoke of our adopting her. I think it would be only kind to help her out in her hour of need when she has let us keep Noelle almost like our own child. She could have claimed her long ago, but she hasn't.'

He looked up at her, dark eyes calculating. 'Has it ever occurred to you, my dear, that she would not want her return because she has not informed her husband of her former indiscretion?'

Daisy wilted a little. 'I've never thought of that.'

'Then I suggest you do.' His expression changed suddenly, softened. 'I do promise you that I shall consider what help I can give your friend. I promise also that we shall soon go to see a specialist of gynaecology.'

Daisy's heart leapt suddenly. All else forgotten, she unstiffened and next thing was throwing herself across the chair arm into his beloved arms.

'I find no reason for your wife not to have a child.' The specialist spoke in German, his tone coldly efficient.

Daisy frowned, not understanding, shot a look at Teddy. 'What's he saying? He doesn't hold out much hope?'

But his smooth sallow face was grinning like some Cheshire cat. 'On the contrary, my dear,' he interpreted, 'There's nothing wrong with you.'

He turned back to the man who had begun addressing him again. Teddy replied, his voice ringing with delight as he translated for Daisy.

'He says he is of the opinion that it must merely be of the mind. None of the tests have shown anything wrong with you. He is of the opinion that you are trying much too hard to conceive. That we both are trying much too hard.'

Daisy frowned again. 'But how else are we going to have a baby? Of course we've been trying.'

'No – you have it incorrectly.' He turned back to the man saying something in German that softened the gynaecologist's stern features, and brought a reply in a far warmer tone than he'd hitherto used.

Translating, Theodore gently took Daisy's arm. 'He is explaining that those so wanting a child may become tense during copulation and such tension will obstruct the normal result of the sexual act. He says we should relax when making love, and in time all will be well.'

'But I've always been relaxed,' Daisy cried.

'Not relaxed enough,' Theodore returned after relaying her words to the gynaecologist. 'What is on your mind when we are making love is, "Will I have a child this time?" You are over-anxious that this time something must happen.'

The specialist was speaking. His face once more stiff and formal. Teddy nodded, colouring as far as his pale complexion would allow.

'We are to enjoy having . . . sex. He advises we do . . . things . . . while making love. That we should . . . enter into fantasy . . . and play games . . . you with me, I with you . . .' He was definitely blushing. 'I am telling you only what the Herr Doktor is saying, you understand?'

Now Daisy was blushing furiously, wishing she could be out of this surgery and as far away from the imperious man gazing at her as she could possibly get. But her heart was already singing.

The gynaecologist regarded them both, his light grey eyes fierce and commanding, trained more on her than on Theodore.

'Now we have concluded our tests, Frau Helgott, and found no reason why you should not conceive of a child, you and your husband will attend a clinic where you will be taught relaxation with each other. You will begin on Tuesday, which is the day of the clinic, promptly at seven in the evening for two consecutive Tuesdays. You will be given your attendance card by the receptionist. You will not miss either appointment. Good day.'

He moved towards the door, opened it, executing a small curt bow as they passed through, his terse *guten Tag* almost as though he bore them a grudge.

Daisy's thank-you smile lay frozen on her lips. All she had understood to any degree apart from the dismissive goodbye, was *die Klinik*, unmistakable in either language, *Dienstag* being Tuesday, and the time appointed them, *sieben Uhr*, but the imperious tone of command had not been missed and she shivered to even dream of disobeying it. Yet the manner of the gynaecologist had instilled her with such confidence that she somehow knew that before long she would be carrying Theodore's baby. As they left, she offered up prayers of grateful thanks to the Almighty that Theodore had brought her to Germany to live.

Cissy sat reading Daisy's letter, the first lines an excited scribble as if a moment wasted might make her wonderful news untrue. It was a good job the postman came early around here, Cissy thought as she went back up the stairs to read over a final cup of tea before going down to open up the shop.

She read at first with joy for Daisy, turning vaguely to concern for what such wonderful news could eventually portend for herself.

Daisy was pregnant. Daisy was overjoyed. 'After all these years of going to specialists in France, them shaking their heads as if they couldn't care less, then a German doctor, such a wonderful, efficient German doctor, has wrought a small miracle – no, a huge miracle. Aren't you just thrilled for me?' Daisy's writing shouted at her for support.

The letter was all about how the specialist had frightened her with his German correctness, almost browbeating her, she'd thought at the time. But oh, how she could kiss his hand now!

Cissy was happy for her, yes, but there was a tremor of foreboding creeping into her heart, especially the following words proving not so cheerful: Noelle, gone down with chickenpox just over a week ago, was getting over it, and wouldn't be scarred at all, the doctor ordering her little fingertips to be bound with soft bandage to stop her scratching off the crusting heads of the spots. She would be as pretty as ever – an accompanying photograph of her taken earlier showed a most pretty four-year-old that Cissy felt a surge of mother love come over her.

There had been of course no question of claiming her back, Eddie knowing nothing about her and hopefully he would never know. She was even thinking seriously of letting Daisy adopt her, but now here was Daisy announcing her pregnancy, would she still want to adopt? Reading on, how Daisy had hardly been off her feet during Noelle's chickenpox, how tired she'd been, how she wondered how she'd cope in her condition if Noelle fell ill again, and so many childish illnesses she hadn't yet had, Cissy's heart, from rising to her friend's wonderful news, now plummeted.

Yet if Daisy was suffering a change of heart how could she feel angry after what she and Theodore had done for her – for Eddie?

Not long after the *Cicely* went down, had come word from Theodore saying he wished to help, enclosing a cheque of an amount near enough to pay off what Eddie owed the bank, thus leaving him the insurance money to buy another tug. He had added that it was not charity but a loan to be repaid in Eddie's own good time, interest at one per cent. One per cent! If that wasn't charity, Cissy thought, overwhelmed by Theodore's generosity, she couldn't say what was.

Eddie, however, had been startlingly ungrateful, waving the cheque in her face as though she had been in on some conspiracy.

'What's this then? I suppose you've been blabbing to your friend how badly off we are, how I can't provide fer me own family.'

'I haven't.' She had been taken aback.

'Tellin' 'er all about how you 'ave ter provide fer us now. You and yer shop. Me with no livelihood to me fingertips. Leading 'er to think you're 'ard done by and I can't keep you without 'elp.'

'Of course she doesn't think that.'

'Then why this? And 'ow does she know all about us?'

'It wasn't a secret what happened, Eddie. I just wrote and told her of our bit of bad news. And I suppose she wanted to help us somehow.'

'Well, they've got money, ain't they? And 'er husband now thinks he can go giving me 'andouts like I was a pauper.'

'It's nothing like that! Daisy and I have been close ever since we first started working together. We've always helped each other out.'

'I bet you 'ave,' he'd shot at her with such venom that it left her bewildered, with no idea what he was alluding to.

It wasn't like Eddie, the Eddie she once knew. Churlish, uncertain of temper, it was the times they were living in, worrying about where the next penny was coming from. He didn't want what he called handouts, yet he could hardly return the money. Throwing it back at them would have, he growled, diminished him even more in that he'd look scared of having to pay back even at one per cent. He had some pride, even though some people tried to put it down.

At the end of February, rather reluctantly but circumstances having the last word, he bought another tug, fortunately a buyer's market in these bad times. When she'd asked if he would be naming it *Cicely*, he had been most offhand; said he'd never give a tug of his that name ever again. She might have taken it as a compliment except for the look he had thrown her, as though blaming her for something she'd done, though she couldn't think what. When she had asked, he hadn't answered. She had written her profound thanks to Daisy and Theodore for their wonderful generosity on Eddie's behalf.

There was more to Daisy's letter, catching up on all the news from the country she now called her home.

'We've had some odd things happen here though I don't bother much about politics, as you know. There was some trouble in Berlin last month. The Reichstag was burned down. It was arson and there's a lot of rumours flying about, though no one is saying who they suspect, I don't think I should say who I think it was either. You never know who could read one's letters and I don't want Teddy to get into any trouble . . .'

Cissy gnawed at her lips. Something wasn't right about the tone of Daisy's letter. Far from her usual happy or carping self as the case may be, it had an ominous ring and Cissy felt apprehension run through her. It was like what she'd read in history books: intrigues of Henry VIII's court, terrors of the Spanish Inquisition, unease of Cromwell's time. With no comparison in modern days, it was the only way she could describe it. It sent a shiver up her back – the friend she'd spent so many carefree days at work with, now writing like some anxious spy. She read on hurriedly:

'The new Chancellor has curtailed all personal liberties and public meetings. Understandable I suppose. Well, it was *the Parliament building. And if* ours *went up in flames . . . But all Jewish shops now have notices on them that they are to be boycotted so maybe the Chancellor suspects Jewish connections. But what worries me is that the girl who used to come to do our house told Teddy she wouldn't be working for us any more because he's Jewish. And we're being snubbed by our neighbours. No one's talking to us.*

Funny, I never think of Teddy as Jewish. It's all a bit worrying and not nice. I expect it'll blow over like most things do, but it's rotten for Teddy. He's such a kind person and I can't see why anyone needs to be nasty to him. He feels it. We both feel it. And yesterday, one of the children in Noelle's kindergarten spat at her, and his mother said he had every right. I wanted to go round to have a row with her over it. After all, you don't do that sort of thing in England and get away with it. But Teddy wouldn't let me, and anyway I still can't speak German enough to have an all out row with someone. I could in England, of course. So I had to do what Teddy asked, and say nothing. But I'm so angry . . .'

Cissy looked at the clock on the mantelpiece and realised how the time had gone on, now she only had two minutes to get downstairs and open up. Putting Daisy's letter aside, she hurried off, thinking less about Germany's problems than about Noelle being spat at and the implication it had – Daisy hinting of tiring of looking after Noelle, that before long something awkward was going to crop up, and what would Eddie say to her having kept secret from him that she had a child living in Germany? She could see no way out of it all coming suddenly to light. It was a worrying prospect, enough to make her feel quite sick as she hurried downstairs.

Chapter Twenty-Seven

'I've got work!' Charlie Farmer's broad face was aglow with triumph and relief as he burst into the steam-filled kitchen, Monday morning being Doris's washday. 'Got meself taken on permanently. I start termorrer.'

Dropping the shirt whose collar she had been scrubbing, Charlie's neck tending to sweat a lot, back into the tub, Doris hurried across to him and, her arms still covered in suds, threw them around him.

'Oh, Charlie! Oh, that's wonderful! Oh, I'm so glad!' Exclamations tumbled from her and she leaned away from him. 'How'd you get it? Oh, it's wonderful news. What sort of work?'

'Lighters. Be workin' for Briggs.'

'Big people!' She knew her companies, did Doris. 'And it's permanent, you say?'

'As permanent as it can be. They said for an indefinite period. Things must be lookin' up at last. Said they wanted someone what's got a few years behind 'im rather than a youngster. That must say something.'

Doris had collected herself, dropped her arms from him. At her age and the length of her married years, wives didn't go mooning around their husbands. But her small round face was alight with hope.

Last week, May had found herself full-time machinist work – lingerie or lingery as she always put it, that was how it was spelled, wasn't it? Nice delicate work. She was pleased for May. And her fiancé had been working for a while, street sweeper, but it was something. Maybe she and her fiancé could get married at last.

That left only Bobby, but Doris had hopes for him too. Eddie had bought another tug after losing that last one like he did. Must've done well with the insurance money. He might have something for Bobby. They weren't doing too bad, Cissy with her shop, modest though it was, the both of them in business – couldn't be that bad off. Yes, Eddie might give Bobby some work. Doris could see a candle at the end of their particular tunnel, and overcome with joy that her breadwinner was a breadwinner once more, she threw herself at him again, and to the Devil with her age and the length of her married years.

It was good to be on the river again, feel the strength of the water under his feet, the breeze in his face. To feel at one with if not in charge of the elements. Himself and an apprentice working a sixty-five-ton craft this fine April morning in the pale clean light of dawn, he had pulled her to the lock on a thirty-one-foot oar. Other craft gathering, a lively exchange of news and banter between lightermen as they waited for the lock gates to open. Good to have like men around him, to feel once more a part of the world he knew. Life was good again.

Standing firm, legs apart to steady himself, the young apprentice he had with him making himself busy as his craft was pulled steadily in on the capstain rope alongside others. There was the familiar rumble of lock gates closing and the rush and gurgle of water draining, lowered until level with that outside. The dripping green-slimed lock walls seemed to rise above him, the gurgle of water dying, gates opening, pulled out by the capstain rope, the tide catching the craft, swinging it round, head to tide. They made the craft fast to the pier head and waited for the tug to arrive taking him to whatever destination he had on his orders.

The one picking him up was the *Milo*, Eddie's new tug. Charlie waved to him in the wheelhouse as he made fast and with his apprentice leapt aboard, his lighter and another secured in tow, signalled 'How goes it, then?' the chugging of the tug too noisy for words. He saw Eddie's thumb go up, his optimistic grin from the wheelhouse signalling back that all was well.

Later they'd probably have a proper chinwag in a coffee shop. He liked Eddie, admired him for taking Cissy back like he had, even if he thought him soft for having done so – he couldn't have forgiven Cissy so easily, hadn't, not for a long time. He had now, of course. With Eddie so forgiving, how could he go on holding a grudge? He just hoped it wouldn't backfire on Eddie one day.

He'd taken Bobby on his payroll again too. For that Charlie felt somewhat awkwardly indebted to him. Good sort, Eddie, but some people could be almost too good for comfort, he rated, tended to make you squirm a bit. But he was doing too much thinking. Getting looks from the bloke from the other lighter, and from his apprentice.

Bobby was coming aft with mugs of tea for them. Soon there'd be four more craft hooked on at various points, and more blokes to bring tea for. He nodded thanks to Bobby as he took his mug, sipped the boiling brew and he left Eddie, Bobby and the other two crew to their work.

The *Milo* was proving a good vessel. Eddie felt at home in her as he'd not done for a long time in the *Cicely* before she'd gone down. He felt a little odd, though, knowing the *Milo* had been acquired with someone else's money. It still had a ring of charity to it rather than of business even though the money would be paid back. He was determined to do that as soon as he possibly could, even wished the interest was a little higher so as to lessen this sense of having accepted charity.

He stood at the wheel, the *Milo* towing her six heavily laden barges as if they were matchsticks, each picked up at various points; Millwall Dock, Deptford Cattle Market, Folly House Roads, heading now for Tilbury Dock. The leading two barges towered blunt-bowed and cliff-like behind her, each rolling a splashing uneven moustache of a bow wave before it with a hollow sloshing and a strong muddy odour of stirred-up river water.

He could see his father-in-law and the other lightermen taking it easy in the stern now, grouped in a pose with two of the *Milo*'s crew for an old box camera one of them had.

With little to do for the time being but to forge ahead, merely keeping an eye out for other craft, Eddie glanced towards Bobby, a little apart from the rest, gazing back from where they'd come. Eddie grinned to himself. No doubt taking his own private pictures in his mind as usual, the river smooth, the fine weather clouds marching across the April sky. Eddie's grin broadened, guessing the poetic wool-gathering his crewmember was indulging in.

He'd taken Bobby on again after procuring the *Milo*; felt obligated, family and all that. After all, having laid him off before, it was only right he should consider him before anyone else. It had pleased Cissy.

A good lighterman, Bobby had got his waterman's licence years ago but hadn't a chance to air his skills, unemployment being what it was. His main trouble, he was a dreamer. Like Cissy in that respect, except that where it had sent her looking for greener pastures he merely dreamed. Less harmful, Eddie concluded. She'd found them not as green as she had thought, but in looking had caused, and was still causing, bitter reverberations in some hearts, mostly in his.

Abruptly, he drew his thoughts purposely back to Bobby, needing to focus them away from her. Bobby's other drawback was forever moaning about Ethel; how she always took their daughter Jean's side against his no matter how naughty the child was; how he wished he had left her and gone to that woman across the river; how he regretted not having got to know the son he'd had – on and on until Eddie felt like telling him to shut up. Yet he was a good hard worker when not daydreaming.

He leaned out of the wheelhouse, alerting him from whatever was absorbing him. 'Be making Tilbury Dock in ten minutes.'

Bobby came to himself with a start. 'Oh . . . yeah . . . right, Eddie.'

Eddie smiled grimly. He had been daydreaming. If only Cissy had been so easily satisfied, things could have been a lot different to what they were now. But here he was again, taking things out on her when it was his own fault he let her go off as she had.

'It really looks as though the shop's picking up.'

Cissy, counting the day's takings, sitting at the dining room table, threw him a smile. The table cleared, pound notes flat, coins stacked, the tip of her tongue visible as she jotted down each count, like some miser, except that she wasn't counting in a dim hidey-hole but in the liquid light of April evening sunshine slanting through the window.

'If it goes on like this, what with the towage business, we might even be able to get out of this flat and find somewhere decent to live. We could put our name down for one of those council houses going up around the suburbs. They say that Dagenham's nice. Very country-like – well, it is country, isn't it? I wouldn't mind Dagenham.'

Eddie looked up from his *Evening Chronicle*. 'Counting chickens.'

'No. But we can't stay here over the shop for much longer. Edward's thirteen months old now and getting a big boy. He can't go on sleeping in our room. We'll be wanting another baby, won't we, eventually, and where will he sleep then?

'Well?' she prompted when he didn't reply. 'You would like to have more children, wouldn't you? At least another one. I know I would.'

He had to say something as she continued to stare across at him. He managed to grunt, ''Spect so.'

It was moments like this that made his heart take a sickening backward leap into the old bitterness. Time had gone on, and in the way time has of blunting edges, he'd forget for days on end about the secret child she had. Yet it only needed her to talk as she was doing now, as though she had only the one child, to bring it all back.

She was frowning at him. 'What do you mean, you expect so? Surely you don't want an only child?'

He could feel himself on the very brink of blurting out: *I've* got an only child, *you've* got two. How about that? But he held his tongue and said. 'I'd like another, yes. But give it time.'

'Can't give it too much time,' she said happily, returning to her counting. 'If we start trying soon, it'd make Edward two and a half, coming up to three – a nice age to have a little brother or sister.'

The inevitable thought sprang to his mind. He's got one already – one he don't know about – one you don't think I know about. But I do – and, oh God, I wish I didn't!

'Oh, my God!' Cissy stared at the letter with the German postmark just arrived with the midday post.

Closing for the lunch hour, she had come upstairs with the slim bundle of envelopes handed her by the postman just a moment earlier: long brown important-looking envelopes, they would be bills; flimsy wide envelopes, they would be circulars, adverts, the usual rubbish, and one firm-looking white one, the one with the German postmark.

This Cissy had torn open first. The bills could wait, those touting for custom, far longer until she felt like going through them. But the one from Daisy was always the one she looked forward to.

Mrs Bennett senior had taken Edward out to the park for the morning, the April weather being so warm and bright, but had come home about half an hour ago to get their usual quick lunch. 'I do so enjoy doing all this,' she never failed to remark on whatever she did around her son and daughter-in-law's little flat. 'I feel ten years younger, looking after me grandson.' And indeed she looked ten years younger.

She popped her head round from the division between kitchen and dining room at Cissy's cry.

'What is it, love? Not bad news, I hope?'

'They've lost all their money,' Cissy burst out, her eyes still scanning the letter, still only half read. 'They've lost everything, Theodore's business, everything.'

'How could it've 'appened?' Mrs Bennett cried, coming to look over her shoulder, butter knife still in her hand where she'd been making something to eat.

Cissy didn't answer, was reading on, disbelief growing with every word she read.

It had taken Daisy two weeks to put her letter together. So many times she had begun, and so many times had torn it up. It was embarrassing, degrading having to write like this to Cissy, who had herself come down in the world and having, she suspected, seen her as opulent, of some standing, would now feel the superior one.

Not that she'd ever wanted to lord it over Cissy. She hadn't. But it had brought a good feeling being the one to succeed where Cissy, the girl who had done it all back in 1925, had finally taken a tumble. She hadn't wished for her downfall of course, but there'd always been the but-for-the-grace-of-God bit hovering in the back of her mind.

Now the tables had turned again, and it was she who found herself taking a tumble, worried out of her mind – no, not worried, terrified. And to think how happy she'd been in March, after all those years of hoping, to find herself pregnant at last. Teddy had been so happy, excited, shaking his head in disbelief.

'I never thought I would be a father,' he'd said, enraptured, and she'd felt so proud; so very proud and good and important, as though this miracle had been wrought by her alone. She'd been so grateful to the German doctor who'd shown her and Teddy what had been lacking. But now her world was falling around her. Having to hint – all she dared do – at Cissy's financial help. After all, Eddie did still owe Teddy.

Cissy felt her blood go icy as she read Daisy's letter:

'I'm so frightened. I'm sure we're in danger. Teddy says there's nothing to worry about and that it will blow over. He may be right of course, and it might be that my condition has made me worry more than I would normally. But I can't help feeling so awfully scared. I want so much to come home, but we can't afford to. We've hardly any money left. I wish I was in England. I don't understand German politics, but

there's something ominous about it. Like the way that doctor spoke when I was trying for a baby. He did help us and what he said did work, but it was how he said it – like a command rather than advice. That's how it seems all the time here. Ominous.

The reason we've got so little money is that last month, the first of April it was – proper April Fools Day – Chancellor Hitler seized all Jewish bank accounts and Teddy's money has been frozen. He has a Jewish bank even though he doesn't make too much of his religion. Now he can't get at his money and we only have what's in the house and now Teddy is insisting his clients pay cash so we've enough to live on for the time being, but I don't know for how much longer. But now a lot of his clients are dropping off. If we had the money to get us back to England, we'd be so grateful, but there is no one here to help. I don't like this Fascist government. It frightens me.'

Cissy's eyes wandered from the letter recalling what had been going on here in London only recently. Sir Oswald Mosely, a Labour MP who'd resigned three years ago, had formed his own party. The New Party he called it, but really it was Fascism – Blackshirts as everyone called them, throwing their weight around as if they were hoping to run the country. Last month the papers had given accounts of demonstrations in the West End with battles between Jews and Fascists. His photo in the papers showed a dynamic man – drawing the wrong sort to him, he could bring Fascism even to England while people's backs were turned.

'Your poor friend do seem worried, don't she?'

Her mother-in-law speaking suddenly over her shoulder from where she had been reading made Cissy jump. Quickly she folded the letter. It was her letter, private, but she gave the well-meaning woman a smile.

'I suppose we all get a bit over-sensitive when we're carrying,' she dismissed.

'I suppose we do,' adjoined the older Mrs Bennett. 'Anyway, your lunch is ready, luv. I done tinned sardines on toast – it's keeping warm under the grill. I'm going ter give Edward a bit ter see 'ow he likes it. It'll be 'is first taste of tinned sardines. I bet 'e pulls a face. Kids do, yer know, at their first taste of anythink a bit stronger than porridge.'

'Yes, I expect they do,' Cissy murmured, her mind on Daisy and Theodore's plight, but more on the situation her daughter could be in, a sudden protective instinct gripping her.

Theodore had felt sure the country wouldn't see its Jewish population threatened without realising how it could rebound on them. A lot of non-Jews had money tied up in banks that dealt with financiers like himself. Freezing Jewish banks would affect them too and they would not stand for it, he was sure of that.

But his beliefs were thrown down when on the 18th May the Fascist Party won the elections in Danzig. The whole of Germany it seemed was behind its saviour, lured on by promises to lead Germany out of the world depression; promises they believed implicitly.

'They will snatch at anything in the dire situation Germany finds herself,' Theodore had said bitterly when news of the political landslide came over the wireless. 'They will learn the truth in time.'

Daisy couldn't share his optimism. She could see a day coming when she could be stranded in a country swiftly losing its attraction for her. By then with no money left to get home on, what would she do? No use asking her family for the fare. None of them had any money. And Cissy? She was feverishly still awaiting a reply from her. Would she take up the hints in her last letter. There had been hints. How could anyone ask outright and look cheap?

'After all,' she said to Theodore, following her train of thought, 'Cissy owes us, for more than just money. And Noelle *is* her daughter. Surely she wouldn't see her in danger.'

He looked stern, his lips tight. 'We do not beg. I hope you have not been writing to her asking for help. It is not shirt buttons we would be expecting.'

On this occasion Daisy hadn't laughed at his usage of her cockney sayings. 'If we don't ask, we won't get,' she flashed at him. 'We need all the help we can get. And I'll grab at any straw that comes along to get me home.'

Yet for all her talk, pride stayed from writing such a blatantly begging letter. Until events in mid-June finally gave her no option.

It was still partially light at ten o'clock. Teddy hadn't yet come home and she was beginning to worry when urgent rapping on her front door made her start. Wondering why she hadn't heard his motorbike, a second-hand one he now used instead of that lovely Daimler he'd once had, she found herself confronted by two stony-faced policemen as she opened the door.

Her first stunned thought sent her blood cold as, in voices curt to a point of rudeness, they informed her that there had been an accident. Her gasp of relief was pure reaction that he hadn't been killed as she was told that he'd been taken to Sankt Marien Hospital. But before she could begin to ask how bad he was or what had happened, they'd turned on their heels back towards a black car without even answering, much less offering to give her a lift to the hospital six miles away in Dusseldorf.

Flustered, frightened, fearing the worst and not knowing quite what to do, she watched the car turn and speed away. Still in shock, she made for her nearest neighbour's house, her only thought to ask if her neighbour's husband would drive her to town. Then came a second shock.

Opening the door to her frantic knocks, the woman stared blankly at her saying her husband was already in bed, and, without another word, closed the door in her face, leaving her staring, stunned. She tried three other neighbours in turn, all with almost the same results. The husband either in bed or going to bed or, worse still, too busy.

It was that last excuse that brought an unpleasant flicker of truth just what her situation was. She hadn't realised it before but this build-up of anti-Semitism was touching even her, Anglican to the core except that she was married to a Jew. Funny, she thought as she stared at the last closed door, as she had once told Cissy, she never thought of Teddy as Jewish, only German.

Now with growing sickness in her heart, she got herself back to her house, knowing that whatever she did now must be done by her alone. Going to the garden shed, she unearthed one of the bicycles she and Teddy used for keeping themselves fit cycling on fine days. Gathering up a sleepy Noelle, she dressed her, settled her in the rear wickerwork child seat and, ignoring the child's whimpering protests at being woken up, set off to pedal the six miles to Sankt Marien, glad that the terrain here was flat, and she was as yet still not too pregnant to push a bike.

At the hospital she was met by the same stony faces of nurses and doctors as the policemen had presented.

'You will find your husband in the general ward,' was all she was told, her frantic enquiries in poor German as to how badly hurt he was ignored. 'You must collect him in two days. He will be strapped up and ready to go home.' And this from the very hospital that only a few months back had helped her so willingly and well to finally become pregnant.

She found him awake and in pain, his chest strapped with wide, frayed bandages beneath a buttonless, grubby pyjama top, his left arm in a splint, his face so swollen and bruised she hardly recognised him. He looked as if he had been hurriedly patched up with whatever had come to hand and left to get on with it; not even a bell beside him to ring should he need help.

Between winces of pain he managed to tell her that he had been set upon by a gang of thugs as he'd gone to his motorbike. They had said something about Jews not being worthy of owning motorbikes. She heard the whispered name, Brownshirts, and knew with a chill of goose pimples that this had been no mere onslaught by a few drunken louts.

It was almost midnight when she returned home. She noticed lights on in her house and realised that in her haste she'd forgotten to turn everything off. The wireless was still playing to itself as she came in – the German Anthem before closing down for the night.

In sudden fury at all that had happened, she took off her shoe and flung it with all her strength at the thing. Her aim accurate, the heel cracked the flimsy fretwork of the speaker in the centre, but the anthem went on playing as though nothing had happened, mocking her almost. 'You'll – not – escape,' the stately, slow, solid rhythm of the anthem seemed to say. 'Not ever – not ever . . .'

Weeping, she gave herself up to her defeat, letting the weeping drain away all the horror of the evening, ignoring a wondering and very sleepy Noelle. Then weary, tears finally exhausted, she got up, turned off the now silent wireless and took her back to her bed, kissing her soft cheek and tucking her in before going to her own bed.

It cost precious Reichmarks to hire a taxi to bring Teddy home two days later. No amount of pleading allowed him any longer stay in hospital, beds were needed for more urgent cases – good Germans, she was brusquely told. Had she been in England, she'd have retaliated against such rudeness, but she wasn't in England. So she left, making no fuss, supporting Teddy as best she could to the taxi, surprised how she, a fiercely proud Cockney, could have changed so much. It was belittling.

For the next few weeks she nursed him, watched him slowly return to normal. But still in no fit state to work, his business was sinking. Soon there'd be no business, no clients, no money coming in. Something had to be done. She saw him settled after crawling like an old man to the table to eat, then took herself off to his empty study to write to Cissy about what had happened. She still could not demean herself to outright begging, filling her letter merely with hints, hoping Cissy might read between the lines and automatically offer help.

But it wasn't the letter she sent. On the way to the postbox a few yards down the road, Noelle toddling beside her, her path was suddenly barred by five uniformed young men who had just got out of a car.

Her name rudely demanded, she felt obliged to tell them, hating the feeling of being cowed. They leered.

'Jew!' One of them spat out.

Regaining some of her courage, she drew herself up, her own small height dwarfed by each young man.

'I am English and Anglican,' she returned in German. 'I was baptised into the Church of England, and that is that!'

'But married to a Jew,' came the statement.

'Yes, but he doesn't . . .'

'And this is your Jewish child.' One of them took hold of Noelle's arm, who, frightened by the stranger, began to cry.

In a rush of motherly defence of her child, her old Cockney temper flaring, Daisy reached out, dragged her back, at the same time landing a sharp smack on the opponent's brown sleeve.

'She's adopted. Leave her be! How dare you!'

To her surprise the man did not grab Noelle back. Laughing, the five moved on, pushing her roughly aside as though she were dirt. Her heart thudding with sickening beats as she bent to wipe Noelle's tears she saw them pause to take note of her house. She straightened up as they came sauntering back.

'A splendid house your Jewish husband has,' one of them drawled. 'It is not proper that Jews should own such a splendid house while many good Germans live in poor tenements. This will be looked into, Fraulein Helgott.'

Getting back into their car, they drove off looking very pleased with themselves.

Their last ominous words echoing in her head, the way they had grabbed Noelle, she didn't tell Teddy of her encounter, but sat down and rewrote her letter to Cissy, this time the begging letter she had put off for so long.

Chapter Twenty-Eight

Cissy looked forward to Thursdays. Thursdays were special.

Early closing, Eddie's mother giving eye to young Edward, it was an opportunity to ride up to Knightsbridge to gaze in the windows of big department stores like Harrods, to dream and masochistically mull over the chances she had missed: with a little thought, how easily she could have played her cards better. But she had gone ahead, had gone against Langley and had her baby; had made a fool of herself because she hadn't learned to be hard. Too late now to start regretting, of course, but it was like a magnet that drew her, this regret; unable to escape its pull – in a way didn't want to escape.

Of course she was tormenting herself, dreaming of Paris, buying wild perfumes, beautiful clothes, jewellery in the exclusive expensive boutiques of the Rue Royale, wearing them for him, luxuriating to have him slowly divest her of the clothes she'd bought as they made love in that fine apartment in Montparnasse. There had been the fun, the crazy madcap escapades of the twenties.

People like that still had mad, mad parties, still did crazy things. No hectic Charleston now, jazz pushed into the background, women in slinky bare-backed satin dresses, hair marcel-waved, faces differently made up, now they rumba'd and tango'd, but they still spent and spent in spite of the continuing Depression in which those like herself must struggle.

The West End with Hollywood films displaying the elegance she had once indulged in; but she was merely a housewife, a mother, a small dealer in ladies knitwear, even the dream of selling Paris fashions gone.

Moving away from the display window of this, one of London's most exclusive shops, its expensively dressed mannequins with painted faces and unbelievably long eyelashes smiling at her, taunting her, she sidestepped to avoid a couple, so busy consulting Harrods' window that they didn't notice her. But Cissy had drawn in a startled gasp.

Langley Makepeace – that slim and elegant grace of him, that suave self-assured expression of his – it was him. He hadn't changed a bit and Cissy's heart seemed to leap with an arousal of what she had once felt for him. She only just managed to stop herself calling his name.

The woman on his arm was also slim and elegant, beautifully dressed – that sleek beige summer dress and wide-brimmed hat could only have come from Harrods itself. She had to be his wife, moving beside him with the easy confidence of the happily married woman. Seeing her arm through his, his hand covering hers the way it had once covered her own, sent a shock of envy through Cissy.

Even as it did, they merged with other shoppers going in through the swing doors and out of sight. He hadn't even noticed her; had he done so, would probably not have recognised her anyway. She still tried to dress reasonably well, but was no longer the person he would remember, she felt suddenly drab, poor; felt as though she had been a kerbside beggar he'd passed. She felt degraded for all he hadn't seen her. All she wanted to do now was run away in case the pair came out and he did recognise her. What an embarrassment. He had no idea that she had borne him a child, must have long ago forgotten her.

She felt sick, the world blurring behind tears which she fought to stem, all that self-destructive pleasure of recalling the old days flushed out of her, she made her way blindly towards the underground that would get her a train back home. That old life she had known was truly gone and couldn't be brought back no matter how she yearned and dreamed and pretended. She knew that now. She knew also that she would not come near Knightsbridge to dream ever again and that Thursday from now on would be just humdrum Thursday.

The letter lay on the living room table. Cissy stared down at it in disbelief and something near to horror. Not at what Daisy had written but the importance it had for herself. There could be no question of not helping her and Theodore. She had to, no matter what it cost. But it would mean having to confess a daughter to Eddie to do so. Everything ruined, her marriage destroyed.

She felt an unbearable anger towards Daisy for putting her into such a position. Unjustifiable she knew, but as she sat alone, Eddie's mother having gone home and Eddie yet to come home, her only thought was how dare Daisy place her into such a situation? She should never have gone to Germany in the first place, and surely Theodore must have known what was going on there. He wasn't an idiot yet had taken Daisy, and more importantly Noelle – her daughter, not theirs – into danger.

More to the point, though, it was herself she was really angry at, but it was easier to aim her fury at Daisy, transferring some of the blame from herself for not having taken more interest in Noelle. And now she would reap the harvest of it all. And yes, it could ruin her marriage but what could she do after all Daisy had done for her once? In a strange way, that made her feel even more angry.

And now she waited with dread for Eddie to come home, wondering how on earth she was going to break the news to him that she had another man's child hidden away in Europe – explain away the long years of not telling him. The tale would be long and laboured, trying to explain how it had been, trying to appeal to his better nature. Better nature? He would have to be a saint to bear this without wanting to half kill her, or, worse still, walk out on their marriage. God, what a mess!

She smoothed the single page and read again the abject, pleading words Daisy had written. How could she ignore them and walk this earth untouched if anything were to happen to them, and to her daughter? She couldn't.

By the time Eddie's footsteps sounded on the stairs up from the street, Cissy was a bag of nerves, filled with fear for Daisy and Noelle, and for herself, still rehearsing how best to tell him.

'Sit down a moment, Eddie,' she said, trying to sound neither too timid and penitent nor too brash and defiant. 'I've something I have to tell you.'

He smiled at her. 'Can't it be after dinner? I'm starved.'

'I don't think I should wait until after dinner,' she said quickly. 'I've had a letter from Daisy. And there's a lot I think you ought to know before I tell you what she says – what she's asking.'

Theodore's expression was dark as he sat watching his wife pace the bedroom. 'You should never have written such a letter to your friend,' he admonished but she continued to pace.

'If you think I'm going to stay here and be persecuted when someone might be able to help us, then you must be mad. We should never have come here in the first place. We were all right in Paris. But you had to drag me here – just so you could put a silly stone on your father's grave. Now we're stuck here. Even if we had enough to go to England, the three of us, who's to say we'd be allowed to leave? We've no extra money for bribes.' Teddy was bankrupt, his clients gone, boycotted by non-Jews, his own people mostly having lost everything, like himself.

'I should think they'd be most happy to let us leave,' Teddy said, watching her pacing. 'If they want Germany for what they term good Germans, I would imagine undesirable elements such as we appear to be would be virtually asked to leave.'

'Then why did they come here to look at our passport? You heard what they said. Ours wasn't worth the paper it's written on. If you can't see beyond that hint, I can.

What if they suddenly take it away, then where will we be? All I want to do is go back home. I'm English. I belong in England.'

'And I am German.'

She stopped pacing to glare at him sitting quietly on the dressing table chair watching her. 'I suppose you're going to say you belong in Germany. You're not German, you're a German Jew. There is a difference or there is now. What's Germany done for you?'

'It is my homeland.'

'One that allows Hitler's mobs to beat you up.' His face still held traces of bruising and his arm was still in plaster, not expected to be rid of it for three more weeks yet. 'One that allows a hospital to throw you out on the street – that lets gangsters, and that's all they are, the SA, beat you up and manhandle our Noelle . . .'

'She is not *our* Noelle,' he reminded calmly. 'She is your friend's child.' He hadn't once risen to her anger. It wasn't in his nature to become easily riled. But his even temper riled her.

'Cissy doesn't want her,' she flared at him. 'You and I love Noelle so she is ours, and if you're happy to stand by and see her mauled by SA thugs, I'm not! If you won't come to England with me. I'll go on my own and take her with me.'

Teddy stood up, frowning, the first real flicker of retaliation she had seen throughout her whole tirade, which had been going on for some twenty minutes unchallenged.

'My dear, you cannot easily use our passport for yourself alone. In most countries that is not allowed unless you have one in your own right, and when we married you gave up your own for a married passport, you may recall. And would you really go and leave me here?'

She was deflated. 'No, of course not.'

'We are a family,' he continued as she stood looking at him, tears filling her eyes. 'We cannot leave each other behind. We cannot do as we please without the agreement of the other, or we are no longer a family. I too regret coming here. I was a fool. I should have foreseen how things were going, but I was blind and sick with longing for my homeland, as you are now for yours. I love Germany. It is my home.'

Daisy was mollified. Her voice came small and wavering. 'I know. But I love mine too. England. It's always been safe in England.'

'It was safe here in Germany once.'

'But it isn't any more, and England is still safe. Oh, Teddy, I want to leave. I have to leave. I'm so homesick. Like you were – remember? I want to see my family and feel safe, have Noelle safe.'

She saw his eyes mist over at the mention of Noelle's safety. He chewed his lip. 'But we have no money.'

'That's why I wrote to Cissy to help us. Eddie still owes us money. She can't ignore that fact. We've helped them, and we helped her when she most needed it. She can't have forgotten. And there's Noelle. I know she let us carry on looking after her, but she is her mother, and when a mother knows her own daughter is in danger, she'll do anything to save her. She might not want her back, but she couldn't stand by and see her at risk. It wouldn't be natural.'

Teddy's expression was solemn as he regarded her. 'But she has so far not replied to your letter. And it is many weeks already.'

Daisy dropped her gaze, closing her eyes tightly against the look he was giving her, against the harsh connotation in that reminder.

Cissy sat at the living room table, the blank sheet of paper before her. It was the hardest decision she'd ever had to make, and she felt she'd made some hard decisions in her life. Eddie had finally told her it was up to her to do what she thought best, leaving it in her lap. But she couldn't blame him for that – in this case.

She had stood before him that evening, twisting her hands as he looked up at her from the chair where she'd asked him to sit. His enquiring expression had been entirely innocent of what she had been about to say, and it had wrung her heart that she could have duped him for so long. How dare she? Love was pouring out of her for him, such love as she had never truly felt before – not even for Langley, but now with Eddie she feared it had come too late, aware that she was about to destroy what they'd had with her belated truths.

She'd begun hesitantly, then taking herself in hand began again. 'Eddie, you know when I went abroad?' He had nodded slowly.

'You see,' she continued laboriously, 'I went away with someone.'

'Yes.' It had sounded to her almost as though he knew all about it. She remembered thinking that he couldn't know, but his quiet 'yes' had made it harder to express what she'd wanted to say.

She'd continued doggedly, telling him how she had stayed with some people; how lovely it had been, the places she was shown, the romance of it all.

'I was carried away by it all,' she said, and then coming to the crucial part, she'd paused, had turned away from his trusting eyes, unable to face them, saying, 'I don't know how to tell you this.'

'You just say what you have to,' she heard his voice behind her. 'Simply.'

Desperation had clutched at her. 'I can't say it . . . simply.'

'Yes you can.' There had been tension in his tone, an earnestness again as though he already knew what she was about to say and he was trying to help her.

Suddenly it had all come out: Langley; the baby; his treatment of her, throwing money at her to get rid of it; how Daisy had taken her in, provided for her while she had the baby, a daughter; had taken charge of the baby while she'd looked for a job; had continued to do so when she returned to England so she could find premises with what had been left from what Langley had given her; how she hadn't dared tell him, Eddie, about her daughter, frightened that their marriage would be sacrificed, that she loved him so – hadn't really loved Langley, only been infatuated by him and the romance of her life in France, the craziness of the company she'd known.

'What's her name?' Eddie had asked suddenly, his quiet tone taking her by surprise where she had expected him to rant and rave.

Near to tears as she told him, she heard him murmur that it was a nice name. Nothing else, just that it was a nice name, Noelle Louise.

Her bad reaction to his acceptance of it all, she supposed, should have been anticipated, but it wasn't. Turning out quite opposite to what people would normally expect – abject gratitude – she had fallen into a fit of self-indulgent fury. 'What's the matter with you? Don't you see what I've done? Can't you just get angry? For God's sake tell me you hate me, Eddie. Tell me! Tell me our marriage is all washed up.'

But he had merely stood up slowly and come over to her. His words would stay with her to her dying day.

'I can't be angry. Not now. It's could've 'appened to any girl blind enough to go off in search of a bit of romance, looking fer a better life than she 'ad. I'm just sorry I wasn't the one to give it to you. I'm not angry, Cissy. I was at one time. I waited and waited fer you to tell me, and when you didn't I felt more and more wounded.'

She'd looked at him aghast. 'Are you telling me you already knew? And you let me go on?'

He shook his head. There was a hint of a smile in his dark eyes – no, more a look of relief than a smile, and again her fury rose.

'You've kept what you knew a secret all this time and said nothing – let me go on suffering, not knowing how I would ever begin to tell you? Was that your way of punishing me?'

She saw the smile desert him. 'I never wanted to punish you, Cissy. I found out the day we got married. Your friend Daisy's mother let it out by mistake. She tried to cover it up, but I realised then what she'd said. I should 'ave faced you with it, but I couldn't. I wanted you to tell me, but you never did, and the longer I waited the more 'urt I felt until I almost began to hate you. I couldn't even look at you at times. I tried to will you to tell me, but you didn't, and I couldn't ask you to tell me, because it wouldn't 'ave been the same – do you understand?'

For a moment she had stared at him, the full import of what he was saying sinking in. Yes, she had understood – how he must have hurt, loving her as he did yet feeling hatred of her actions, or the lack of them, hurt by his own stifled anger towards her. She had fallen into his arms, crying out, 'Oh, Eddie, can you ever forgive me?'

'I can – now.' He'd held her close. The next thing, she was crying on his shoulder, overwhelmed by the simplicity of his forgiveness, the unnecessary web she'd made for herself finally disentangled.

Now she sat looking down at the blank sheet of paper and thinking about it all, she picked up the pen, dipped the nib in the bottle of Swan ink and began to write, her decision made.

'Daisy. I, Eddie and I, have decided to sell my shop. We can't possibly let Eddie's business go, but my shop's expendable and, after all, he should be the breadwinner. I think he might have always been a little bit upset, jealous if you like, of my being independent in a way. You know what men are like – they don't care to be made to feel inferior. So to get enough money to bring you all back to England if we can, that's what I, we, have decided. The building is rented, but I've found a buyer for my business.'

She paused, staring down at what she had written, then with an afterthought scratched out the 'we'. Eddie had left it entirely up to her what she did. It hadn't been churlish on his part, merely that he couldn't make that decision for her and feel easy in his heart.

But she wasn't going to dwell on that, only that she had never felt so grateful to anyone in her life as she felt at this moment to him. She didn't deserve him, and she still cringed at the thought of all the pain she had inflicted on him by her silliness. But now wasn't the time to think of that. She had shown him photos of Noelle and he had agreed that she must be brought back to England as soon as they could drum up enough money for it. He had been so worried. She knew he was looking at his tug business being sacrificed, and what could she do but offer her own small business instead?

'What we must do, is make arrangements for me and Eddie to come over as visitors. We're getting a passport, a short one is quicker, and we'll be with you as soon as we can. We'll stay with you on a Friday and then on Saturday morning we'll all go to Switzerland as if for a few days' holiday. There'll be you, me, Eddie and Noelle as English visitors you might say, and Teddy might be taken for granted, we hope, as just holidaying with us. There shouldn't be any fuss as far as I can see. Just leave the house as it is. Don't go closing it up or it might look as if you're leaving the country. Just leave it all behind as though you will be coming back to it after a short holiday. In Switzerland we'll catch a train through France, then a Channel steamer to here. And don't worry about the cost. It's been all worked out. I've been lucky to find someone to buy my business. With that and a loan Eddie has been able to get from the bank, we'll just manage if

we go very easy. Everything is going to be all right. You'll see.'

She didn't say that it would leave them vastly in debt with only Eddie's money now, that very little after paying back the interest every week. What Daisy didn't know about wouldn't hurt her.

She sealed the letter without showing it to Eddie – he would only have been even more embarrassed than he was, and hurriedly posted it. The ball had been set rolling. There was nothing she could do now, even if she had wanted to change her mind.

Taking a night-crossing Channel steamer, sleeping in chairs to save money on a cabin, travelling by train through France in the early hours, they made Germany by mid-morning, where they would stop for a modest early lunch.

What she'd expected to find in Germany, Cissy didn't know. Resentment perhaps? An overpowering sense of peril; hostile interrogation at the German border as their passports were examined?

What she did find was an incredible friendliness, English holiday visitors gladly welcomed with warm smiles and pleasant faces. Everyone she and Eddie met were charming, from the waitress with a smattering of English at their luncheon table to someone in the street similarly gifted, from whom they had to ask directions, ready to interpret their needs, and the only questions asked were what was England like, had they ever met their King George and Queen Mary, and what did they think of German food after plain stodgy English cooking?

They arrived at Daisy and Theodore's house mid-afternoon. From the outside it looked huge and opulent after the flat over her shop, now vacated of course, she and Eddie back with his mother, one bedroom and sharing the use of her living room and kitchen.

Daisy, looking strained but healthily pregnant, and Theodore, were at the door to greet them. Noelle was asleep upstairs they were told.

'Oh, God, Cissy!' Daisy cried, falling emotionally on her friend's neck the moment of greeting her. 'Oh, it's so good to see you again, it really is. It's been so long since we've seen each other.'

Theodore solemnly shook Eddie's hand, very German and formal. 'I am most happy to met you, sir.' Then he kissed Cissy's hand with a small sharp bow. 'I am delighted to see you again, Fraulein Bennett.'

'Cissy, call me Cissy,' she laughed as they conducted her and Eddie into the house, at the same time aware of someone pruning roses in the front of a nearby house pausing to watch the goings-on with interest.

As she glanced towards the woman, she felt for the first time an apprehensive shiver run through her. No sense of friendliness that she could detect emanated from that concentrated look, and she made up her mind there and then that first thing tomorrow they must be on their way, leaving noisily with bright baggage and clothing as though they were anticipating a short fun-filled holiday with friends.

The interior of Daisy and Theodore's home was a shock. Traces of recent wealth were still evident, silk wallpaper faintly faded where large paintings had been, a comfortable three-piece suite, a few fine chairs and a table, but the window drapes were cheap and there were no ornaments, carpet and little other furniture, their absence bearing witness to the terrible disquiet and unease behind hasty sales to keep money coming in enough to live on, but she ignored the significance.

'It's a lovely house,' she said as, leaving the men to talk in the sitting room, she followed Daisy into the vast kitchen to make coffee.

'It *was* a lovely house,' Daisy stressed. 'But it's not like it's ours any more. Any moment it could be taken away from us, confiscated.'

'Why?' Cissy was aghast.

'Because Teddy's Jewish.'

'Can they do that?'

Daisy had her gaze on the coffee percolator, beginning to bubble. 'Easily. They can do anything they like. They've done it to others. We just spend our time waiting. I think they've left us alone so far because they realise I'm English and that Noelle's not Teddy's child, that we are only fostering her and she belongs to an Englishwoman and was born in France. It's left them in a bit of a dilemma, I think, so they've let us be for a time. But it is only a matter of time.'

She turned abruptly to Cissy, her brown eyes swimming. 'Oh, Cissy, I'm so afraid.'

Confronted by that awful look, Cissy felt the full intensity of the fear that dogged her friend, an intensity of fear no amount of letter writing could convey. It had to be seen for itself to really know it.

'Never mind,' she said inadequately, vaguely embarrassed by its rawness, but Daisy brightened almost as though she too had become embarrassed, hurriedly changing the subject on to Noelle.

'How much does Eddie know about Noelle?' she enquired, her old self again, her whisper melodramatic, her eyes on the half-closed kitchen door. Her fear of her situation here in Germany pushed aside, she was once more the Daisy that Cissy had known when they'd tried to be one of the bright young things, but now mature and blooming, glowing, with her condition suiting her. Cissy would ask about her pregnancy later, but just now, her own fear for Daisy put aside, devilment crept into her head, a light-hearted need to punish, just a little. She had Daisy where she wanted her – a little something gossiping Daisy must pay for, if only mildly.

'I told him everything.'

'What, *everything*?'

'Yes.'

Daisy paused from setting out coffee cups and saucers to look at her, her eyes, dry now, wide with disbelief. 'How did he take it?'

'Surprisingly well, really.'

'You don't mean it!'

'Yes, I do.'

'You mean he never batted an eyelid?'

'He already knew.' Cissy felt her eyes dancing. 'Ever since our wedding day.'

'You mean you told him then? You never said anything to me.'

'*I* didn't tell him.' Cissy lowered her eyes, began arranging the biscuits onto a plate Daisy had got down from a white-fronted cabinet. 'Someone else did.'

'My God! Who? Who could have known other than you and me?'

'Your mother.' She wasn't angry, more amused. She could have been angry that Daisy had betrayed her – would have been had Eddie not been so readily forgiving. Had he not been, she would have been very angry, blaming Daisy for the ruin of her marriage, but as it was she was merely amused. And it didn't do any harm to see the loquacious Daisy squirm a little. She wasn't disappointed. Daisy stood transfixed, coffee percolator in her hand about to pour into the cups.

'Oh, Cissy . . . I never meant to.' Her cheeks had begun to flame. 'It just came out by accident, once when I was visiting her. I could have bitten off my tongue, I never thought she'd go and . . .'

Cissy's laugh cut short her babbled excuses. 'I'm not annoyed. The way Eddie told it, your mother did the same as you, spoke without even thinking. But it's done now. And I'm glad it's out in the open. I even feel grateful to you, Daisy. It's myself I have to blame. If I'd only been honest with Eddie from the first, so much strain would have been taken off our marriage. It was there, you know, and I couldn't understand it. He'd been waiting for me to tell him. I hurt him terribly, and I never realised it. The terrible things we do to each other by not being honest.'

She had long ago ceased laughing, and at the sadness now on her face, Daisy quickly put down the percolator and came over to her.

'Come here, you silly!' she burst out as the two hugged each other. 'It's all in the past now. Everything's all right. And I'm so grateful you're here. So very glad. I feel so much safer.'

'Yes.' She watched as Daisy recovered herself, resuming pouring the coffee, setting milk and sugar on a tray beside the coffee for those who wanted it, with the plate of plain biscuits on another.

'And now we'd better think about what we're doing tomorrow,' Cissy went on briskly as they carried the two trays into the sitting room. 'There's a lot to think about.'

There was also Noelle to talk about and that she didn't relish.

Chapter Twenty-Nine

'Come on, darling, time to wake up . . .'

Noelle became aware of her arm being gently patted. At first she thought it was the dream. She had been in a wonderful place, full of children, all smaller than her, and they had been dancing and playing games and she had been included in every one. One little girl was patting her arm gently, begging to join the fun. But the voice had grown deeper, more adult, more immediate.

'Come on, darling, wake up. Dinner'll be ready soon. And you've slept and slept. And there's someone downstairs to see you.'

Now she was awake. The lovely dream had faded, its colours gone, in its place the solid shape of her bedroom and Auntie bending over her. She felt disappointed. They'd been such friendly children, speaking to her in French and English. Not German. She didn't like German that much even though she used it. Children said nasty things to her in German, sometimes chanting *Jude! Jude!* Nastily, as if it were a rude word. She didn't know what it meant and no one told her. Someone had once said to her that soon she wouldn't be allowed to come to this kindergarten because they didn't want any *Jude* '*balg*' – meaning all sorts of horrid things like urchin or brat, here.

Disappointment changed in turn to the reality knowing that outside of dreams, she had no friends. Very few at kindergarten asking her to join their games. Even the person in charge, Fraulein Lotte as the children called her, was nasty to her all the time. Where she always petted and played with everyone else she ignored Noelle as if she wasn't there, sometimes even giving her a sharp smack when she didn't even know what she had done to offend. Soon she'd be going on to an infant school and she hoped they'd be nicer there. Thinking of it her lower lip pouted. Seeing it, Auntie gathered her up.

'Now don't cry, darling. You always wake up miserable, don't you? But you must be happy today. Today we've got a nice surprise for you. We're all going on a holiday.'

Instantly the heavy feeling in her heart went away.

'A holiday!' she cried, out of Auntie's arms in a second. 'What holiday?'

'It's a surprise. You're not to say anything to anyone.'

How could she say anything to anyone when she had no one but Auntie and *Vater* to talk to?

'Promise?'

'Promise,' she answered, looking serious.

'Come on then.' Auntie held her hand as they went downstairs.

There were people in the sitting room. She vaguely recognised the lady, though not the man. She had a vague memory of seeing her after having been on a boat. There'd been a shabby room with lots of boxes, though where it had been she didn't know. Auntie had said she was Mummy. It seemed odd that she was never with them if she was supposed to be Mummy, though it didn't worry her that much. Auntie was too nice and lovely for her to long for anyone else.

Auntie led her up to her now. She was very pretty, smiling, and there were tears in her bright blue eyes as she crouched down to greet her.

'Noelle, you remember your mummy?'

Solemnly Noelle nodded. There were photo albums with her and Auntie in them, both of them with arms linked, both shown in loose dresses and hats that went right down over their eyes and with no hair to be seen. This Mummy had fair hair curling around her ears and she wore a blue and white plaid dress with a bow at her neck, not at all like her photos though the smile was the same. So this was the Mummy her auntie often mentioned. 'One day you'll see her,' she would say and she would have a sad look when she said that. But lately she had looked a lot less sad when she said the name. Perhaps it had something to do with the little brother or sister that Auntie kept saying would be coming to join them before long.

'Hello,' Noelle said dutifully.

'Oh . . . Noelle,' it sounded like someone in pain and then she found herself suddenly snatched up and held close. 'Oh, Noelle, I've missed you so much. I never thought I did, but I have. I have.'

Eddie stood watching the two being reunited, mother and daughter, and found himself pushing away an uninvited prickle of jealousy. How could he have expected otherwise, blood being thicker than water every time? True, Cissy loved their Edward with equal abandon, but there was something painfully poignant in those kisses and cuddles. Leaving Cissy to her reunion, Daisy going to join in, the two of them falling into deep discussion while they both caressed and cuddled the child, he took Theodore to one side.

'I 'ope you don't think me as taking charge, Mr Helgott,' he began. 'But we've got some 'ard thinking ter do. I saw some ole gel . . . woman . . . in 'er garden watchin' us. I didn't like the *way* she was watching.'

'I too saw her,' Theodore said, his dark brows drawn into a frown.

'It might be best to leave as early in the morning as we can.'

'Not too early. Such haste could draw suspicion.'

'Yeah, I see what you mean.'

On the far side of the room, they went into deep discussion. Their plan of action finally resolved, they returned to the women, bringing them out of their happy absorption with the four-year-old Noelle.

'Tomorrow morning,' Theodore informed them, 'we go to Switzerland. Tonight, we'll each pack a medium-sized case, tomorrow wear our holiday clothes. There is a bus to Dusseldorf at eight forty-five. This we will board, making a lot of happy noise for our neigbours to think we are going on a small weekend trip. This is most important.'

Lying beside her in the room they'd been given, Eddie seemed to her to be cold and aloof, his body rigid, a little removed from hers.

Preoccupied, she thought, with the prospect of tomorrow. It was going to be a bit dramatic, almost like acting out a play, though this wasn't going to be any play. She still couldn't grasp the immediate seriousness of it all. Life in England bore no resemblance to this, yet it was hardly believable that this was all happening to her. She almost wanted to burst out laughing, but it would be nervous laughter, springing from a sense of eeriness that wouldn't take any definite shape or form.

She turned over towards Eddie, a need to have him cuddle away the strange unformed feeling, but felt him move even further from her.

'What's wrong, love? It will be all right tomorrow, I'm sure it will. Don't worry.'

But he didn't reply, and later she heard him snoring softly.

He was his old self again by the morning, noticeably tense before the journey ahead of them, maybe feeling a little responsible for everyone, but his peculiar coolness last night in bed was gone.

Cissy wished she knew what had made him so cool towards her, as though she had done something wrong. But in the throes of getting ready to leave, eating a quick breakfast of moist dark rye bread and some smoked cheese, the leftover perishable foodstuffs consigned to the garden waste tip as anyone would going away on holiday, a final look round to see if anything had been left undone, she dismissed it.

That was until just before setting off, she picked Noelle up and cuddled her. The child made no attempt to wriggle free, even put her little arms about her. Slender, dark-haired, eyes bright blue, and her face oval but not as oval as that of most four-year-olds, promising the high cheekbones and firm cheeks of good bone structure; the child of her father, with his handsome looks – she was already beautiful.

But Langley was in the past. Noelle was now, and was hers. Holding her close, savouring the moment before putting her down ready to be off, in her heart regretting the years away from her, Cissy glanced towards Eddie. His brown eyes were watching her, taking in the scene. They were dark and brooding, and then she knew what was eating into him. So he hadn't entirely forgiven her. Or was it not that he hadn't forgiven her, but felt left out now? Was he jealous? Was it of the man whose child she held or the child herself. She couldn't tell.

Quickly she put Noelle down, smiled at him; receiving an answering smile. A little stiff perhaps, but a smile, and at least he hadn't turned away. She vowed that she must be more careful about Noelle in his sight, make her errors up to him as best she could, keeping away from her as much as possible. But it was going to be so hard, the way Noelle had fitted so naturally in her arms after all those years away from her, she believing neither of them capable of being close.

'Are we ready then?' Theodore said, taking one last look about the house he had bought for Daisy.

Daisy gave a little sniff, and he put a brief arm about her waist, one that was visibly beginning to thicken under her loose-cut summer dress. 'One day we will return here, when this is all over, *mein liebling*, my darling.'

Daisy sniffed even more audibly. 'I don't ever want to come back to Germany. All I want now is to go back to England. And stay there!'

His arm dropped away from her, but he smiled sadly. 'As you wish, my dear. As you wish. Perhaps you are right.'

With Noelle's hand in hers, Cissy deliberately making no attempt to approach the child, they filed out of the house some few minutes before the autobus into town would be due.

'Look happy,' Theodore warned as he pocketed the main door key. 'We are to look pleased to be going away on a few days joyous vacation.' And he smiled at a woman, a slightly known neighbour, passing them, her gaze curious.

'*Guten morgen*, Frau Schmitt,' he said affably as she paused, her interest aroused, continued in German, 'an old friend of my wife, and her husband, have come to visit us for a holiday. We are taking the weekend to show them around. We will be returning on Monday.'

The woman, taken a little aback by his candour, muttered, '*Nimm dich ja in acht*,' bidding them to take care, and continued on her way, apparently satisfied.

Cissy wondered what all the trepidation had been about as they boarded the train south. They hadn't been challenged. No one took much notice of them except, hearing English spoken, someone asked where they came from. Eddie said London, then fell to talking to Cissy to avoid the inevitable enquiries about his country.

The journey proved pleasant as they travelled south, dozing, eating sandwiches and drinking flasks of coffee brought with them, disdaining to pay out for lunch on the train, enjoying passing views of orchards, blossom gone, fruit not yet formed, the uniform trees lovely to look at just the same; then nearing Stuttgart glimpsing the Bavarian Alps on the horizon to the south-east, the Black Forest to the west. Finally at Stuttgart, they found the cheapest decent lodgings they could for the night, boarding a train for Switzerland next morning. They could have been ordinary holidaymakers.

Anxiety came at the Swiss border, the inevitable German guards clambering aboard to examine passports, starting at either end of the train. Sitting quiet, tense, Cissy could hear carriage doors opening and closing, the sounds drawing closer like pincers slowly tightening, all the way along the crowded train carrying mostly summer holidaymakers at this time of year.

She blessed their good thinking in choosing the centre of the long train, trusting the tedious repetition of opening doors and going through each crowded compartment examining and stamping passports would promote some sloppiness by the time their turn came.

The time arriving, Cissy and Eddie presenting their visitors' ones, then as Theodore held out their joint passport, Daisy let out a piercing cry holding her side, words tumbling out in her best Cockney.

'Ooh . . . Teddy . . . I've got such an 'orrible pain! Ooh, cripes . . . it's the baby! Oo-er!'

Her stomach stuck out as far as she could get it, she fell sideways into his arms so that he had to catch her. Cissy, on cue, took the passport from him, half presented it, then distracted by another cry, bent over the whimpering Daisy offering comfort.

The guard was looking alarmed, most likely with visions of having to deliver a child on the spot. His face florid, he asked in German if there was anything he should do to help.

Neither Cissy nor Eddie genuinely understood him. Theodore was too taken up with his wife's plight to reply, while Daisy gave another screech and swore colourfully in Cockney.

'Bleedin' 'ell! Oh, bleedin' 'ell. Oh, 'elp!'

Whether the guard understood English or not, much less Cockney, the sentiments were plain enough. But he had his job to do. Quickly he stamped Theodore's passport, hardly glancing at it except to see it was a German one.

'I'm taking my visitors to Switzerland for the week-end,' Theodore explained hurriedly between efforts to support the writhing Daisy, 'before they return to Germany to spend the rest of their holiday.'

The guard nodded, handed back the passport, glanced at the four-year-old child with them, also crying and trying to pat the distraught Englishwoman's hand, and again asked if there was anything he could do. But Daisy was recovering, was sitting up, face flushed, eyes brimming tears.

'It's goin', the pain. Gawd, what a pain that was. Must've bin somefink I et. Gawd, that's better. Much better. Gawd . . .'

'No need to overdo it,' Cissy whispered, still bending over her as the guard moved off. 'You're not on the stage now.'

It was all she could do to control a giggle as fellow passengers ranged along the opposite seat looked on, each face a picture. But Daisy, sitting up and fully recovered, managed a smile for them.

'It must've bin a false alarm. I really fought I was 'avin' a miscarriage. I really did.'

'You've said enough,' Cissy warned again, but she was smiling too. Daisy, always a caution as the Cockney saying went, had done well, though she did look a bit shaken. In her condition it couldn't have done her all that much good.

Cissy took charge of the still whimpering Noelle to give Daisy a little respite in which to recover.

'Is Auntie not well?' Noelle sniffled.

'She is fine now,' Cissy told her and took her on to her lap, soothing and cuddling her. It felt so natural that she didn't put her down back on to her seat beside Daisy, and finally Noelle fell asleep in her arms.

Feeling comfortable with her, pleased with herself that she should be, Cissy gave Eddie a smile, surprised that he looked away immediately to glance down at his watch. She'd bought it for him just after their wedding. He still wore it, mainly unable to afford any other. Then he glanced through the window at the frontier buildings, avoiding her gaze. But she needed some response from him.

'Why couldn't we have gone straight through into France? It would have saved an awful lot of money.'

'You know why,' he said, looking away from the window but not directly at her. 'It was too obvious. No one goes to France from Germany for 'oliday. They go to Switzerland or Bavaria.'

She nodded, shaken and a little angry at the uncalled for sourness of his tone, and didn't further the conversation.

The train was moving, trundling across the frontier, boarded again by guards in a different uniform and with a totally different manner, calling for anything to be declared. Then on again, through countryside that took Cissy's breath away. Her first ever close-up view of mountains, she wasn't prepared for them. Snow glittering on their peaks they didn't so much appear big, as the houses beneath took on a toylike look, even those near at hand – an optical illusion if ever there was one, she thought. And yet the air was so clear that each peak seemed near enough to touch. It gave her a strange feeling watching them go by slowly, majestically. It was only when she caught sight of one rearing through an already high cloud, its peak protruding above it as clear as crystal, that their true height suddenly overwhelmed her sense of proportion, making her feel quite dizzy.

'How small we all are,' she whispered, pointing out the optical illusion to Eddie. 'Us with our petty worries and fears.'

'Our *petty* worries and fears are real enough to us,' he returned quietly but morosely, and again she fell silent, feeling even more angry with him, and stayed that way until they finally piled off the train into the warm Zurich afternoon sunshine.

Zurich was no more than a brief overnight stay in a modest hotel, breakfast, then a train going to Basle where the borders of Germany, Switzerland and France met. Nor was it a pleasant stay. Eddie was quiet and sombre, seemed to have gone into himself even more, not joining the light-hearted atmosphere that now existed between the four of them, feeling safe. His only response to her goodnight kiss in bed was a grunted reply before he turned over, his back to her.

Once she asked what was wrong but he mumbled, 'I'm tired. Been a long day,' leaving her to lie awake, questions running through her own weary brain until finally she concluded that of course he was tired. She was tired. They were all tired. Noelle grizzling for much of the time had borne out the weariness in all of them.

It hadn't been like going on a real holiday with everyone knowing that on arrival, only fun and games lay ahead. There had been tension all the way and still more to come – still a long journey to make. She could forgive – had to forgive – Eddie his peevishness. Even so, she was glad when they left next morning and he seemed refreshed.

The rest of the journey was uneventful – a little fraught maybe, aware how near Basle was to Germany, but it went smoothly.

The problem now was money, rapidly running out. No sandwiches brought from Theodore's home to supplement the expense of eating bought ones, they filled up on coffee and croissants, she and Daisy taking it in turns to nurse a fractious Noelle, wanting ice cream and sweets, and sooth her natural yearning for something more.

Eddie was quiet, and Theodore thoughtful, perhaps thinking of the homeland he was leaving behind. The two days going through France began to feel more like a week, with yet another overnight stop in Paris.

Raining slightly, the cobbled back-streets where they found rooms at a reasonable rate were dark, slippery and badly lit. Cissy thought of the brilliance of the Champs Élysées, white lights of shops and lamps reflected in the wet pavements like endless arrays of dancing silvery columns. But no one had money to waste on sightseeing.

First thing next morning they were on their way again, to Dieppe for the cross-Channel boat to Newhaven – a longer but far cheaper crossing – and home.

It was an uncomfortable night, tossing and turning in chairs using jackets for pillows. Cissy with Noelle fast asleep on her lap felt her legs going to sleep too, so that she had to hand her to Theodore, the two of them taking turns at nursing her, Daisy, worn out by her ordeal in her condition, sleeping like a log, snoring gently.

Eddie was still withdrawn – though as far as she could see there was no cause to be now that the worst was over – and spent the crossing mostly walking the deck. She would have followed him, tried to delve into what was bothering him, but something said she should leave him alone to come round in his own time. She had long ago become accustomed to these bouts of surliness of his, but sometimes they bewildered and hurt.

No one ate any breakfast apart from a cup of tea and a piece of cheap cake for Noelle to stop her whimpering.

'There's just enough money left to get us 'ome,' Eddie said, totting up what they had, 'with about three quid left over. We should 'ang on to that if we can, in case of emergencies.'

Eight o'clock that evening, after what had been a hot July day, even for England, the small group of travellers made their way from the bus stop at Canning Town, turning into Woodham Road where Eddie's mother lived, those last few hundred yards feeling like the very worst. Utterly worn out, famished, in need of a good wash, each holding their small suitcase as though it weighed a ton, they looked and felt like refugees.

Eddie had thought it best to go first to his mother's rather than to Daisy's parents, giving them a chance to wash and brush up and have a decent bite to eat before going on. 'Fish and chips,' he suggested, adding, 'cheap and cheerful and good for the sole.' Theodore had looked a little askance at the odd joke but could only nod in agreement.

'Fish and chips . . . nice to be nearly home,' Cissy couldn't help remarking and got a wan smile from Daisy.

Noelle had ceased her intermittent whimpering. Too worn out for even a miserable snivel, she dragged on her mother's hand. Hers, not Daisy's, Cissy was gratified to note as they trudged those last few yards to Eddie's mother's door. It had been settled on the train to London – Noelle was to go with her mother and Eddie. Daisy had something other to look forward to now.

'What do you think about it?' Cissy had turned to Eddie as the decision was made between her and Noelle's erstwhile foster parents, but he had merely given an indifferent shrug.

'It's all right with me, I guess,' he'd murmured. 'You do what you think best – she's your daughter.'

She hadn't known which way to take the remark but had been too tired to query it. Now she had hold of Noelle's hand, encouraging her those last few steps. 'You're going to see your nanna,' she encouraged, 'and she'll have some nice cake and perhaps sweets. That'll cheer you up, won't it?' And she felt Noelle's step grow a fraction lighter.

After the clarity of Switzerland, the heat of France, Canning Town didn't just seem drab, it was drab. But oh, the relief to be here and feel the security of its dull, featureless look.

It wasn't just her, she could see it on everyone's face, shining like a beacon in the dingy street as their steps quickened towards the narrow two-up-two-down terraced house, undistinguishable from its neighbours but for its number and perhaps a different pattern of cheap lace curtains.

How Eddie's mother was going to accommodate them all in her tiny front room before Daisy and Theodore left for Daisy's parents' home, she didn't know. She could visualise the squash and the thought hit her with a bubble of amusement. She chuckled and had Eddie glance questioningly at her.

'Something went through my mind,' she excused, more easy in herself than she'd been for days.

They were broke – all of them. Had barely enough for a taxi to get Daisy and her husband to her house in Plaistow. One pound four shillings and sixpence ha'penny, by Eddie's last count. When money grew scarce it was amazing how well an exact record can be kept to the very last ha'penny. The rich had no need of such exact counting. Even when Cissy had been going careful with the money Langley had thrown at her, she hadn't counted so miserly.

But she had no intention of dwelling on those humiliating days now. Broke – she had never been so broke – she felt far more her own worth than at any time with Langley and all his money. No matter how broke she and Eddie became, they would pull themselves up out of the mire. With him she would hold up her head and face whatever came.

'We're going to be all right, Eddie,' she said confidently and had a sudden desire to laugh out loud.

She looked across at him, expecting him to laugh with her, instead met his unsmiling face and instantly the laughter inside her died, leaving a strange uncertainty and bewilderment, though she wasn't sure why.

Putting down his case, Eddie fished in his pocket for his door key – such a small domestic action after all they'd been through, that tears came to Cissy's eyes and she forgot the small hurt his unsmiling face had caused. She stood close to him as the key turned.

'We're home, Eddie, love,' she whispered. 'Whatever's wrong between us, it'll be better now.' She saw him nod, but he said nothing.

The door opened, not by him pushing it, but by Mrs Bennett on the other side, having heard their arrival. Her square face was wreathed in smiles of relief. In her arms, little Edward was giving an immense yawn, his fresh little face stretched about his wide open mouth.

Cissy felt a surge of love go through her – almost like a pain.

'Oh, Edward! My lovely pet! I've missed you so!'

Letting go Noelle's hand, which she had been clutching for so long, she reached out and hugged him to her, kissing the sleepy face. Tears of relief at being home, seeing her baby again, trickling down her cheeks, she pressed her face against his warm soft chubby one. Even that didn't seem enough as she kissed and kissed him.

She heard Eddie laugh. An odd relieved sort of laugh. The first laugh she'd heard from him in months it seemed. So unexpected.

'Don't eat him!' His light quip came close to her ear – Eddie who for so long had never resorted to quips.

Cissy was laughing again now, everyone else forgotten but him and Edward.

'I *could* eat him! I could eat him all up!' she cried, and she felt Eddie's arm come around her waist, guiding her as she took their son into the tiny front room, the others following them.

After Daisy and Theodore had been put into a taxi, leaving Noelle behind, too tired to cry for her auntie, Noelle put to bed in Edward's cramped cot, Edward was to share his grandmother's bed that night – an early night for everyone – Cissy and Eddie lay side by side staring up at the narrow ceiling, still lit by the fading sunset through the drawn curtains.

Cissy's voice came softly. 'There's something the matter, Eddie. I can feel it. I've felt it for years and I don't know what it is.'

'It's nothing.' His voice sounded hollow. 'Nothing at all now.'

'But there was – something,' she persisted.

'Pressures, I suppose.'

'We'll always have pressures.'

'I know.'

Their voices softly droning.

'We've got no money.'

'We'll 'ave to start concentrating on getting some business. We'll be paying back the bank loan for years yet.'

Cissy lay very still beside him, 'We,' he had said, not 'I' – I have to. Something inside her leapt in joy. But she continued to lie still. 'But I'm worried – about you and Edward . . .' She paused. 'And Noelle,' she ventured, making it sound like an afterthought. She knew now what had been nagging at him. She didn't want to raise that particular bugbear again, but Eddie's voice came evenly and softly.

'You love her.'

'I hardly know her. She's my child, but I don't know her . . . not the way I know Edward. He's mine. Somehow she doesn't yet seem mine. I'm going to have to work hard to make it feel so . . .'

She broke off and turned to him. 'Oh, Eddie, I'm so sorry about not telling you. I was so wrong, and I . . .'

He laid a hand over her mouth. 'It don't matter no more, Cissy. We'll be a family, the four of us. We'll find the money again to live decently. One day it'll be all right, you see.'

Gently he kissed her, then less gently, more in urgency, and as she melted into his arms, he made love to her with a passion that took her wholly by surprise.

'We've come full circle,' he mumbled once against her lips.

Yes, she thought, rags to riches and back to rags, right to where I started. But she didn't tell him that as she gave herself up to his love.

Acknowledgements

My grateful thanks to:

Ron Sewell, retired lighterman, Freeman of the Company of Watermen and Lightermen of the River Thames, who gave me the idea for this book and for all his ready advice and information on Thames lightermen.

I should also like to thank Mrs Beryl Meadows for the loan of the book concerning an old family connection, *a hundred years of towage, 1833–1933,*[*] which has provided me with invaluable information on the towage business for part of this fictional book.

* The history of Messrs. Wm. Watkins Ltd., by Frank C. Bowen, 1933.

Also by Maggie Ford:

The Soldier's Bride
A Mother's Love
Call Nurse Jenny
A Woman's Place
The Factory Girl
A Girl in Wartime
A Soldier's Girl

Maggie Ford was born in the East End of London but at the age of six she moved to Essex, where she has lived ever since. After the death of her first husband, when she was only twenty-six, she went to work as a legal secretary until she remarried in 1968. She has a son and two daughters, all married; her second husband died in 1984.

She has been writing short stories since the early 1970s.